The Chilbury Ladies' Choir

JENNIFER RYAN grew up in Kent and now lives in the Washington, DC area with her husband and two children. She was previously a nonfiction book editor. *The Chilbury Ladies' Choir* is her first novel.

'I adored it, it made me want to sing with joy'

ALEX BROWN, author of
The Secret of Orchard Cottage

'Delightful . . . it manages to be sad and funny, exciting and heart-warming, all at the same time. Quite an achievement' BARBARA ERSKINE, author of *Sleeper's Castle*

'I adored *The Chilbury Ladies' Choir*! The pages sing with such wonderful characters, and through them wartime England really comes alive. Warm, witty, touching and uplifting, I will be recommending this to all my friends'

HAZEL GAYNOR, author of *The Girl from the Savoy*

'There's so much happening in Chilbury: intrigue, romance and a charming cast of characters who aren't always as they appear. *The Chilbury Ladies' Choir* is a charming slice of English wartime life that warms the soul like a hot toddy'

MARTHA HALL KELLY, *New York Times*
bestselling author of *Lilac Girls*

'Wonderfully warm . . . the descriptions of the togetherness of a choir are spot-on . . . an extremely impressibely researched and tender debut' *Liverpool Echo*

'A charming story' *Prima*

'A wonderfully warm debut . . . a life-affirming tale of the power of community spirit' *Scotsman*

The Chilbury Ladies' Choir

JENNIFER RYAN

THE BOROUGH PRESS

The Borough Press
An imprint of HarperCollins*Publishers*
1 London Bridge Street
London SE1 9GF

www.harpercollins.co.uk

First published by HarperCollins*Publishers* 2017

This paperback edition 2018
3

A catalogue record for this book
is available from the British Library

ISBN: 978-0-00-816373-0

Printed and bound in the UK by
CPI Group (UK) Ltd, Croydon, CR0 4YY

To my grandmother, Mrs Eileen Beckley,
and the women of the Home Front

Notice pinned to the Chilbury village hall noticeboard,
Sunday, 24th March, 1940

As all our male voices have gone to war, the
village choir is to close following Cmdr Edmund
Winthrop's funeral next Tuesday.

The Vicar

Mrs Tilling's Journal

❦

Tuesday, 26th March, 1940

First funeral of the war, and our little village choir simply couldn't sing in tune. 'Holy, holy, holy' limped out as if we were a crump of warbling sparrows. But it wasn't because of the war, or the young scoundrel Edmund Winthrop torpedoed in his submarine, or even the Vicar's abysmal conducting. No, it was because this was the final performance of the Chilbury Choir. Our swan song.

'I don't see why we have to be closed down,' Mrs B snapped afterwards as we congregated in the foggy graveyard. 'It's not as if we're a threat to national security.'

'All the men have gone,' I whispered back, aware of our voices carrying uncomfortably through the funeral crowd. 'The Vicar says we can't have a choir without men.'

'Just because the men have gone to war, why do we have to close the choir? And precisely when we need it most! I mean, what'll he disband next? His beloved bell ringers? Church on Sundays? Christmas? I expect not!' She folded her arms in annoyance. 'First they whisk our men away to fight, then they force us women into work, then they ration food, and now they're closing our choir. By the time the Nazis get here there'll be nothing left except a bunch of drab women ready to surrender.'

'But there's a war on,' I said, trying to placate her loud complaining. 'We women have to take on extra work, help the cause. I don't mind doing hospital nurse duties, although it's busy keeping up the village clinic too.'

'The choir has been part of the Chilbury way since time began. There's something bolstering about singing together.' She puffed her chest out, her large, square frame like an abundant field marshall.

The funeral party began to head to Chilbury Manor for the obligatory glass of sherry and cucumber sandwich. 'Edmund Winthrop,' I sighed. 'Only twenty and blown up in the North Sea.'

'He was a vicious bully, and well you know it,' Mrs B barked. 'Remember how he tried to drown your David in the village pond?'

'Yes, but that was years ago,' I whispered. 'In any case, Edmund was bound to be unstable with his father forever thrashing him. I'm sure Brigadier Winthrop must be feeling more than a trace of regret now that Edmund's dead.'

Or clearly not, I thought as we looked over to him, thwacking his cane against his military boot, the veins on his neck and forehead livid with rage.

'He's furious because he's lost his heir,' Mrs B snipped. 'The Winthrops need a male to inherit, so the family estate is lost. He doesn't care a jot about the daughters.' We glanced over at young Kitty and the beautiful Venetia. 'Status is everything. At least Mrs Winthrop's pregnant again. Let's hope it's a boy this time round.'

Mrs Winthrop was cowering like a crushed sparrow under the weight of Edmund's loss. *It could be me next*, I thought, as my David came over, all grown up in his new army uniform.

His shoulders are broader since training, but his smile and softness are just the same. I knew he'd sign up when he turned eighteen, but why did it happen so fast? He's being sent to France next month, and I can't help worrying how I'll survive if anything happens to him. He's all I have since Harold passed away. Edmund and David often played as boys, soldiers or pirates, some kind of battle that Edmund was sure to win. I can only pray that David's fight doesn't end the same way.

The war has been ominously quiet so far, Hitler busy taking the rest of Europe. But I know they're coming, and soon we'll be surrounded by death. It'll be like the last war, when a whole generation of men was wiped out, my own father included. I remember the day the telegram came. We were sitting down for luncheon, the sun spilling into the dining room as the gramophone played Vivaldi. I heard the front door open, then the slump of my mother's body as she hit the floor, the sunshine streaming in, unaware.

Now our lives are going into turmoil all over again: more deaths, more work, more making do. And our lovely choir gone too. I've half a mind to write to the Vicar in protest. But then again, I probably won't. I've never been one to make a fuss. My mother told me that women do better when they smile and agree. Yet sometimes I feel so frustrated with everything. I just want to shout it out.

I suppose that's why I started a journal, so that I can express the things I don't want to say out loud. A programme on the wireless said that keeping a journal can help you feel better if you have loved ones away, so I popped out yesterday and bought one. I'm sure it'll be filled up soon, especially once David leaves and I'm on my own, thoughts surging through my head with nowhere to be let out. I've always dreamt of being a writer, and I suppose this is the closest I'll get.

Taking David's arm and following the crowd to Chilbury Manor, I looked back at the crumbling old church. 'I'll miss the choir.'

To which Mrs B roundly retorted, 'I haven't seen you instructing the Vicar to reverse his decision.'

'But, Mrs B,' David said with a smirk. 'We always leave it up to you to make a stink about everything. You usually do.'

I had to hide a smile behind my hand, waiting for Mrs B's wrath. But at that moment, the Vicar himself flew past us, trotting at speed after the Brigadier, who was striding up to the Manor.

Mrs B took one look, seized her umbrella with grim determination, and began stomping after him, calling, 'I'll have a word with you, Vicar,' her usual forthright battle cry.

The Vicar turned and, seeing her gaining pace, sprinted for all he was worth.

Letter from Miss Edwina Paltry to her sister, Clara

3 Church Row
Chilbury
Kent

Tuesday, 26th March, 1940

Brace yourself, Clara, for we are about to be rich! I've been offered the most unscrupulous deal you'll ever believe! I knew this ruddy war would turn up some gems – whoever would have thought that midwifery could be so lucrative! But I couldn't have imagined such a grubby nugget of a deal coming from snooty Brigadier Winthrop, the upper-class tyrant who thinks he owns this prissy little village. I know you'll say it's immoral, even by my standards, but I need to get away from being a cooped-up, put-down midwife. I need to get back to the old house where I can live my own life and be free.

Don't you see, Clara? Soon I can pay back the money I owe, like I promised, and you'll finally realise how clever I am, how I can make up for mistakes of the past. We can put everything behind us, and never mention what happened with Bill (although I always say I saved you from him). Then I'll buy back our childhood house in Birnham Wood, all fields and cliffs beside the sea, and we can live safe and happy just like before Mum died. I'll be finished with births and babies and nasty rashes in people's nether regions, people bossing me about and laughing behind my back. I'll be back to being my own person, no one watching over me.

But let me tell you about the deal from the beginning, as I know how you are about details. It was the funeral of Edmund Winthrop, the Brigadier's despicable son who was blown up in a submarine last week. Only twenty he was – one minute a repulsive reptile, the next a feast for the fishes.

The morning of the funeral was cold and wet as a slap round the face with a fresh-caught cod. We might have been in the North Sea ourselves for the ferocious winds and grisly clouds, a monstrous hawk circling above us looking for a victim. 'Rather fitting,' I heard someone murmur as we plunged headlong with our umbrellas through the bedraggled graveyard and into the dim, musty church.

Packed to the rafters, the place was buzzing with gossipy onlookers. At the front, the Winthrops and their aristocrat friends were sitting all plumed and groomed like a row of black swans. A splatter of khaki and grey-blue uniforms appeared as per usual, uniformed men thinking they're special when they're just plain stupid. More like uninformed, I always say.

The rest of us locals (mostly wool-coated women these days) had to crowd around behind them, listening to the thin excuse of a choir, a few off-key voices hazarding 'Holy, holy, holy.' The posh women of the village are upset at the choir's closing, but after a performance like that I'd rather hear a cats' chorus.

Throughout the dreary service, the dead soldier's mother snivelled into her hands, quaking under her black suit. She's pregnant again, late in life – although she's still in her late thirties. They say her nasty father forced her to marry the Brigadier when she was barely sixteen, and she's been terrorised by him ever since.

She was the only tearful one though. The rest of us weren't so blind to Edmund's brutish, arrogant ways – just like his father. I'm sure there were even a few present who felt a justified retribution at his early demise.

Hardly attempting to look sad, the two sisters, now eighteen and thirteen, sat dutifully beside their grieving mother. The older one, Venetia, with her golden hair and coquettish ways, was more interested in batting her eyelashes at that handsome new artist than in the funeral. Young Kitty, gangly as a growing fawn, glanced around like she'd seen a ghost, her pointed face like a pixie's in the purple-blue glow of the stained-glass window towering over the altar. Beside her, that foreign evacuee girl looked petrified, like she'd seen death before and a lot more besides.

The Brigadier glared on like a domineering vulture, the burnished medals and his upper-class prestige ranking him above everyone else in the church. He was rhythmically thwacking his silver-tipped horsewhip against his boot. His violent temper is legendary, and no one was going to cross him today. You see, not only had he lost his only son, he'd also lost the family fortune. The Chilbury Manor estate must go to a male heir, and Edmund's death has plunged the family into turmoil. The Brigadier would be branded a fool if the family fortune was lost under his watch. But I know his type. He won't take this lying down.

After the gruelling service, we grabbed our gas mask boxes and traipsed gloomily through horizontal daggers of icy rain up to Chilbury Manor, a Georgian monstrosity that some past Winthrop brutally erected.

I puffed up the steps to the big door, hoping for a glass of something and a big comfy sofa, but the place was already crammed with damp-smelling mourners and wet umbrellas. It was noisy as King's Cross, what with the marbled galleried hallway echoing with ladies' heels and noisy chatter. The Winthrops are an old, wealthy family, and the locals are scavenging toads, all hanging around in case they can get their grubby hands on some of the spoils.

And me? I already have my hand in their pocket, and that makes it my business to keep track of events around here. You see, the Brigadier has already been paying me to keep my mouth shut about his affairs, including that unwanted pregnancy last year, and his nasty son spreading disease around this village faster than you can say 'the clap'. This war means opportunity for me. Any midwife worth her salt must realise the potential such a situation can bring, especially with the likes of these smutty gentry who think they're beyond reproach. They're easy prey for extortion – twenty here, forty there. It all adds up.

As I entered, my eyes caught a pretty twist of a maid, standing on the stairs to avoid the rush, a tray of sherry glasses balanced on one hand, her long neck elegant but her mouth sour as curd. She came to me with gonorrhoea she'd got from Cmdr Edmund last year, just like half the bleeding village. She told me he'd promised to marry her, promised her money, freedom, love, and then he'd vanished into the Navy as soon as war broke out. I felt sorry for her, so I told her about his other women – the previous maid, the gardener's wife, the Vicar's daughter – all with the same condition. I treated them all, and Edmund too, the disgusting beast. Elsie was the maid's name. I think she was a bit unsettled that I told her everyone's secrets, worried about her own, no doubt. But I told her it was because we were friends, her and I.

I smiled at her in a conspiratorial way, and took a glass of sherry from her tray. You never know when these people could come in handy.

I joined the condolence line behind gloomy Mrs Tilling, nurse, choir member, and deplorable do-gooder. 'He will always be remembered a hero,' she was saying with immense feeling. She is so excruciatingly well-meaning it makes me want to plunge her long face into a barrel of ale to perk her up.

'Never should have happened,' snapped Mrs B, another member of the choir, all upright with traditional upper-class fervour, the insufferable next to the insupportable. Her full name is Mrs Brampton-Boyd, and it exasperates her that everyone calls her Mrs B.

As I came to the front, Mrs Tilling sucked her cheeks in with annoyance. She's never approved of me. I've stepped into her nursing territory, become too close to her village community. She may also have heard about some of my less orthodox practices. Or the payoffs.

'It's so terribly tragic,' I said in my best voice. 'He was taken so young.' Planting a closed-lipped smile on my face, I swiftly moved away to the side, standing alone, people glancing over from time to time to wonder what business I had there.

Just as I was thinking of opening a few doors and having a little nosy around, a hunched goblin of a butler directed me into the drawing room, where I was rather hoping to partake of some upper-class funeral fare but found myself alone in the big, still room.

The distant clang of someone banging out the *Moonlight Sonata* on a piano clunked uneasily around the ornate ceiling as I ran my fingers over the crusted gold brocade couch. Then I picked up a bronze sculpture of a naked Greek, heavy in my fist like a lethal weapon. The opulence of the room was dazzling, with the floor-length blue silk drapes, the majestic portraits of repulsive forebears, the porcelain statues, the antiquity, the inequity.

I couldn't help thinking that if I had that sort of cash I'd do a much better job, cheery the place up a bit. It smelt like death, as old as the dead men on the walls, as fusty as the eyes of the disembodied deer watching from the oak-panelled wall, the settle of dust and ashes. I was reminded of the last war, the Great War, when all the money in the world couldn't buy an escape from mortality. It was the one great leveller. Funny how things went back to normal again so quick – the rich in charge, us struggling below.

I pulled out my packet of fags and lit one, the sinewy smoke meandering into the drapes, making itself at home.

A gruff voice came from behind. 'May I have a word?' A hand grasped my elbow, and before I knew it I was being pulled to a door at the back of the room. I turned to see the Brigadier, purple veins livid on his temples – he must have been at the Scotch late last night. He shoved me into a study, thick with male undercurrent, lots of leather chairs and piles of papers and files. The tang of cigars mingled unpleasantly with the dead-dog smell of rank breath.

As he twisted the key in the lock behind him, I knew this was going to mean money.

'I'm sorry for your loss,' I said, surveying the surroundings, trying to cover up any trepidation. The Brigadier's a bigwig, an overpowering presence, officious and rude and unlikeable, yet powerful and ruthless. He's one of the old types, the ones who think the upper class can still bluster their way through everything. The ones who think they can boss the rest of us around and act like they own the country.

'I knew you'd come,' he muttered in an irritated way, his voice slurring from drink. 'Which is why I had Proggett put you in the back drawing room. I have a service for you to perform. Time is of the essence.' He sat down behind his vast desk, all businesslike, leaving me standing on the other side, the servant awaiting instruction. I considered pulling over a chair, but fancied this act of rebellion might lose me a few bob, so I just plonked my black bag on the floor and waited.

'Before I begin, I must know I have your full confidence,' he said, narrowing his eyes as if this were an official war deal, when I knew outright it was going to be nothing of the sort.

'Of course you have it, like you always do,' I lied, glowering at him for even doubting my integrity. He didn't scare me with his upper-class military ways. 'I'm a professional, Brigadier. If that's what you mean? I'm never surprised by what is asked of me. And I always keep my mouth shut.'

'I need a job done,' he said brusquely. 'I've heard you're willing to go beyond the usual services?'

'That depends on what the service in question is,' I said. 'And how much I'll be paid.'

A gleam came to his eye, and he sat up. I was speaking the language he wanted to hear – more interested in the money than the nature of the deed. 'A lot of money could be yours.'

'What exactly do you have in mind?'

By now I'd guessed he was about to come out with something big, something that would line my pockets well and good. My bet would have been another affair gone wrong (perhaps a high-profile woman involved, maybe someone from the village), so *shocked* doesn't describe how I felt when he came out with it.

'Our baby must be a boy.'

There was a pause as I wondered what he meant. He took in my reaction, his eyes scrutinising me, debating whether I had the requisite bravery, deceit, greed.

'Ours is not the only birth to happen in the village this spring,' he continued, acting like he was giving complex orders on the front line. 'And ours must be a boy. If there were a way to ensure that this might be the case—'

The penny dropped. It was outrageous. He wanted me to swap his baby with a baby boy from the village, if his was a girl. I sucked in my lips, working hard to keep the ruddy great smile off my face. I'd take him to the bank for this! But I had to keep calm. Play it for all it was worth.

'I think it would be a tremendous risk, as well as an immense personal compromise,' I clipped.

He leant forward, dropping his façade for a moment, his eyeballs shooting out, bloody and globular. 'But could it be done?'

'Possibly,' I said elusively. But I knew I could do it. I have a vicious herbal potion that induces babies to come forth very promptly, and the village is small, you can get from one house to another in minutes.

'Anyone who could help that to occur would certainly be well compensated,' he said evenly, his fingers toying with his moustache as if it were a battlefield conundrum.

'How well?'

There was a scuffle from outside the door that made him pull back. 'We can discuss that at another time and place.' He stood up and went to the window. There was a French door that overlooked a muddle of fields and valleys down to the English Channel, grey and churning like dirty dishwater.

'We'll meet the Thursday after next at ten in the outhouse in Peasepotter Wood,' he said in a low voice.

'I'll be there,' I whispered.

'You may leave now,' he added. Then his head shot round and his eyes dug into me with threatening revulsion. 'And mention this to no one.'

Only too happy to get away, I spun round and bolted for the door, fiddling with the key in the lock and then closing the door gently behind me, before sallying out into the thronging hall. My stride widened as I swooped in and out of the black-clad mourners, the uniforms, the nosy neighbours. I marched straight out of the front door without so much as bye your leave. People were still arriving in the expansive driveway, so I had to refrain from skipping for joy as I trotted briskly back to the village.

Once I was at my drab little home, I gave a well-earned cheer, throwing my arms up into the air and laughing with utter delight. This is going to work.

I'll show you that you can forgive me for what happened with Bill, and for taking the money when we ran off. How was I to know he'd grab the cash and vanish as soon as he could?

We can be happy again, you and me, like when we were young. Funny, you never think how lucky you are until it's all whisked away, first Mum dying, then staying with disgusting Uncle Cyril when Dad was in jail, shut in his attic like slaves. But enough of that. We'll put the past behind us, Clara.

It's time to gird our loins. There are two other women in the village who are expecting around the same time as Mrs Winthrop. Droopy Mrs Dawkins from the farm is on her fourth, so that should be simple. Less easy would be the goody-two-shoes school teacher Hattie Lovell, whose husband is away at sea. Hattie is chummy with that niggling nurse, Mrs Tilling, who's done the midwifery course and sees fit to poke her nose into my birthing business. Every time I go round to Hattie's, she's there, hanging around like a superior matron, saying she's going to be midwife at the birth. She doesn't understand. This village is only big enough for one midwife.

I'll write again after the meeting with the Brigadier. Who would have known such an upper-class gentleman could stoop so low? I'm going to tap him for the biggest money he's ever known. I won't let you down this time, Clara. You'll get the money I owe you, I swear.

Edwina

Kitty Winthrop's Diary

Saturday, 30th March, 1940

They announced on the wireless that keeping a diary in these
difficult times is excellent for the stamina, so I've decided to
write down all my thoughts and dreams in my old school
notebook. Nobody is allowed to read it, except perhaps when
I'm old or dead, and then it should be published in a book, I
think.

Important things about me

I am thirteen years old and want to be a singer when I grow
up, wearing glorious gowns and singing before adoring audi-
ences in London and Paris, and maybe even New York too. I
think I will handle the fame well and become renowned for
being terribly levelheaded.

I live in an antiquated village full of old buildings that
always smell of damp and mothballs. There is a green with a
duck pond, a shop, a village hall, and a medieval church with
an overgrown graveyard. The church is where we used to
have choir until the Vicar decided we couldn't go on without
any men. I've been pestering him to change his mind, but
he's simply not listening. In the meantime I've been trying

to set up a choir at the school. I used to go to a boarding school, but they evacuated it to Wales and Mama didn't want me to go. So now our butler, Proggett, has to drive me five miles to school in Litchfield every day. It's not a bad place, except no one wants to join my choir.

I have one vile sister, Venetia, who is eighteen, and I used to have a brother until he was bombed in the North Sea. We live in the big house of the village, Chilbury Manor, which is terribly grand but freezing in the winter. It's not as pristine as Brampton Hall, where Henry Brampton-Boyd lived before he joined the RAF to fight Nazis in his Spitfire. When I am old enough we are to be married, and we'll have four children, three cats, and a big dog called Mozart. We'll live a life of luxury, although we'll have to wait until old Mr Brampton-Boyd passes away to inherit Brampton Hall, and since he prefers to spend his time in India, who knows when that may be. Venetia jokes that he only stays there to avoid his wife, bossy Mrs B, and if I were him I'd be tempted to do the same.

About the war

This war has been going on far too long – it's been well over six months now. Life has been insufferable. Everyone's busy, there's no food, no new clothes, no servants, no lights after dark, and no men around. We have to lug gas masks everywhere, and plod into air raid shelters every time the sirens go off (although they haven't very often so far). Every evening we have to draw thick black curtains across every window to stop the light from alerting Nazi planes to our whereabouts. The crackling of the news broadcasts on the radio is interminable, with people forever shushing and banning me from playing the piano.

Daddy is a brigadier, though I have no idea why as he never does any fighting, only occasionally going to London on what he calls 'war business'. I think he's trying to get into the War Office meetings, but they keep making excuses to keep him out. He has been especially cross, his horsewhip always at the ready to give one of us a reminder of our place. Venetia and I try to stay away from the house as much as we can. Mama's petrified of him and also extremely pregnant, so no one's around to watch us apart from old Nanny Godwin, and she's far too old and has never been able to stop us from doing anything anyway.

Some of the papers say the war's going to end soon, since there's no fighting and the Nazis seem happy occupying Eastern Europe. But Daddy says it's all nonsense, and the war is just beginning.

'The papers are written by fools.' He's fond of picking up the offending newspaper and slamming it down on a table or desk. 'Hitler's taking his time in Poland, then he'll turn his attention on us. Mark my words, the way this war's going, France will fall before the end of the year. And then we'll be next.'

'But it's so quiet and normal,' I say. 'My teacher is calling it the Phoney War because nothing's really happening. Half of the children evacuated from London have gone back already. He says our troops will be home by Christmas.'

'Your teacher is an imbecile who can't see beyond his own four walls,' Daddy cut in angrily. 'Look at Poland, Czechoslovakia, Finland. Look at all the ships sunk, the submarines, and our own Edmund.'

We had to end the conversation there as Mama started crying again.

My brother Edmund's death

The next thing I need to tell you about is Edmund, my brother who was blown up in his submarine. We're supposed to be in mourning, and I feel dreadful for saying this, but I don't miss him at all. He was a disgusting bully, and I loathed him. I've never forgiven him for shutting me in the well, the freezing water edging up to my mouth until Nanny Godwin found me. Or for the time he used me as a target in archery practice. Although he did promise to teach me to drive when I was older, which I suppose was quite nice.

Mama is beside herself and desperate for the new baby to be a boy, as is Daddy. He thinks girls are pointless, Venetia slightly less so because of her yellow hair. I am so utterly pointless I think he's forgotten I exist, except perhaps when he needs someone to blame. Sometimes I go to Mama to see if she can stop him from being so horrid, but she can't do anything. She only tells me to make sure I choose a decent, kind sort of man to marry. I wonder if she's terribly unhappy.

Every evening, Mama has the maid set Edmund's place for dinner, as if he's about to come in any minute, sitting and stretching his legs in his usual arrogant manner, making some cruel joke at someone else's expense, usually Venetia's or mine. Then he'd let out a few breaths of laughter, smoothing back his hair, as if it were simply super to be him. Sometimes it's hard to believe he's just gone. It was his funeral last week, without a body to bury. It seems so strange. Where did he go?

Death is at the forefront of my mind again this week, as David Tilling is leaving for France and he may never come back, especially since he's so hopeless at getting anything done. I heard Mrs B say yesterday that he was the type that a bullet would find faster than the rest, and I worry that she might be right.

I can't believe the group of children we grew up with here in Chilbury are all suddenly scattering – Edmund killed, David on his way to war, Henry flying Spitfires over Germany, Victor Lovell on a ship somewhere, Angela Quail in London, and only Hattie and vile Venetia left. I'll miss David especially. He was always the one waiting for me to catch up with the rest, a bit like a brother, only nicer. In a few weeks' time he'll be home after training, and everyone's invited to the Tillings' for a surprise leaving party before he heads off to the front. I know we're supposed to be cheerful these days, even if we know someone might die, but it's hard to forget that this could be the last time I see him.

List of things to make note of before someone leaves for war
The shape of their body – the blank cutout that will be
    left when they're gone
The way they move, the gait of their walk, the speed at
    which they turn to look
The crush of smells and scents that linger only so long
Their colour, the radiance that veils everything they
    do, including their death

People's colours

I like to see people as colours, a kind of aura or halo surrounding them, shading their outsides with the various flavours of their insides.

> Me – purple, as brilliant and dark as the sky on a
>   thundery night
> Mama – a very pale pink, like a baby mouse
> Daddy – soot black (Edmund was also black, but black
>   like a starless sky)
> Mrs Tilling – light green, like a shoot trying to come
>   up through the snow
> Mrs B – navy blue (correct and traditional)

Henry is a deep azure blue, to match his eyes. I'm always reminded of the flawless July day during our school holidays when he spoke of marriage, a year ago now. The sky was an endless blue, the stream beside our picnic spot trickling with late-afternoon laziness. Henry had joined Edmund, Venetia, and me, and we were tearing all over the countryside, Mama never having a clue where any of us had got to. Of course, because it was all out of the blue, Henry didn't have a ring, and we've never made it official. But he remembers, deep down in his heart.

I know he remembers.

My beastly sister, Venetia

In complete contrast to the rest of us, Venetia is clearly enjoying this war immensely, and not only because no one's around to keep an eye on her. It's shuffled everything around, made everyone more adoring, and Edmund's death has promoted her to top spot in the family. Venetia's colour is a vile greenish yellow, like the sea on a tempestuous day, sucking the living daylights out of anything good around her, dragging down young men into her murky depths, spewing them out unconscious on distant shores.

I find it tremendously funny that she's having trouble engaging the attention of the handsome newcomer, Mr Alastair Slater. He's an artist escaping potential bombs in London, like all the writers and artists desperate to save themselves. Daddy says they're running away, avoiding their duty. Mr Slater looks like Cary Grant – all groomed and sophisticated, unlike the boys around here. His colour is a dark grey to match his debonair suits and formal standoffishness. He seems completely uninterested in Venetia, even though she's parading herself around him day and night. I overheard her telling Hattie that she's made a bet with her friend Angela Quail that she'll have him eating out of her hand before midsummer, but the way things are looking, she'll have to work a little harder.

Angela Quail is the most flirtatious and despicable girl I know – it's impossible to believe she's the daughter of the Vicar. Her colour is tart red, all lips and slinky dresses and no morals whatsoever. She used to work with Venetia at the new War Command Centre in Litchfield Park, which is a gorgeous old manor house on the outskirts of Litchfield, complete with Georgian pillars and rolling gardens. It was requisitioned by the Government for the war a few months ago, and Lady Worthing is having to stay with her sister in Cheswick Castle, poor her. It's now a terrifically important place, and since it's only five miles from Chilbury, we're on special alert in case the Nazis try to bomb it. Venetia has a clerical job there and thinks she plays a vital role when all she does is type notes and relay telephone messages to London.

Last month Angela was moved from there to the real War Office in London, where she is almost certainly toying with every man available. Angela is without doubt the most accomplished flirt this side of the English Channel. Venetia's distraught that Angela's gone to London as she's her best friend, and who else can she share her conquests with? I was hoping that Venetia might become a bit nicer without Angela's evil presence, but she seems worse than ever.

Our Czech evacuee, Silvie

Now I must tell you about Silvie, our ten-year-old Jewish evacuee. The Nazis have invaded her home in Czechoslovakia, but her parents managed to get her here before war broke out. Her family is supposed to follow her, when they can get away. Uncle Nicky, Mama's youngest brother and my very favourite member of our family, was organising the children's evacuation and got us to take Silvie last summer before the war started.

'We had to stop the evacuation because the borders closed, which is terribly sad for the children left behind,' he told us. 'The Nazis run half of Eastern Europe now. It's desperate over there. They're thugs and arrest people if they don't obey the rules. They can do what they want. Everyone's petrified.'

Daddy wasn't happy about having Silvie at all. But then a few months later war was declared and hundreds of grotty

London evacuees turned up wanting homes. Suddenly he was overjoyed we had lovely, clean, quiet Silvie and no space for anyone else. The Vicar and Mrs Quail took in a dreadful woman with four squalling children who had lice and fleas and no table manners at all. The woman was forever arguing with Mrs Quail, and then upped and left back to London because the war didn't seem to be happening. She didn't even say thank you.

I've yet to decide what Silvie's colour is. She doesn't say much, or smile much either. We've been trying to make life a little jollier for her and helping her practise her English. And she told me she has a secret that she can't tell a soul.

'I am completely trustworthy,' I reassured her. But she refused to budge, her little lips tightly shut to warn me away.

She arrived without even a suitcase, which had been lost on the way. There had been a difficult border crossing into Holland, and they had to hurry everyone through. It was a group of about a hundred, some of them as young as five or six – she said they cried for their mothers all the way, for three whole days. The loss of the cases was especially traumatic as they had their favourite toys, photographs from home, everything that was familiar. We gave Silvie a doll when she arrived, but she put it on a chair at the side of the room, her face to the wardrobe, as if it were a magical doorway to a better world.

The new music tutor, Prim

But I almost forgot. There's some excellent news! A music tutor has moved into Chilbury. She came down from London to teach in Litchfield University. Her name is Miss Primrose

Trent, but she told us to call her Prim, which is funny as she's not prim at all but frightfully unkempt. With her frizz of greying hair and her sweeping black cloak, she looks more like a wizened witch with a stack of music under one arm. Her colour is dark green, like a shadowy woodland walk on a midsummer's night.

Mrs Tilling introduced me to her yesterday in the shop, and I felt bold enough to tell her my dreams of becoming a famous singer.

'Practise, my dear!' she boomed, her dramatic voice causing the tins to rattle on the shelves. 'You must have the courage of your convictions.' She swept her arm out gracefully as if on a grand stage. 'I can give you extra lessons if you have time.'

What an opportunity! 'I'll ask Mama to arrange one straight away. You see, we've had some disastrous news. The Vicar has disbanded the village choir, so we're stuck without any singing.'

'Well, that's no good, is it! To close down a choir. Especially at a time like this!'

I'm hoping with every inch of me that she'll persuade the Vicar to reopen the choir, although I can't see what either of them can do. With no men around, what hope do we have? In the meantime though, I have singing lessons to look forward to as Mama agreed. That'll propel me into the spotlight, I can tell by the way Prim's eyes twinkled.

Letter from Venetia Winthrop
to Angela Quail

Wednesday, 3rd April, 1940

Dear Angela,

The bet still stands! Mr Slater is tiresomely resisting my advances. I've tried my best tricks, even knocking on his door and asking if he had any spare paint as I was attempting 'a frightfully difficult landscape', but he simply handed some paint over and politely waved me off. I'd spent all day getting ready, wearing my green silk dress, my hair curled to perfection. Perplexing, my dear. *Perplexing* isn't the word!

But you must stop proclaiming victory, as I'll have him soon enough. He is truly captivating, Angie, and a romantic artist too. I've always thought of them as bohemian willowy types, but he is more athletic, with the look of a gentleman fencer – *en garde* and all that. Beneath those crisp suits I can make out his muscular arms, thighs even. How I long to run my fingers over him. But Angie, it's more than that.

There's something about him that makes me feel we're meant to be together. The way he looks at me, as if he's looking through me to a different person inside.

I miss having you here, even though things are improving. Everyone is finally calming down after Edmund's death, although Mama remains weepy and Daddy furious. I miss him too, in my way, the antics we'd get up to. Funny how one forgets how beastly someone can be when they're dead. I suppose the threat of him is gone.

I've been rekindling my friendship with Hattie, even though she's been as boring as boiled cabbage since she's become pregnant. I went around for afternoon tea yesterday. She'd redecorated the baby's room a ghastly green as that's the only paint she could find. Her terraced house on Church Row is excruciatingly tiny. I don't know how she can bear it.

'But it's next door to Miss Paltry, the midwife!' she exclaimed, inexplicable joy on her pretty face, her long dark hair especially unruly since she's been pregnant. 'Don't you see how useful that is? Although Mrs Tilling is to be my main attendant at the birth. She's like family to me with my parents gone.'

'And Mr Slater lives on the other side of you. That's infinitely more exciting,' I laughed, wondering if all this tedium was ruining my lipstick. I didn't want to bump right into him without looking perfect.

'How is your bet going?' she asked.

'Not well. I confess I don't know what to make of him.'

'I know what you mean. I do wonder what he's up to. I always see him going out, in his motorcar or on foot, with not so much as a paintbrush, and he doesn't come home for hours.' Hattie's always acting the sensible older one. She thinks being two years older makes her wiser. And now that she's going to have a baby, she's insufferable.

'Maybe he's really a movie star!' I laughed. 'He certainly has the looks.'

She didn't laugh. 'Maybe you're better off chasing someone else.'

I looked at her, in her dreadful maternity dress, the lonely quietness of the pokey little house, but I knew she was tediously happy. I have to confess that a flash of envy crossed my mind. But don't worry, I soon snapped out of it. Who wants Victor Lovell, after all? Who wants to be pregnant when there's so much excitement with this war? All the new things a girl can do. We'd never have got our clerical jobs with the War Office, and you would never have been sent to live in London by yourself. All the parties and freedom. I heard that Constance Worthing is even ferrying planes for the war effort.

I suppose Hattie's always been the sensible one, but she seems so annoyingly settled. I remember when we were young, the three of us in the Pixie Ring shouting, *We are as strong as the snakes, as fierce as the wolves, and as free as the stars.*

'I'm still the same person as before,' she said suddenly, as if reading my mind – funny how she does that – and I knew she hadn't changed at all.

I thought about Hattie having a baby as I walked home. I'm not sure I'd like being a mother, but perhaps it isn't as bad as all that.

Silvie came into my room when I was home, her quiet little feet treading carefully to the dressing table. She scoured it for treasures, asking me what various items were. Sometimes I make up stories about them: a necklace from the deep, a lipstick lost by a princess.

'Do you like Mr Slater?'

'How do you know about that?'

'Kitty told me,' she said simply. 'I hope he is kind. Like you.'

I smiled and gave her a cuddle. I'll have to make sure Kitty regrets telling my secrets, and doesn't hear any more.

Do write soon, Angie, as I heartily miss your mischief making. I do wish they'd send me to London with you, although now that I have Mr Slater to tantalise me, perhaps not quite yet.

Much love,
Venetia

Letter from Miss Edwina Paltry
to her sister, Clara

3 Church Row
Chilbury
Kent

Thursday, 4th April, 1940

Dear Clara,

The deal is done. We'll be wealthy beyond our wildest
dreams, dear sister. I went to meet the Brigadier,
as arranged, in the deserted stone outhouse in the
wood.

He was already there, crossly getting out his silver
pocket watch. 'You're late.'

'Am I?' I smiled politely. 'What a shame!'

He snorted at the unmistakable irony in my voice. 'Well?
Do you think you can do it?'

'Swap the babies, you mean?' I kept the smile off my face,
although I still found it hilarious that he was suggesting
just that. 'Nip between the births and make both women
believe they gave birth to a different baby?'

'Yes, damn it, woman,' he shouted. 'Or should I find
someone else?'

'I doubt you'll find anyone as trustworthy.' Then I added with a little laugh, 'Although Mrs Tilling has midwife training, if you'd like to ask her?'

'Don't be absurd,' he bellowed. 'Just answer me. Will you do it?'

'Depends how much we're talking.'

He snorted like a disgruntled bull. 'I'll give you five thousand.'

I stopped breathing for a split second. Five thousand pounds is a vast sum – ten times what I earn in a year. But I wasn't willing to leave it there. The old rascal is worth far more than that. I've seen the finery, the crystal chandeliers, the crown sodding jewels.

'I wouldn't be able to work again, and I'd need to leave the village afterwards,' I said, looking as sorrowful as I could. 'I'd need twenty to give it a thought.'

He was furious. 'Eight thousand then. That should be plenty for a woman like you.'

'A woman like me?' My face shot up to meet his gaze, and I raised an eyebrow. 'A woman like me can kick up a good storm, you know?'

'Are you threatening me?' he hissed. 'If you are, I'll deny it. They'll never believe your word over mine.'

'Don't count on it, Brigadier,' I said. 'The days of you toffs being in charge are long gone.'

'I'll get you strung up for something, you mark my words.'

'Ten and I'll do it,' I said resolutely. 'Provided I get the money regardless if it works out or not.'

'You'll do exactly what I tell you, Miss Paltry, or you'll never work here again. Do you hear me?' He came up close. 'You'll get your money when I get my boy.'

'You give me the money beforehand, and if no boys are born, there ain't a jot I can do about it. But if there is a boy' – I smiled with enticement – 'I will make him yours.'

He clenched his fists. He hadn't been bargaining for this. Since arriving here five years ago I have been careful to build a reputation of even dealings, especially following my miscalculations in that village in Somerset. (You'll remember how they hounded me out after I gave wart patients the wrong ointment that resulted in purple-coloured nether regions. It caused three marriage breakups, a major punch-up, the disappearance of a young woman, and at least two angry men trying to hunt me down.) No, Clara. I've played my game carefully in Chilbury, hushed up my past, played by their rules.

Now it's time to reap the rewards.

'All right, you'll get ten thousand. But it'll be half before and half after,' he roared. 'And if Mrs Winthrop gives birth to a boy, you'll settle with half.' He looked me over scowling. 'How am I to trust a woman capable of doing such a business?'

'Women are capable of many things, Brigadier. You just haven't noticed it until now.' I gave a quick smile. 'I will need the first half of the money, in cash, two weeks from today.'

He blustered around the scrub, and I suddenly realised how much this deal meant to him. I should have taken him for fifty. He would have done it. He would have done virtually anything.

'You'll get your money,' he growled under his breath. 'Come back here on that date at ten, and it'll be ready.' He came towards me, his eyes scrunched up like Ebenezer

Scrooge. 'And mind you keep your mouth closed, or the deal's off. Not a word to my wife either. She is not to know. Do you hear me?'

'I hear you, Brigadier.' I spoke quietly. 'Loud and clear.'

With that I turned and strode out into the wood, leaving him pacing around, cursing under his breath.

Taking a deep breath of newly fresh air, I danced out of the bracken and onto the path. This will work, Clara. As a precaution, I have decided to get chummy with the nuisance Tilling woman. Keep my ear to the ground. This is big money, and my attention to detail merciless. I'll write closer with details, just as you said you wanted in your letter. I know you think I'll mess it up like usual, but I won't let you down this time. You'll be rich before the spring is out, I swear.

Edwina

Notice pinned to the Chilbury village hall noticeboard,
Monday, 15th April, 1940

Rehearsals for the new Chilbury Ladies' Choir
will commence in the church on Wednesday
evening, 7 o'clock prompt.

Miss Primrose Trent, Professor of Music,
Litchfield University

Mrs Tilling's Journal

Wednesday, 17th April, 1940

Prim's notice in the church hall announcing a new 'Ladies choir' has caused uproar in our tiny community. Last night before the Women's Voluntary Service meeting (or the WVS as we say these days), Mrs B told me she'd gone straight to the Vicar to find out the truth.

"'Have you allowed this woman – this newcomer – to take over the choir and debase it beyond recognition?" I demanded of him, and do you know what he said? The Vicar, who is supposed to be a Man of God, told me, "Well, she was awfully forceful and I really couldn't object." I didn't know what to say!'

'Gosh,' I said. I was rather excited about the whole adventure. At least we'd be singing again. I'd missed it. 'I know it's unusual, but why don't we go along and see what Prim has to say. There's no harm in it, after all.'

'No harm in it?' she bellowed back at me. 'No harm in ruining the reputation of our village? I can't imagine what Lady Worthing will have to say to me about it. She's such a stickler for doing things the way they've always been done.'

A few of the other WVS ladies joined in, the Sewing Ladies tutting about it over their troops' pyjamas, the canteen ladies unsure how it would work. So you can imagine my curiosity as I peeked into the church this evening, nipping in out of the rain.

I was one of the first to arrive, and the place looked enchanted, the candles at the altar throwing dark shadows around the nave. One by one the ladies began to arrive: Mrs Gibbs from the shop, Mrs B, Mrs Quail at the organ, and even Hattie, who's heavily pregnant now but said she wouldn't miss it for the world. Miss Paltry made an appearance – it seems she is turning a new leaf, even speaking to me at the end about becoming involved in the WVS. Kitty and Mrs Winthrop bounded in enthusiastically, bringing their evacuee, Silvie, who for once was almost smiling. Venetia strolled in, perfectly dressed in case she bumps into Mr Slater. She's become astoundingly unpleasant. But maybe there's hope for her now that Angela Quail's out of proximity.

By seven the place was packed, in spite of the downpour, and a buzz of chatter and anticipation filled the chilly air; even Our Lady of Grace seemed to look down in readiness. Meanwhile, a firm contingent of naysayers clucked like a bunch of unhappy hens in front of the altos' pew, urged on by Mrs B.

Suddenly, the massive double doors flung open, and Prim, majestic in her black, sweeping cloak, swooshed down the aisle towards us, her footsteps cascading through the wooden awnings, scaring a few bats in the belfry. She swirled off her cloak and shook off the rain, her hair looking especially frazzled. With a look of pomp and ceremony in her eyes, she plumped a pile of music on a chair and pranced theatrically up the steps to the pulpit.

'May I have everyone's attention, please,' she called, her pronunciation resounding richly through the cloisters. 'I'm proud to announce the creation of the Chilbury Ladies' Choir.'

From one half of the crowd, a round of applause burst forth. I felt a warm glow inside me. This might become a reality.

But on the other side, Mrs B, hands on hips, stood defiant, guarding her territory and supporters with a firm, unyielding presence.

Prim continued, her bright grey eyes bulging with purpose. 'I know that everyone's been feeling downcast at the choir's demise, which is why,' she announced jubilantly with a flourish of her baton, 'I proposed to the Vicar that the village's dear choir should become a women's-only choir.'

'And how exactly did you do that?' Mrs B asked in her usual condescending way.

'I explained that now that there's a war going on, we're far more in need of a choir than ever before. We need to be able to come together and sing, to make wonderful music and help ourselves through this dreadful time.' She paused, turning towards a tall candle beside her so that its flickers reflected thoughtfully in her eyes. 'Some of us remember the last war, the endless suffering and death it caused. It is time for us women to do what we can as a group to support each other and keep our spirits up. Just because there are no men, it doesn't mean we can't do it by ourselves.'

'Don't be ridiculous.' Mrs B stepped forward, her pompous form bristling up to the pulpit. She was dressed in her usual tweed shooting jacket and skirt, puffing out her chest in what her friends and neighbours know to be her fighting stance. 'What will we do without the basses and tenors?'

'We will sing arrangements for female voices, or I will rearrange them for us. We don't need the men! We are a complete choir all by ourselves!'

'In any case,' Mrs Quail laughed from the organ, 'the only bass we had was old Mr Dawkins. And he hasn't been singing in tune for at least two years.'

A few titters came from younger members, but Mrs B was not disheartened, looking around for her supporters to speak up.

'What will God think?' one of the Sewing Ladies piped up. 'He couldn't have intended women to sing on their own. Just think of the Hallelujah Chorus – where would that be without men?'

'There are plenty of male-only choirs, aren't there?' Prim chuckled. 'Think of the great choirs of Cambridge, not to mention St Paul's Cathedral. I can't imagine any God would dislike a spot of singing.'

'But it goes against the natural order of things,' Mrs B said.

I felt like clearing my throat and telling her that she was wrong, and before I knew it, I was saying out loud, 'Maybe we've been told that women can't do things so many times that we've actually started to believe it. In any case, the natural order of things has been temporarily changed because there are no men around.' I glanced around for inspiration. 'Mrs Gibbs makes her own milk deliveries now, and Mrs Quail has taken on the role of bus driver, like a lot of us taking on new jobs. The war's mixed everything else up. Why shouldn't it change the choir too?'

A few claps went round, as well as one or two cheers of 'Hear, hear!' and 'That's the spirit!' I still couldn't believe I'd stood up and spoken, and to Mrs B as well, who was watching me in a highly disapproving way.

'Indeed, Mrs Tilling?' Mrs B snipped. 'I don't know which part of that address shocks me the most! The notion of having to lower our moral standards because of the war, or the fact that you, my dear, seem to have joined the fray.' She turned to the group, clustered on the altar between the two choir stalls. 'We will end this once and for all with a show of hands. Whoever agrees with this preposterous notion, please raise your hand.'

Now Mrs B is not a spirited loser. Even as she counted and recounted the hands that went up, an indignant frown took form. She glowered at us as if we were somehow beyond reproach. 'Don't think this won't have its consequences. I'll be watching. Carefully.' And with that she huffed off, making a great show of it, and then, not being able to quite leave, plonked herself down in the last pew. She obviously felt she could guilt us into changing our minds, but as the voices around me grew, I knew she had no such chance.

'What a jolly idea,' Hattie said. 'I can't think why we didn't come up with it before.'

'Yes, and such a splendid name too,' Venetia declared. 'The Chilbury Ladies' Choir. It has a ring about it.'

I hadn't thought of it before, but now I found myself wondering why we'd been closed down in the first place, why the Vicar had so much say over us. And, more to the point, why we'd simply let him do it.

Prim passed around some copies of 'Be Thou My Vision'. 'Let's get ourselves organised. Stand in your usual places in the choir stalls, or wherever you'd like to be, and try to sing along with your part.'

We muddled around, and Mrs B huffed into the altos beside me. 'I need to be here to see what a mess she's going to make of the whole thing.'

'It'll be fine,' I said, but I was holding my breath, praying that we'd do well. I didn't want it to fall through right from the start, for Prim to be disheartened by our terrible voices. We needed to show her that this could work.

With a look of confidence on her face, Prim lifted her baton, looked to Mrs Quail to begin the introduction, and then brought us in. The sound of our voices filling the space, echoing through the little stone church, brought a burst of joy inside of me: the thrill of singing as a group again, the soft music of intertwining voices, for once staying in tune. I wondered if everyone was putting in a little more effort. Trying to make this work.

'That was wonderful,' Prim gushed when the final tapering of the last notes ebbed away into the still air. 'We've got some talented singers here!'

We all smiled and hoped she was talking about us. Even Mrs B's little group seemed to come under the spell of the music, forgetting the objections.

Mrs B, however, wasn't ready to give up the fight. 'I'll have to speak to the Vicar about this,' she announced, and flounced down the altar and out of the double doors. I'll hear soon enough how that goes.

Afterwards, I wandered home in a trance, trapped between the euphoria of song and the pinpricks of fear reminding me that David is leaving soon. The Nazis invaded Norway last week, and we're sending a force to try to push them out. I hope they don't send David there.

Slowly, softly, I began to sing to myself 'Be Thou My

Vision'. Everything was black in the moonless night, the blackout rules forcing all the light out of the world. But with a cautious smile, I realised that there are no laws against singing, and I found my voice becoming louder, in defiance of this war.

In defiance of my right to be heard.

Kitty Winthrop's Diary

Thursday, 18th April, 1940

What a breathtaking day! My first singing lesson with the superb and masterful Prim took place at her house on Church Row at five o'clock. I have never been more excited, and arrived a whole ten minutes early, waiting for her to get back from the university.

Prim arrived on her bicycle, her cloaked body balancing precariously on the narrow frame. 'You're here early,' she chortled. 'I always say that enthusiasm paves every path with a shining light.' She climbed off and leant the bicycle against the front of the house. 'Come in, and we'll make some tea before we start.'

The small house was exactly the same size and shape as Hattie's, except it was completely filled with extraordinary things and smelt as musty as an antique shop. In the corner, a gold elephant stood on his hind legs. On the wall above were paintings of distant mountain peaks, and the burnt oranges and reds of a desert sunset. A small table was crammed with decorated boxes of different shapes and sizes, covered with shells or brightly coloured silks – peacock blue, emerald green, cerise.

'Open one,' she said, as she watched my eyes flitting over everything.

I picked up an emerald one with gold-coloured cord. There was a small latch that opened it, and inside the black velvet interior was a tiny silver ring, a child's, with a St Christopher motif on the front.

'Was this yours?' I asked hesitantly.

'Yes,' she laughed. 'It was given to me when I was a child. It came from India, where I grew up. India has always been my favourite place – the colours, the noise, the vibrancy, the people.' She pointed to a picture of a beautiful white temple on the wall beside her. 'We lived close to this majestic edifice, the Taj Mahal. It's a mausoleum built by an emperor for his wife, who died in childbirth. He visited here every day, it is said, to grieve.'

'Can you imagine loving someone so much that you create such a wonderful building?'

'Well,' she said. 'It depends how rich and powerful one happens to be, I expect. Most people wouldn't be able to afford it. But that doesn't make one's love any less. We can show our grief in simpler ways. Is not the beauty and power of funeral song just as great as such a palace?'

I nodded, peering into the sitting room that was beaming with the brightness of antiquities. 'Do all of these things come from India?'

'Not at all. I travelled across Asia. There's a mesmerising world out there, where people live in all kinds of different ways.' She led the way into the room so that I could see. Gold gleamed from every corner: gold urns, gold statues, gold silk drapes around the windows, tiny gold miniatures as small as my thumb – an elephant, an old woman, a falcon.

'Other cultures are rather odd, don't you think?' I said.

'No, quite the contrary. Other cultures often make me think that we're the strange ones.' She chuckled to herself, then headed for the kitchen. 'Let's make some tea.'

As the kettle boiled, I looked around. A series of old decorated jugs sat on the windowsill, and bunches of dried herbs lined the far wall, giving off scents of rosemary, thyme, and lavender. A waist-high seagull watched us from the corner.

'Oh that's Earnest, made of papier-mâché,' she chirped. 'He was one of the props for a play we put on in London years ago. He's always here in the morning, looking hungry.'

I laughed and gave him a pat on the head.

Around the sink were a number of bottles full of liquids and powders and potions, and I leapt back. Was Prim a witch?

She saw me stare, and smiled. 'Those are my medicines,' she said. 'I once was very ill indeed, and I need the medicine to prevent me from getting ill again.'

I stood back, looking at her. She looked pretty normal – well, normal in a kind of witchy way. 'It's not catching, is it?'

'No, I caught it from a nasty mosquito in India, but we don't have mosquitoes here.' She rearranged the bottles, then made the tea. 'The disease is called malaria.'

'Were you terribly ill?'

'It was almost the end of me. I was about the same age as your sister, my whole life ahead of me, with plenty of music and laughter, and romance too. There was a boy whom I was to marry.' She smiled at the distant memory of him. 'He was the most beautiful creature, a butterfly collector, brilliantly clever.'

'Why didn't you marry him?'

'He died,' she said simply. 'He contracted malaria at the same time as me, and didn't make it. We'd grown up as neighbours and then fell in love. We became ill at the same time. But the malaria ran its course and passed out of me. I was alive.'

'But brokenhearted!'

'Exactly, and ever since then I've felt destined to live a double life for both me and my butterfly collector, alone yet not.' She found a floral porcelain sugar bowl and milk jug. 'It taught me that you have to live your own life. Don't let anyone hold you back.'

I found myself blurting out, 'I want to be a singer, but Daddy insists that I can't. He wants me to make a good marriage, to be a good wife. But Mama tells me to take care when choosing a husband, or my life will be a misery.'

'You need to make your own path,' she said, leading the way into the back room. 'Decide what you want to do, and then all you have to do is work out how to achieve it.'

The room was full of musical instruments. There was a huge harp, an upright piano, a harpsichord, a stand with a clarinet, and a silver piccolo lying across the table like a fairy had just flown off after doing a spot of practice.

Prim perched the tray on a tiny round table and pulled over the piano seat, gesturing for me to sit on the harpsichord chair.

'Is that why you never married? Do you still love the butterfly collector?'

'I don't know.' She smiled, pouring out the tea. 'Sometimes we do things without fully understanding. You shouldn't try to know everything, Kitty. Often it's beyond our comprehension.' She put the teapot back on the tray. 'Now before we start, I want you to sing me a note, as clearly as you can.'

I sang a long, high 'laaaa'.

'Beautiful,' she said, picking up the cup and saucer again and handing it over to me. 'Did you think about that too much before singing?'

'No,' I said, sipping the hot tea.

'Sometimes the magic of life is beyond thought. It's the sparkle of intuition, of bringing your own personal energy into your music.'

'But don't I need to worry about singing the right words to the right notes?'

'The most important part of singing is the feeling.' She leant forward. 'Remember, Kitty. I have faith in you.'

That afternoon we sang 'Ave verum corpus' by Mozart, my favourite composer. I sang better and stronger than I ever have before.

'There is a tragic tale about Mozart,' she told me. 'He wrote his Requiem, one of the saddest funereal pieces ever written, as he himself was dying, telling his wife, "I fear I am writing a requiem for myself." On the eve of his death, he and some friends sang it together, and it was at the most poignant song of his Requiem, the 'Lacrimosa', that he let the papers drop and began to weep for his very own death. He died in the early morning. Can you imagine writing your own death music?'

I gasped. 'That's dreadful. Do you think the music made him die?'

'Perhaps it was that he knew deep down inside that he was dying, and put that fear into the music.' She looked back at the 'Ave verum corpus'. 'Why don't you try this again, just like before, only this time, think about Mozart writing for his own death. Put your heart into it.'

She began the introduction, and I felt the sound of my voice come from deep inside, and I found myself thinking of the fear you must feel before you die.

A strange elation came over me when I'd finished, like I was a pure white dove's feather being whooshed up into the air by the lightness of the breeze. And later, as I wandered home, I drew a deep breath of the crisp spring air, and I felt suddenly jubilant to be alive.

Letter from Miss Edwina Paltry
to her sister, Clara

3 Church Row
Chilbury
Kent

Friday, 19th April, 1940

Dear Clara,

A large pile of crisp hundred-pound notes is now hidden in a secret hole under my floorboards, wrapped in an old envelope and done up neatly with a piece of string knotted twice. In less than a month, the deed will be done, the money will be double, and we can away, you and I, to our new life in Birnham Wood.

Yesterday I met the Brigadier for the exchange, the bundle of money gripped firmly in his sinewy fingers, the tight old git. To say he was reluctant to hand it over would be putting it mild. But I finally wrenched it away and fled, the money safe in my hands.

That was the easy part.

Now I have to deliver the boy.

You see, much to my infuriation, Mrs Dawkins from the farm gave birth last Friday. I wanted to push its scrawny head back in, but then I saw that it was a girl, so it wouldn't have been any good anyway.

Now my hopes are pinned on goody-two-shoes Hattie. She's due a week after Mrs Winthrop, so at least I won't have any issues with early births. Problem is the Tilling woman's hovering around like a bleeding fairy godmother. Now she's gone and promised to be midwife at the birth, even though I tried to talk Hattie out of it. I mean, who would take a misery like Mrs Tilling instead of an experienced, well equipped professional like myself? But she was adamant, whining that Mrs Tilling was the closest to family that she has in a pathetically sentimental way. God damn the girl!

Unspeakable as it was, I decided to befriend the nauseating Tilling woman. I had to persuade her out of it, or find out when she'd be out of town. If all else fails, I could give her a major injury, push her down some stairs or collide into her with my bicycle. I hadn't wanted to go that route frankly. There's a fine line between a broken arm and manslaughter, after all.

As a first effort, I joined the new choir to cosy up next to her, and I couldn't believe my luck when I walked in and spotted a place right beside her.

'I'm surprised to see you here, Miss Paltry,' she said snootily, shuffling over. 'It's not often we see you in church.'

'I always come on Sundays,' I smiled warmly, although I bet she's the type to count and see who's absent.

There was a lot of kerfuffle about starting a women's choir, which was patently ridiculous. Of course women can sing without men. I do it every week in the bath.

Then we sang some rather dreary hymns, and after practice was over, I saw my chance.

'I feel it my duty, Mrs Tilling, to lighten your load and take over Hattie's birth,' I began. 'I live next door to her, after all, and you're so incredibly busy these days. I have all the equipment and medicines at my house should anything happen. I even have a mechanical ventilator,' I lied.

'What? In your own home?' Mrs Tilling frowned with disbelief. 'Did the hospital lend it to you?'

'Yes, that's it,' I said quick as a fox, hoping she wouldn't check. 'You'd be surprised how often I need it to get the baby breathing proper. First-time pregnancies can be hazardous, you know.'

'But you're busy too, and Hattie's made her mind up to have me there.'

'I may be busy, but duty first!' I bounced back. 'I feel a responsibility, deep down inside.' I thrust a fist up against my heart at this point, looking all patriotic. 'And if anything should happen, I'd feel tormented for the rest of my days.' I tried to push out a few tears at this point, but there's only so much you can do.

'Quite,' Mrs Tilling said, stepping back, a look of distaste on her lips. I sensed that she smelt something fishy. I must have overdone the theatrics. So I quickly changed tack.

'But you do so much for our little community, what with the WVS always helping people out – all this on top of your own nursing duties.'

'Yes, the WVS is a great force. You should join. There's a meeting in Litchfield a fortnight from today, distributing the Bundles for Britain from America. Why don't you come along and see how it works.'

I smiled a gleeful smile, as that was precisely what I was looking for! A date when the Tilling woman would be out of town. And perfect timing too – a day before Mrs Winthrop's due date, and a week before Hattie's. 'Is it an all-day event?'

'Yes, all day Friday the third of May.'

She looked slightly bemused at my enthusiasm. So I stopped smiling and added with my usual despondency, 'I'll have to check my dates, but I'll try to come.'

Fortunately, Kitty descended on her with ludicrous cheers for the new choir, so I scooped up my bag and fled, dashing home before my elation exploded.

What a stroke of luck! Now all I have to do is check that she keeps her WVS meeting and hone my plan for the births.

I have become quite the professional, you see, Clara. My herbal potion brings babies out with impressive speed. Now, to give the potion to Mrs Winthrop, who is a timid, compliant sort of woman, will be no problem. This is her fourth baby, so I expect the baby to pop out within the hour. After calling out that it's a boy, I'll pretend the baby's not breathing proper, that I need to whisk it to my house for resuscitation with the mechanical ventilator. (Who's to know I haven't got one?)

Hattie, however, will be a more difficult matter. Not only will it be gruelling to get her to take the potion as she is so nauseatingly proper, but then it'll take four or five hours to get the baby out, it being her first child. Meanwhile, I'll need someone to watch the Winthrop child.

That's why I decided to enlist the Winthrops' maid, Elsie. Not only could she lend a sense of propriety by coming with me when I whisk off the Winthrops' baby, but she could also help look after the mite while I'm busy with Hattie. So when I spotted her in the shop yesterday, I invited her for tea and mentioned that I may be in need of her assistance at the birth.

'What you're saying is you want me to help with Mrs Winthrop's birth, and then come to your house if you have to take the baby away for emergency help?' She screwed her eyes up with distaste, suspecting it was down-and-dirty business. But she didn't ask questions, came from a background like that, see — ask no questions, take the money, leg it.

'That's right, love,' I said, offering her another biscuit. 'I'd just need someone to help me look after the baby for a short while.'

She took two biscuits, and I could see her thinking it through, her beautiful face pondering like a deer listening for danger. 'I could do it,' she said at last. 'But how much will you give me?'

'I'd give you ten bob for your trouble, provided you kept quiet.'

'Ten bob?' she uttered. 'More like ten quid, I'd say.'

'Five quid then,' I said. What a pain this girl was being!

'Oh, all right then,' she said, getting up. 'I'd love to get me own back on that cheating bastard, even if it's just his family.'

'You're worth a thousand of him, Elsie,' I said, leading her to the door. 'You need to find yourself a proper gentleman.'

'Yeah, p'rhaps I will.' She poked her head out the door and looked up into the puffy grey clouds. 'You just wait, I'll find someone far better than that scoundrel.'

Then she darted out, her long slim form gracefully flitting through droplets of rain, and I settled back to my plan with relish.

This will work, sister! I wish you'd stop pestering me with your doubts. I have no time to think about whether it's right or wrong, and who cares anyway? How can I think of all that morality nonsense when we've got a chance to get back to where we belong, safe and free? I shall let you know when the deed is done. Keep hush, as usual.

Edwina

Silvie's Diary

Saturday, 20th April, 1940

Kitty told me to write a diary. It is good for my English. I have to write about our house. It is big and grand. Mrs Winthrop is quiet. Nanny Godwin is old. Kitty is nice but a bit bossy. Venetia is my friend. Brigadier Winthrop is very angry. There is a grumpy maid and a strange butler who has a hump. The new baby is nearly here. I hope they will still want me then.

There is a new choir and I am a soprano. Singing is good. Kitty helps me with the words. I like the horses too. Amadeus is my favourite. I fell off at Bullsend Brook last week. Mr Slater helped me walk home. He is the man Venetia likes. He spoke a little Czech. It was terrible. My English is much better.

Kitty Winthrop's Diary

Tuesday, 23rd April, 1940

David Tilling's leaving party

Tonight Mrs Tilling was throwing a party for David. He's back from training and heading to the front in France tomorrow.

But I was much more focused on Henry, who was on forty-eight-hour leave from his aerodrome. One has to take advantage of these moments if one has eternal happiness in mind. I spent the afternoon perfecting my appearance. Floating around in Venetia's lilac chiffon dress, I knew I would be the focus of everyone's attention. People would say, 'Is that Kitty? Who would have known she'd be so beautiful', and, 'She puts Venetia quite in the shade.' Henry would watch from afar, unable to tear his eyes away. Then, when the music started, he would take me in his arms and express the endless depths of his love.

Maybe it wouldn't happen exactly like that. There might not be dancing, after all. But I was determined that this was the night that would secure our future together.

'The dress is too big,' Silvie muttered when I asked her how I looked.

I'd already padded myself up a little on top, but decided to throw an extra stocking down each one, just to be on the safe side.

'That's better,' I said, smoothing down the dress in front of the mirror. 'He won't be able to resist me, don't you think?'

Silvie sighed. 'I think he likes Venetia.'

I laughed. Silvie's definitely coming out of her shell a bit more, but I don't know where she gets some of her ideas. I'm far more interested in hearing about her secret, and badger her to tell me all the time. But she just goes quiet and runs off.

Venetia wanted to make a late entrance so she stayed behind, as did Daddy, who was tied up with work. Norway is going horribly wrong, he says. The Nazis are walking all over us, and it looks like we might have to back out fast. Everyone's worried they'll invade Belgium and France next, although apparently we have all routes covered, so we should be fine.

So it was only Mama, Silvie, and I who plunged into the cool evening air. We beamed our torches around because it's scary walking down the lane next to Peasepotter Wood. Just as we were saying that you never know who might be lurking in there, there was a crunch of bracken and who should appear but Proggett. He shook himself off, bid us good evening, and headed back to the house. How very odd.

We pressed on. As Mama is incredibly pregnant now, Silvie and I had to take an arm on each side to help her along, which made it rather jolly.

The sky was curdled with dimples of darkening dusk, and apart from the odd hoot of a barn owl, it was silent, like we were treading into an enchanted land. Tiny threads of pollen dusted the air, the sweetly scented yellow specks plunging me into a reminder of last summer, before this beastly war, when everything was just right – as it should be.

The Tillings' home, Ivy House, is one of my favourite places in the village. Not as imposing as Chilbury Manor, nor as ornate as Brampton Hall, it has a quiet serenity about it, a flavour of Mrs Tilling's thoughtfulness lacing itself through the fairy-tale gardens, the tiny rosebuds growing over a series of pagodas, and a birdbath and feeder, as Mrs Tilling loves all living creatures. She now has six hens for eggs, and a healthy vegetable patch to help the war effort. Ivy House used to be the vet's office before Dr Tilling died ten years ago, and there is still an air of purpose around the place, as if, at its very heart, it remains a haven for lost or harmed creatures.

As we opened the front door, a lively throng surged out into the garden, and we hurried in to avoid blackout fines. (Mrs B dishes them out like a strict school ma'am – even if only a smidgen of light is let out for a split second she'll slap a fine in your hand and bellow, 'We don't want the Jerries to see us, do we?')

Inside, the house was merry with flickering candles and jaunty music, which sat oddly with the dreadful fear that David might not come back. Red, white, and blue bunting was draped across the walls, probably borrowed from Mrs B after the extravaganza she threw for Henry. The crowd of chattering villagers stood around gossiping, each clutching a rationed-out glass of sherry.

Venetia made her grand entrance not long after we'd arrived, bringing the room to a standstill by loudly proclaiming, 'I hope I'm not late!' Standing out from the rest of us, she was wearing a dress of glistening green and gold, twirling it this way and that so that the sequins caught the light, trailing around her legs with a tempting fluidity. Within an instant, there was a crowd of men surrounding her, mostly friends of David's on their way to war. She rewarded each with her special flirty attention, all pouty lips whispering little secrets into their ears. I wondered if I could craftily trip her up.

Before long Mrs Tilling hushed us, sending a wave of shushes around the room, and went to fetch David down from his room. We cheered as he came in, dressed in full, pressed khaki uniform, looking terribly grown up. But as I watched, I realised with a flash of both relief and worry that he was still the same David – relief that a uniform doesn't change a person, then worry that the clumsy lad was going to the front line. He was still the same foolish nine-year-old who'd got stuck up the cherry tree on the green, the same lanky twelve-year-old who I'd punched for pulling my pigtails, the same idiot fourteen-year-old who'd crashed the Dawkinses' tractor into a perfectly innocent hedge. His colour is yellow, although not for cowardice, but rather a kind of blindness to reality, and I couldn't help but worry for him. Even now, the eager and dazed look in his eyes showed the way he embraced every challenge in life, with a tireless naivety, like a fox gambolling into the hunt, half expecting to be caught, not thinking about how it all might end.

'Wow!' he gasped as he came into the glistening sitting room. 'You shouldn't have gone to so much effort.' He put his arm around Mrs Tilling in his chaotically warm way. 'Thank you for coming, everyone!' He stepped forward to us. 'Lovely to see you, Mrs B, I thought you'd be far too busy giving someone what for. Have you persuaded Mr Churchill to come and give the Chilbury WVS a speech yet? Bet he doesn't know he has his top fan club here!'

Everyone laughed, and someone called, 'He will do soon enough!'

David then turned to Venetia, taking her hand and kissing it. 'And the beautiful Venetia, a last sight of you to cherish on my journey.' His eyes remained on her as his smile lurched wetly.

Venetia was all modesty, looking up at him with fluttering eyelashes and glossy red lips. 'David, you'll come back my hero,' she said in a voice breaking with tears. I wanted to laugh, until I met Mrs Tilling's sour look from across the room. We all know Venetia doesn't care a farthing for David. I have no idea why she insists on playing stupid games with him.

Mrs Tilling asked me to offer around a plate of rather chewy cheese straws (with so many rations no one ever knows what people put into recipes these days). So I mingled around, watching Henry, who was talking to a very pregnant Hattie. He was looking terrifically handsome with his sandy hair cropped and his pristine RAF uniform. His new moustache is devilishly dashing, like all the best fighter pilots. It makes his nose look a little less beaky, I think. And he looks older too, even though he's already nineteen – a real man, someone who'll know how to take care of me. He didn't seem to notice me watching, until Hattie drew me over to join them.

'What a gorgeous dress, Kitty,' she said, fingering the fabric. 'Don't you think so, Henry?'

'Yes indeed. You look lovely, Kitty,' he said, grinning, and I found myself dissolving into his eyes. But then he added,

'You'll follow in your sister's footsteps soon and become quite the beauty.' His eyes swept over to Venetia, who was holding forth in a crowd of men beside the piano. Why does she feel she has to get the attention of every man in the room, including Henry, when she's not even interested in any of them?

'I don't want to look like her,' I said, annoyed, making him look back to me. 'I want to be a beauty in my own right.' I felt Hattie let out a sigh, I have no idea why.

'Of course you're a beauty in your own right, Kitty!' Henry declared jovially, putting his hand warmly on my upper arm and giving me a special smile. I felt a surge of heat where he touched me, like a flame lighting up my body. I waited for him to take me in his arms—

But suddenly I felt his attention melt away – Venetia was approaching. Her dress fluttered as she twirled from one man to the next, like a dazzling dragonfly soaring around in search of prey. Her blonde hair hung low over her pearly white shoulders, while a stream of pungent perfume oozed from her soft, white neck. Henry's hand lost contact with my arm, which suddenly felt cold and lost, and when I looked up at him, he had turned to face her.

'Come and sit down with me, Henry darling, and tell me all about your bombing raids,' she chanted loudly, scrolling her fingertips under his chin and softly directing his mouth towards her carefully painted lips. 'I hear you've been fighting over Norway.'

'I thought you were busy with the other men,' he said under his breath.

'They don't mean a thing to me,' she said, pouting. Then she leant her head to one side, her thick blonde hair forming a shimmering curtain to conceal her from the rest of the room, and she whispered something into his ear, her long red fingernails barely touching the other side of his neck.

He responded by whispering something back, his hand moving her hair back as his lips hovered closely to her ear.

A man's voice called her from the other side of the room, and she pulled away.

'I'll have to think it over,' she said, a menacing gleam in her eyes, and spun off into the throng. Henry followed briskly, calling her name. 'Venetia!'

And me? I was abandoned, alone, in the middle of the room, mutely holding the plate of cheese straws in my hand. How could she do this to me? And why did he follow her? Doesn't he know that she's using him, that she says he's boring and his nose is like a giant wart? Doesn't he know she doesn't care a toss about anyone except herself, lining up the men to prove she's top? But worst of all, knowing how I love him, she revels in keeping him away from me, another of her little tricks at keeping everyone else beneath her, preening over us like she's some kind of vicious queen. It's not fair.

She snaked her way through the throng to Mr Slater, who was looking as impeccable as ever, his dark hair smoothed, a detached manliness about him making David and his friends look like halfwit schoolboys. Venetia's been fanatical trying to get his attention, but he seems immune to her charms – possibly the first man ever. She's stepping up her game, or else she'll lose her bet with Angela. And Venetia always has to win. She calls herself the empress of this little place, and she is determined to keep it that way.

I wandered over to Daddy, who had dragged himself away from his office and was looking ferociously at Venetia, with

Mrs B prattling away beside him. He wants Venetia to marry Henry and inherit Brampton Hall, which is just plain ridiculous. I simply can't imagine them together, and even more horrible is the thought of Henry being my brother-in-law. Whenever we'd see each other, the tension would be insurmountable. But we would never give way to our secret passions, holding them inside like tragic lovers. Perhaps there'd be the occasional moment when we'd meet on the veranda. 'Oh, Kitty,' he'd say, surprised to see me. 'Henry, I didn't think you'd be here—' I'd reply, looking at the ground, then back towards the open French door, a white drape spilling out in the soft summer breeze. 'Nor I. I just have to say—' 'No, don't, Henry. Don't make things harder.' 'But Kitty, darling ...' and so forth, until one of us dies.

Daddy was muttering about Mr Slater again. 'That Slater's a worthless coward for sitting out the war.'

'Mr Slater is exempt from fighting as he is flat-footed,' Mrs B told him pointedly. She's taken a fancy to Mr Slater, imagining him a great artist ready for her to discover. Trying to prove herself frightfully cultured, she's attempting to take him under her wing, Heaven help him. Although I have no idea whether he's any good. I don't think Mrs B has the ability to discern a masterpiece from a school art project.

'Slater's a down-and-out skiver shirking his responsibilities.' Daddy gulped down his sherry. 'Cowardly laziness, that's what it's all about. He doesn't realise that it's fighting that makes a real man.'

I thought of Edmund blown to bits in the North Sea, and poor David on the brink of a bullet in France, and couldn't help wondering if it had less to do with courage and more to do with common sense. Sending people off to their deaths seems completely ludicrous. I've begun imagining what it's like being blown up in a submarine, the radar blipping warning signals of one's approaching death, everyone saluting and singing the national anthem, 'God save our gracious King'. Then boom. Nothing. Only gnawed pieces of fingers and ears washing up on unsuspecting beaches.

As I watched Mr Slater, I couldn't help thinking that he can't be all bad. He helped Silvie home last week when she came off Amadeus. She should never have tried to clear Bullsend Brook. It was lucky he was there. Although I wonder what he was doing at Bullsend Brook. It's the other side of Peasepotter Wood – the middle of the countryside.

Daddy's eyes narrowed on Venetia, who was busy with Mr Slater, all witty replies and feigned boredom. Even though Daddy will have words with her later, he can't control Venetia at all. Every time he tells her to leave Slater alone, she simply shrugs and smiles and says she's 'Daddy's little poppet', and then carries on as usual. It makes me sick.

Henry was standing behind Venetia's shoulder protectively, trying to get into the conversation. He didn't have to try hard as Mr Slater seemed pleased to include him, speaking to him directly, making jokes as they both laughed. It was as if he was avoiding Venetia's attention. Henry put his hand on Venetia's arm, and I saw his eyes glance at her face, her throat, her cleavage beneath the low-cut dress. She shook off his hand, but he stayed close, and I wondered why he let her play games with him. But then I remembered how clever he is – he must be playing some kind of game himself.

Then I realised I wasn't the only one watching Venetia. David Tilling was gazing over at her from the window, leaning against the wall, engulfed by her presence. He's been in love with Venetia since he was in breeches. I never thought it was so serious, but his eyes were like those of a big gulping fish, drinking her up. Venetia needs to watch herself there. David's become a lot more forthright since army training.

'Let's get the piano out,' Mrs Tilling called. 'Can I dare Kitty with a song or two?' Mrs Quail (whose colour is a cheery orange) plumped her very ample behind on the piano stool, while Mrs B grasped my elbow and marched me up beside her. Everyone knows I plan to be a singer when I grow up, so I'm always the first one called for a song or two. Prim gave me a special smile from the crowd, and I felt determined to make a good impression.

'Come on, Kitty,' everyone cheered, and I must confess I was touched and took the score. Mrs Quail had given me 'Greensleeves', that beautiful song that was supposedly written by King Henry VIII, although I bet he asked someone to help him as you can't be king and write lovely music at the same time. Especially if you're busy beheading wives.

Mrs Quail began the opening, and I entered with the wonderful tune. It was perfect for showing off my top notes. When I finished, Prim gave me a little nod, as if to say *Well done*, and I felt a surge of delight. At long last my skills have been noticed!

I glanced over and caught Henry's eyes, and it was as if the world slowed down as our gaze met across the crowded room. He smiled, his whole face lit with joy and love, until Venetia nudged him with some remark or other. Trust her to interfere.

In the next song, Gilbert and Sullivan's 'I Am the Very Model of a Modern Major General', Mrs Quail started playing faster to trip me up on purpose. It was hilarious.

'You should be on stage as a comedian, not a singer, Kitty,' Hattie joked. Her colour is lilac, pretty and uplifting, and I have no idea why she's such good friends with vile Venetia and awful Angela Quail. Perhaps she's trying to rescue them from utter loathsomeness.

The pregnancy is making her tired – I could tell from her big brown eyes sagging with the weight of the evening – and yet she's always so lively, perking us up with her jokes and smiles. It must be difficult for her with Victor stuck on a ship in the Atlantic. I still can't get used to them being married. They were friends for years and then, as if someone turned on a giant light, war was about to break out and they fell in love and got married within the week. It's happening every-where, apparently. Obviously, it's all about death. How strange that love and death suddenly become so tightly knit in a time of war.

Why everyone's getting married in a hurry

If you're in love, why wait for a tomorrow that never
   comes?

People are being moved around, so if you want to stay
   with someone, you'd better marry them

Do you want to have children before it's all too late?

Do you want to be notified when your someone special
   is killed?

Do you want to get some money if they're killed in
   action?

Do you want someone special to pray for, live for?
   Who will be left at the end, after all?

As we left, I gave David a peck on the cheek. 'Don't let Venetia get you down,' I whispered, feeling the need to give him a word or two of support. 'You need to forget about her, find someone who'll treat you right.'

He frowned at me. 'What are you saying, Kitty?' he said, a cocky smirk coming over his mouth. 'Just because you're labouring after a lost cause, don't think we all are.'

I was shocked. The old David – the David before training – would never have said something like that. I wasn't entirely sure I understood what he meant. Who exactly is the lost cause around here?

Henry was leaving, so I had to forget about all that and rush off to steal a last moment with him. He was in the hall fetching his jacket – the special bomber pilot's one with leather and fur lining.

'When will I see you again?' I asked, standing in front of him on my toes, my eyes level with his lips, soft and beckoning beneath his neat moustache.

'You'll see me, young lady, when we've fought off those Nazis,' he said, taking my chin between his fingers. I tilted my face upward, closing my eyes, waiting for our lips to meet—

But then Mama came through and said we had to go, so we were forced apart. There was a smile on his face as I pushed my arms through the sleeves of my coat and followed Mama and Silvie out into the cold blackness outside. But as I turned to take one last look at him, he gave me a wink, and my heart exploded with joy, knowing only one truth. He loves me, and soon we will be together.

Mrs Tilling's Journal

Wednesday, 24th April, 1940

Today my son left for war, and I have adopted a brittle façade, a limp smile that wavers in and out like a broken tune on a worn-out wireless. I keep trembling as I remember the last war, all those soldiers who never returned, the neighbour's lad gone only a month before the telegram arrived.

They say this war is different, but a horror overcomes me if I dare to think of David out there, trying to stay sane through the gore. They say we have bombers and tanks and there won't be trenches like last time. But when I close my eyes, all I hear is the unbearable yells of men in pain, crushed by the colossal theatre of war.

You see, I saw them come home after the last war, the cripples, the amputees, the ones so disturbed they'd never sleep soundly again, haunted by their dead friends, guilt-stricken that they were somehow allowed to live. They were never the same again.

This morning was filled with much running up and down the stairs, the fresh scents of shampoo, hair cream, and clean laundry cutting the fraught air. I watched out of the hall window for the van, as slow, grey clouds mottled the outside world. Ralph Gibbs from the shop was leaving too, and Mrs

Gibbs was driving them both to Litchfield in her grocery van.

'Look at you,' I said as David came downstairs for the last time. He was wearing his uniform and looking all tidy and grown up. I straightened his already straight collar; I just wanted to touch him, to feel his mass under my fingertips. He looked down at me and grinned in his cheery way.

'Well, best be off then, Mum,' he said. 'Or I'll be in trouble before I've even started.' He laughed a little, and I clenched my mouth into a tight smile so that I didn't cry.

As he opened the front door, the clouds broke apart, and the sun came out, making the wet trees and grass glisten silently for a brief moment. Then a fine rain began, sprinkling the air with a dewy sparkle that made it feel almost unreal, like a slip in time.

We said goodbye at the gate in the ethereal drizzle. With a glance back at the house, his home for all these years, he put his arms around me.

I gripped him tight.

'You know you don't have to go,' I whimpered, praying for one insane moment that he'd change his mind.

He smiled and wiped away a tear. 'Chin up, Mum! Someone's got to teach those Jerries a lesson, eh?'

Pulling away, he ambled off to the van, and I studied his broad back, his lazy lilting walk, his state of being that would no longer be mine to watch, mine to grasp. A vision came back to me of him as a boy, scampering down this very path, late for school, turning and grinning, lopsided by his heavy satchel.

And just as I remembered, he turned back to me then with that same look, as if the world were a great adventure for him to behold and relish, and I felt the rain washing the tears down my face for all our precious years together.

He got into the van and opened the window to wave, and then, as it revved up and pulled away, his lips touched the palm of his hand and he blew me a kiss, something he hasn't done since he was a child. It was as if on the edge of manhood he too remembered everything we had shared, that he was the man who was still, in his heart, my little boy, late for school.

And then he was gone.

I went into the house and moped around the kitchen, my head throbbing as it does so readily these days. I looked out of the window into the rain that still fell, the grass that still grew, the birds that still sung.

But now I was alone.

After a few dreadful minutes, I got up, unable to help creeping into his small, sparse room, still warm from his presence. Running my hand down his soft blue bedcover, I remembered how many times I'd pulled it over his small frame at bedtime, and kneeling down next to the bed, I took a deep breath, filling my lungs with his essence, that unmistakable smell he's had since he was a baby. I'd recognise it anywhere, all salt and warm honey.

That evening, when I'd stopped crying, I realised that this was a feeling I was going to have to get used to. Keeping busy, stopping my head from thinking the most abysmal things, never knowing where he is or whether he's still alive.

David is all that I have. I know he must go and do his duty, even though I wish with every ounce of me that he might have been given a desk job or kept home to refuel planes. I can only pray that God is watching over him. I suppose I am just one of the millions of mothers around the world standing by a door, watching our children walk down the road away from us, kit bag on backs, unsure if they'll ever return. We have prayer enough to light up the whole universe, like a thousand stars breathing life into our deepest fears.

I had to pull myself together for tonight's choir practice, at once looking forward to expelling some pent-up feelings into the air, and also fearful that I'd collapse, breaking our silent vows to keep it tucked inside, keep spirits up.

I went to the church early, wandering up to the altar and thinking about the finality of death. Then a hand on my arm made me turn around, and there was Prim nodding her understanding. As if she knew, she saw straight inside me at the emptiness and fear.

'Are you all right?'

'Loneliness seems to follow me,' I said with a sad smile.

'It's never the end,' she said softly. 'Love is always there. You just need to embrace it.'

'But—' I wasn't sure what she meant. Where is the love when my family have gone?

'You need to cherish your memories of people. You can't ask anything more from them now.'

The door squeaked open and Kitty and Silvie dashed in, breaking up our talk with their chatter.

'Did David leave today?' Kitty asked, breathless from running.

'Yes,' I replied. 'He left this morning.'

'Did he remember everything?'

'I suppose so,' I replied stiffly, not wanting to talk about it.

Silvie's little hand tucked into mine, and when I looked down, I saw her eyes large and fraught. The poor child's seen far too much of this war. I can only pray it never comes here.

Soon the choir stalls were packed, people clamouring to hear news of the war from anyone who knew anything. A few of us remained quiet, listening in a half-tuned-in way as our thoughts were drawn away. Some of the women who also had loved ones away came to give me their sympathy, their scared eyes welcoming me into their haunted world.

Prim turned to the choir, requesting that we sing 'Love Divine' for Sunday. Gathering up the sleeves of her dramatic damask cloak, she held her baton high in readiness, and we plunged into it, bathing in the glow of song. At the end, Mrs Quail tottered to the front and had a word with Prim, to which she nodded and directed Mrs Quail back to the organ.

'By special request, we'll have a good old sing of "The Lord's My Shepherd".' We gathered up our song sheets and looked towards her to begin. I knew Mrs Quail had done it for me. She knew it was one of my favourite hymns. I caught her eye to say thank you, and as the slow, methodical introduction began, I felt the blood pumping faster through my veins.

The most beautiful sound, the choir in full voice was singing softly, hesitantly to begin with, and then opening our voices straight from our very hearts.

> *The Lord's my Shepherd, I'll not want;*
> *He makes me down to lie*
> *In pastures green; He leadeth me*
> *The quiet waters by.*

The volume swelled with passion and deliberation as we poured our emotions into every darkened corner of the church. Every dusty cloister and crevice reverberated, reaching a crescendo in the final chorus, a vocal unison of thirteen villagers that cold, still night, pouring out our longings, our anxieties, our deepest fears.

Letter from Flt Lt Henry Brampton-Boyd to Venetia Winthrop

Air base 9463
Daws Hill
Buckinghamshire

Thursday, 25th April, 1940

My darling Venetia,

I have felt little except the wild beats of my heart since we parted last Tuesday. The way you looked, the way you moved in that dress, I feel mesmerised, put under an enchanted spell by your elegance and beauty. When you told me that you would consider my offer of marriage, I could only rejoice in the knowledge that you might one day be mine. I only hope that I may survive this war long enough to know you properly as my wife.

I am not due back to Chilbury until July, and when I arrive, I hope you might have had time to consider my proposal. I have plenty to offer, after all, my darling. Brampton Hall will be yours, as will our illustrious family name, and my everlasting passion and devotion. Timely weddings are usual these days, and I am anxious to be wed as soon as you give the word. They give the newly wedded an extra few days' leave. I have a good notion of the perfect place for our honeymoon, where we shall get to know each other in a wonderfully whole way. I truly cannot wait!

Wishing you all my love, my darling, and hoping that while I am away you remain mine, in the same way that I will remain completely and undeniably yours,

Henry

Letter from Venetia Winthrop
to Angela Quail

Chilbury Manor
Chilbury
Kent

Friday, 26th April, 1940

Dear Angela,

So much to tell! First of all, you missed David Tilling's
spectacular leaving party on Tuesday evening. Well, maybe
more predictably pleasant than spectacular. You know how
these Chilbury events are. Everyone was there, including
Hattie and Mama, who are both taking pregnancy in such
different ways, Hattie all excitement and joy, and Mama
with a weepy hope that she'll get a boy for Daddy.

Mr Slater stubbornly refuses to be tempted by me. He
skilfully redirects any questions and provokingly ignores
any flirtation. Your idea of showing him some suitable
landscapes might hold some opportunities. I am
formulating a plan that cannot fail.

Henry asked me to marry him again. Obviously I was
vague. I can't bear to let the poor man down every six
months. When will he get the message? Meanwhile, Kitty

pathetically hangs on his every word. He politely fobs her off, which is rather cruel, don't you think?

Hattie is preparing the school children for her departure when the baby arrives. In typical Hattie fashion, she's enormously guilty about the whole thing, and feels that it's frightfully selfish to be having a baby.

'Don't be silly, Hattie. You're a born mother. You can't pass that up just to teach a few school children,' I tell her.

But she only says, 'You don't know how much they depend on me, Venetia. You don't understand.'

Clearly I don't.

The new choir mistress, Prim, made an extraordinary announcement at choir practice on Wednesday, and everyone's up in arms once again. She surged in with her usual melodrama, but instead of handing out music scores, she quickly climbed the pulpit, and we knew something special was afoot.

'I have entered the Chilbury Ladies' Choir into a public choir competition in Litchfield three weeks from Saturday.'

'What in Heaven's name are you thinking?' Mrs B stood up and strode over with the determination of a tank. 'We're not parading any nonsensical women's choir in a public competition. We'd be a laughingstock!'

'The competition is in aid of weapon production and is considered a tremendous boost for Home Front morale,' Prim said, jubilantly. 'It'll be in all the papers, cheering spirits across the country. I can't imagine anyone will be thinking badly of us.'

'All over the country?' Mrs B thundered, the stained-glass windows jittering. 'Our respectable, historic village will be dragged into the national press?' She took out her ticking-off finger and began wagging it fiercely. 'Are we to find ourselves shut out of polite society?'

'Now don't be a spoilsport, Mrs B.' I stepped forward, smiling sweetly. 'Everyone will think us wonderfully modern.'

'And it would be so much fun to perform on a stage, wouldn't it?' Kitty added.

'What complete and utter tosh,' Mrs B snapped. 'We'll look absurd. A bunch of women muddling along without any men! Where's your sense of pride?'

Then a strange thing happened. Hattie came forward.

'I know you want everything to stay the same, Mrs B, but there's a war on and we're trying to get on as best as we can. There are no rules about singing without men. In fact, there are no rules about anything any more. So let's be amongst the first to herald this new opportunity. It's part of the Home Front effort to keep spirits up, after all,' she went on. 'So we're doing our bit for the war simply by entering.'

'Count me in,' Mrs Quail called over from the organ.

'I'm in,' said Mrs Gibbs, and another voice spoke out, 'Let's give it a go!'

'Yes, let's give it all we've got!' Mrs Tilling said cautiously. 'Just because we've never done something before, it doesn't mean we shouldn't try.'

Mrs B, pouting like a restrained child, wasn't ready to step down. 'Has everyone lost their minds around here?'

'Not at all!' Prim spread her arms wide with pride. 'We may be a late entry, but I know that we have what it takes. We have some great voices – Kitty and Venetia are already first-class sopranos, and Mrs Tilling is the mainstay in the altos. Everyone has a fine voice, but to compete against the

big choirs we have to use our finest asset, the one that will
mark us out as truly exceptional.'

She looked from person to person. 'Music is about
passion. It's about humanity. We need to bring our own
passions to our voices.' She wound her baton thoughtfully
through the air. 'We have to imbue every note, every word,
with our own stories. Think of what our members can
bring: Kitty's exuberance, Silvie's courage, Mrs Quail's
joviality, Hattie's gentleness, Mrs Tilling's diligence. Even
you, Mrs B, bring a gusto and verve to our singing. Every
joy, every pain we are feeling from this war will be put to
use in our music.' She paused momentarily. 'That plus an
extra practice on Fridays.'

Mrs B looked annoyed. 'Where is the competition to be
held?'

Prim leant forward dramatically, speaking in a theatrical
whisper. 'Litchfield Cathedral, probably the most spiritual
and inspiring edifice of them all. The acoustics are amongst
the finest in the country. And if we win, we'll be in the
finals in none other than St Paul's Cathedral in London.'

'That sounds jolly grand.' Kitty beamed. 'Let's try and
win, shall we?' She went over to Mrs B. 'Go on, Mrs B,
you'll help us, won't you?'

'I suppose I may as well give you my support,' she sniffed
petulantly. 'Only because it's for the war, mind you.' I knew
she wouldn't be able to stay away, although she stepped
haughtily back to the choir stalls like they smelt of horse
manure, shooting Mrs Tilling a look of disgust.

Prim sifted through a pile of sheet music and began to
hand it around. 'Righty-ho. We're going to start with a new
piece for the competition.'

The sheets went around, and we all shuddered.

'"Ave Maria",' she began, 'is a prayer to the Virgin Mary, calling for her divine help in a time of war. I have arranged the piece especially for our choir. Are we ready to try it?'

We gave it the best shot we could, then she took each part through, first the sopranos, then the altos. I could tell that Prim was delighted.

'You see, you made the most glorious sound. I have no doubts now that, with some more practice, we will make it work wonderfully. We can stand together and strong and be a force to be reckoned with.'

At the end, Prim mentioned that if anyone would like to try a solo, she should step forward to audition.

'There are two verses in the arrangement, so two different voices are required. Do we have any takers?'

Kitty was there in a trice. 'I'll do it!'

I couldn't let Kitty have all the glory, so I stepped forward too. 'I'm sure I can give it a good go.'

Prim waited a few minutes, then raised her voice over the throng. 'How about you, Mrs Tilling? Don't you think you have voice enough to share with the world?'

She blushed, picked up her handbag, and came over. 'Do you really think I could?'

'Well, that's up to you,' Prim said. 'You certainly have the voice. But do you have the nerve?'

A flush went over Mrs Tilling's gaunt cheeks.

Prim went over and had a word with Mrs Quail at the organ, then returned to us.

'We're going to hear you sing the first verse one at a time.' Mrs Tilling looked like she might faint, while Kitty simply couldn't wait.

'Kitty, why don't you go first?' Prim said, and motioned to Mrs Quail to start playing.

Kitty sang like she was on stage in front of several thousand adoring opera-goers. She raised her eyes to the ceiling when hitting those tricky high notes, and even did that awful warbling sound. It was ghastly.

'Bravo,' Prim gushed at the end.

And I wondered if she was being tactful until Mrs Tilling joined in. 'What a beautiful voice you have, Kitty!'

Kitty grinned in an infuriating manner.

I was considering backing out, except Prim quickly decided it was my turn, Mrs Quail already playing the introduction.

I sang as well as I could, stumbling over a few words, and not hitting the top notes quite as well as Kitty. But really, my voice is so much nicer than hers. Much more natural sounding.

At the end, Prim and Mrs Tilling gave a small round of applause and agreed that I had a lovely mellow voice. Kitty looked smugly on, thinking she'd won.

Then it was Mrs Tilling's turn, and we know that she sings terrifically well, has done since we can remember. Without her the choir would have been in a lot of trouble. She sang perfectly in tune, all the words right, never wavering from her enchanting alto tone.

'Wonderful, Mrs Tilling,' Prim said. 'The perfect voice for one of our solos.' Then she looked at me, the inevitable coming. 'And I'm afraid, Venetia, that I'm going to pick Kitty this time. We'll need some extra work, and I imagine she has a lot more time than you do, with the War Office job.'

'Yes, you're completely right,' I said. 'I shouldn't have auditioned really as I don't have any spare time these days. Maybe next time.'

And with that, seeing Kitty delightedly jumping up and down in the corner of my eye, I got my coat and walked majestically out of the building.

Since then Kitty's been lording it over me ad nauseam. Silvie and I had to retire to my bedroom to escape. I did her hair up beautifully while she tried on my lipstick. She's such a sweet creature.

On that note, I must away to get my beauty sleep. I will let you know how my plan to get Mr Slater proceeds. Success will be mine.

Venetia

Kitty Winthrop's Diary

Saturday, 27th April, 1940

The question of Venetia's virginity

Why is it that just when you think you know how everything works, something explodes right under your nose and you have to rethink it all through? There was I, merrily going through life thinking that no one did anything except perhaps one or two kisses before they got married, and then, boom! I see the whole act unfold in front of my very eyes.

Things I would dearly like to know
Was Venetia as pure as the driven snow, as we've
   always been taught to be?
Will she have to marry Mr Slater now?
Will this mean she'll stop playing her evil games with
   Henry?
Does anyone else do this before they're married?
Will I have to?

First of all, let me state that as far as I was concerned, before I saw what I did, Venetia was still a virgin. Mama told both of us that one has to stay a virgin until one gets married, and I must say it has never crossed my mind to question this instruction. I've seen plenty of copulation before, so don't think I'm naïve – bulls mounting cows in the fields, that time Mr Dawkins brought his mare over for Amadeus to get her pregnant, and the dogs in the stables are at it all the time. And I know what it leads to – babies. So why was Venetia doing it? She's not married and, as far as I know, she doesn't want a baby. It was disgusting.

Then I wondered if she'd done it with anyone else, and a cloud of memories flew into my head like a photograph album of every boy she's ever toyed with. Now that I came to think about it, she could have done it with any of them: Cecil Worthing, David Tilling, even Victor Lovell or, Heaven forbid, Henry. They'd known each other since they were children, grew up as friends, spent many evenings together at parties, perhaps sneaking out into the night for a quiet kiss that may have led to more. Maybe this was her awful hold over them.

Could Venetia be a harlot?

Angela Quail is most definitely a harlot. I'm sure she did it with Edmund, as they were always touching each other in a most embarrassing way. I think she wanted to be with Henry too, because she always seemed odd around him, all fluttery. I wonder if he rejected her and chose me instead because he likes proper girls and Angela wears her depravity like a badge of honour. I suppose being the Vicar's daughter has made her more unruly.

But with Venetia, Daddy would hit the roof.

It all started after my singing lesson with Prim this afternoon, which had gone particularly well as she told me that I had perfect pitch. I couldn't wait to tell Silvie, and since she wasn't at home, I trotted off to the stables to see if she was there. It was such a delicious day, all buttery and golden, and I felt as if the world made complete sense. The cherry blossom was just past its best, and pink and white petals cascaded over me as I crossed through the orchard – it was wondrous, like it was snowing tiny soft cushions.

As I passed through the whiffy stable yard, I thought I heard voices by Amadeus's door. For a brief moment, I wondered if Venetia had taken a funny turn and decided to pay her old horse a bit of attention – she's completely neglected him since she stopped dressage.

No such luck.

It was Venetia's voice all right, but she wasn't talking to Amadeus. I stood on tiptoe to look through a gap in the wooden door and had the perfect view of Mr Slater, immaculate in grey suit and tie. He looked incredibly out of place in the stable setting, which ponged of sweaty horses and saddle leather. I would have been surprised to see him there, had it not been for Venetia's little bet with Angela.

But this didn't seem like a little bet at all.

She was standing close to him looking up at him in the most ridiculous way, her blonde hair swept to the side and over one shoulder. Even from where I stood, the gusto of her peachy perfume overpowered the sinewy whiff of manure. She was wearing a dress I've never seen before. It was sunflower yellow and shone like silk, with a flowing skirt and low in the front, exposing her cleavage with startling fullness. A white cardigan was draped around her smooth shoulders, making her look young – playful kitten one minute, conniving minx the next.

'What do you have for me?' she said, standing before him, inches away.

'Do you deserve anything?' he asked with a strange half smile on his handsome lips, one eyebrow raised.

'Maybe,' she giggled, twirling her hips so that the gleaming skirt slunk around his legs for a moment, and then cascaded back around hers.

He slid his hand into his inside pocket and slipped out a package. She took it and stood away laughing, opening it. I wanted her to get on and rip it open, but she wavered and hesitated, opening and then closing, running her forefinger over and under the brown paper packaging in a ludicrous way.

Eventually she pulled out a pair of stockings, holding them up in the dim light. Two sheens of slender brown gauze moving gently in the still air, transparent in the dappled light of the dusty window.

With careful deliberation, she took one shoe off, standing as she was in the middle of the small stable and, casting one of the stockings at him, she slipped the other onto her foot and up over her ankle. I felt instantly uncomfortable, as did Mr Slater, who turned away, busying himself with folding the stocking he held in his hand.

'What do you think of that?' She prompted him to look as she drew the top over her knee and rucked up her dress to pull it up.

He glanced down, and I saw his eyes engage with her long, smooth thigh, now half-covered with the stocking, beige brown below and pearly white skin above.

'They'll do well enough,' he said, looking away. But his eyes strayed back to her as she kicked off her other shoe.

'Give me the other one,' she breathed, and he handed her the other stocking.

She unfurled it, letting it cascade down in front of her, and then she raised her foot and slipped it over, shimmying the beige haze up her other leg. Again she rucked up her dress, this time to show a white lace garter, to which she carefully attached the top of the stocking. You could even see a glimpse of her undergarments as she brazenly displayed herself in front of him.

'I don't think you should be doing that,' he said. He hadn't turned away this time. He was just standing there watching, immersed.

'I wanted to let you see what they look like. A kind of thank-you gift.' She stood up straight but held the skirt of her dress up so that he could view his gift in full glory. See what I mean about her poise, as if she's played every step before? Then she slipped her shoes back on and raised her skirt a touch higher, placing one foot in front of the other like some kind of actress or showgirl.

'I told you. You'd better leave me be,' he answered, his voice slipping out of his usual witty, upper-class front, his hand pushing back through his hair. Then he recollected himself and added with a half smile, 'Or I might not be a perfect gentleman.'

She smirked, a look of determination in her eyes. This was the problem with Venetia – she could never see herself beaten. She wanted Slater, regardless of the price. She took a step towards him and took his hand. I couldn't see what happened next as she now had her back to me, but I think she must have put his hand on her thigh.

'Venetia,' he whispered. 'Do you know what you're doing?'

'Yes,' she replied, velvet self-assurance in her voice. 'I know exactly what I'm doing.'

'I don't think you do.'

He lowered his face and kissed her extremely forcefully indeed, his other hand coming around the back of her pale shoulders, pulling her in towards him. They stood locked, writhing like that against each other for a few minutes, and then, I have no idea how, they eased themselves onto the hay without stopping kissing. I couldn't see them as the hole in the door was too narrow, but I knew what they were doing. Like animals in a stable.

Flinging myself out of the yard, I decided to go back home and do some thinking about what I just saw, which is where you find me now. None of my questions seem to be answered, but I now know some things for sure.

Things I know for sure
Venetia has almost certainly done this before
She might have done it more than once before too
    (although didn't have a baby)
She might have done it with Henry, which is why he
    follows her around
Angela Quail has clearly done it, Vicar's daughter or
    not
Now that I come to think of it, there is a lot more of it
    going on than I thought
I'm still not going to do it until I'm married
Venetia is more serious about Mr Slater than I thought
    (or Daddy thought, for that matter)
Daddy will be furious if he ever finds out
This piece of information might come in very useful

With that, I have decided to close the matter, although the image of her standing there is etched onto my mind. How come she's got it into her mind she can do these things, when we've been told that we can't?

Then I realised. It's the war. No one cares any more about saving ourselves for marriage. It's all about the here and now, letting everything go, enjoying life while we can. Virginity is old hat because we could be dead tomorrow or, worse, be occupied by the Nazis.

That said, I'm not sure I fancy the idea of doing it that much, so I think I'll just keep mine for now. I'll have to perfect my solos so that I can become so famous and successful that I never have to think about Venetia and her disgusting little affairs ever again.

Letter from Miss Edwina Paltry
to her sister, Clara

3 Church Row
Chilbury
Kent

Friday, 3rd May, 1940

Dear Clara,

You have a champion for a sister! Triumphant is how I am,
as it wasn't easy – like Hercules getting through the ruddy
Twelve Labours, except that it was only two screaming
babies being swapped. But I wasn't going to let that reward
run away from me. Not this time, Clara. Let me tell you the
whole.

After a good breakfast spent watching Mrs Tilling,
smartly dressed in her ghastly green WVS uniform, arrive
and then depart from Hattie's house for her usual morning
check, I gathered my black bag and moved into the first
part of my plan: feeding Hattie the potion.

'Anybody in?' I called as I knocked at the door and
pushed it ajar, putting on the most friendly voice I could
muster. 'Hattie? It's me, Miss Paltry. Are you upstairs?'

'In the kitchen,' she chanted in her singsong voice.

I walked in to find her pottering around the tiny room, surrounded by soil-coated vegetables dug up from the garden, a sizable leek in one hand.

'I'm glad I found you in,' I smiled. 'I saw a midwife friend in Faversham yesterday, and the most remarkable coincidence. I was telling her about your tiredness, and how there was nothing you could take for it, and she told me about a new remedy. She said she has been giving it out for months and every woman has been so happy that she's quite run out of the stuff!'

'Can I get it anywhere?' Hattie turned, putting down the leek. 'I haven't been able to get out for days now, and I need to visit the children in Litchfield Hospital. I've been giving them extra lessons in my spare time, and—'

'As it happened she received a new box while I was there, and I begged her to let me have some for you.'

'You did? How marvellous!' She took a few steps towards me in eagerness, fixing a thick strand of dark hair that had slipped out of its pins. 'How much do I owe you?'

'It was quite pricey, dear, because it's so much in demand,' I said, putting my head on one side to add an extra cheeriness. 'But I'll give you a special price of thruppence ha'penny for the dose.'

She got some change from her purse and handed me a few coins. I checked the money (it was a ha'penny short, but I decided not to press her for it) and then I took the brown bottle out of my bag, along with a teaspoon.

'How much do I have to take?' She took the bottle and eyed it, her rosy mouth pinched with fear.

'A teaspoon will do the trick. Let me pour it out for you.' I took the bottle and got her a glass of water. 'There's nothing like having a proper midwife to help you with these things.'

I stepped back to open the mixture, as the smell can knock you out. Breathing through my mouth, I poured the globuled liquid, and a faint green-grey effervescence lifted off as the smell of dog meat and motor oil crept up my nostrils unaware. I handed it over.

'Are you sure?' She dithered, grimacing at the powerful concoction.

'I know it doesn't look appetising, but what medicines do?' I eased her elbow up, lifting the spoon towards her mouth, and down it jolly well went.

She turned rather green, and I worried she might throw up, or worse, faint. It wasn't an official medication as such, and I'd heard about some of the side effects – internal bleeding, convulsions, coma – and for a moment she gasped for air and her eyes seemed to pass backward into her head. I sat her down (before she fell) and patted her heartily on the back, and at last she choked violently and seemed more herself, clutching the bottle like it was a blooming lifesaver. I stayed with her a few minutes, trying to get the bottle away. I wasn't going to leave any evidence for that interfering Tilling woman to examine. In the end I had to grab it and run, as time was moving fast.

'But, Miss Paltry, I feel something happening,' she gasped, grabbing my hand.

'Early days, early days,' I said kindly, yanking my hand away and running for the door. You see I had to get the Winthrop baby out quick, before this one gave birth. It was all a matter of timing, and I wasn't letting pleasantries get in my way.

I rushed out and strode up to the Winthrop house. To get to Chilbury Manor, you only need to cross the green and the square and take the lane up to the driveway. It's ten minutes on a usual day, five if you're in a hurry, less if you run. Hopefully it wouldn't come to that.

Elsie met me at the side door, looking alarmingly dishevelled, hair falling out from under her cap.

'I don't know if I can watch the baby for you. I mean, if I had to,' she said. 'Nanny Godwin stays in her quarters in the mornings, and there's no one else about. I don't know if I'd be able to get away.'

'You must,' I urged, taking her slim wrist and digging my grubby nails into the soft underside.

A gasp of pain escaped her. 'I'll do what I can.'

'You'll explain that it's for the baby's sake, your duty as a servant.'

She looked bewildered, and as I followed her upstairs, I let out a sigh, thinking, *God help me if the idiot girl ruins the whole thing!*

Wimpy Mrs Winthrop took the medicine without any qualms, only grateful that I should be thinking of her. Since it was her fourth child, labour began almost instantly, and the child's head was peeking out before Elsie had got back with the hot water. There was a moment, I recall, where I wondered if luck would be with me, and it would be male. But before I could even cross my fingers, the baby was born, and as she plopped out in front of me, my eyes homed in on the ominous lack of boy parts.

'It's a boy!' I announced, containing my disappointment while snipping the cord and swiftly swaddling the baby in a blanket. I tried to be fast so Elsie wouldn't see, but as I turned, there she was, a look of anguish on her face.

'But it's a girl,' she said, quiet like.

'No, Elsie,' I said through gritted teeth. 'It's a boy.' I frowned at her and jerked my head towards the door, and I saw her eyes narrowing as the penny dropped.

Luckily the lady didn't hear Elsie. 'It's a boy!' she cried meekly, 'Thank God it's a boy!'

'But he's having trouble breathing,' I gasped, trying not to make it sound rehearsed. 'I have a mechanical ventilator at my house. I'll have to rush him away quickly. This maid can come with me. Will the nanny be able to help with the afterbirth?'

Elsie ran off to get the nanny, and I was left with Mrs Winthrop begging me to see the child.

'Please, please, I want to see my baby!'

'No, no, no, Mrs Winthrop. I need to get him away as soon as I can.'

She just kept on and on. Lucky she wasn't strong enough to haul herself out of bed or else I'd have been in trouble.

Elsie returned promptly with the old nanny, who looked both tired and dismayed. I told her about the afterbirth, clamped the baby to my chest, and darted down the stairs and out the door. As I strode down to the village, Elsie trotted along beside me asking pointless questions and being worried about getting found out. I wished I'd never employed the stupid girl.

Back in my kitchen, I had a nice box for the baby and a bottle of milk made up from powder. The way I saw it, I'd only be gone a few minutes and she'd be fine with Elsie for that short time. As I laid her down, the baby looked up with her big china blue eyes, just like her sister Venetia's, and I briefly wondered what it would be like to be a mother, to have such a lamb. I might have been a mother if that stupid Ida didn't get pregnant and force Geoffrey to marry her instead of me. He didn't even have proof it was his, the fool that he was. He could have asked me to help. I'd have sorted her out, well and proper.

'I know what you're up to, and I want none of it,' Elsie suddenly announced, lifting up the baby. 'I'm taking her back to her mum.'

'No, you're ruddy well not,' I said, snatching the baby back and returning her to the box. 'You'll stay here and do as you're told, or you won't get a penny off me.'

'I don't care about the money. It's wrong, it is.' She brought a hankie to her little nose and blew it loud as a baby elephant, her pretty eyes begging me. 'Can't you see that? Can't you give it back?'

'It's being done for the right and proper reasons, and that's all you need to know,' I told her.

'Well I'm not having any of it,' she sniffed. 'I'm going back to the Manor.'

'You'll do no such thing.' I stood between her and the door. 'I can't have you ruining my plan!'

She tried to barge past me. I could hear the faint caterwauling of Hattie in labour next door and panicked that everything was about to collapse around me. 'I'll let you go if you promise not to tell anyone.'

She pondered for a moment. 'I'll not mention a word provided you give me my five quid.'

I seethed. It's completely immoral to demand money for a service she'd failed to finish. But, like Hercules

overcoming another obstacle, I reached into my black bag
for the money. 'You keep your mouth shut or it'll be
curtains.' She snatched the money away and barged past me
into the sunshine. I fretted about what she'd say to Mrs
Winthrop, but then I imagined her dainty throat between
my hands and focused on the task at hand, grabbing my
bag and hurrying off to Hattie's, leaving the baby girl to
fend for herself in the box.

After a few knocks I let myself in to find Hattie slumped
by the door, moaning loudly.

I leapt down to her, and checked her – thank God the
baby was still moving around inside. I prayed it was the
boy I needed. Once I'd helped her up to bed, she moaned
and strained, the baby refusing to budge.

That's when I began panicking about the baby girl in the
box in my kitchen. She would need milk by now, but I
couldn't get away from Hattie, who held my hand with a
vice-like grip. Would she be all right?

At last Hattie's screams grew almost inhuman, and I felt
panic rising – what would happen if she didn't have a boy?
Would the Brigadier have me disposed of in some gruesome
way? I was petrified as a ferret in a snare by the time the
baby eventually squirmed its way out.

But the surge of joy – it was a boy!

'It's a girl!' I announced.

'Let me see her, let me hold her!' Hattie cried, leaning
forward and trying to grasp the baby from my arms.

'No, she's not breathing properly. I need to take her to
my house to resuscitate her with my mechanical ventilator.'

Hattie screamed, 'My baby!' And she was on him,
dragging the blanketed little fellow out with all her might.

Scared to damage the baby, yet adamant to salvage the plan, I yanked him back with a lunging turn towards the door. 'I have to go!' I screamed, pushing her back on the bed with a firm shove.

Her screams of 'No' echoed through the house as I surged down the stairs and out the door, not knowing what I'd find when I got back to my house. The horror of finding the baby girl dead, white-blue and stiff, her big eyes glazed like a doll's? Or maybe stupid Elsie had called the police, and I'd find the village matrons gathered to witness my downfall.

But the house was ominously quiet. My heart began to race. I am not the most saintly of people, I know, but I couldn't bear to have caused the death of a baby. The vision of her lying dead in the box came to me, and I dashed for the kitchen.

I could hardly breathe as I looked into the box. There she was, pale and limp, her eyes closed. This couldn't happen! My hand darted to her neck to feel her pulse. I felt a faint fluttering, and she opened her toothless mouth as wide as a baby hippo, and let out an ear-piercing screech.

I took her out of the box and thrust the bottle of milk into her gob.

'Don't you worry, baby girl,' I muttered to her. 'You're about to have the most adoring mother this side of London.'

I placed the boy baby in the box, fitting a blanket around him as he seemed a scrawny kind of lad, the type to catch a chill. Then scooping the girl back up, I headed back to Hattie's.

Hattie was just inside the front door, desperate for me to

return, still in her bloody nightdress, her dark curls wet and matted. 'Is she all right?' she cried, panic on her face. 'Is she going to be all right?'

'Yes,' I smiled. 'She's going to be fine.' I handed the baby into her outstretched arms, and she gazed at the perfect little face with blue, blue eyes and a little pointy chin, a coating of pale blonde hair over her head. She truly was an exceptionally beautiful baby – and take it from me, most of them aren't.

The afterbirth came promptly, with a little help, and after promising to be back as soon as I could, I wrenched myself away to deal with the boy. I could hear him bawling as soon as I opened the door, the little bugger, and had to stuff his mouth with a bottle as soon as I got to him. I took him in my arms, bottle and all, and headed for the door, but as I was nipping onto the green, I saw a group of women in the square. It was the WVS ladies just off the bus from Litchfield, Mrs B holding forth with Mrs Quail and the dreaded Tilling woman.

'Lovely day!' she said cheerfully as she spotted me trying to creep back inside.

'Yes, glorious weather,' I enthused, concealing the baby inside my coat. 'I'll have to get my hat!' I disappeared in, grabbed my hat, and knew there was nothing else for it, I was going to have to stuff the baby into my black bag, and hope he didn't jolt around too much.

I emptied the contents, and the crumbs at the bottom, put the baby inside, trying to balance the bottle against his mouth, and crept out once again. The women were thick in discussion, and I decided to make a dash for it across the green.

'Hello there, Miss Paltry,' Mrs Tilling called as I darted to the lane. 'You should have been with us today for the meeting.'

'We were just saying how uplifting it was,' added Mrs Quail, her round face puce with pleasure.

'Oh, how marvellous,' I said, keeping a distance. A crowd had gathered outside the shop, all in green uniforms like pecking budgies, and I was stuck listening to their nonsense for a few minutes. It was ridiculous. How a bunch of women can honestly believe that a cake sale and some raggedy sewing can win a war, I have no idea.

'Lady Worthing was there,' Mrs B preened. 'We have been so fortunate to have her as our benefactor.'

The baby boy in the black bag began snivelling, quietly at first, and then louder, and I knew I had to leave. Now.

'Must dash,' I said, making off.

'What was that noise?' Mrs Tilling said with a start, looking around the green.

'Oh, the ducks are such a menace at this time of year,' I said cheerily. 'They keep me up half the night with their mating rituals,' I added with some quick thinking.

'Oh,' she said primly. I'm sure she'd consider any allusions to reproduction inherently coarse.

Only then a distinct baby's cry came from my black bag, and she glared at it, her mouth open to speak, yet unable to decide what to say.

I strode off faster than a hen escaping the pot, petrified the woman would start asking questions. But as I rushed up the lane, with the boy's vocal cords reaching a fine volume, I knew that I could corroborate any questioning with a half-truth of sorts. I would say that the baby in my bag had been Mrs Winthrop's son, who I had whisked to my house for resuscitation. On returning him to his mother, I felt it best to keep him hidden so that she could see him first, before the village folk. Yes, it was perfect.

No one would suspect a thing.

When I reached Chilbury Manor, I took the baby out before knocking at the side door – it wouldn't be considered proper for a midwife to be going around with newborns in bags.

The door was promptly opened by Kitty of all people, the little evacuee brat hanging around in the background.

'Where have you been?' she demanded in a way that made me wonder if she knew somehow. Could she have intuitively guessed the whole thing? Did she understand her father well enough, and me sufficiently, to fathom the entire scheme? Her big eyes glanced from me to the baby to the black bag, and back again, the scowl stiff on her face like I'd ruined her life.

I shook my head briefly to remember the right storyline. 'The baby is alive!'

'Why did it take so long?' she muttered, leading me through the grand entrance and up the marble staircase to the long gallery. 'What could you possibly have been doing?'

'It took as long as it did,' I said crossly. I wasn't so scared of Kitty, you see. I was in her father's employ, after all. He would get her to shut up if need be. So perhaps I wasn't as cautious as I could have been. I might have made a big error there. Kitty is close as clams with the Tilling woman.

Mrs Winthrop was still in bed, snivelling in her usual way, when I handed her the whimpering baby boy with his dark fluff of hair. The perfect family.

'Dear, dear little boy,' she crooned, bringing him to her chest. 'How can I ever repay you for saving his life, Miss Paltry?'

'The Brigadier will pay what's due,' I said with the best smile I could muster. I could hear Kitty sniff moodily beside me, the nosy evacuee girl watching with a keen interest. 'What are you going to call him?'

'His name will be Lawrence Edmund,' she smiled. 'Edmund after our dear lost son.' That set her off weeping again.

I didn't want to mess it up now, the end so clearly in sight, so I checked the afterbirth and waited patient like I was the Queen herself, and when it had calmed down, I promised to visit in the morning and backed out of the room.

Nipping down the back stairs and into the kitchen, I was heading for the door – for freedom! – when who should turn up but Elsie.

'I know your game,' she sneered.

There was no one around, so I took her by the scruff of her maid's uniform and pulled her close. 'You'd better not breathe a word or you'll be found in Bullsend Brook before you know it.'

I let go, and she fell back onto the floor. Trembling she was, so I think I did a worthy job. Threatening has always been a skill of mine.

Stepping over her, giving a small kick for good measure, I headed for the door, and with a sharp tug of the handle, I was out in the open at long ruddy last. Skipping for joy down the drive, one hand carrying my now-empty black bag, the other waving around wildly like a jubilant cowboy.

I'd done it!

I'd escaped ambush, gotten over hurdles, avoided pitfalls, and arrived victorious, babies swapped, both mothers happy, and me wealthy. The hero of the day.

No one else could have done it, Clara. I swear there's not a woman out there who could have made it through the way I did, always keeping calm, using my quick thinking. The rest of my well-earned money will be with me within the week, and I will be on my way to you, Clara, to begin our new life together.

Edwina

Letter from Venetia Winthrop
to Angela Quail

Chilbury Manor
Chilbury
Kent

Friday, 3rd May, 1940

Dear Angela,

You owe me cocktails at the Ritz, my dear, as I have won our little bet! Mr Slater, who I now call darling Alastair, has joined the throng of admirers who worship the ground I walk on. I knew I could do it, given some time, although I have to confess that this one was quite resistant. It took some of my more sophisticated moves to prompt action, but now he's mine.

And what a man he is! I never dreamt he'd be so fascinating. He's transformed his sitting room into a studio – he has the house next to Hattie's on Church Row – and it's crammed with canvases and oils and piles of paintings. Every evening he lights candles and paints while we listen to the wireless. One night they played 'All of Me', and we danced around like we were in a tiny ballroom of our very own, spinning through a haze of flickering lights as if in a different world.

But listen, this gets scandalous! I've been such a naughty girl, even by your standards! Having seduced him in the stable last weekend, all raw and naked in the hay just as I had planned, I slipped out of work early yesterday and surprised him at his studio. Luckily he wasn't busy, just trying to mend some typewriter contraption, so I began flipping through his pictures. I didn't know what to expect, but my eyes almost popped out of my head: weird shapes plastered with clashing colours, blacks and greys and yellows, violins sliced in half and deranged, figures made monstrous with mutations and distortions.

'What's this supposed to be?' I asked him, wondering if he hadn't finished it properly.

'It's modern art, darling,' he said, chuckling. 'It's all the rage in the continent, and London too.'

Then I came across a smaller sketched image, a single nude, an almost transient figure blurred with charcoal as she flew wisplike across the page. 'I say,' I said nonchalantly. 'Who's she?'

He pondered for a moment. 'A girl I knew in London.'

She was well formed, agile, but there was an urgency about her, her head glancing back over her shoulder as if she were being pursued. He was staring at her, as if remembering something. Who was this girl?

You know me, Angie. I can't bear a man to prefer someone else. So I hastily put the picture back in the collection and gave him a saucy smile. 'Why don't you paint me like that?'

The room had become stifling with warmth, sunshine bursting in through the little windows, sparkles of dust spinning endlessly through the air. 'I want you to paint me, so you can always remember how I look right now, before I'm old. Come on.' I twirled in front of him.

He laughed. 'Venetia, I really don't think – it's not what girls like you do. You're the Brigadier's daughter, after all.'

'Stuff that! If I say it's all right, then that's that.' I went to the mirror above the fireplace and let down my hair. 'That girl did it. Why can't I?'

'That girl was—' He paused, searching for the right word. 'She wasn't at all like you, Venetia.'

'You mean she wasn't respectable?' I glanced over my shoulder at him, shaking down my hair.

'I mean she was different. She was a bohemian, mixed in different circles. She was older than you.'

'I'm eighteen, you know?'

'I know.'

'We don't need to tell anyone, or show anyone,' I said. 'It'll be our little secret.'

'There's a wild gleam in your eye, Venetia,' he said, coming and toying with a strand of hair on my neck.

'There always is.' I smirked. 'It's one of my greatest charms.'

You know how I get when I have my mind set, and there was something about his refusal that was goading me on, making me do and say things. I had to show him that I was just as daring, just as sophisticated as his city girls. And to be so incredibly naughty, posing nude is far more risqué than sex, don't you think? Just imagine what my father would have to say!

I began slowly removing my clothes, first one shoulder and then the other, and before long my dress was flung to the floor. Then I began slipping off my petticoat and peeling down my stockings. I knew it was having an effect as he folded up his collection and watched me with a smile.

'All right, my little minx. You shall have your nude.' He attached a clean canvas onto his easel and began selecting the paints.

I draped myself on the thick crimson rug in front of the fireplace, lying on my side, my legs tucked slightly, somewhat modest and yet magnificently naked. It was such a freedom, lying there without a jot on, his eyes flickering over me every few moments, focusing on my body in a way that I've never encountered. Parts of my body normally clothed felt the softness of the rug, the freshness of the breeze from the window, the exposure. It was Heaven.

Yet as he painted, I felt his attention floating away, as if he were in a different world, listening to the news on the wireless, an intent frown over his face. For an artist and a pacifist, he takes an unhealthy interest in the war. His ears seem on continual alert for news, especially now that the Nazis are pushing us out of Norway.

Am I mad, Angie? Is this all too absurd of me, to go falling in love with an unknown stranger? Having my portrait painted nude? I laugh when I think of what Daddy would say if he ever found out, which of course he won't. I wish you were here and you could see for yourself what an incredible man Alastair is. I know this started out as a little bet, but I never expected it would turn into – well, one never knows how these things end, does one? All I know is that he's done something to me, Angie. It's as if he's reached deep inside me and grabbed hold of my heart.

Write again soon and give me more advice, Angie darling. Oh, I almost forgot to say! Mama has given birth

to a very scrawny and highly vocal baby boy. Everyone's
ecstatic, as you would imagine, especially Daddy, who
needed his male heir, and Mama, who needed to keep
Daddy happy. But as a matter of fact, the little baby is a
godsend for me too – keeping everyone so busy that no one
knows where I am and what I'm doing. From now on,
Angie, I'm free to live my life to the full.

Much love,
Venetia

Letter from Miss Edwina Paltry
to her sister, Clara

3 Church Row
Chilbury
Kent

Saturday, 4th May, 1940

Dear Clara,

I'm as flustered as a bluebottle in a jam jar. I can't believe it
has all led to such a catastrophe! There I was late last
night, settling in for the evening after an exhausting day,
when there was a sharp knock at the door.

'Tell me how it happened.' It was the Tilling woman,
storming over from Hattie's house to accost me. 'Why did
the baby stop breathing?'

Reluctant to bring her into my house, where she might
want to see the mechanical ventilator that wasn't there, I
insisted that we go round to Hattie's to go over the details.
She seemed to want to discuss it in private – accuse me,
more like it!

'It's only right that Hattie's present if we're speaking
about her,' I said, shoving her back down the path. There's
no arguing with that, and I knew it.

Hattie was in a fresh pink nightgown, dividing her time between our conversation and the baby, whose name is Rose, I was informed.

'I'm rather tired, you know,' I said in a huffy manner, hovering close to the door of Hattie's little sitting room so I could make a clean getaway. 'Two births in one day, you see. Although the Winthrop baby was easier, it being her fourth.'

Mrs Tilling was watching me in rapt interest, seeping up every gesture, scrutinising it for any slip-ups. 'Yes, and all on the day I was in Litchfield,' she snipped. Then she turned to Hattie. 'I'm sorry I couldn't have been here to help you through it all.' I could see that she felt genuinely guilty for taking the day off to go to the WVS meeting. 'I shouldn't have left you.' She looked back over to me, a storm cloud coming over her face. 'Although I thought Hattie might have gone on another week or more.'

I felt a stab of panic that Hattie had told her about the brown bottle, the smell of the grimy green mulch lurking inside. 'You can't blame yourself. The WVS needs you too. You do such marvellous work for us all.'

'But when I was gone there was an emergency,' she stammered. 'And I couldn't be here in your hour of need, Hattie.' I thought she might burst into tears, which would round off my day like a thwack around the ankles with a dead rat. 'Tell me how it happened, Miss Paltry. Tell us how you got the baby breathing.'

'Well, when babies are born I usually give them a little smack and off they go, crying and all. But this little one—' I leaned across and stroked the soft little cheek in the crook of Hattie's arm. 'This little one didn't cry at all. It really

was incredibly fortunate that I was there and knew what to
do. And of course I had the right equipment.' I swept my
hands together, as if concluding that my experience was
worth a hundred times Mrs Tilling's.

Silence hung in the air for a few moments, and then
Hattie began weeping. I know that pregnancy and
motherhood make women prone to tears, but Hattie has no
thought for others. I wanted to give her a good hard slap
and tell her to pull herself together. The baby's fine now.
She should be happy she got the pretty one.

Mrs Tilling then insisted that I give her a blow-by-blow
account of the long, laborious birth. She was new to the
midwife game and appeared enthusiastic to learn, and I
decided it was education that was driving her rather than
gathering details against me.

Until the very end, that is. After we'd gone through the
whole thing several times, I once again announced that I'd
had a long day and really needed to be getting home.

'I'll walk you to the door,' Mrs Tilling said, getting up
and leading the way into the hallway.

She held the front door open, and I walked out into the
peaceful night air, thinking for a wondrous moment that
the ordeal was over. It was dark, the ducks turning in for
the night, seeking out a comfy spot on the edge of the
pond. A cool grassy breeze made me pull my cardigan
close.

'I have just one more question for you,' Mrs Tilling said,
stepping out behind me onto Hattie's path. 'I want to know
about the medicine you gave Hattie this morning.'

'Oh, that,' I said. 'It's for tiredness, but I suppose she
didn't need it after all!'

'Could I have a look at it?'

'No, you can't,' I snapped, and then, pulling myself together, added, 'It was used up, so I threw the bottle away.'

'Can I see the empty bottle?'

'No,' I stammered, quashing down a panic that whipped up my throat like a poisonous snake. 'I think I must have left it at the Manor.'

She pondered. 'Don't you think it may have been the reason she went into labour? She wasn't supposed to be giving birth for another week.'

'I'm not sure,' I said. 'She may have got her dates wrong. The baby is a fine size for her small frame, and perfectly formed. She was definitely ready to come out today, if not sooner. I've seen it happen dozens of times, dates all mixed up.' I looked at her, smiling as if to emphasise my superior understanding of such things. 'Especially with first-timers.'

I looked at my front door. 'I really need to get home now.' I gave her a final pat on the arm, then headed down the path.

Once inside my own house, I leant against the door for support and slid down onto the floor, lying there for a while, curled up in a question mark, exhausted, confused, and – I have to admit it – scared. It's clear that the Tilling woman smells something fishy. I only hope she doesn't speak to Mrs Winthrop about her birth. Having two births the same day with the same minor emergency will almost certainly rouse suspicion.

Why didn't I think of that?

Why didn't I think of so many things? I was stupid enough to think this would be simple as cracking a rooster's neck. I should have been planning, thinking about how I could cover my tracks. At least I know that proof will be almost impossible – she'll have to piece a lot more together to make the whole story. It makes me feel all tied up in knots to think that I could be at the mercy of this wretched woman.

Or the Brigadier! I know he'd have to step in for me if the Tilling woman brings the law into it – after all it'd be his moth-eaten backside on the line too. But if he gets wind that Mrs Tilling suspects, then I'll never see the other half of my money, and I'll have him on my back as well.

I'd had enough of it all, and tried to forget about it and get on to bed. Except I keep hearing Hattie's cries in my head, screaming at me not to take her baby.

I will carry on as usual for now, keep my head down and wait for the money from the Brigadier. But the whole thing has given me the willies, and you must promise me to burn this letter as soon as you've read it. The walls have ears these days.

Until I have more news,
Edwina

Mrs Tilling's Journal

❋

Friday, 10th May, 1940

Today the Nazis invaded Holland and Belgium. I feel almost numb with horror, the sheer brutality and viciousness of these people. Now that they're so much closer to us, they'll almost certainly be using the air bases in Holland and Belgium to make raids over England, especially over us in the southeast. France will be invaded next, and after that?

Our Prime Minister, Mr Chamberlain, has stepped down because he underestimated Hitler, tried to appease him, and it is said that Mr Churchill will replace him. We all know that Churchill wants to take us into all-out war, regardless of the fact that they're bigger and stronger and likely to win. Doesn't he remember the millions of men killed in the last one? What about David? Will his life be wasted on a battle-field because of some idiotic notion that we have to try?

'Winston Churchill will be much better for this war,' Mrs B chortled when we met at the shop. 'He's such a ruthless old bulldog! The Nazis are petrified of him. He's the only one who can win it.'

'But he can't stop them. They'll overrun us, like they're overrunning everyone else. Surely it's better if we negotiate peace now?'

'It's talk like that that makes us look like cowards,' she said sharply. 'Where's your fighting spirit, Mrs Tilling?'

I nodded weakly and studied the shelves of tinned peas for a few moments, before deciding to leave the shop without buying anything. You see, I don't have a fighting spirit. The thought of all-out war overwhelms me. I feel like Britain is a bird wounded from the last battle, and there's a savage crow right there, ready to push us out of our nest and take over.

I had to get on. Apart from my other visits, I had to check on Mrs Winthrop and baby Lawrence. The Brigadier has been keeping me away, insisting that Miss Paltry is seeing to her, which is ridiculous as I'm just as well qualified. But today I heard that the Brigadier was going to London, which left the coast clear. I was desperate to hear about her birth story, find out how it fit in with Hattie's. So I trudged determinedly up to the Manor.

Mrs Winthrop was looking exhausted. 'He can't stop crying, poor lamb,' she sniffed. 'Nanny Godwin says she's never seen anything like it.'

'I'm afraid some babies are like that. It'll pass with time.' I scooped him up to calm him down, his dark, scraggy hair glued to his scalp with the sweat of crying. 'Now tell me about the birth. Did Miss Paltry give you some medicine at all?'

'Yes, some nasty green stuff. I thought I was going to be sick, but then the contractions started. It might even have brought them on,' she mumbled, almost as if she were talking to herself. 'But the dreadful part was when the baby came and she had to rush him away to her house because of the breathing problem.'

What? I thought. *Another breathing problem?* 'Did you see that he wasn't breathing?'

'No, I hardly saw him before she took him away.'

'Tell me exactly what happened.'

She gushed forth about how Miss Paltry saved baby Lawrence's life by whisking him away to her house to use the ventilating machine. It seems incredible that two babies had the same breathing problem in the same day. Perhaps it had something to do with the medicine? But no matter how many questions I asked, I simply couldn't get to the bottom of it.

After I left, I had to deal with a billeting problem. Since I am the Billeting Officer in Chilbury, I'm responsible for finding spare bedrooms for evacuees or war workers, and because Chilbury is five miles from the Litchfield Park War Centre, I'm continually getting called upon to find more beds for their people. Now they need another two rooms for senior staff. I tried half the village before giving up.

'But what about your David's room?' Mrs B snapped as we congregated for choir practice. 'He's in France now. There's no reason for you to keep his room empty when there's so much need.'

'Yes,' Mrs Quail stepped in. 'Here you are foisting goodness-knows-who on everyone else, and you're not even prepared to take one yourself.'

'David's only just left. You can't expect me to give up his room just like that?' I thought I was going to burst into tears but quickly pulled myself together. 'In any case, I don't see you giving up Henry's room,' I retorted to Mrs B.

'He's an RAF pilot and comes home on leave.' She puffed herself up a little. I can't bear how she goes on about

RAF pilots and how they're the crème de la crème of the military, as if David's some little nobody worthy of a bullet or two.

'That's not the point,' Mrs Quail came to the rescue, but then turned on me again. 'But, Mrs Tilling, you can't call yourself a Billeting Officer if you don't billet yourself. It's not fair.'

'Indeed. You said these new billets are for important bigwigs at Litchfield Park,' Mrs B snipped. 'Ivy House is the perfect place for someone to stay whilst working their hardest to win this war. And you have a telephone too, and there aren't many houses in the village with one of those. It's your duty, Mrs Tilling, to take one in.'

'Don't you have a telephone, Mrs B?' Mrs Quail snipped back. 'Surely you can find space for a bigwig?'

As if by magic, Prim swooped down the aisle.

'Ladies, it's time to rehearse.'

Everyone fell quiet and went to their places, except for Mrs B, who was still quietly smarting.

'We need to focus on "Ave Maria" tonight for the competition. Let's start at the beginning and take it to the end of the chorus.'

Mrs Quail pounded out the introduction, and then we jumbled the entry and were off key and far too loud.

'What a muddle!' Prim said when we'd come to the end. 'You're all out of balance with each other. Now, let's try a few arpeggios.'

We did some arpeggios, and then some scales, and sounded a little more together, but the argument had put us out of keel. During one of the scales, Mrs B thumped her music score down and marched off out of the church.

'Right, let's try "Ave Maria" again,' Prim continued, ignoring the departure.

It was better, but still not good.

'It's simply too difficult,' Kitty whined.

'Perhaps we should pull out,' I said quietly.

'We'll do nothing of the sort,' Prim said in a jovial way. 'We'll jolly well do our best and enjoy it, as will our audience. No, we may not win, but taking part is what counts. Being there, being heard. Being alive.'

She smiled, and I found myself smiling too. And as I looked around me I realised that everyone else had cheered up. Prim was right. It's not about winning. It's about finding humanity in the face of this war. It's about finding hope when everything around us is collapsing.

Including my own precious home.

Letter from Venetia Winthrop
to Angela Quail

Chilbury Manor
Chilbury
Kent

Tuesday, 14th May, 1940

My dearest Angela,

I know you told me not to fall in love with him, but I just can't help myself. It's been only a few weeks, but we're virtually inseparable. I've taken to popping out after dinner every evening so that Alastair can continue his work on my nude. We talk a lot, but he's still extremely secretive, never serious and changing the subject every time it's about him.

'What inspired you to be an artist?' I asked him the other day.

'It's a long and dull story, and I don't want to bore you, sweet Venetia.'

That's what he calls me. Sweet Venetia. I don't think anyone has ever called me sweet before. It's rather charming, don't you think? Even so, I do worry that he thinks I really am sweet, all young and naïve. I keep telling him how I'm famed for my raciness, but he simply isn't surprised by me, not in the way that the others are. He's heard all my witty lines, and seems to have played this game a thousand times. It's as if he sees the real Venetia inside. And do you know what, Angie? I don't want to pretend any more. I want to be the real Venetia, not just what's fashionable or daring, but someone complicated and substantial. And he's the one who's opening it up for me.

Last night, we talked about poetry, and he made up a poem about his love for me, as beautiful as a summer breeze. I won't bore you with the details, but honestly, Angie, there's nothing like hearing the man you love expressing his adoration for you with such eloquence and fervour.

He always has more intellectual matters on his mind, talking about Greek philosophy or medieval politics. The wireless is continually on, sputtering out the latest war news, and once he surprised me by getting quite cross at something they said. The news was about the Nazi invasion of Belgium, which has caught our war chiefs by surprise. They used an indirect route while we were busy guarding the proper way, the one they'd used last time.

'What a military catastrophe!' he muttered under his breath.

'I thought you were a pacifist,' I said nonchalantly.

He picked up his brush again, as if remembering I was there. 'Of course I am. But what a dreadful pack of idiots we are to underestimate the Nazis, eh?'

'Why don't you sign up? See if you can do better?'

'Are you trying to get rid of me, darling?' he replied in a playful singsong way. 'Push me out of your life forever?'

He paused and looked at me again, stretched out before

him. 'Oh, Venetia!' he said with gentle amusement. 'Do you know how beautiful you are?'

I must have looked at him in such a way, as then something came over him, and he put his brush down and came around the easel and lay next to me on the great red rug, pulling my naked body towards his fully clothed one.

'I need you, Venetia,' he whispered into my ear, so blunt and direct that I was taken aback. 'I need you and you need me. We need to be together.' I shifted back and looked into his dark, cavernous eyes, finding an intensity that was disarming but crushingly compelling.

The whole thing was exhilarating, Angie, and in an odd kind of way a little frightening. As I returned his gaze, something new inside me seemed to explode open, like the cherry blossoms bursting open, and everything else seemed to dissolve into nothing, all the messing and the conniving and the boys, all the little games and affairs. I suddenly knew that this is what it's for. I've finally met my match.

Now all I need to do is get to the bottom of him.

Meanwhile, more village news. Hattie named her baby Rose after her poor mother. She invited the Chilbury Ladies' Choir around to her house to wet the baby's head with a few glasses of sherry and one or two songs. We're frightfully worried about the competition on Saturday, so quiet hopefulness rather than the usual squabbling seemed to be the dominant feeling, although Mrs B remains adamant that it's all an embarrassing mistake. Kitty is being incredibly nice for a change, although that's probably because she's still gloating about her soloist victory.

Hattie brought the gorgeous baby out of her crib and sat down beside me on the sofa.

'She's beautiful,' I said. And for once I meant it. Rose is the most gorgeous baby you'd ever see. Even you would think her a gem, with her big blue eyes and gurgling smile. 'It's odd seeing you all grown up with a baby now,' I said to Hattie. 'It seems like yesterday the three of us were making that pact in the Pixie Ring, that we would stay together come what may. How funny it seems now.'

'It does seem a long time ago, doesn't it?' She smiled, and suddenly I felt so very close to her again. 'Venetia, I'd like you to be Rose's godmother. Victor and I talked about it in our letters over these last few months, and both knew that you were the right choice,' she said. 'I know that Rose will grow to love you, as I do.'

'As I do you,' I said hastily, feeling immensely touched and overwhelmed. 'Thank you, Hattie. I'd love to be her godmother. What a wonderful idea. I'll make sure no harm ever comes to her.'

I looked down at the beautiful child, and I must admit, Angie, that with such an old friend as Hattie producing an angel like Rose, it made me wonder about having a baby myself. I'm sure the magnificent Mr Slater would make the very best of fathers, don't you think?

Hattie's being tremendously brave, but I know she's terribly worried about Victor. He's out in the Atlantic until next year, they say, and she hardly gets word from one month to the next. With news of ships torpedoed every week, I know she's wondering if he'll get back at all, if little Rose will grow up without a father.

Oh, wouldn't it have been nice to be born fifty years from now, when all this is over, and we'll be back to normal. Imagine what the world would look like then! Will we be married and happy, our children grown up with children of their own? Or shall we be famous for something or other, some daring deed or great invention? Obviously, that's assuming we'll still be here, and our dear country makes it through in one piece.

I know you think I'm silly to fall in love, but Angie, maybe I'm just not the same as you, busily seducing every man in London. Maybe I need to do my own thing. I'll write again soon.

Venetia

Mrs Tilling's Journal

Thursday, 16th May, 1940

The Litchfield Park bigwig who is billeted to stay in my house arrived this afternoon amidst much confusion. He was supposed to come next week, so when I heard the doorbell I thought it was the postman and became flustered (the poor postman is the harbinger of sorrow these days). But when I opened the door, an extremely tall middle-aged man stood on the doorstep, in the pouring rain. His tan raincoat was soaked and clingy around his bulk, and his brown hair clumped wetly when he took off his sodden hat, exposing a big, squashy face with a nose that looked like it had been broken at least once.

'Oh,' I uttered, looking at him accusingly. 'You're not the postman.'

'No. May I come in?' he said bad-temperedly, barging past me into the hallway, trying to brush off some of the rain. He put his somewhat shabby suitcase down next to the stairs.

'May I ask who you are?' I said, rather crossly.

'Colonel Mallard,' he muttered.

'As in the duck?' I asked vaguely. He didn't look like a colonel. He was wearing civvies and was frankly more than a little unkempt.

He nodded, his eyes flickering over the dilapidated hall. The servants' dwindling has taken its toll on my poor house, although I was relieved when Mrs Peck left, as I couldn't work out who was in charge of whom any more.

'I'm afraid I'm in a bit of a hurry,' the Colonel said, turning towards the stairs.

I glared at him, wondering what on earth he was doing. 'Well, I don't know what you're in a hurry about, or what it has to do with me, but I would be grateful if you could tell me what you're doing here.'

'I've been billeted here.' After scrambling around through his pockets, he dragged out a crumpled, soggy letter and handed it to me.

'Oh!' I had a quick look. 'I was told to expect you next week. Your room's not even ready yet.'

'Well, I'll just have to make do with it the way it is, won't I,' he said, looking at the stairs impatiently.

I led the way up, the man's heavy footsteps following me. Hardly bearing the notion of him inside David's room, I eased the door open, taking one last glimpse, one last breath of its peaceful air before it became someone else's.

The Colonel was well over six foot, and the room suddenly seemed terribly small as he entered. I hurried back to the door, feeling a little claustrophobic. 'I'll be downstairs if you need anything,' I said, and disappeared off before I became teary.

What a dreadful man! Although I suppose it could be a lot worse; he could smell of cow dung, or whistle, or even more dire, take up residence in my sitting room. It'll be awkward sharing my house with a stranger, so unlike the soft warmth of David. I wondered what Colonel Mallard does at Litchfield, as I worry that the war may be lost if this is the general countenance of the people we have in charge. He hardly looks like one of Mrs B's 'important bigwigs'. He's far too dishevelled and disorganised, like a big old cardboard box.

As I began peeling the potatoes for dinner, thinking of going over to see Hattie as soon as I could get away, I heard the door upstairs open, and for a split second I thought it was David, and his cheery voice would carry down the hall, 'I'll be off now, Mum!'

The heavy tramp down the stairs jolted me back.

'Mrs Tilling,' he called from the hallway.

'Colonel Mallard,' I replied, hurrying out of the kitchen, wiping my hands on my apron. 'Will you be requiring dinner in the evening? If so, I'll need your ration book.'

'No, I'll eat at the canteen,' he said, and then added, 'Thank you', in an officious way.

He held out a tattered satchel. I recognised it immediately as David's, realising that I must have left it in the room when I began tidying everything away. I snatched it from him in annoyance. Why can't he leave everything alone?

'Is that all?' I said, desperate for him to leave. But he stood for a moment looking through me, as if trying to remember if he had everything, and then turned and headed for the door, muttering a sullen 'Goodbye'.

I closed the front door and wandered numbly back to the kitchen. From the window over the sink I can see the tumble-down tower of the church, and if you climb to the top of that tower on a clear day, you can see the yellow-brown turrets and pinnacles of Litchfield University. I stood and thought about how my dreams have become smaller over the years, from when I was young and yearned to study, to meeting

Harold and dreaming of my own family, to Harold dying and my world circulating around David, the only light left in my sad little life.

And now all I dream is that he doesn't die. Everything else, including the new intruder, means nothing.

To calm my nerves, I went for a brisk walk, and found myself in the church, sitting in the pew at the back on the left, piecing together the new world around me.

'All right there?' A voice came from behind, instantly recognisable as Prim.

'Yes, just coming to terms with a strange colonel staying in my house. He's billeted with me.'

'Before I found my house in Church Row, I stayed with a lovely old gentleman. He still joins me for tea from time to time. Perhaps it'll improve as you get to know each other.'

'He's such a grumpy curmudgeon, I can't imagine ever getting on with him. I'll have to see if I can find another room for him somewhere else.'

'I'm sure that if you take the time to talk to him you'll realise he's just like you or your son, or anyone else. There's a war on. Why not give him a chance?'

She had that twinkling little smile on her face, and I couldn't help but smile too. 'That's the ticket,' she said, and continued her hurrying in and out with various music stands and scores.

'Prim,' I began as she scuttled by. 'You coming here and reinstalling our choir has been such a tremendous lift for us. Do you really believe that singing will help us get through this gruesome war?'

'Music takes us out of ourselves, away from our worries and tragedies, helps us look into a different world, a bigger picture. All those cadences and beautiful chord changes, every one of them makes you feel a different splendour of life.'

'I wish I had your enthusiasm for something,' I murmured.

'But you do, Mrs Tilling. You do. Not for music but for other things. You only need to stand back and see.'

'I don't know how to do that,' I said glumly.

'Well, let's start by cheering you up with a little singing.'

She took my arm and led me to the front. Standing me in the middle of the altar, she went back and plumped herself down on one of the front row seats.

'Now sing, Mrs Tilling. Open your heart and sing. Just pick your favourite hymn.'

'Well, that's "I Vow to Thee My Country",' I said, the thought of this powerful hymn making me warm to the idea. 'But I can't just sing, here on my own.'

'There's no one here except me. It doesn't matter if you do it wrong.'

I imagined the organ introduction and softly began humming it, until I opened my mouth and began to sing the first poignant words, sending them echoing clearly through the apse.

> *I vow to Thee, my country, all earthly things above,*
> *Entire and whole and perfect, the service of my love.*

The hymn was sung at my father's funeral, as it was for so many of those men who died in the Great War. And then we sang it again at my mother's funeral, and then at Harold's. As I was singing it out alone in the church, it took on a new horror. I realised that I have been trapped by those deaths, that I had let them take over.

And I now see that it is time to let them go.

Kitty Winthrop's Diary

Saturday, 18th May, 1940

The choir competition

What an extraordinary evening! I am completely exhausted, dear diary, but I simply have to stay awake and write down everything, right from the very beginning.

We were on tenterhooks as our small huddle gathered on the green watching for the bus, which was late. Hardly noticing the first few bulging raindrops plunging around us, we worried whether we'd even make it on time, let alone sing well.

'We'll be humiliated in front of the whole of Kent,' Mrs B kept saying, unable to get over the brass-bones fact that we're a women's-only choir now.

'But we'd be a women's-only choir whether we wanted to be or not,' Mrs Quail snapped. 'There's no men left. Or would you rather have no choir at all?'

'We are a group of upstanding ladies, Mrs Quail. Not an unruly singing spectacle,' snapped Mrs B, barging past her to be first in line as the bus swung dangerously around the square. 'Lady Worthing will have plenty to say about it, not to mention the Archbishop.'

'Then why are you bothering to come?' Mrs Quail climbed on the bus after her.

Mrs B swung around. 'Someone has to witness the catastrophe.'

Mrs Tilling looked like she was about to have her fingernails pulled out. 'We simply haven't practised enough. I don't know what the *Litchfield Times* will say about a ladies' choir, but surely it would help if we were exceptionally good.'

'Better to give it a try though,' I said, trying to rally everyone, but all I got were fraught faces and scoffs. Silvie sat glued to my side, whispering to me, 'It will be fine', in a very unconvincing way. She loves the choir as much as I do, and has been helping with my solo by being an appreciative, and only sporadically critical, audience. Only Venetia looked unaffected. She's been in a world of her own since Mr Slater came on the scene. She's only doing the competition because the choirs have their photographs in the papers.

We finally arrived. Litchfield Cathedral is like a magical fairyland castle, with its dwindling spires and ornate buttresses, and is surrounded by roses of the palest of pinks and yellows, incredibly grand yet impossibly romantic. The architect must have been in love. It's where Henry and I are to be married, I have decided.

Today, however, the roses hung loosely as the rain battered down on us, and we joined the throng of people rushing in for the competition. Mrs B battled her way through the crowded vestibule to see the list that had been pinned to a noticeboard.

'We're going last,' she announced when she huffed back to the group.

'That's good,' Mrs Quail said cheerily. 'We can watch the competition and see who we have to beat.'

'Nothing of the sort,' Mrs B snapped. 'Our voices will be quite ruined by that time of night. It's becoming more of a disaster with every turn.'

Prim's theatrical voice rang out. 'We'll end the evening on a high note.'

We took our seats in the old stone interior. The lovely stained-glass windows had been covered with blackout material, making us feel enveloped in a massive underground burrow.

As the place became full, the gnome-like Bishop of Litchfield walked to the front and asked for quiet in strong nasal tones, making me think that his wire spectacles were too tight. He quickly presented the puffed-up Mayor, complete in full red robes, who pompously began a lengthy speech about the joys of song in the horrors of war, and the terms 'uplifting the spirit', 'heralding a new tomorrow' and 'striving onward' were all trotted out. Ever since Mr Churchill has started broadcasting wonderful speeches, everyone else is trying it out.

There were four choirs in the competition, the other three being normal men-and-women choirs. We were to sing in order, followed by brief refreshments, and then the judging panel would announce the results.

I trembled in my shoes and looked over to Prim. She was looking very pleased with herself, her hands clasped across her rounded midriff, eyes twinkling and the little V of a smile on her lips. Even though I think she's the best choir mistress in the whole country, I couldn't help a nagging suspicion that maybe we weren't ready for this. Maybe the countryside wasn't ready for a women's-only choir. But then she caught me looking at her and gave me a flicker of a wink, and I knew then that everything would be all right. With her at the helm, we'd be fine.

Heavy rain began, spattering the roof and engulfing us, as if we were all sheltering under the same umbrella. A clap of thunder echoed around the vaulted ceilings, and we huddled together, more in fear than anything else, while the other choirs trooped up to the front to perform.

All about our competitors
1. The small Riseholme Choir – sang a very nice 'Jesu, Joy of Man's Desiring'
2. The huge Litchfield Choir – incredibly good, and we agreed they were going to win (followed by more suggestions that we should back out)
3. The Belton Choir – not so good, which perked us up, thinking we might not be last

Next was us. My heart was clattering like castanets as the Bishop announced us. A series of murmurs echoed around the church, people questioning whether they'd heard right, no doubt.

'Did he say, the Chilbury *Ladies*' Choir?' I heard someone behind us say with astonishment. We looked to Prim with anguish, but she was standing ready to file out to the aisle, beckoning us to follow suit.

We sat terrified, glued to our seats like a huddle of wild rabbits in hunting season.

But then, suddenly, a deafening crack of thunder came. The congregation stopped in unison and looked to the ceiling, as the lights blinkered, then blinkered again, and died. We were plunged into darkness, the kind of blackness that makes you feel like you haven't got your eyes open when you know you have.

Everyone began frantically whispering.

'At least we can go home now,' Mrs B sniffed. 'Escape this dreadful ordeal.'

Then came the nasal voice of the Bishop. 'Don't worry, everyone. Just stay where you are, and we'll get some candles.' The whispers grew until, from behind us, a glimmer of light came from the vestry as a single candle was carried to the altar. It was a girl, maybe about ten years old, holding her hand around it to stop it from flickering as she moved slowly forward. Another girl came up behind her, a few years older, and then a woman, and then more people, each holding a lit candle, coming up the aisle, and dividing at the altar to place their candle in a new dark corner. After a few minutes, candles of different lengths and shapes had been placed around the massive ancient interior, some in candlesticks of silver and gold, others long pillars of angelic white. Soon the scent of the hundreds of glowing wicks wafted around, the shifting shadows bringing the ancient statues to flickering life.

'Will we still be able to sing?' I whispered. 'What about the organ? It's not going to work now we don't have electricity.'

'We'll do it without,' Prim said jauntily, as if it were a bit of a lark and not a colossal disaster.

'How will we know the right note to start?' I was panicking. We were barely ready to sing, let alone this!

'I shall hum the first note for the altos as they come in

first, and I'm afraid the sopranos are going to have to use that note to find their own. Kitty, we will have to rely on your keen skills.' She grinned at me, and I was at once elated and terrified.

We got up quietly, the hammering of the rain drowning our chairs and feet as we worked our way to the front and took our places on the altar step. There was a slight rustle of papers as we found our music, hands shaking with nerves. Prim was holding her baton aloft, her eyes large and bright as she caught each of ours ready to begin. In the silence, we heard her hum a single note, flowing through the candlelight like a small, silver dart. I saw her catch Mrs Tilling's eye and nod – if Mrs Tilling had the note, we knew the altos would be all right. Prim lifted her baton, eyes closed as if in prayer, and as she brought her arms down, Mrs Tilling's clear, held note rang out through the church, surrounding the mass with glowing warmth. The other altos joined in for a wonderful full sound.

I was petrified. The sopranos would be counting on me to guide us in. I thought I had the note – knew I had the note – but did I have the confidence to sing it out? What if I just opened my mouth and nothing happened?

But the moment had arrived. Prim's eyes narrowed on me. She raised her arms and then brought them down, both baton and forefinger pointing at me, and I heard our first note carrying through the flickering candlelight like pure-cut crystal. Someone else must have got it, I thought, until I realised that it was my own voice I was hearing. I looked over at Prim, praying I'd got it right. But she had her eyes closed, a smile of serene contentment on her face. The sound swelled as the other voices joined mine. I had done it! Me, Kitty

Winthrop. I'd saved the choir. A surge of exhilaration gushed through me, knowing that Prim had recognised my talent, had faith in me. I had carried the choir through and made them proud of me.

The solitary beauty of our unaccompanied voices soared up in the desolate, dim church, weaving in and out, climbing higher and more passionately until the breathtaking climax. It was magnificent, angelic, even I could tell.

My solo was up first, and I felt my throat dry to nothing as the chorus came to an end, marking the place where I came in. Prim's eyes were on me, her baton poised, and then I opened my mouth for the first note to ring out. 'Ave Maria'. I slowed slightly – my nerves were getting to me – but the top notes were firm, clear, crisp, lingering as all eyes were on me, and then I continued, as the notes swept down, and I suddenly felt an elation, as if the piece of music belonged to me, and I sang as if it were part of me, from some new reserve deep inside.

I came to the end, allowing the final note to slowly ebb away, catching Prim's eyes, her nod, and I knew that it was the best performance I could have given. The best I have ever sung.

The chorus resounded beautifully around me, and we began looking at Mrs Tilling as it was her solo next. She had been incredibly nervous beforehand, repeating that she didn't want to let us down.

'But you won't,' said Prim. 'You have to trust your voice.'

The chorus drew to an end, and I watched Prim look at her, lift her baton, and bring it down. Mrs Tilling's voice was superb, the mellowness deep and rich like a late summer's night. She paused slightly before the high note, making it even more poignant, even more beautiful, and after that the notes seemed to flow like gold from her, straight from her heart.

The rest of the choir joined in for the final chorus, the wonderful fullness of sound surrounding us again. Then came the calming lull of the slowly undulating final notes, dissipating into the eerie darkness.

There was a pause through the cathedral, only the drumming of the rain echoing through the apse.

Then the applause started, growing to a hearty surge, and I found a tear coming down my face. We had made it! *I* had made it!

Prim beamed a look of gratitude at me as we went back to our seats, and inside I rejoiced. I didn't care if we won or lost. I had saved the day, as had Mrs Tilling.

The nasal Bishop came to the front again. 'I'm afraid that refreshments have to be cancelled because of our diminishing candle supplies. So please could everyone keep their seats for a few minutes, and hopefully we can give you the results shortly.'

Everyone began whispering, except for Mrs B, who loudly proclaimed that Mrs Gibbs had sung off key for the entire performance and that, should we lose, we'd know where the blame should be placed.

'Either that or we'll be eliminated for not having men,' she sniffed.

'We have nothing to worry about,' Prim smiled, and I suddenly began to doubt if she really knew the countryside, how attached everyone is to tradition around here. There's something called conventional wisdom, which means we have to carry on doing things the same way, even when it doesn't make sense. That's what the countryside's about. Litchfield especially.

A minute later, the nasal Bishop returned to the front, this time with the Mayor beside him to announce the winner. The Mayor began to give another speech, and then, thankfully, the Bishop leaned over and had a word in his ear, which was probably 'Get on with it,' and he started to announce the runner-up.

'Litchfield,' he announced, as the choirmaster tottered up and received the certificate. That would mean, we thought, that the winners would be Riseholme, as surely no one would vote for Belton.

'And the winner, who will represent the Litchfield area in St Paul's Cathedral in the finals' – he rustled some papers annoyingly – 'is the Chilbury Ladies' Choir.'

We leapt out of our seats.

Mrs Quail gasped, 'What did he say?'

Mrs Tilling sputtered, 'We weren't eliminated?'

Mrs Gibbs said, 'Was that really us?'

Then Mrs B pushed her way through to the aisle. 'Pull yourselves together. Of course we won. What were you expecting?'

We followed her up the aisle, where she was busy pumping the Bishop's hand as if she were solely responsible for the entire thing. I looked around for Prim, and serene as ever, she was floating up the aisle after us, her long cloak flowing behind her like a great protective owl.

After we took a bow, we got together for photographs. Of course Venetia made sure she was centre stage, hair perfect, which was funny as she was standing beside Mrs Gibbs, who looked like an unhinged hen, with coats and scarves at all angles and hair like a bird's nest.

There were some photographers there from the *Kent Times* and even a national paper – they're grabbing any happy stories they can these days.

We filed over to shake hands with the judges, who were sitting at a fold-up table at the front. First was the Mayor and beside him Mrs Mandelson, who is the rather severe Litchfield WVS leader. Then there was pompous Lady Worthing, who stood proffering her white-gloved hand as if we were diseased. Mrs B was doing her hideous false laugh at something she said, and we grimaced with embarrassment.

The final judge was the Head of Litchfield Park, a giant of a man who looked untidy even though he was in uniform. Mrs Tilling whispered to Mrs Quail that he's the man billeted at her house.

'I didn't realise he was the Head of Litchfield Park,' she muttered, irritated. 'What a strange choice!'

I wondered why she was being such a sourpuss, but then I saw that he, too, frosted over as she pushed her hand out to shake his.

'Well done, Mrs Tilling,' he said noncommittally.

She flustered, embarrassed. 'I didn't realise you were one of the judges. I really don't know what—'

'Thank you for voting for us!' I said quickly, as it was a bit mean to question his judging ability when we'd just won.

He smiled warmly at me. 'It was an easy choice, especially with your solo performances.' Maybe he wasn't so bad after all.

Mrs Tilling tried to ignore him, making a small *hmph* sound before turning to me and saying in a very forced way, 'Come on, Kitty. And you, Silvie. We need to find Prim.' And making a bolt for the vestry.

The rest of the evening was a blur of congratulations, with cheers and patting on backs, and the other choirs pretending they were pleased for us. A journalist asked us how we felt being a women's-only choir.

'We're starting a new trend,' Venetia declared, preening before him. 'We're all the rage, didn't you know?'

The man stood gawping at her until Mrs B barged in, saying, 'We always believed we would win. Men or no men.' And we all nodded and smiled.

After a while, the crowds began to dwindle, and the Bishop had to shoo us out, so we made our jolly way back to the bus and set off jubilantly for Chilbury, singing all the way. But we didn't sing 'Ave Maria'. No, we sang old music hall songs, including my new favourite, 'Can't Get Away to Marry You Today, My Wife Won't Let Me!'

Letter from Colonel Mallard to his sister, Mrs Maud Green, in Oxford

Ivy House
Litchfield Road
Chilbury
Kent

Monday, 20th May, 1940

Dear Maud,

Apologies for my lack of contact, but I have been caught up with the recent events in Belgium and northern France. This letter comes to you from my new billet in Chilbury – have you been here on your travels? Please tell the girls to write to me here as letters to the MOD always get diverted via London. Do encourage them to write; frankly their letters are the only things that keep me going in this dreadful war. Once again, many thanks for looking after the three of them – I do hope they're behaving themselves. I know that Vera would be happy knowing they are with you, God rest her soul. I can't believe it is five years on Wednesday that she died. I can still hardly get used to the fact that she has gone.

I'll be here for the summer, I'd imagine, probably beyond. The woman who owns the house, a Mrs Tilling, is a nurse who seems to disapprove of everything and everyone, and especially me. She's a stick of a woman with a never-ending supply of dull grey housecoats. Hardly speaks a word, except to give me polite orders, and has been particularly bad-tempered since I asked if I could have dinner at home, demanding my ration book and crashing pots around the kitchen in annoyance.

'I'd like it, Colonel Mallard,' she said crisply to me last night, 'if you could let me know at what time you will be home for dinner.' I had only been an hour late the previous night.

Similarly, one evening I decided to move the small chest of drawers as it makes much better space if it goes in the nook beside the wardrobe. The next day it had been returned to its usual position, and I decided not to attempt any further furniture rearrangements.

But then on Saturday I was forced into being a judge for a choir competition, and would you believe it, she sang a solo, and it was so wonderful and expressive. It was as if she was a different person. I can't make head or tail of her.

Most evenings when I come in, she disappears completely. I hear a door slam upstairs or see the curtain swing in the front room window as I approach. It would be nice to have some company, but I usually end up trudging upstairs to be by myself. Her son has just left for France, and she is openly resentful that I am staying in his room. There's not much to be resentful about, if you ask me: a small, lumpy bed and a picture of the solar system on the wall – we are a tiny, self-destructive dot in a mass of grey blackness.

Enough for now. I'll write to the girls Wednesday, after I've been to the church to say a prayer for Vera. I hope she's watching down on us, keeping us safe.

Much love, Anthony

Kitty Winthrop's Diary

Saturday, 25th May, 1940

The eventful picnic

Since it was such a heavenly morning, I decided that Silvie and I deserved a treat after our choir competition victory. I felt an urge to pretend — at least for one day — that the war wasn't happening.

So I flung open my bedroom window to feel the warm yellow sunlight on my face, smelling that fresh piney scent of a sumptuous spring morning. It was so utterly perfect that I decided to dedicate the day to a search for lost time, and to recapture some of my childhood.

On days like these before the war, we used to get dressed up and go on picnics with the Tillings or the Brampton-Boyds, the girls in summer frocks, the boys in smart suits. Proggett would get Cook, who has now left to make tanks in Tonbridge, to prepare a picnic luncheon packed with pies and cherries and madeleines. Mmm, the smell of those delicious buttery cakes always takes me back to waiting eagerly in the kitchen before tasting the first warm bite of the fresh cakes as they came off the cooling racks. Today we had to make do with Elsie putting some jam sandwiches together in a terrifically offhand manner, asking all kinds of questions about Henry.

Questions Elsie wanted to know about Henry
What's his favourite food? Roast pheasant, of course,
and spotted dick pudding
What's his favourite sport? Shooting, fox hunting, and
cricket
Does he like Venetia? No, of course not
Does he have a girlfriend at his base in Hampshire?
No, of course not
What's his favourite colour? Azure blue
What does he like to do for fun? Picnics, parties, and
he's rather good at croquet

I think she was trying to help me win him over, although she wasn't being terribly useful. Silvie nudged me, whispering that I shouldn't tell her anything, although I have no idea why. Sometimes Silvie seems to completely misunderstand what's going on.

After we'd sorted out the sandwiches, Silvie and I had the important task of choosing our dresses. I took Silvie to my room and found one of my old ones for her, the white one with tiny turquoise flowers, the one that I wore the time Henry proposed to me. It brought back the flood of memories – boating on the lake, Venetia storming off up the banks, Henry stumbling after her and landing me in the bracken, getting my dress muddy, him promising to love me forever if I forgave him, and then roaming the countryside with him, calling Venetia's name until we found her on top of a hill sulking beneath a sprawling oak tree. She refused to speak to

Henry and would only come back to the picnic with me, gloomily trudging back as I skipped for joy, thrilled that my future had been mapped out to perfection.

In the spirit of remembering, I decided that I should wear Venetia's sky-blue dress, as that was the one she was wearing that day, and I stole into her room to borrow it. Although it was a little large, it was perfect.

Silvie and I sneaked into Mama's dressing room to peer at ourselves in her big mahogany mirror. We looked impeccable. The sky-blue dress was just the thing for a picnic, and Silvie looked lovely too, in the white frock. She's a pretty girl, with her unruly dark curls always plastered behind her ears, although she hardly says a word. We used to think she was quiet because her English wasn't very good, but now we know that her English isn't bad at all – except when she misunderstands things, like the whole Henry situation. So when she doesn't talk it's simply because she doesn't want to. I sometimes ask her about her secret, but she looks very alarmed and stops speaking immediately.

I often wonder what her life was like back in Czechoslovakia. The food was different, that's for certain. She barely touched anything for weeks when she arrived and has been living on bread rolls and jam for the main part. Mama tries to tempt her with bacon or roast beef, but she won't touch a thing.

The difference between Czechoslovakia and Chilbury, from what I can gather
Czechoslovakia has more chocolate (Silvie adores
    chocolate, and it's rare here now the war's on)
Chilbury has hills with fields and woods, whereas
    Czechoslovakia has more forests

They both have horses (Silvie loves horses)

In Czechoslovakia, Christmas is always snowy and
  there are magical Christmas markets

There was no war in Czechoslovakia, the Nazis simply
  took over one day

All Silvie's belongings are in Czechoslovakia, in her
  big house with a veranda

All Silvie's family are in Czechoslovakia, waiting for
  her by the front door, her mother wearing a white
  spring dress like the day she waved goodbye at the
  station, her father in his suit and hat with a big smile
  warming her chilling bones, and her baby brother,
  Mila, giggling in his blue blanket as she takes him
  from her mother's arms for one final kiss

With a last look at our reflections in the glass, we decided we
were ready, and dashed downstairs, scooping up the picnic
basket as we raced through the kitchen and side door into the
pale, clear morning.

The tall grass in the meadow was still wet from the rain
last night, the multitude of droplets glistening like a thousand
fallen stars in the thick field of the brightest green. There was
that smell you get after a big storm, a new freshness as if the
rain has washed away all the dust and dirt and horrid things
that people shout at each other and are left reverberating in
the air, waiting for the thunder to deafen it all out.

I decided that we'd go down to the little wooden bridge
beside the Dawkinses' beehives, as there are lots of wild
flowers, and you can play stepping stones across the stream.
We went there on a picnic a few years ago when the motorcar
wasn't working.

No one got stung that time.

It was quite a walk, and when we got there, exhausted and ready for our picnic, we were rather peeved to find it already occupied. A boy was building a dam.

'Hello there!' he called. Standing shakily on a tree branch that was covering half the width then, steadying himself, he trotted over to the bank to greet us. He was older than I thought, tall and lanky like big boys are before they become men, his tatty shorts and rather unkempt appearance making him look younger from afar. He had a curious face, kind of spoon-shaped, his chin and forehead jutting out further than the rest of it. Handsome. Not handsome like Henry, but still not bad-looking for a boy. Clearly enjoying himself, he grinned in the sunshine, putting a dirty hand up to shield his eyes from the sun as he hollered up the bank to us.

'Come down and join in.' His voice was thick and Cockney.

Since Silvie was already halfway down the slope, I felt obliged to add my protection, and we were soon beside him.

'I'm Tom,' he said, still smiling, his mouth open as he panted, hands on hips as he appraised his dam.

'How do you do,' I said, unsure whether to shake hands. 'My name is Kitty and this is Silvie.' Silvie actually smiled. Did she like him?

'What are you children doing 'round 'ere?' Tom said.

'We are not children!' I corrected.

'She is,' he said, jabbing his head towards Silvie and laughing.

'Yes,' I relented, infuriated by his rudeness. 'I suppose she is. But I'm not.'

'How old are you? Twelve?'

'Fourteen,' I smarted, my hand nudging against Silvie to stop her from calling me a liar. I am almost fourteen, after all. Well, almost-almost. 'But more to the point, what are *you* doing here?' I asked crossly. The land belongs to the farm. As do the bees.

'We're here for the hop picking.' He jerked his head behind to the hop pickers' huts by the barn. Every year Dawkins Farm gets about fifty Londoners to come and help out with farm work, then pick the hops when they're ready. They live in rows of huts. It all seems frightfully squalid to me, but apparently it's exactly how they live in London – better even.

'How long have you been here?' I demanded, my eyes narrowing with distrust. I was still miffed he'd called me a child.

'I only came last week with me auntie. Me mum had to go help out in a factory, and no one knew what to do with me. I told them I wanted to fight.' He thrust a few tidy punches into the air. 'But they said I'm too young.'

'How old are you?'

'Nearly fourteen. Strong as any man – probably stronger.' He showed us his biceps, which were puny, but we didn't say anything. I felt sorry for him. His face was so open and funny that you couldn't possibly think he was up to no good.

'Come and help me with the dam,' he ordered. 'Get that branch there and bring it along.'

Fortunately, the dam was stable enough for us to totter to the halfway point.

Unfortunately, we'd quite forgotten about the bees, which suddenly surrounded us, buzzing furiously at Silvie.

'Tom to the rescue,' Tom cried, flailing his arms around like a deranged orangutan.

'No, not like that,' I cried. This city idiot clearly hadn't got a clue about bees. 'Keep still. Keep still, and they'll go away.'

I trotted as fast as I could back to the bank, almost falling in once, picked up a long, narrow branch, and held it out to Silvie for her to make her way back without panicking too much – although I must say she was the calmest of us all, an amused little smile on her lips like the Mona Lisa having some kind of private joke.

Once on land, I opened our basket, found a jam sandwich, and as the bees headed straight for it, I flung it as far as I could up the bank, in the direction of the beehives. It did the trick all right, luring the bees away, although one of them stung me on the elbow as he went past, the monster.

I screamed, and Tom came bounding over, grabbing my arm in a most ungentlemanly way. We all looked down at the growing mound of pink.

'You'll need some vinegar on that,' he said.

'Don't be ridiculous,' I said sharply. Didn't this boy know anything? 'We need honey.'

'If you want honey, I know where to get some.'

'Do you?' I asked warily. Honey wasn't easy to get these days. He brushed down his rather tatty shorts and then pointed out his arm. 'Step this way, young ladies.'

We collected our things and followed him up the bank, giving the basket to him to carry since my arm hurt and Silvie is too small. He led us back along the side of the orchard to Peasepotter Wood, and at the cusp of the wood, he turned, glanced around furtively, then headed in. We hurried in after him.

After a short walk, he pushed his way into a massive bush, the type that is hollow on the inside and packed with tiny close leaves around the edge. After a minute or so of rummaging in the shrubbery, he reversed back out.

In his hand was a jar of honey. It must have been home produced as it had a blue gingham cover and a white label saying *Allicot Farm* – I couldn't help wondering where I'd heard that name before. He took off the top and stuck a grubby finger in, stuffing the yellow fingerful in his mouth. I wanted to stop him. He was tainting all that honey. It was disgusting!

'It's honey all right.' He chomped his mouth about, savouring the flavour. 'Try some.'

Silvie stuck her finger in and tentatively put it in her mouth, and the look of pleasure on her face finally made me give in and try it too.

It was the most divine honey I'd ever tasted, all rose petals and syrupy sweetness. We all took another fingerful, and I smeared a little on my sting.

'What's it doing in the bush?'

'I've seen Old George put it there,' Tom said. 'He's an old crook who stays in one of the hop huts. We don't bother him much.' He bit his lip awkwardly. 'He's got a knife and things. Threatened our Charlie, so we leave him well alone.'

'Should we be taking his things?'

'S'pose not,' Tom said, with a small lilt of a skinny shoulder. 'It's black-market, of course. I only take a few bits at a time. Nothing he would notice.'

A noise in the bracken startled us. We looked around, but there was nothing there. It could have been a fox, but the trees were so dense it was hard to see.

'Should we go?' I whispered.

The rustling became louder – it was definitely a person – and we crept quietly behind a broad tree. When I turned, I saw a fat, angry-looking bald man stalk into the clearing, his whiskers grey and scraggy, a greenish stain on his shirt. With him was Mr Slater, of all people. I always suspected he was up to no good. I wonder if Venetia knows about this.

'It's Old George. Let's get out of here,' Tom said urgently, pulling me away.

As we turned, I saw Mr Slater's face look round to us. Did he see us?

We fled, our legs pounding the ground like a whirl, the bracken and dead leaves crackling under our feet, darting deeper into the wood, nipping around heavy trunks and tucking between dense bushes until all we could hear was the sound of our own rhythmic footsteps in the silent surroundings.

Suddenly, as if a heavy curtain had been swept open, we tumbled out of the wood, and the vast expanse of English countryside lay before us, a colossal spread of multicoloured hues bathed magnificently in the brilliant golden sunshine.

We fell down, gasping for breath, laughing, checking behind us for the shadow of Old George on our trail, but there was nothing, only the light whisper of the leaves as a breeze lifted them to and fro, and the songs of the birds flitting busily around the edge of the greeny-gold field of wheat before us.

'We'd better go home,' I said.

'You know where to find me,' Tom said, helping us up. 'At the hop pickers' huts.' And with that he turned and began a wide-strided walk down the hill to the river.

'Bye,' Silvie said quietly, which meant that she liked him,

and I had to admit, as we picked up our picnic basket and headed home, that it was rather fun having an adventure of our own.

As we trotted around the edge of the wood, I asked Silvie if she'd ever seen anyone sneaking around the wood.

'Proggett,' she replied.

'Proggett? Where?'

'In Peasepotter, behind trees, in the Pixie Ring, down by Bullsend Brook,' she said quietly in her taut Czech voice. I know she disappears off by herself quite a lot, but I never knew she'd been wandering all over the countryside. 'He meets men,' she added.

'What kind of men?'

'Just men.' She glanced away. 'Boring men.'

'Were you scared?'

She shook herself up, running ahead of me with bravado. 'No.'

As I sped up behind her, I remembered where I had heard the name Allicot Farm. It's a place on the other side of Litchfield. Mrs Gibbs started selling their honey in the shop last month. I wonder how Old George came across his assortment of goodies – how Mrs Gibbs got her hands on it. And how exactly Mr Slater was involved. I have decided not to inform Venetia quite yet. Let her come crawling to me. Or, better still, keep it tucked away for a time when it might be put to good use.

Telegram from General Winchester to
Colonel Mallard

Monday, 27th May, 1940

Operation Dynamo is underway. All civilian boats
sent to Dunkirk to collect 300,000 British and
French troops stranded on beach. All local facilities,
military, and medics on standby.

Mrs Tilling's Journal

Wednesday, 29th May, 1940

Who'd have thought such a disaster could happen! And that I would be caught up in the midst of it! Tonight I am in Dover, working fast to patch up the soldiers coming off the boats from Dunkirk. Hundreds of thousands of troops surrounded and trapped on a beach in France, the Luftwaffe strafing them with bullets, and all we can do is get everyone who has a boat to go off and rescue them, from fishing boats to ferries and yachts even. It's as if we've gone back to medieval times!

Dover is a mass of activity. Teams of men pouring off boats of all shapes and sizes and tramping through the town to the railway station. Most of them, thank goodness, seem to be in good humour, overjoyed to be home. But many others look like they've been through a nightmare. Then there are those on stretchers, bleeding and delirious, or silently dying.

The thick mess of fresh blood, fresh casualties, is relentless in our surgery, an old workhouse converted into a hospital, reeking of human death lightly confused by the acidic stench of sterilisation. The medics are too few for so many brutally wounded men. But we are trying our best, working from one patient to the next with gruesome practicality.

They picked me up at dawn in a bus packed with available doctors and nurses from the area, and we're here for a few days at least. It's now well past midnight, and I'm sitting in a dusty back room with an hour off to catch whatever rest I can. They've set up a few beds, but every time I close my eyes all I see is blood and gore, and I can still hear the screams of men as the pain gets too much, or worse, the sudden disconcerting quiet of death.

I'm trying not to think about David, but it's like a throbbing beacon at the back of my brain. I know he was in France – almost all our troops were – so he must be somewhere in this chaos. I hope.

We have some desperate cases here. Earlier today I was called to help a bloody mess of a young officer by the name of Berkeley who had a vast gash of shrapnel in his side. I quickly realised that it was too late for surgery, too late for anything. His bleeding was relentless, spurts pulsating into the drenched poultice that I pushed desperately into his rib cage.

'You're going to be all right. You'll be just fine,' I said softly.

'I'm going to die, aren't I?' he murmured, his refined tones sounding very young indeed. He must have been just out of school, the same as David.

'No, you'll be fine,' I lied, inwardly panicking. What should I do? Should I tell him he's going to die in case he has something he needs to say? I felt so utterly unprepared: What was I doing here? What was I playing at?

'If,' he stammered quietly. 'If I die, w-will you give my ring to someone?' He tried to raise his hand, and I saw the gold band loose on his finger.

'Of course,' I said, slipping it off and holding it out in my hand. It was a man's signet ring, heavy, old, valuable.

'Give it to Carrington,' he murmured, his voice breaking as he spoke the name. 'In Parnham, near Litchfield.'

'That's close, I can get it there,' I said gently. 'Is there a message?'

'Say *I love you*,' he choked horribly.

'Of course I'll give it to her,' I said.

'He's a man,' he whispered, his eyes looking into mine, large with dread, scared that he'd asked too much, said too much. He could be hanged for this. If he wasn't dead already.

A surge of blood rushed to my face. I've never met a homosexual before. I'd heard of them, of course, but always thought they were different, living in an underworld, as if they didn't really exist at all. But here was a gentle, handsome, dying youth telling me to send his last message to his friend, who he loved. I was speechless for a moment, unravelling the dense mesh between morality and reality.

'I'll tell him,' I whispered.

Then, as if something had suddenly occurred to him, he opened his eyes wide and gasped, 'You won't, you won't hand him in, will you?'

'No,' I said, meeting his gaze. 'You can trust me.'

'I, I wasn't thinking. I forgot that I could land him in trouble. I couldn't bear for anything to happen to him.' His lean body began to shudder with tears.

I wanted to wrap my arms around him, but I couldn't take my hands away from the thickening maroon of blood flooding the dressing. All I could do was find his hand and squeeze it tight.

'You're the brave one,' I said. 'You're the hero. Carrington will be fine. Don't worry about him. Just rest and breathe easily.'

And his breath became easier, and easier, until it stopped. I looked around for help, someone to tell, someone to acknowledge this death.

But no one was there. They were too busy.

Another life just begun and already over. A faraway star glows brighter and then disappears into the void.

What an insignificant, unprepared army of souls we are.

Letter from Flt Lt Henry Brampton-Boyd to Venetia Winthrop

Air base 9463
Daws Hill
Buckinghamshire

Tuesday, 4th June, 1940

Dear Venetia,

My darling, I can't tell you how incredibly hard we've fought these last weeks, keeping the Luftwaffe from bombing the men being rescued at Dunkirk. The last boats left today, and we flew wearily back to base to celebrate our successes, and my name has been bandied around as something of a hero, no less.

Our dogfighting happened mostly inland, heading off the Luftwaffe before they got to Dunkirk, and it wasn't until the fourth day that I went after three Messerschmitts into the fray, shooting them all down. They're making a tremendous fuss about it back here at the base, even though I keep insisting it was nothing.

I will be home on leave in a month or so, and have asked Mother to arrange an engagement celebration of sorts. I

can't wait for our honeymoon, my dearest, when you will
finally be mine.

All my love, Henry

Kitty Winthrop's Diary

Wednesday, 12th June, 1940

*Nothing for ages, and now we're right
in the midst of war!*

Dunkirk was astounding! We rescued almost all the British troops and most of the French troops too. Far more than anyone had hoped. Everyone says it's all thanks to the 'little ships', all those ordinary people dropping everything to hurry off in boats and pick up our soldiers off the beach. Daddy took his yacht over and says he saved over three hundred soldiers. 'Bombed all the way!' he says. He has been incredibly pleased with himself, with people lining up to shake hands in the village square.

'We small boats were central to operations,' he told a gathering. 'We could go right up to the beach, carry the men to the big ships in deeper waters ready to head for England. It was a fearful scene. Crowds of men crawling the beach like ants, wading into the water, sometimes up to their shoulders, while overhead Nazi planes strafed us with bullets. I'll never forget hauling those men out of the murky water, some badly wounded, all exhausted, the bullets pummelling the choppy sea around us.'

Luckily David Tilling came home all right, although exhausted and starved. Mrs Tilling was incredibly relieved and kept him in bed for two days to recover. Fortunately, the Colonel gave up his room and has taken a hotel room in Litchfield, or I think we'd have had a war right here in Chilbury.

Ralph Gibbs from the shop came back in a bit of a state, with his shoulder dislocated and some broken ribs. He is prone to fighting, and we can't help wondering if his injuries were from the enemy or from trouble in the ranks. He gets to stay at home for now, while David Tilling has to go back again in a few weeks, probably heading to North Africa. And very unhappy he is too, mooching around trying to woo Venetia, who is far too busy with Mr Slater to even notice him.

Henry is a hero at last, and bound to get a medal, Mrs B says. He downed three Nazi planes over Dunkirk! I was hoping he'd have leave too, but they're busy helping poor France, who are being overrun.

Sadly, the son of Mrs Poultice, one of the Sewing Ladies, didn't make it. He was in a small boat that was bombed by a Nazi plane. Another boat dragged him out of the water, but he was too injured and died before they reached Dover. She hasn't spoken a word since, just slowly sews. We managed to convince her to join the choir, which might help a little.

Mr Churchill says we're not giving in!

Daddy's glad that Mr Churchill became Prime Minister, even though a lot of people say he's wrong. They want to make a settlement with the Nazis rather than fight, as frankly our chances don't look terribly good.

'They're cowards!' Daddy roared. 'It's more honourable to go down fighting than to give in. We can't just let them walk all over us.'

Mr Churchill says this war is going to be fought in the air, and we've been asked to give our pots and pans to the Government so that they can be melted down and made into bombers. I found eleven in our kitchen, which surely must amount to a wing at least.

Invasion

If we don't give in, we're the next ones after France to be invaded. Since Chilbury is only seven miles from the coast, there's a chance we'll be overrun by Nazi troops before we've even heard about it. We'll be woken in the middle of the night by the sound of tanks crashing down our doors.

What will happen if we get taken over by the Nazis
We'll all starve as they'll take our food to give to Nazi soldiers
They'll take anyone left who can fight and send them to the front line, or get shot
They'll force the rest of us into factories, even children like me
We'll have to have Nazi soldiers staying at our houses, or shoving us onto the street so they can live there
We won't be able to go anywhere except by walking or bicycle as they'll take our motorcars and we won't be able to get on trains

They'll imprison or shoot anyone who doesn't do what
    they say
They'll imprison or shoot anyone they don't like

People have started moving away. The Dunns have gone to
Wales as Lizzie is deaf and Hitler doesn't like children like
that. The synagogue where we take Silvie is looking rather
empty as many Jewish people are moving away from the
coast, even though the synagogue is determined to stay open
for the Jewish people in the troops. We're petrified about
Silvie, of course. Mama wanted us to go and stay with a
cousin in Scotland, but Daddy refused.

'I have complete confidence that we'll always remain British,
even if those Nazis try anything silly.' He looked all gruff and
proud, thwacking his horsewhip against the unsuspecting leg
of an armchair, and I felt at once glad to be part of such a
fearless national spirit and frightened to death that it's no help
at all when you have half a dozen Nazi guns pointing at you.

Everyone's going mad accusing people of being spies.
They've rounded up all the Germans and Italians and sent
them to camps on the Isle of Man, even Mama's frightfully
nice bridge partner, Mrs Barone. I can't imagine her in a
camp at all – where would she store all her fur coats and
fancy hats? We've been told to look out for spies amongst us,
keep an eye on our neighbours and turn in anyone doing
anything suspicious. I considered telling someone about
Proggett, as he's forever sneaking around – I even found him
in Daddy's study last week, leafing through a few papers,
telling me he was trying to locate a lost cuff link – but Daddy
would beat me if they carted off Proggett. He's got to be the
last available butler this side of London.

We've been told there'll probably be Nazi planes coming over to drop bombs on us soon, and the Vicar's taken the job of Air Raid Warden. Most people have dug great holes in their gardens to put in Anderson bomb shelters, which are little metal huts that look far too flimsy to survive a bomb. I'm glad we've got a cellar that's big enough to sleep in, even though it's thick with dust and home to a highly prolific spider community.

The Government has circulated leaflets about what to do when the Nazis invade (stay calm) and what we're not to do (panic and run away). There are pictures of Nazi soldiers and a list of what to do if we find one (go to the police) and what not to do (try to reason with them and get shot as a result). We've been busy removing signposts so that when they arrive at least they won't know where they are.

Apparently the rest of Europe was overrun easily because the people weren't prepared and they simply panicked. I'm not entirely certain how the Government intends us to stop a cavalry of well-equipped Huns, but this is what they have told us to do.

Preparation for invasion

Keep calm – don't run away

Don't believe rumours and be distrustful of orders –
   check that orders are from the Government

Hide all maps, food, fuel, tools and other supplies – a
   parachutist will prey on you for these items

Put concrete pillboxes, land mines, or barbed wire
   defences on beaches, fields, and roads

Dig anti-tank ditches on roads and tracks – a line
   across the country stops the Nazis from going north

Block the roads with motorcars and other big
   obstacles, or by felling trees
If necessary, use wire or chains to block a road with an
   imitation bomb (box with cable)
Only ring church bells to warn of invasion
Form a group of Local Defence Volunteers from men
   still in the village – Daddy is organising the few
   men left
Form a village Invasion Committee to work out how
   your village aims to defend itself

The Chilbury Invasion Committee (CIC)

Mrs B has taken it upon herself to coordinate the CIC
(everything is abbreviated nowadays because it sounds more
official). She's been especially bossy as her remaining servants have left, so now she's fending for herself, asking for
recipes from Mrs Tilling (although we suspect she's living
off hampers sent down from Claridge's). She called the WVS
ladies for a special CIC meeting in the village hall this
afternoon.

'As your leader, I feel it my duty to prepare our ladies for
the coming invasion. First of all, I'd like some suggestions of
what we can do if a troop of abominable Nazi thugs stomp
into the village square tomorrow morning.'

'But we don't know it's going to happen for certain, do
we?' Mrs Gibbs stammered. A haunted look has overtaken
her face since Ralph's been back. I'm not sure if she's more
scared of Ralph or the Nazis.

Mrs B marched up to her, putting her face close like a
sergeant major. 'We have to be ready,' she roared. Then,

turning to the rest of us, she continued, 'I'm looking for serious suggestions.'

'I'd get my husband's old air rifle,' Mrs Tilling suggested.
'I don't know how to use it, but it would look good, wouldn't
it?'

'Well, you must learn how to use it,' Mrs B shouted.
'Everyone who has access to firearms, clean 'em, make sure
you know how to use 'em, then load 'em.' She looked around
menacingly. 'Mrs Quail, what about you?'

'I'm quite dapper with a kitchen knife,' she said confidently,
and I exchanged a smirk with Hattie, who was rocking Rose's
pram. Imagine Mrs Quail getting cross with the Vicar over
tea and whipping out a carving knife!

Mrs B, clearly disappointed with our lack of pluck, demon-
strated how to lunge and attack using household objects, such
as a fire poker, a table lamp, or a three-tiered silver cake stand.
We all enjoyed it thoroughly and left feeling awfully brave.

Of course the next meeting wasn't as straightforward as
that, because the Chilbury Defence Volunteers (CDV) showed
up halfway through.

The Chilbury Defence Volunteers (CDV) vs the Chilbury Invasion Committee (CIC)

Daddy has taken it upon himself to start the Chilbury
Defence Volunteers (CDV). We think he did it because Mrs B
'stole' the CIC from under his nose, and he needed a troop of
his very own.

The Chilbury Defence Volunteers consists of a motley
collection of men left in the village preparing to defend us if
or when the Nazis come. All a lovely idea, but in reality it's

Daddy, Proggett, old Mr Dawkins and the two farmhands, some other old men in various stages of decay, the Vicar, Ralph Gibbs (although he has yet to put in an appearance), and would you believe it, Mr Slater, who apparently finds the entire thing 'rather amusing', according to Venetia.

They meet twice a week and Daddy shouts a lot while they pretend to be a real army, marching up and down and trying to stab each other with pitchforks, since they don't have any proper weapons yet.

The problem is that Mrs B's Invasion Committee also meets in the church hall twice a week, and yesterday the men began arriving with their pitchforks just as Mrs B was perfecting her three-tiered-cake-stand lunge, surrounded by a group of women practising the very same move. 'Point, lunge, thrust.'

'We're supposed to have the hall now,' Daddy announced pompously. 'Will you clear your women out of here immediately.'

'I shall do no such thing,' Mrs B retaliated, swinging her cake stand in his direction.

'We have important invasion preparations.' Daddy was starting to raise his voice. 'Get your blasted women out of here.'

'Brigadier, I'd like to remind you that my Invasion Committee is the most important body for invasion prevention in our village. As you can see, we are in the middle of crucial combat practice.'

'But we have booked the hall, haven't we, Vicar?' He turned and searched for the Vicar, who was hiding behind Mr Slater, and dragged him by the collar to the front. 'Haven't we, Vicar?'

'Well, yes, but the hall is meant for all of us to share—'

'Never mind that,' Mrs B said, pushing the Vicar roughly to one side. 'We were here first, and you'll have to wait until we're finished.'

'In that case, we'll have to come in and take over.' He turned to the group of men, who were starting to edge back towards the door, and bellowed, 'Company, fall in!'

The men shuffled into the room amongst the women and got into line, pitchforks at attention.

The women just stood and looked at them in dismay, until Mrs B yelled, 'Point, lunge, thrust.'

The women obediently lunged, mostly at the men who were in the way, which was clearly Mrs B's intention.

Mayhem ensued. Many of the older men and women made an escape to the door, some nursing injuries. But the rest continued for a few minutes until the door slammed shut and a sharp teacherlike voice clipped, 'What's going on here?'

Everyone looked around. It was Hattie, standing at the door with her blue pram. 'What on earth are you all doing?'

'The Brigadier started it,' Mrs B began. 'It's our rightful turn to use the hall and they barged in and tried to intimidate us.' She looked proudly around at the ladies. 'But we showed them, didn't we?'

'It was our turn and they wouldn't leave,' Daddy said, nose in the air as if even discussing it were beneath him.

'Well, I suggest that everyone put down their weapons and shake hands,' Hattie said. 'And then after that let's put on the wireless and listen to news of a real war.'

Everyone quietly began putting things away, although Mrs B snapped, 'That's precisely what I've been telling them to do all along.'

Bad news for the choir — and my singing career

The choir competition has been postponed indefinitely. Prim announced it at practice, although she quickly said we'd have a special choir practice next week, and everyone in the village is invited. At least I still have singing lessons. Prim has lent me a pile of modern records for me to try to sing along to at home. Some are jazz, which is quite thrilling. We're to try them out in our singing lessons.

Tonight at choir practice, we sung an especially aggressive rendition of 'Jerusalem', becoming quite raucous towards the end as we're so peeved with the Nazis for preventing us from singing in St Paul's Cathedral. You'd have thought that our higgledy-piggledy assortment of ladies was ready to pick up handbags and charge towards the enemy. Does Hitler have any idea of the force and determination of thirteen impassioned women? At the very least, I suspect he's never considered the lethal potential of a three-tiered cake stand.

Note from Miss Edwina Paltry
to Brigadier Winthrop

3 Church Row
Chilbury
Kent

Monday, 17th June, 1940

Dear Brigadier,

After waiting more than a month for the money owed which is rightfully mine, I have taken it upon myself to remind you that we had a deal, and you owe me the second half of my money. I carried out my role, and now you must fulfil yours.

I will be waiting at the outhouse Saturday morning at 10.

Miss E M Paltry

Notice pinned to the Chilbury village hall noticeboard,
Monday, 17th June, 1940

There will be a special choir practice on
Wednesday evening in commemoration of those
lost in Dunkirk. It will be open to all the village, both
men and women.

Prim

Mrs Tilling's Journal

Wednesday, 19th June, 1940

We arrived early for Prim's special choir practice, some chattering about what Prim had for us, others with our own thoughts after Dunkirk. I had convinced one of the Sewing Ladies, Mrs Poultice, to come. She lost her only son at Dunkirk. She hasn't spoken a word since, just sews, in her own world.

I was surprised that so many people were there. The whole of the Chilbury Ladies' Choir, the Sewing Ladies, and some other women not in the choir. Then there were men too, including the Vicar and Mr Slater, and even Colonel Mallard. I tried to ignore him, but he insisted on coming to speak to me. Fortunately, as he came near, the heavy door swung open and Prim came down the aisle and we were saved the need to speak to each other.

Instead of her usual dramatic voice, Prim gestured for us to be quiet.

'Tonight is a special evening for us to come to terms with what has happened and what is upon us. Please take a chair from the back and bring it to the altar, making a circle.'

We all did so. I had poor Mrs Poultice beside me, looking so pale and sad, as if something inside her had stopped living but her body lived and moved, like a lifeless machine.

'In my youth,' Prim began, 'I travelled to Italy, and it was there that I learnt a different type of song. A song to bring peace and acceptance of the natural cycle of life and death. The chant.' She put out her hands on either side. 'Let us take each other's hands, complete the circle.'

We gingerly held hands. Such a simple, childish thing, but so rare in our busy, untouching world. I felt the back of Mrs Poultice's wrinkled, veined hand in mine, and felt her tremble slightly with the strange intimacy of it all. It was as if we'd torn down our everyday masks to expose the scared children inside.

'Now let's close our eyes, and start with a single held hum.'

The sound of a faint hum, a middle note, neither high nor low, emanated from Prim, at first soft and then growing with confidence.

Then I heard Kitty's soft tones joining in, then Mrs Quail's, and before long a sonorous single note was echoing around us, filling all the gaps between us with a vibrating connection. A noise that drowned out all the mess.

The hum petered out, thinning into the air until it was a whisper, or an echo of a whisper.

After a few poignant moments of silence she handed out some music. 'This is a simple Gregorian chant,' she told us. 'It is for the mourning of the dead.'

She hummed the note to begin, and then we all came in, Kitty's voice leading the descant. It was beautiful. At the end, when the echoes had faded into silence, we sat a few moments in the warmth of the silence, our hands linked.

Prim was the first to get up, ushering everyone to follow suit, quietly taking her chair to the back, finding her music bag.

'Keep calm and peaceful for the rest of the night,' she said gently, and drifted out as if on a wave of calm.

We slowly began to get up, chattering softly amongst ourselves. Even Mrs B seemed pacified for a moment. 'What an extraordinary evening,' she said. 'I really wasn't sure at the beginning, but it was like we were nuns,' she chortled.

Funny how a bit of singing brings us together. There we were in our own little worlds, with our own problems, and then suddenly they seemed to dissolve, and we realised that it's us here now, living through this, supporting each other.

That's what counts.

Silvie's Diary

Wednesday, 19th June, 1940

Everyone is sad after Dunkirk. Prim had a special choir practice with chanting. I sat beside Kitty and Mrs Poultice. Her
son died at Dunkirk. Her hand shook, so I gripped it tight.

Then we sang a Gregorian chant.

It was beautiful. I began to cry. It made me think of sitting
shiva when Grandpa died and there was chanting every
evening. Mrs Poultice was crying too.

The Nazis will be here soon. Mrs Winthrop will hide me
in the attic. When they came to Czechoslovakia, they found
everyone who hid. They beat people in the street. They took
that screaming woman into a house. Then she had blood and
cuts, nearly dead.

I try not to think. But it is there.

I sang Kitty our mourning chant, the Kaddish. She wrote
it down. Maybe we can sing it for Mrs Poultice.

Letter from Miss Edwina Paltry
to her sister, Clara

3 Church Row
Chilbury
Kent

Saturday, 22nd June, 1940

Dear Clara,

All is not yet lost, Clara, although I must confess we have
had a few setbacks, the first entailing the Brigadier
handing over the rest of the money. I met him at the
outhouse today, fuming he was, and he told me he wasn't
giving it over.

'Why not?' I demanded, clutching my black bag, ready to
give him a good clout.

'Because, my dear woman, you weren't terribly good at
covering your tracks, were you?' He was all controlled
anger, waiting to snap like a tethered wolf. I felt my knees
wobble but put up a good front.

'No one knows a thing. I did a clean job. Always do.'

'But what about the rumours?' He took a step closer,
threateningly, so I took a step back right into the nettles. I
could feel them pinch under my stockings. 'Mrs Tilling has

been asking my wife questions about the birth. Couldn't you have come up with something better than the mechanical ventilator? A different problem for the other child?'

'I don't think you understand the difficulties of the task, Brigadier,' I said haughtily. 'We made a deal, did we not? And I fulfilled my part. So I want my money.'

'I told you there'd be no money if you aroused suspicion. If that woman pieces it together because of your carelessness, then you'll be paying me,' he snarled, his face coming up to mine like a fierce army general. 'With your blood.'

The smell of his breath at such short range made me fall over backward into the bracken, and he looked smugly on as I picked myself up and pulled off twigs. He's a woman hater, that man. I can tell one anywhere. In my line of business you hear all sorts of stories from women, sometimes even the men themselves, thinking they're so clever abusing some poor woman. I can tell the Brigadier thinks women are only good for serving men and having babies. And sex, of course. Doesn't realise that we're human too. With heads and hearts and pockets to line.

'She'll never catch on,' I said. 'It'll blow over, same as everything. You owe me that money, and I can raise a stink about it if you don't give it to me.'

'You know better than to make a fuss about something that'll put you in jail,' he said shrewdly, twiddling his moustache. 'But I'll make you a deal. If I hear no other gossip before the end of the summer, you'll have your money. Until that time, I expect no more stupid blunders, no more rumours, and no more notes – I'd have thought you'd know better than to pass letters between us. You could have had us both arrested within the hour if it had fallen into the wrong hands.'

He shoved my note, all scrunched up, into my hand and stormed off, leaving me picking bracken off my skirt and feeling relief about two things: first, that the Tilling woman didn't know anything for sure, and second, that I'd just have to sit tight and the rest of the money would be making its way to me soon.

Not ideal, but better than only getting half.

My next problem was that stupid girl Elsie. She came to my house thinking she had one over me.

'I know your deal,' she said, striding in and lounging on my sofa like a sleek cat. 'And I want my cut.'

'Whatever are you talking about?' I said, smiling with puzzlement.

'Your deal, swapping the babies. I know all about it.'

'What on earth are you talking about, my dear?'

'Don't act all nonchalant with me. I saw you swap them. I know you did it and got paid.'

'Who could possibly have asked me to do that?' I said, all astonishment.

'The Brigadier. See, I've been thinking, putting it together. I'm not as stupid as I look, you know?'

'Believe me, Elsie. You look far cleverer than you really are.'

She ignored my comment, or didn't understand it. 'He gave you money so he could have his son, didn't he? And I want my cut.'

'But you didn't do anything,' I said, deciding to get down to business.

'I helped you escape with one of them. In any case, I
know all about it, and I can tell people. Isn't that
enough? I want two hundred pounds, please.' She stuck her
hand out towards me, face up, all white and skinny like a
corpse's.

'How do you know how much he gave me?'

'A woman like you wouldn't have done it for less than
twenty thousand.'

I grimaced. I knew I should have asked him for more.

'I'll give you fifty and that'll be that. If I hear you've told
anyone, you'll have to pay me my dues,' I added, taking a
leaf from the Brigadier's book and looking all menacing.
'With your own blood.'

I left the room and got out the large notes. Wretched
girl, I knew I should never have trusted her. Anyone
capable of fooling around with Edmund Winthrop was
bound to be immoral.

I slapped them on her hand, and she leapt up.

'You'll have no worries from me. I'm heading out of this
dingy place as soon as I've finished some business here.
The Brigadier can stuff his stupid job. No one wants to be a
maid these days, and it's easy to see why. I've been slaving
for them for pennies, and now I've got my chance.' She
glanced at the money bulging in her old coat pocket. 'Now
I've got the money, I'm getting a new life. I got myself
Edmund, didn't I? So now I'll get another one of them toffs.
Once one of them gets a taste of Elsie, I'll have him eating
out of my hand. Just you watch! The next time you'll see
me, you'll hardly recognise me.'

With that she flounced out, and I thought how stupid the
girl was. If she couldn't hold down an idiot like Edmund

Winthrop, she'd have no hope with anyone even slightly sensible. Still, I do wonder who she has her eye on.

So, Clara, for now I'm stuck in this village like a splodge of sour tar, unable to move until I get the rest of the money, trying desperately to ensure the nasty secret doesn't leak out. Burn this after reading it, and I'll be in touch soon.

Edwina

Letter from Venetia Winthrop
to Angela Quail

Wednesday, 3rd July, 1940

Dear Angela,

You will never guess what happened here yesterday. I'm
hoping it won't cause any commotion, but I think it's
terrifically funny. It all started yesterday evening at
Alastair's house. It was around midnight, just as they were
closing up the bar at the Fox & Ferret. I could hear the
men's voices in the square; they've become much rowdier
since the soldiers came home after Dunkirk. Ralph Gibbs
has been causing trouble, I've heard, giving someone a
bloody nose last week and threatening someone else with a
knife. They say he's become involved in the black market.

When I arrived yesterday evening, Alastair had cooked
me dinner, would you believe it? Baked cod, no less. He'd
laid the small table and found a pink rose from somewhere,
one of those floppy perfumed ones put in a jam jar with
water.

'Where did you learn to cook?' I asked.

'Here and there.' He smiled, again not giving anything away. 'I'm glad you approve.'

He brought a candle over to the table and watched me in the flickering glow. 'Wouldn't it be wonderful if we could do this every night?'

'Yes,' I said. 'But tediously I have to dine with my family most evenings.'

He grinned. 'Actually I only know two other dishes. So we'd be out of options by the end of the week.'

We laughed, and he tidied a piece of my hair behind my ear, stroking my cheek and my neck. 'I'd love to have you here always,' he said gently. 'You could let your hair down, let me see the real you, the real Venetia, not the showy one who pretends to be mischievous and confident.' He smiled, but there was that disarming seriousness about him again, a look of intensity behind his eyes.

I pulled away, uncomfortably. 'But that's who I am,' I said serenely, although I'm not sure if it really is any more.

After dinner we went to the sitting room. He'd lit a few candles and dotted them like glowing stars around our dark little studio, their waxy scent filling the air, all warm with velvet cushions and the deep, thick rug. I stripped naked and posed for my portrait as usual. It's astonishing how one gets used to having no clothes on, baring one's all for the sake of art. The portrait has been coming on very nicely, even though Alastair stops every few moments to come and whisper sweet nothings in my ear. But tonight, as he was close to putting on the finishing touches, there was a sharp knock at the door, or rather a bang, like someone was using their fist.

'Slater, I know you're in there,' a rough voice shouted. I knew instantly who it was, as did Alastair, as we both exchanged looks, and I smirked.

'Open this door, Slater,' the voice growled, slurring from drink.

It was David Tilling. He was clearly worse for wear from a few pints at the pub and looking for some kind of retaliation. Since he returned from Dunkirk, he's been bragging about how he'd made it back as if he were some kind of hero, which of course he's not when you think about Henry shooting down three Nazi planes in a single day. David has an embryo RAF moustache, which looks ridiculous, and he's taken up smoking. It's too hilarious.

He found out about my affair with Alastair after following me around; Alastair and I spend all our free time together, such is our newfound love! Since then, David's been making these snide little comments, such as 'Slater's not good enough for you, Venetia. What are you doing with a coward?' Or the rather damning: 'You're letting yourself down, Venetia.' I can only conclude that he's learnt a lot more in the army than just fighting; he'd never have come out with something like that before he left.

Back to last night, when he was banging on the door. Alastair put his brush down and went leisurely into the hallway, pulling the sitting room door closed behind him. I slipped my dress back on without putting any underwear on first, which was rather naughty, don't you think?

'Ah, good evening, David,' Alastair announced as I heard the door opening. 'What brings you here?'

'I wanna word with you, Slater,' David slurred loudly, sounding so young and foolish next to Alastair's poise.

After this there were a few loud bangs, as if someone had been hit, and the clank of something hitting the ground. I was worried, as David is tall and just back from army training. He must have thrown a few punches at Alastair.

I peeked into the hallway.

But there was Alastair, not a hair out of place, holding David in a kind of vice grip, a broken beer bottle lying on the floor, which I can only assume was David's.

I found myself looking at Alastair with renewed awe. Where did he learn *those* combat skills?

'I'm not entirely sure what it is that you want, David,' Alastair said lightly. 'But trying to bottle me is not a good means of communication.'

'I know she's in here, Slater.' David's voice was getting louder. 'Get out of my way.'

Next thing I knew he had bombarded past Alastair and was bursting into the sitting room, where I now sat, good as gold, perched on the sofa, my hands together in my lap, my green floral dress delicately creased, and a small smile on my lips. 'Hello, David.'

'Venetia,' he said, dismayed, his big floppy mouth gaping open. I can only wonder how dazzled he'd have been if he caught me with no clothes on.

He came up to me and sat beside me, taking my hands in his. 'Venetia, I need to see you. I'm leaving tomorrow.' He was drunker than I thought, his hands moist and clammy, his breath virtually toxic. 'I wanted one last kiss, since you're giving yourself to every man in the village.'

I slapped him, although not hard. I knew it was just another line he was trotting out. 'David, I can be with who I want. You need to learn that no one owns me, especially with this war going on. We all need to be ourselves, free.'

I laughed as I said it; I'm no more free than he is. Alastair has me completely smitten.

Suddenly David lunged for me, trying to kiss me, his flabby lips like a cold fish slurping me up.

'David, please, stop!' I cried.

Alastair pried him away from me, and David stood and turned to punch him, but Alastair ducked, sending David flying over to the other side of the room, completely off balance, crashing on the floor in the corner.

Then he turned and saw the picture.

'My God, Venetia,' he gasped, gazing up at it flabbergasted.

I remained perched on the sofa as if butter wouldn't melt in my mouth, as Alastair dashed over and covered the easel with a large black sheet.

'Done from imagination, I hope you understand,' Alastair said lightly, trying to hide a compulsion to laugh.

'Venetia, you were posing nude for this scoundrel?' He got up and whisked the black sheet away, taking it all in, the curves, the – well, I'll leave the rest to your imagination, Angie. Suffice to say, he saw it all.

'It's art, David,' I said simply, shaking my hair back in a nonchalant fashion. 'It's what artists do.'

'You took your clothes off for this bastard,' he snarled, his face set in a reddening grimace. 'You let him paint you. You let him touch you, didn't you?'

'David, I'm a grown woman.'

'And I'm a grown man.' He stood looking from me to the portrait in seething silence.

'David, I know you're leaving tomorrow, but you need to go now. This is Mr Slater's house. You can't just go around barging into people's houses like this—'

'I'll tell your father.' He broke in decisively. 'He'll have Slater's guts for garters.' His strangled laugh came out somewhat awkwardly. 'He'll put a stop to him.'

'Don't tell him, David.' This was getting out of hand. Daddy would kill Alastair, and probably me too. 'I know you won't betray me like this.'

He looked me in the eye, and then his eyes travelled down my body, and I felt he was groping me in his mind, lifting my dress, his hands all over me.

Then, quick as a flash, David grabbed the picture and was out into the cold midnight air, slamming the door shut in my face as I raced out after him. I yanked it open and ran into the darkness, but the blackout had him out of sight in seconds.

Alastair came alongside me, and we darted around the village green trying to listen for his escape route, but he'd vanished. I never thought he'd be so extraordinarily daring. Or so incredibly fast.

Our search ended when I tripped over a rock and went tumbling down towards the pond, surprising a few snoozing ducks.

'Are you all right?' Alastair whispered, coming up beside me.

But before he could utter another word, I dragged him towards me, and we began kissing right there on the village green.

What would Mrs B say to that, do you think?

So we never found David, who disappeared off to war this morning. I wondered if he'd have had time to run over to show the painting to Daddy, but he evidently didn't as Daddy hasn't murdered anyone. In any case, he'd be risking his own life by being the messenger; Daddy can be a lunatic with a shotgun. Remember what happened to that poacher last year?

I don't know what David would have done with my portrait, as it would have been too big to take with him, and he certainly wouldn't have left it at home for Mrs Tilling to stumble across. Perhaps he gave it to someone for safekeeping, and I'm hoping it's not someone who knows me, like Ralph Gibbs.

Meanwhile, I've been begging Alastair to tell me how exactly he has all this defence training, but he always changes the subject. The more I get to know him, Angie, the more I think he's up to something.

There was a surprising incident after church on Sunday, on the path outside, where everyone always gathers. Alastair was there – he says he loves to come and hear us sing in the choir – and Mrs B rushed up to him.

'You must let me introduce you to people,' she insisted, taking him around her flock.

The thing is, when they got to Colonel Mallard, I saw him hold back slightly.

'I really need to be getting on, Mrs B,' he said, all politeness, backing away.

'Don't be ridiculous,' Mrs B boomed. 'You need to know everyone here if you mean to make some money, eh what?' She nudged him, chortling.

The odd thing was that Colonel Mallard also seemed uncomfortable. He was in no mood to meet Alastair, so when Mrs B inevitably pulled them together, the scene was a little awkward, to say the least.

'How do you do,' they both said together, and then there was nothing for a long moment.

'Lovely weather, wouldn't you say?' Alastair began, but – could I have been correct? – was he amused at something? His lips smiled in their usual polite way, and his upright stance was relaxed as ever, and yet there was a trace of humour in his voice.

It was as if they had met before. And not under these circumstances.

'Probably won't last.' Colonel Mallard seemed to sneer at him, then turned quickly and found important things to discuss with the Vicar, baffling as that might seem.

Does Alastair know Colonel Mallard? And if so, in what capacity? It was all so terribly perplexing, so I decided to ask Hattie what she thought when I popped in for tea after church.

'What do you know about the Colonel who's staying with Mrs Tilling?'

'He's tremendously rude, according to Mrs Tilling, and hardly manages a conversation with her,' she said. 'But she's barely civil to him, especially since he had the audacity to offer her a lift home from Litchfield last week. It was pouring with rain and he stopped next to her on her bicycle and practically forced her into his car.' She giggled. 'Can you imagine the tension in the air as they drove home?

'But he did give his room up to David when he came back, went to stay in a hotel in Litchfield. Although she tells me that's only what was expected.' She shrugged. 'If you ask me they're tripping over each other, neither ready to call a truce. Why do you ask?'

'He had a peculiar exchange with Mr Slater, as if they know each other, and not necessarily in a nice way. It makes me wonder if he's doing something illegal, like the black market.'

'Oh dear,' she began, looking down. 'I meant to tell you earlier, but I wasn't sure how to put it. I was up with Rose the other night, and I saw him leaving his house at two in the morning. He strode off over the square. Heaven knows what he was doing.'

'Are you sure?' I couldn't believe it was true. 'When did he come back?'

'I didn't see him come back, although I was up until three.' She rearranged Rose in her arms. 'Venetia, he seems to be always popping out, and now Colonel Mallard is awkward around him. It does seem to indicate that he's up to no good.'

'But everyone else in the village adores him. He put up the tables for the jumble sale last week – Mrs Quail was in a complete state before he came. And he's also been helping the Sewing Ladies transport their balaclavas to Litchfield in his car. And you know how he helped Silvie home after she came off her horse by Bullsend Brook. She thinks he's wonderful.'

'But what was he was doing by Bullsend Brook in the middle of the afternoon? It simply doesn't add up,' Hattie said.

'Maybe he's just dabbling in the black market a little, saving himself a bit of money?'

'That would be fine, but he seems positively rolling in money, with the motorcar, the fine clothes, all the presents he gives you.'

'Maybe he's selling his paintings?' I tried. 'Mrs B has always been keen to get her hands on his works of art.'

'Are any of them gone?'

'No.' I shrugged, feeling the fight drain out of me. 'He hasn't sold so much as a sketch to Mrs B, avoids her if he can. And all his paintings are still in his portfolio.' *Except the one that David Tilling stole*, I thought, *and Lord knows where that is.* 'It doesn't bode well, does it?'

'No, I'm sorry, Venetia,' Hattie said.

I sat feeling rather sorry for myself for a while, then pulled myself together. 'Well, there's nothing else for it then. I'll have to follow him.'

'Oh, Venetia! It might be dangerous. Why don't you see if you can find out other evidence before you do that?' Hattie asked.

We discussed it at length, and she persuaded me to ask some more questions, give it one last try. I promised I would, but it seems so hopeless. When I'm with him everything seems perfect and I feel such an idiot for even doubting him, but then when we're apart, and all these strange things come up, I can't help but wonder. Who is he?

I must be boring you senseless, dear Angie, so I'll leave you there and write again soon with any more news. I know you think I should move on to my next victim, but Alastair is truly the man for me. Even though I'm not exactly sure what kind of man he is. I'll write again as soon as there's news.

Much love,
Venetia

Mrs Tilling's Journal

Saturday, 13th July, 1940

Today I took the bus to Parnham to give Berkeley's ring to Carrington. I've been putting it off for weeks, and honestly wish I hadn't been so quick to promise I'd do it. I didn't even know who Carrington would be, or indeed which Carrington should there happen to be more than one. But I knew I had to go, now that the Nazis have started bombing the ports. Dover was smashed last week, buildings in piles on the ground and people dead. It won't be long before they're upon us and we'll be prisoners in our own country, not allowed to travel and forced to work incredibly long hours. I try not to think of it as it scares me to death.

On the bus, I thought it all through. I've never known any homosexuals, apart from now Berkeley of course. I suppose I've always thought it's a phase or something, some adolescent crush gone on too long. Harold used to say there was something wrong with them, and I wondered what kind of a man I was going to meet. How he would react. I hoped he wasn't dangerous as you can never tell, especially if there really was something wrong inside. What ridiculous situations this wretched war has put us in! What was I thinking agreeing to it?

I changed buses at Litchfield, heading out to Parnham, and found myself seated next to an extremely talkative lady who was clearly the village gossip. This was a terrific stroke of luck, if vaguely annoying, and I asked if she knew where I could find Carrington.

'Why, didn't you know? He lives in Parnham House. Viscount Carrington, if you please,' she joked, putting on a posh accent.

'Oh, I didn't know,' I said, not finding it the least bit funny. That's all I needed. A viscount! 'Is he a young man?'

'No, but there's two sons. The eldest is away with the RAF, bit of an upper-class snob. Then there's the younger one, leg wounded in France, at home recuperating. He's a nice lad. Doesn't seem to get on with the Viscount though.'

'The Viscount is his father, right?'

'Yes,' she sniffed. 'Very proud and traditional. Doesn't like the way the boy hangs about. If you ask me, he can't stand the sight of him.' She pursed her lips, nodding in a most disparaging manner. 'We hear things from the servants, you know.'

Before long, the bus dropped me off in the village, and I only had the walk to the great house to collect myself. My meetings with aristocracy have been few and far between, and even though they don't have the authority they once did, they still send a wave of panic through me. If only I had been Mrs B with her so-called royal connections and indefatigable self-confidence – although I very much doubt Mrs B would have agreed to this undertaking, especially since it involves something both unsavoury and illegal. Heaven help poor Carrington, as she would have him marched off to Parnham Police Station within the hour.

I was also incredibly nervous that my task was neither pleasant nor straightforward. Which son was I supposed to tell? What if the Viscount was the only one there and insisted on knowing my errand? What was I to say?

After a long walk through the mansion parkland, the main house came into sight, a sprawling Regency façade, a double staircase separating and converging up to the massive front door. I shuddered as I approached, knowing that I was being observed as a shadow disappeared from behind a ground-floor window, my pull on the bell anticipated, my purpose already considered.

Holding the door ajar and waiting for my swift departure, the antiquated butler informed me promptly and pompously that the Viscount was not at home.

'I've come to see his son,' I said quickly, snaking around him into the hall. I hadn't come this far to be palmed off.

'I shall enquire within,' he said snootily, and showed me into a chilly drawing room.

The interior was grand and austere but empty-looking and rather dismal. The faded colours – sage green, dove blue – had become grey with age, and I knew for a certainty that if I saw a duster lying around I wouldn't have been able to help myself. The smell of wax polish and antique mothballs added to the starchy gloom. I felt completely alien and distinctly uncomfortable.

The door presently opened and a young man entered. Thank goodness, I knew straightaway that he was the one. Still slim from youth, he was medium height and rather dark in complexion and looks, walking in with a self-conscious deliberation, steady, slow, ponderous. One of his legs was obviously wounded, his trouser leg bulking with bandages as he limped forward, and when he looked up at me, his eyes avoided mine, glancing out of the great terrace window, and then at the fireplace. He seemed so vulnerable. There was some deep discomfort in him, an estrangement from everything surrounding him.

'Hello,' I smiled warmly, suddenly conscious that my mission was about to bring me closer to this man than most of the people he knew. 'I'm Mrs Margaret Tilling from Chilbury.'

'Do take a seat,' he said in a very upper-class voice. He didn't return my smile, which I thought was both painfully understandable yet incredibly rude. Although how was he to know my horrific errand? I perched on the edge of a taut beige brocade sofa.

He limped over to the couch opposite and gently picked up a cushion before sitting down, measuring every movement as to the effect on his leg. He sighed and looked out of the window again, over the folds of hills to the bittersweet blue of the sea, Nazi-occupied France only twenty miles across the water, snarling on the horizon like an evil inevitability.

'What brings you to these parts, Mrs Tilling?' he said, as if reading from an etiquette manual, exasperated by the need to deal with me.

'I have a message from Berkeley.'

His eyes darted straight to mine, his eye contact at once total and gripped. His bottom lip fell open slightly, taking in what I had said. A cascade of thoughts must have flooded his brain.

'What message?' he breathed.

'I was the nurse looking after him at Dover. He made me promise to give you this.' I opened my hand and held out the ring.

Carrington spluttered a cough, although I think he was covering a cry. He didn't rush to look at the ring; he must have already known the object: seen it, touched it, held it. He sat for a while, then came over and took it, tucking it away in an inside pocket. Then he walked over to the terrace window, looking over the manicured gardens and hills, the parallel lines of classical statues and symmetrical garrisons of topiary bushes.

'It's mine, you know,' he said quietly, 'the ring.' He turned to me. 'I gave it to him, four years ago. We were at boarding school together.' He became self-conscious and examined his hands. 'What did he say?'

'He told me to tell you he loved you.' I shuddered silently. 'He was so terribly weak.' My words faded out, and the brutal memory of Berkeley came back to me, the hopeless fear in his eyes, his young form turning limp and lifeless.

I looked at Carrington. His eyes seemed broken as he struggled to regain his countenance. He looked out of the window, away onto the horizon, tears welling uncontrollably. A few dreadful minutes passed. I suddenly wondered if I'd been wrong. Perhaps he didn't already know that his friend had died. Had I unconsciously broken the worst news he could ever want to hear?

'I'm sorry,' I stammered. 'I thought you knew. I thought, well, I didn't know what to think.'

'I did know,' he mumbled, clearing his throat. 'His mother telephoned. She knew we were friends, although she never knew——' He cut off, frowning inscrutably. 'I don't mind if you hand me in, you know,' he said, a stern pride controlling his tears. 'You can do your worst. I don't care. I have nothing left to hide.' He looked pensively at the drifting clouds and added in a rather dreamy way, 'I have nothing left at all.'

'I'm not going to hand you in,' I said as gently as I could. 'I made a promise to him.' I paused, thinking this was all far stranger than I had imagined.

He came and sat back down on the sofa opposite me. 'Tell me what happened.'

'He kept talking about you – how you'd be lost without each other, that he was the lucky one for dying first – and then he rolled over, his breath slowing until it finally slowed' – my words were fizzling out – 'to a stop.'

I know it didn't happen exactly like that, but this is surely what Berkeley would have wanted me to say. I remember when Harold died, yearning for him to speak my name, or give me a message. But he didn't, and the best that I can do is to find some kind of peace by giving this gift to someone else.

Carrington put his head down and wept into his large hands. I sat watching for a while, feeling like I was intruding, wondering if I should leave. Then I looked out onto the horizon myself and realised that loss is the same wherever you go: overwhelming, inexorable, deafening. How resilient human beings are that we can learn slowly to carry on when we are left all alone, left to fill the void as best we can.

Or disappear into it.

I went over and sat next to him and, after a minute or two, I put my arm around him and he turned and wept silently into my shoulder. I wondered if I was the only person who knew, the only shoulder he had.

The sound of a distant door opening and heavy footsteps in the hall announced the return of the Viscount, and

Carrington stood quickly and limped over to the window, promptly composing himself, wiping his face with a handkerchief.

'That's my father,' he said without looking around. 'He wouldn't understand.'

'No, I imagine he wouldn't.'

'Thank you for coming,' he added slowly, and I took this to be my cue to leave. He clearly didn't want his father enquiring after my purpose for calling.

As I stood and straightened myself, he turned and said, 'Really, thank you, Mrs, er—'

'Mrs Tilling.'

He smiled, and I caught a glimpse of a different man, a different world, a handsome youth who might have enjoyed life had he not been wrenched into the centre of a bloody war.

'Mrs Tilling,' he said. 'May I visit you some time? I mean, if I survive this beastly war.'

I shrugged. 'Of course you can. I live in Chilbury, Ivy House.' He smiled again, genuine connection in his eyes, and I knew that I would see him again, hopefully on a better day, under happier circumstances. 'Things will get easier, you know.'

He opened the door for me, and we went into the magnificent hallway. A dual staircase rolled up on both sides and came together in a type of royal balcony overlooking the expanse of parquet flooring. A clock ticked interminably, and I just wanted to get out, launch myself away from this oppressive place and into the fresh and wild outdoors.

The butler was waiting for us, his gaze meeting my eye. Then he turned and gave a rather circumspect grimace to young Carrington.

'I informed the Viscount that you had a visitor, and he requested to meet her,' he said pompously. 'If you would be so kind as to wait here, madam, I will fetch him directly.' He bowed again and strode off into the passage.

I felt a thud in my stomach. I was going to meet the Viscount whether I liked it or not. Carrington had gone rather pale. 'I expect he just wants to see if you're a young lady. Some romantic hopeful, if you know what I mean,' he said, attempting a smile.

'Yes,' I said wearily, hoping but not expecting him to be right.

He wasn't. The Viscount stormed into the hall bellowing, 'What's all this then?' He was a large man, in all senses of the word, with a full head of greying hair curling around his burgundy necktie. He looked both immaculate and furious, stalking up to me and declaring rudely, 'Who, may I ask, are you? And what do you want with my son?'

'I'm Mrs Margaret Tilling,' I said in the best voice I could muster, praying that something clever would come out of my mouth. 'I was a nurse at Dover, and I had a message from a friend of your son's.' I paused, while he looked at me expecting more. 'He never made it.'

'If it was that swine Berkeley, he's better off dead.' He snarled at Carrington, who looked through him with practised calm. 'Poisoning my son with these notions—'

'He *is* dead.' I heard my own voice pipe up strong and audible through the vast hall. 'He died that night at Dover, from a wound fighting off the Nazis at Dunkirk. He was a brave soldier, and deserves to be remembered as such.'

'He deserves to be remembered as nothing but a degenerate. He should have been hanged.'

'And yet it was all right that he gave his life – his *life!* – for this country? Why can't you take off your blinkered glasses and see what is in front of your eyes? The man was nothing but a boy, trying to fight, trying to stay alive, helping you and your country survive for another day.'

Carrington's look of complete alarm brought me back to earth with a bump. I was never going to convince this tyrant of anything. I just needed to get out and stop making it worse for Carrington. We all knew that as soon as the door was closed behind me, that poor young man would be chastised and denigrated until his life was hardly worth living either.

'I think you should leave now,' the Viscount said dismissively. 'I don't know who you are, but I heartily suggest that you learn some manners, my good woman.'

I took a brief look at Carrington – pensive, measured, silent – and then strode for the door.

The butler was now holding it open for me, and I sailed straight out and walked down the majestic stone staircase to the driveway, exemplary lawns metered out on either side, beyond which the wild, rolling hills and forests were packed with their own teeming hierarchies, playing out their own chains of command.

As I marched down the drive with a swing in my stride, I took a deep breath of the syrupy sweetness of summer, suffused with bees and birds, and I thought to myself how beautiful this world can be. How lucky we are to be here, to be part of it, for however long we have.

I took the bus back to Chilbury, uneasy about the way that I had left things with the Viscount. The malevolence and pride of these people is ruthless, clinging to their advantage in the face of our total annihilation. Human nature defeats me sometimes; how greed and spite can lurk so divisively around the utmost courage and sacrifice.

A sense of responsibility – or was it guilt? – hung over me, that I was in some way at fault because of cowering to all these pompous men all these years, when I should have had the bravery to reclaim my own mind. That if we women had done this years ago, before the last war, before this one, we'd be in a very different world.

And what about Carrington? That poor, devastated young man! Meeting him, and Berkeley even just briefly, makes me wonder why everyone makes such a fuss about homosexuality. Surely it's not so terribly wrong? And isn't love between two people better than hatred, in this world of violence and mourning? There seemed to me a fragile kindness in their love that survived through this poisonous war. Even though one of them hadn't.

By the time I reached Chilbury, just as the sun was stretching long shadows over the shop and the square, I was feeling quite fraught. I decided to visit the church to see if that would settle me. I end up in the church more and more these days, waiting for the silence to seep inside. As I slipped through the overgrown graveyard, the mellow evening air rich with wild lavender and hawthorn, I found myself pausing by the ornate old grave of a young hero, a weathered statue of a sleeping lion resting over the top, its fat paws coveting the valuable body laid inside.

But valuable to who? Two hundred years later, who is there left to remember this man, so carefully laid to rest, once so loved and real? Now all that would be left is a pile of dust, laid roughly in the shape of a human being, the frailness of our form putrid beside the enduring carved rock lion above it.

I found tears coming fast. This war is too much for me. I'm not the kind of woman to be battling it out with a viscount. I'm not built to deal with my son at war, maybe suffering just like Berkeley, his fragile body left to decay like all human flesh. The war will be the end of me.

I crumpled onto the grassy ground beside the grave, my face in my hands, wishing I could crawl away from all of this, pull the clock back to before the war started and sleep for a thousand years.

A few drops of rain brought me back into the present, trickling down my back like a shiver of reality. I stood up slowly, the rain coming faster now, and turned to the church.

Easing open the arched double doors, I slid silently into the wooden pew at the back and sat quietly. Here in the back row I could take my thoughts out for inspection without fear of them spreading through my brain and taking me hostage.

Today there was a figure a few rows from the front, tucked into the left side like me. The light from the shafts of stained-glass windows above the altar broke a blue and purple haze over him as he bent his head into his hands.

It was Colonel Mallard.

Was he invading my church now? Infuriated by his presence, I forgot my worries and found myself angry and frustrated with this war, these men bossing us about. I thought about leaving, but decided to stay for a short while and hopefully leave before he did. But my plan was ruined a few minutes later when he got up and turned to come back down the aisle. I saw him pause as he spotted me, but then he pressed on, nodding obliquely as he passed. I pretended that

I hadn't noticed him, forcing my thoughts away as they kept flitting back to his presence.

After the door shut behind him, I sat for a while, and then, suddenly feeling the need for normality, I got up and bustled out into the world, heading straight out of the graveyard and down the hill towards home, my lovely warm house.

As I walked, I found myself thinking about how my view of the world has changed. Fancy me giving a viscount a few strong words! And defying the law – taking a decision into my own hands to help this wounded young man. Perhaps there is something good that has come from this war: everything has been turned around, all the unfairness made grimly plain. It has given us everyday women a voice – dared us to stand up for ourselves, and to stand up for others.

We have less to lose in this world of chaos and death, after all.

Kitty Winthrop's Diary

Wednesday, 24th July, 1940

News about Silvie's parents

Today we had a visit from Uncle Nicky. I was so excited as I love the little conversations we have, usually sitting on the terrace if the evening's fine, talking about the world, and being all grown up. But today he had no time for talks. He'd come with some news for Silvie, and instead of the terrace, we sat solemnly in the drawing room.

'I'm afraid your parents and brother have disappeared, Silvie. It's thought that they are in hiding from the Nazis, maybe in someone's cellar, or they might be trying to escape overland to come and join you here. We obviously hope it's the latter, and that they can somehow make their way over, although it might be more difficult now with the Nazis controlling all the ports and borders.'

She stared on with her big dark eyes, not saying anything, not even shedding a single tear.

'We have to be strong,' Uncle Nicky said, taking her hands in his and holding them tightly. 'And hope for the best.'

She made a little curtsy, as if she couldn't open her mouth to say thank you, and trod carefully out of the room, closed the door, and then we heard the darting footsteps running through the hall and up the stairs and the bang of her bedroom door.

Mama asked me to go and see if she was all right. Everyone knows I'm the best person for such a role. I quietly went upstairs and knocked on her door, but she didn't answer, so in the end I just went in. She shouldn't be on her own, after all.

She was lying on her bed, her face turned away from me, silent.

'Please cheer up, Silvie,' I said, sitting on the bed. 'They're probably on their way here.'

But the awful part is that the journey will be incredibly dangerous, with almost all of mainland Europe under Nazi control. Even here we can feel the Nazis encroaching on us. The planes have started to come over the coastal town and ports, bombing Dover almost weekly now. I know Silvie thinks they're coming for her, the fear behind her eyes obvious whenever we hear those unbearable drones.

'They are getting closer,' she whispers to me, barely audibly.

I sometimes wonder if she saw something back in Czechoslovakia, the Nazis in their full horror. Maybe she's replaying some gruesomely violent scene in her mind, only the victim is her or her family.

Before he left, I asked Uncle Nicky what happened in Czechoslovakia when the Nazis took over.

What happened to Silvie, from what I can gather
Hitler claimed the western part of Czechoslovakia in
    1938, and then last year tanks and troops rolled into

the rest of Czechoslovakia, stealing food and
everything else, hitting people who stood in their
way, imprisoning people

Lots of homes and shops were destroyed, and lots of
swastikas were put up by black-uniformed SS
soldiers parading the streets

A lot of the people in prison were shot, their families
forced to pay for their executions

The Jews had their identification papers marked, so
Silvie had to leave quickly before anything happened
to her

I've been incredibly lovely to Silvie after learning all this. She
still doesn't say anything, but perhaps I wouldn't if I'd gone
through all that.

That evening I asked Mama what would happen to Silvie
if her parents don't make it here until the war's over.

'Sadly we can't keep Silvie here for long as Daddy wouldn't
like it. But she can stay for a while, until it can be decided
where she would do well.' Mama wiped a tear from her eye.
She wants Silvie to stay with us, but she has to do everything
Daddy says.

When I saw Daddy later, I tentatively brought up
the subject of letting Silvie stay, but he was as stubborn as
ever.

'We can't have little evacuees from Lord knows where
staying with us, becoming part of the family and so forth,' he
said. 'What a ridiculous notion you have, Kitty, and your
mother too.' He stormed around the room picking up papers
and books and slamming them down. 'Do you know there's
a war on?' he shouted. 'There are Nazi planes in our skies –

one came down last week close to Dover, and the Local Defence Volunteers haven't found the damned pilot yet. The country's in grave danger, and all you can think about is a blasted evacuee!'

And that was that. Obviously I'll have to think up some marvellous plan that will make him capitulate.

Another fight with Venetia

Venetia is being completely intolerable. This morning she stormed into my bedroom in her petticoat, hands on hips, furiously looking around.

'Where's my sky-blue dress, you thief?'

'It doesn't fit you any more, so I requisitioned it.' I gave her a sharp smile. 'I know that Mama would have told me to do the same.'

'It does still fit me, you little twerp. All my dresses have gone missing, and I knew it was you,' she spat. 'In any case, it's courteous to ask before you take something.'

She had come right up to me, standing a foot away, putting her crazed, pursed-up face right into mine. I backed away.

'I only borrowed this one,' I said. 'I don't know where the others have gone. Maybe the maid's been taking them. I needed this one for a picnic.'

'A picnic? With who?'

'Silvie and I went on our very own little picnic. I wanted to show her what it was like in the good old days. You know, before the war.'

'Remember the time we went to Box Hill with Henry?' She stood up straight again and seemed to forget the dress dispute for a moment, her mind flitting back to that July day.

'That was the first time Henry proposed to me,' she laughed. 'What a funny day that was! Do you remember how I—'

I cut in, feeling the blood gush hot into my face. 'But he proposed to *me* that day!' I couldn't believe what she was saying. 'He proposed to *me*!'

'Don't be ridiculous, Kitty,' she smirked. 'He could only have proposed to one of us.' She stood back, arms folded, laughing slightly.

'And it was me.' I stood firm. I think I might have been gripping my fists by my sides because I wanted to punch her ridiculous mouth.

'Ah, but now I remember, I declined his proposal, so perhaps you're right after all,' she joked in a patronising tone. 'Perhaps he was saddened and desperate after being turned down, and then saw little you and felt sorry for you. We all know you've been infatuated with him for years.'

If I'd had Daddy's shotgun with me right there and then, I would have taken it out and pulled the trigger straight into her vile, spiteful heart.

'But he asked me, and I said yes,' I fumed.

'He was only joking with you, Kitty.' She laughed. 'Of course he isn't interested in a stupid child like you. It's me he wants, a real woman.' With this she did that ludicrous pouting with her lips, like a big wet salmon, and I pulled back in disgust.

'Whatever you've got, I don't want it, and neither does Henry.'

'Of course he does, darling.' The look on her face was utter, determined domination. 'He's crazy about me.'

'So why didn't you accept him if he proposed to you?' I demanded.

'Because I'm waiting for someone better.'

'Like that weasel Slater?'

'He's not a weasel.' She looked away, and I glimpsed a flicker of uncertainty. 'He's worth a million of Henry.'

'Really, Venetia?' And I took out my trump card. 'A black-market dealer is better than Henry?'

She unfolded her arms, and something in her posture crumpled.

'You know?' She didn't seem shocked, just wary, treading carefully, trying to understand.

Now it was my turn to be smug. 'I saw him in Peasepotter Wood doing business with a crook called Old George.'

'When?'

'I don't see why I should tell you.' I moved to the dressing table and started tidying my hair clips. 'You'll have to beg me first, and apologise about what you said about Henry not proposing to me.'

She stood completely still for a moment, then turned to the door. 'I'll do no such thing, you little shrew. I'll just have to go and find out for myself.'

And off she stormed back to her room, forgetting about the dress, the picnic, the proposal. I found the sky-blue dress and tried it on again. I'll have to wear it next time I see Henry to remind him of our engagement. I'm sure it'll trigger his memory.

Letter from Lt Carrington
to Mrs Tilling

Parnham House
Parnham
Kent
Telephone: Parnham 47

Friday, 26th July, 1940

Dear Mrs Tilling,

I want to thank you for coming all the way to Parnham to give me the ring. I imagine it was not a pleasant task, and realise that you had no obligation to come, which makes me all the more grateful for your visit and concern.

Since then, I have become employed, which serves a dual purpose of getting me out of the house and providing me with more to think about than the war and lost friends. The surgeon came and deemed me unfit to fight for the time being, and so I have been given a job at Litchfield Park, pushing pieces of paper around and phoning people up to tell them what's on the pieces of paper. It's rather dreary but they say they'll move me into something more interesting as soon as they can. I'm hoping to be sent to London, which would mean a lodging to myself.

If ever you are in the area, please do come and say hello, as I feel I wasn't as polite as I could have been, and want to thank you properly for coming so far out of your way to visit. If there is anything I could possibly do for you, please do not hesitate to ask. I would only be too delighted to reciprocate in whatever way I can.

With thanks and very best wishes,
Lt Rupert Carrington

Letter from Venetia Winthrop
to Angela Quail

Chilbury Manor
Chilbury
Kent

Saturday, 27th July, 1940

Dearest Angie,

Everything is getting more complicated at every turn. I was sent to Dover yesterday to assess the bomb damage, and the place was half demolished and fast earning its nickname 'Hell-Fire Corner'. Even while I was there enemy planes appeared in the sky, circling loudly, their Nazi swastikas clearly visible on their sides. I thought I was going to be sick. A few of our chaps in Spitfires and Hurricanes came along to drive them out, and it became a bit of a dogfight, right there in the skies above us. Some of the locals came out of shops and stood in the High Street cheering them on, but I couldn't bear it. All this charade for more deaths, more ruined lives. What has become of us?

A great deal seems to have happened since last I wrote. The main news is that I think I'm pregnant. I'm not at all sure how to feel about this, and I'm rather hoping that I'm not. I thought I was being careful, but I suppose one never knows with these things. Obviously I haven't breathed a word to Alastair or anyone else. I do so wish you were here, Angie. I know you're thinking that it's all frightfully simple, Alastair and I will have to get married. But, you see, I've also come to suspect that Alastair is involved in the black market. Instead of being the wife of a romantic artist, living in a tumbledown castle on an island in a river, I would be the wife of a hardened criminal, always on the run, always afraid. Frankly, Angie, it's not the life I had planned at all.

I found out through Kitty, of all people, in the middle of one of our stupid rows. Just as I thought we'd finished, she rounded on me, announcing that she'd spotted Alastair in Peasepotter Wood doing business with a common crook. I can't get over it. It seems so unlike him, so contrary to the gentle, sophisticated artist. I know I've had my suspicions. But this!

I stormed off, but then I had to pull myself together for Rose's christening, which was this afternoon.

We'd done some extra practicing so that the Chilbury Ladies' Choir could do something special, processing out of the choir stalls and surrounding Hattie and Rose, singing a gorgeous rendition of 'All Things Bright and Beautiful'. When it reached the part that goes, 'Each little flower that opens, each little bird that sings', we were all gathered round them, and Hattie looked like she'd burst with joy.

After the service, everyone went to Hattie's house in Church Row for a small afternoon tea party, and I stayed to tidy up afterwards, although I was more keen to get her advice about Alastair.

'Kitty saw him in Peasepotter Wood with a black marketeer. He was doing business with him, Hattie!' I was getting a bit upset, pacing up and down the sitting room clearing the plates and crashing them into the sink.

'Goodness,' Hattie said, moving Rose's pram away from the activity – she's getting frightfully mother-hennish. 'Well, perhaps it's time to give him up, Venetia. I don't mean to be heartless, but I worry about you, and I don't think getting involved with him will bring you any happiness.'

'I don't know.' I flopped down in a chair. 'All I know for certain is that I can't stop being with him without breaking my heart in the process. I know it sounds ridiculous, but I can't leave without getting to the bottom of it. It simply means too much to me.'

'What does your mother think of all this?'

'Mama is completely taken up with baby Lawrence, who still won't keep down any milk. She's also busy with Daddy as he's become so volatile. Kitty's running amuck, and Silvie's being looked after by Kitty and old Nanny Godwin from what I can gather. No one seems to care what we do or what's happening.'

'Well, don't worry about them for now. Think of what you need to do.' She patted my hand gently. 'Isn't there a way you could find out more before deciding?'

'I've made up my mind to follow him,' I told her with sudden conviction.

She sighed a great sigh, and it dawned on me that she's the only one who ever really looked after me. 'Well, just be careful,' she said. 'And please give up if it gets too dangerous, Venetia. You don't always have to be the brave and daring one.'

I went to the door and looked back, feeling such warmth and concern from her. 'I'll let you know how it goes.'

'You know I'll always worry about you, Venetia,' she said, and I suddenly felt like crying. So I quickly turned and paced determinedly across the green, the ducks waddling fast to avoid my feet. I took a deep breath of the warm summer air, and prayed I'd come out of this alive.

I'll write as soon as I can and tell you how it all goes, fingers crossed.

Venetia

Mrs Tilling's Journal

❦

Monday, 29th July, 1940

What an odd thought occurred to me today. I'm still trying
to think it all through. The morning was quite usual, as I
popped over to the surgery to help deal with everyone's
aches and pains. Since the war started, people come to see me
when they're out of sorts, even if there isn't much wrong
with them. Mrs Turner, whose husband was killed in one of
the air raids on Dover, has developed an ongoing cough with
no apparent cause. She comes in most days to see me. I try to
offer kind words, but she edges back as if unable to bear it,
her face grey like a ghost's. All we can do is make more tea
and give her some aspirin. Mrs Quail got her to join the
choir and, although she remained silent for a full half hour,
she finally managed a few lines of 'Praise My Soul'. It was an
oddly moving moment for all of us, as if we were trying to
bring a crushed bird back to life with nothing but song.

After luncheon I had to pop over to Hattie's, where she
tried to convince me that little Rose is the image of Victor,
and I couldn't help thinking it odd that she doesn't look like
either of them. In fact, baby Lawrence with his sprouts of
dark hair looks more like Hattie, and then I remembered
noticing at the christening that Rose had the same colouring

as her godmother, Venetia. And that started me thinking about it all: the nasty medicine, the fact that both births happened on the same afternoon – the afternoon that I was in Litchfield. Then they both had the same breathing problem, both requiring resuscitation at Miss Paltry's house.

And when I'd met Miss Paltry in the square that day, I'd imagined – ridiculously, I thought at the time! – that there was a noise coming from her bag. Could it have been a child? Could she have swapped the babies? I shuddered at the horror of the idea. I think I must have looked a little dazed as Hattie touched my elbow and said, 'Are you all right, Mrs Tilling?'

I pulled myself together sharply. I can't have anyone suspecting anything until I have more time to think it all through. Until I have proof.

'It's fine, dear,' I said, smiling. 'I just remembered I need to hurry a little today because I need to check on Mrs Winthrop's little one too.' I pondered a moment, then asked, 'Do you remember when poor Rose had that breathing problem after she was born?'

'How could I forget it? It was the worst moment of my life.'

'Did you see little Rose at all before Miss Paltry took her away?'

Her eyes looked doubtful, questioning my question, and I had to quickly put her at ease.

'I mean, you should have at least been able to hold her before she was whisked away from you?'

Hattie's thin face crumpled into tears. 'No, I hardly saw her pretty little face before she was rushed out.' She looked down at the baby in her arms, and her shoulders relaxed. 'She was gone a whole five minutes. I was beside myself. I pulled myself out of bed and hauled myself down to the front door, and Miss Paltry was back, with my precious little baby.'

She gave Rose a little kiss, their faces together and opposite, hers slim and delicate, the baby's heart-shaped and blonde, and I suddenly questioned the value of revealing any ideas I had. After all, wasn't Mrs Winthrop delighted with her boy too? Didn't they need a boy to keep the inheritance?

That's when it dawned on me. Perhaps this wasn't simply the whim of an unscrupulous midwife. Perhaps there was more to it than met the eye.

I took my leave and made haste to Chilbury Manor, where Mrs Winthrop was at home. We sat in the drawing room, and she asked Elsie to bring some tea, and it felt almost as if the war had never happened. She looked tired and harassed, which must mean the Brigadier's being unbearable again.

'I'm doing some studies on babies born with breathing problems, so I wondered if I could ask you a few more questions about Lawrence's birth,' I began carefully. I didn't want her to suspect anything fishy.

'I thought I'd gone through it all with you.' She sighed. 'It was so distressing. I'm not sure I'm quite up for going through it again.'

'Just a few questions. Did Miss Paltry take the baby away straightaway, or did she let you see or hold him first?'

'No, she had to leave immediately. He was in great distress.'

Her story collaborated with my theory. I quickly pressed on.

'Was she carrying baby Lawrence in her black bag when she returned with him?'

'Of course not!' Mrs Winthrop exclaimed, and I realised I'd gone too far. In any case, even Miss Paltry would have the intelligence to take the baby out of the bag beforehand.

Elsie had come in with the tea, and I wondered if she'd overheard. She smiled a little. 'Would you like sugar?'

I had to stay and talk about normal things for a while before I could get away, and then I rushed back home to sit and think it all through. It seems such a ridiculous notion, such a dramatic act for a person to do.

Unless someone was paying her.

Kitty Winthrop's Diary

Wednesday, 31st July, 1940

Prim had the most wonderful idea. We're to have a Memorial Service for everyone to come together and help those grieving. I think Mrs Tilling prompted her by mentioning Mrs Turner, whose husband was killed in a bombing raid over Dover. And there's poor Mrs Poultice too.

'It's important for them to know that we're grieving with them,' Prim told me in my singing lesson today, which was held in the church for extra acoustics. I sang the Lord's Prayer, the fullness of the sound making my voice sound extremely professional. She said I could sing it as a solo for the Memorial Service, which is to be in a few weeks' time.

I always arrive early for choir practice as it's a wonderful moment, the excitement of singing, everyone glad to see each other, and today was no different, especially since we have the Nazis on our backs, ready to invade, so we have to make the most of everything while we can.

'I've been working hard all day preparing for the WVS meeting,' Mrs B was complaining. 'Never getting a word of thanks or any rest.'

'You have to let us know how we can help,' Mrs Tilling said.

'Unfortunately I'm the only one who can handle leadership around here.'

Mrs Tilling began, 'I could—'

'There's no other way around it.' Mrs B's voice rose over Mrs Tilling's, like a tornado overwhelming a welcome breeze.

'And Mrs Quail said she—' Mrs Tilling pressed on.

'If you need something done,' Mrs B boomed, and we all knew what was coming, so we joined in: 'You have to do it yourself.'

Prim arrived in time to hear the end of this, and to see Mrs B fuming as some of us giggled behind our hands.

'Let's get organised, ladies,' Prim said, hiding a smile and handing around some new music scores. 'We are to have a Memorial Service for the Chilbury community, to help us join together in our time of grief.'

Everyone quietly agreed and opened the music scores.

'I've chosen a piece from Mozart's Requiem, "Lacrimosa", which means tearful, beautifully describing this heartfelt piece. It's more complicated than our usual hymns and anthems, but I think we can give it a try. It's one of my favourite pieces of music, a massive ocean of sorrow.'

We opened our music scores to see the complicated patterns of notes.

'Shall we try it out? Let's all stand. Just try your best, feel the music take hold of you, and don't worry if you sing anything wrong.'

The introduction began, and I knew exactly what she meant. The piece is like a series of waves gushing over you, becoming larger and more powerful as it goes on, until the incredible, strident *Amen* at the end, as if we have survived it all, stronger than ever.

'Lovely,' Prim said as she brought the finale to a close, sniffing a little with the emotion of it. 'Let's try it again, shall we? This time, let's try to feel the sadness of it. Let yourself flow into the music. Let it speak your own grief.'

The introduction began again, this time slower, more thoughtfully, and then we came in with the first tentative notes.

As we sang, Mrs Turner crumpled into the altos' choir stall, her hands over her face, her hunched body shuddering with tears. Mrs Poultice sat down beside her, putting her arm around her shoulder, beginning to cry herself. And a new dread crept into our singing, as if we were singing for them, for everyone who had lost someone, or could.

By the time we reached the powerful chords towards the end, we were almost crying with our song, louder, more raucous than before, until the final *Amen*, when we all stood together, firm in the power of our choir to face this war together.

'Let's finish for tonight,' Prim said quietly.

We silently folded our music scores and went over to Mrs Turner and Mrs Poultice, putting our arms around them, holding their hands, whispering our condolences. People were putting their hands around Mama as well as she is still mourning Edmund, and Silvie, so far from her family, and Mrs Tilling and the other mothers and wives, all worried about their loved ones in this horrific war.

'You always have us,' Mrs Quail said to Mrs Turner. 'I know we can't replace your husband, but remember we are here, all together. The Chilbury Ladies' Choir stands with you.'

Letter from Venetia Winthrop
to Angela Quail

Thursday, 1st August, 1940

My dearest Angie,

I was awake at dawn almost paralysed with fear, as today I
was resolved to follow Alastair. I knew that he was busy
this morning with his so-called meetings as I'd tried to
arrange something and he resolutely refused.

Of course I hardly slept a wink. I was so certain that I'd
face probable death on this outing that I almost let myself
off the hook, snuggling down under the counterpane for
extra protection. What made me get up in the end was the
thought that my pregnancy is becoming less of a
possibility and more of a reality. I have to know what to
do.

I got up around four, dressed quietly, and took one last
look around me – would I ever see my dear bedroom again?
Stealing softly down the back stairs and through the
pantry, I stepped out into the still, dark air.

I slowly crept into the lane, feeling like the only person alive, although I'm sure some of the farmhands down in Dawkins Farm would have been hard at work in the fields. There was a light mist that lingered in the air, coating the village with a wordless hush.

As I reached the square, silver grey in mist, I almost collided with a small black van that was parked outside the shop, one of Ralph Gibbs's black-market deliveries no doubt, which hopefully had nothing to do with Alastair. Had I noticed him speaking to Ralph? Not that I could recall. But did that mean anything? Did any of my recollections mean anything, or have I been living in a world that is only half complete, a dream within a dream?

I went round to my spying spot at the end of Church Row, where I could see both the front and back of Alastair's house from behind a hedge. Then I began my wait. Sitting in the dark waiting for someone to appear is extremely tedious, especially as I was in two minds about whether this was a good plan after all, and I was just checking that my wristwatch was working properly at around six when finally he appeared on the path in the back garden, heading out of the little gate and into the pasture. Immaculate as usual, with a beige raincoat over his suit, he walked briskly away from me, pausing momentarily to smell the morning air – dawn had lifted the mist, and it had blossomed into a heavenly morning, all pale yellow and crisp with dew. How I longed for this wretched scheme to be over!

I hopped nimbly out from behind the hedge and crouched beside it as he stalked down the edge of the field away from me, going at quite a pace. After he'd gone into the next field, he headed towards the Manor, which I thought an odd route. I trotted after him, watching him take an abrupt detour through the bushes at the verge and dashing across the lane, and then making a couple of quick turns towards Peasepotter Wood. I was finding it hard to watch where he was going without being seen, and suspected his circuitous route had been created in order to avoid meeting people and lose any trailers.

He certainly wasn't losing me though.

Before he reached the wood, he crossed a very exposed field with no bushes or hedges on either side, and I had to stay at the bottom until he was virtually in the trees. It was there, as I was hiding in a rather prickly bush, that he turned to scrutinise the scene, and I felt that his eyes may have lingered on me for a split second before he vanished into the trees. I didn't think that he saw me. Surely he would have come and got me if he had? But that brief moment made me draw breath. I had to be more careful.

I sprinted up the narrow path and plunged into the wood. I hadn't been in Peasepotter Wood for years, and yet I still remembered all the tracks, the path to the Pixie Ring. Alastair was heading into the Chestnut Patch, the place Kitty and I used to play as children, their broad, barrel-like trunks as old and sturdy as the whole of England. I thought about her, and how we'd been friends, so long ago.

Alastair suddenly stopped in a clearing, so I darted behind one of the larger chestnuts, peeking my head around the side where I could watch through the shrubbery.

Then I spotted a man up ahead approaching him. He was stocky and powerful, built like a gladiator and dressed in an old suit that was obviously not his as it was too short in the legs and arms.

They spoke for a while in low voices, and I stared at the stranger. He must be a criminal in hiding, living rough, perhaps in the wood itself.

He was furious about something, that was for certain, and I was suddenly afraid for Alastair, afraid for our little village, and utterly petrified of what might happen if he found me there.

Alastair was calmly engaging with him, his hands gesticulating as if trying to pacify him. He took a small packet from his inside pocket and handed it over, and the stranger took it cautiously and went to put it in his pocket, but then changed his mind and wrenched it open, examining the contents. For some reason I'd expected it to be a wad of money, but it wasn't. There were two little black booklets, and as he turned them over in his hands, I recognised first a ration book and then a passport. Alastair was helping this man to escape the country.

The stranger was getting more heated, flinging the booklets back in the packet and shoving it into his pocket, and as his voice became louder, snarling through the bracken, a flash of frozen horror shot through me as I realised that he wasn't speaking English. The language he was using, without any doubt, was German.

What was he doing here? Was he a spy? How did he get here? Had he parachuted in? Why was he wearing odd clothes? Was he going to kill us all? We've been told to keep a lookout for the enemy, but I never imagined I'd actually see one.

Or that he'd be meeting with Alastair.

Straining my ears to listen for Alastair's reply, I almost retched when I heard German words come out of his mouth, so alien from his normal English tones. I abruptly grasped the full weight of the situation. How little I really knew him.

After a few final enraged words, the man strode off into the wood, thankfully in the opposite direction to me. Alastair stood watching him leave for a minute, and then turned and, to my complete dismay, headed straight towards the place where I was hiding.

I sprang behind the tree and held my breath, pinning my back and arms to the sheltering trunk, listening to the rustle of his footsteps through the undergrowth as they came closer and closer. I didn't have a clue whether he'd seen me, whether he was heading back out of the wood or coming in my direction to root me out. What would he do to me? I swallowed hard, fighting back a growing panic.

It was when he stopped next to the tree, on the other side of me, that I became certain that he knew I was there. I heard him again quietly treading around the tree, and saw him slowly appear, his finger on his lips. He eased his way around until he was beside me, his back next to mine against the broad trunk, and as we both stood there, his fingers moved over and found my fingers, and interlaced them softly between his. I felt heat surge up through my hand and arm and into my head. What is wrong with me, Angie? I was terrified he'd pull me against him and slit my throat, and yet I longed for him so badly I could hardly breathe.

He did neither. He just turned his head to look at me, and I could see a different look in his eyes, a melancholy I'd never seen in him before.

After a few minutes he broke his gaze, then pulled away and glanced around the side of the tree, and then, just like that, off he went, grasping my hand and pulling me after him, darting through the trees as fast as we could go. I almost stumbled a few times, but the tug of his hand dragged me onward. I was petrified and exhausted. What did he intend to do with me?

All of a sudden, we tumbled into a clearing, the golden morning sunshine tunnelling through the gap in the treetops; it was as if the world had survived after all, glorious and resplendent in the pale early-morning glow.

'Which way?' he whispered, panting in the warm air.

'Here,' I said, quietly, catching his hand, leading him down through the trees. 'The edge of the wood is just down here, and then we can skirt the orchard down to Bullsend Brook. It leads to the back of Dawkins Farm, and you can go back to the village from the other side.' I was thinking of the fastest route to the fields where the men would be working, someone to hear my cry for help if need be.

As we came out of the orchard and entered the copse around the brook, we began to slow down. He still kept hold of my hand, his thumb brushing the back of my fingers. It was strange, as we never like to be seen together in public. I am cautious about Daddy seeing us, and he is, well, just cautious, which doesn't seem surprising now. But there we were, hand in hand like young lovers, water trickling over the smooth grey rocks below as we walked through the glistening trees, in and out of the shade of the branches, in a strange juxtaposition between good and evil.

'You're more than I bargained for, Venetia,' he said quietly.

'So are you!' I spluttered, not really knowing where to begin.

'Why did you follow me?' he asked.

'I couldn't believe you were involved in the black market,' I replied. 'And yet it seems to be the least of your ventures.'

He looked confused for a moment, then said, 'Oh, Kitty must have told you,' as if that cleared up everything.

'I followed you because I had to find out more about the black marketing. Obviously I had no idea I'd find out you're a Nazi spy too,' I snipped. 'Are there any illegal activities you don't do, Alastair?'

He smiled. Yes, *smiled*, as if he were proud of himself. 'Well, I don't do many at all, unless you count house burglary. I dabbled in a spot of forgery once, which was quite interesting. I felt it improved my art actually.'

I was stunned, and stopped walking for a moment to take it all in. I mean, I knew he was a black marketeer and everything, but he sounded like a completely renegade criminal, who clearly had no conscience whatsoever.

'And now you're a traitor too,' I said limply. I looked up into his clear brown eyes, the word so ugly and clumsy in my mouth, so repulsive. 'How could you help the enemy, and on our own soil too?' I was angry with him for letting me down, angry for what he was doing. 'I never knew you spoke German! How many other people are you, Alastair?'

'Many,' he said simply. 'I speak French too, if it's any consolation.'

'Why would that be a consolation?' I said, and started walking again.

'It's a lot more complicated, Venetia. I can't tell you about it right now, but you have to trust me.' He came after me, trying to take my hand.

'How could it get more complicated?' I spat, snatching my hand away. 'You're a criminal and a traitor. Most people would be satisfied with just one: criminal *or* traitor, but, no, Alastair Slater has to be both.' Then I added, 'And a very poor artist just in case that's not enough.'

He laughed. 'Oh Venetia, I'm not really that bad an artist, am I?'

'Yes.' I smarted. 'You had my portrait completely wrong. You don't know me at all. You've had me wrong all along.'

'I see that I have,' he smirked, although I could see he was getting ruffled. 'I'll change it, Venetia. I'll find the painting and I'll change it. I'll make you into the gentle goddess that you are.'

'Why should you bother?' I shouted. 'I'd have thought another minx would be exactly your style!' I turned to face him. 'You have a nerve asking me to trust you, when all you've done is lie and cover up.'

He took my hand. 'Venetia, I may be a lot of things, but I have always been true to you.' His voice was velvet smooth, steady and serious. 'I love you, Venetia. I thought you loved me too, felt it inside. We're meant to be together.'

'I don't know if I can be with a traitor,' I said, my voice breaking, tears beginning to well up in my eyes, and then I made a feeble wobbly laugh. 'Black marketeer was fine,' I said, 'but not a traitor.' My face dropped, and I began to cry, right there in the wood, the trees silently standing around us, conveying on the world their stoical constancy.

'It's not that bad, Venetia.' He put his arms around me and pulled me in tight, trying to recapture our cosy nighttime world. 'You have to trust me. It's far more complicated.'

I sank into his warm body like it was a sustaining or intoxicating drink that kept me alive, and yet I knew deep inside that the morning's endeavours had put a different light on him, on us.

'Tell me then!' I pulled back, angry with him for ruining everything. 'Tell me how it's so very complicated.'

'I can't,' he said simply, a look of utter remorse in his eyes. 'I can only tell you that I love you, and that you need to believe me.' He put his hand into his pocket and pulled something out, a tiny pendant. There was no chain, no necklace, just the little silver object, the etching worn.

'Take it,' he said.

I was unsure whether to or not, but my curiosity got the better of me and I took it, turning it over in my palm. It was a St Christopher, a good-luck charm.

'It's from my grandfather,' he said softly, a memory making him smile. 'John MacIntyre, the man I thought to be the cleverest in all the world.' He closed my hand around it. 'Take it.'

'No,' I said, flashing my hand open again. 'You're the one who needs it.' I gave a frail laugh. 'I'm sure you have dozens of criminals and spies after you, not to mention the police and military intelligence.'

'Losing you scares me more than any of them.'

There was something strange in his look, a look I couldn't read; was it sadness or a kind of plea, a prayer?

I glanced at him, uncertain. 'You never told me about your grandfather,' I said. It was such an odd moment, as if the world had stopped turning, all the air abruptly still, the silence complete.

'I don't like to talk about myself,' he whispered, taking my hand in his. 'But you know how I feel about you. When all this is over, we can be married.'

The wind blew through the branches, sending a chill over my neck and face. I felt tangled up with the enormity of everything, what might be ahead of me: the shame, the hatred, the poverty, the loss. The baby growing inside me. I took an unsteady step back.

'I need time to think about everything,' I said hesitantly, and then, on hearing my voice feeble and scared, added in a more bold way, 'And I'm sure that you need time to get rid of the Nazi in the wood.' I shook my head in disbelief, trying to erase the image out of my mind. 'Aren't you worried that I'll hand you in?' I asked, intrigued that he hadn't brought it up.

'No,' he replied quietly.

'Golly, you're mighty confident, aren't you?' I blurted back. 'Do you think you have me so smitten?'

'No, Venetia. I'm just not afraid of being handed in,' he said gently, his hand reaching up and picking up a fallen emerald leaf from the hair on my shoulder. 'I'm far more afraid of losing you.' And there was a longing in his eyes that I knew would take me over if I stayed for much longer.

'I don't know who you are, Alastair Slater,' I blustered, furious that he was being so evasive. 'And I don't know your game, but you can jolly well find yourself a new muse.'

With that, I turned my back on him and stalked out of the copse to the orchard, each gentle breeze shifting the delicate shadows of the branches, like life flickering between light and dark. Above me a great bird of prey circled, wings spread wide and powerful in the pale dawn light.

As I approached the edge of the wood, I couldn't help but take one last glance back at him, and he was still there, standing at the edge of the glistening trees, silently watching me. Huffing, I turned away and marched up into the wood, beginning to run all the way home.

And so here I sit, confused and angry and not knowing what on earth to do. I *long* for him. And yet, how could I love a traitor? I may have his baby growing inside me, yet how could I ever trust this man who can betray our country, our world, our beloved little village? Everywhere I look, our choir, the Sewing Ladies, Mrs B, Hattie and her little baby Rose, Silvie, even Kitty in her own way, are all so incredibly dear to me. How could he put us at risk? How could he aid our destruction in such a direct and final way?

Just as I was thinking the worst, I felt something in my pocket. It was the St Christopher. I must have slipped it in when I was angry. I took it out and rolled it over in my hand, remembering the moment when time stopped, when he told me it was more complicated. When he told me to trust him. I want to, Angie. Yet how can I?

There was a small knock at my door. It was Kitty.

'I heard you crying,' she whispered as she stepped carefully into the room. 'I wanted to make sure you're all right.'

'Well, I'm not, if you want the whole of it.' I suddenly felt close to her again, and beckoned her to come and sit on the bed with me. We huddled close, like we did when Daddy roared at us as children, and we would flee out into the woods, gripping each other for dear life.

'Can I do anything?' Kitty asked.

'Not really. It's just that I don't feel well, right down in the pit of my stomach.'

'You should go and see Mrs Tilling. She always manages to make me feel better.'

And as we shared a moment of alliance, I decided that perhaps it wasn't such a bad idea to pay Mrs Tilling a visit after all.

I promise to write soon,
Venetia

Mrs Tilling's Journal

Thursday, 1st August, 1940

This afternoon as I returned from the hospital, I saw that I had a most unexpected visitor. The blue bicycle leaning against the whitewashed wall by the door belonged to Venetia, although there was no sign of her anywhere.

What now? I thought as I went in search of her. In the end, I went around the back of the house, and there she was on one of my wicker chairs on the terrace, the magnolia tree over her like an ivory-pink sun shade. She was leaning back, her eyes closed, her hair gleaming in the sunshine. She made quite a picture; she is such a beautiful girl, especially in the lovely floral green dress, with her golden hair and soft pale skin. It's a shame she's so reckless, although the influence of Angela Quail doesn't help. I'm sure she's not such a bad girl underneath all that makeup and pretence.

'Venetia,' I said, putting my hand gently on her arm.

She blinked her eyes open, and I could see she was tired. Her job at Litchfield Park has long hours, and I've reason to believe she's been spending long hours somewhere else too.

'I must have dozed off,' she said, sitting up straight and brushing herself down in a haze, a different world.

'Have you come to see me about something?' I asked. I had dinner to prepare, and a busy afternoon planned, and I hoped she wasn't going to waste my time.

'Yes, I have.' She looked at me nervously for a moment, her pearly hands pushing against the arms of the chair, easing herself forward and up. 'Could we go inside?'

I opened the back door, and she came in behind me, through the kitchen and the hall to the sitting room. I'd left the window open this morning, and the wonderful scent of the lavender bush from my front garden supplied the room with a brisk freshness, like washed sheets. The white net curtain was fluttering in and out of the window, as if the summer warmth were oblivious to the war.

I sat in the beige armchair, and she perched opposite on the sofa. I decided not to offer her tea, being busy and everything.

'Well,' I said, wishing she'd just come out with it.

And then she did.

'I think I'm pregnant.'

There was a long pause. She looked at her hands, which were moving in and out of each other on her lap. I didn't want to think about the things that sprang into my head all too readily, so I pressed on.

'Do you know how long?'

'I don't really know—'

'Do you remember when you had your last monthly?'

'Oh, about five or six weeks.'

She looked up and caught my expression, which obviously bespoke my disapproval.

'It was a mistake,' she said quietly. 'It's all a big mistake. I—' She broke off and started to cry, such a strange sight for the tough and headstrong girl she's become, and reminding me of the small girl I once knew, the girl running scared from her father or brother. I went over and put my arm around her, her turmoil dissolving the distance between us like fingers of dawn threading light into a new day.

'It's Mr Slater's, isn't it?'

'Yes,' she muttered through her sobs. 'What should I do?'

'Have you told him?'

'No.' She pulled away, as if with determination in spite of the circumstance. 'I want to be sure. I want to work out how I feel about it before I tell him.' She abruptly looked at me, scared and restless. 'You won't tell anyone, will you?'

'No, of course I won't.' I took her hand. 'But people are going to have to know sooner or later.'

She began crying again, this time harder, with more concentrated sobs of desperation. 'I want to find someone to get rid of it. I've heard there are women who—'

'You don't need to know about that, Venetia,' I butted in. I'm not having her go to the likes of Mrs Nees in a back street in Litchfield. 'It's illegal and dangerous.'

'But I can't have a baby!' She flew into a rage and began pacing the room. 'I can't believe this has happened to me! There has to be someone who can help?'

'Venetia,' I said gently, trying to calm her down. 'Firstly, we know how it happened, don't we? Let's not be coy here.'

She looked at the ground, reddening, her beautiful face crushed.

'And secondly, women like Mrs Nees don't know what they're doing. She may get rid of your baby, yes – but at what cost? Do you want an infection that might strip you of your ability to have children? Or may lead to your own death?'

'But that's rare, surely?'

'She uses old scissors, blunt and rusty.' I found a few tears coming from my eyes. 'There was a girl in the hospital last year, only fifteen, taken advantage by an uncle popping in and finding her alone. She spoke of the pain, the hour-long wrestling with various instruments, none of them cleaned, on the woman's filthy sitting room floor. Then she collapsed on the street and a policeman took her to hospital.'

Venetia had sat back down and was focusing on the pattern on the rug.

'She died, Venetia.' I swallowed, pursing my lips with the horror of the memory. 'She contracted septicaemia. She died.'

Silence sat haphazardly in the still room, although I could almost feel the turbulence in Venetia's mind, her eyes darting over the rug as if weighing the costs.

'How can she get away with it? Letting women die like that?' she eventually said quietly.

'It's illegal, Venetia. She can get away with whatever she wants.'

'Surely there's someone out there who would do it properly, with the right equipment?'

'No, Venetia. There are other people who would do it, but not properly, with the right equipment sterilised, the right procedure, the right clinical experience. It's a tremendous risk, Venetia, and I will do everything in my power to stop you from taking it.'

'What about you? Couldn't you get rid of this baby for me?'

I was stunned into silence for a moment.

'No, Venetia. I'm not qualified to give you an abortion, nor would it be within my powers. It is illegal. We would both be criminals.'

'But no one would find out – no one else knows I'm pregnant.'

'I don't care, Venetia. I don't know how to do it, and I'm not putting myself in a situation where I might be responsible for your death.'

She went quiet. Then came the tears.

'I don't know what I'm going to do.'

'You can do what most girls do in this situation. Tell Slater and get him to marry you.'

At that point she burst into a whole new wave of tears. 'I'm not sure I want to marry him any more.'

'What on earth are you talking about?' I was getting a bit cross. 'You've been carrying on with him these past months, getting yourself pregnant. Why wouldn't you want to marry him? I thought you rather liked him?'

'I do. I mean, I love him like my heart will explode, but he isn't who he says he is, and I'm scared, Mrs Tilling.' I put an arm around her and she turned into my shoulder. 'I'm so terribly scared.'

'What are you so scared of, child?'

'I can't tell you.' She looked up, her eyes full of tears, great pools that seemed to be drowning her.

'Do you want to keep the baby?'

'Of course I do, but I can't imagine how my life would be. I can't marry him, and Daddy will turn me out, and everything will be horrific.' She looked up at me. 'Please help me get rid of it, Mrs Tilling.'

I sat uncomfortably with her head against my shoulder, weighing the moral and practical implications of illegal abortion. Since the whole Carrington situation made me reconsider the moral standpoint of homosexuality, I've spent more time contemplating my own values, asking myself questions that I thought I'd always known the answer to. That juxtaposition between society and humanity, of what it is to be human, in all its guises.

'No, Venetia,' I said finally. 'I can't help. And I refuse to let you see Mrs Nees or anyone else who might kill you.'

She sat up and blew her nose, as if she knew it was pointless pushing me.

'What should I do?'

'You should talk to Mr Slater.'

She got up, thrust her handkerchief in her bag, and replied sharply, 'I can't go to him.' And then with a furious look at me, she added, 'I'll have to go and see Miss Paltry then. I'm sure she'll be able to help me.'

'Please, Venetia,' I begged. 'Whatever you do, stay away from the likes of Mrs Nees.'

'But Miss Paltry knows—'

'Miss Paltry doesn't always have her patients' best interests at heart, and I'm sure there's money in it for her if she refers you to a butcher like Mrs Nees.' I came up next to her, taking her wrist in my hand as if she were a small child. 'If you can't tell Mr Slater, then come to me and I'll help you through the pregnancy and to have the baby. We can hide it.'

Her eyes shone with doubt and hope and a richness of fear that seemed to loop around her mind, switching back and forth between horror and pain, and then she briskly flinched her wrist out of my hand and strode out of the door, without even saying goodbye.

As she got on her bicycle and left, I took a deep breath, a breath that acknowledged that I was involved in this now, and that I was the one she would come to when everything gets too much. With that I went inside and cleared out the back storage room. There's a small sofa in there, under some boxes and chests, and you never know, Venetia might need somewhere to sleep when the Brigadier finds out.

Colonel Mallard arrived home as I was scurrying around upstairs with sheets and blankets, and he watched me pensively. 'Can I help?'

'No, thank you,' I snapped, going into the tiny room and shifting boxes to make some space.

'Are we to expect a guest?' he said, coming up behind me and trying to help with a chest.

'Over there,' I muttered, reluctantly accepting the help. He's a large, strong man, after all, and he may as well be of some use.

He shunted around some of the other big items, putting boxes on top of the chest, clearing the sofa to use as a bed and making a good space.

'Thank you,' I said begrudgingly. 'And no, we're not expecting a guest.' I looked out of the small window to the treetops in the back garden, where a lone magpie stood watching me from the branches. 'At least, not yet.'

Letter from Miss Edwina Paltry
to her sister, Clara

3 Church Row
Chilbury
Kent

Thursday, 1st August, 1940

Dear Clara,

Today I happened upon some extremely useful
information, a trump card to trump all trumps. The
morsel of which I speak is news that the Brigadier's unwed
daughter is pregnant. And you'll never guess where
I found this nugget of dirt – it was from the foolish girl
herself.

There was a muffled knock at my door at about four this
afternoon, and when I answered, there she was, all prettily
done up but clearly flustered. She almost barged past me
into the sitting room, looking behind her to check if anyone
saw. Her rudeness was outstanding, but such was my
intrigue that I planted a welcoming smile on my lips and
followed behind.

'I need you to help me, Miss Paltry,' she said in quivering
tones.

I sat down, brightening at the prospect. 'Of course I can help, my dear. What do you need?'

'I need an abortion,' she said through gritted teeth, and the elation within me rose like a choir invisible, singing the praises of a new unprecedented opportunity.

And you know me, Clara. I wasn't going to let it get away.

'How many people know you're pregnant?' I asked quickly.

'But can you help me?' she snapped. She was in a trough of a mood, her face contorting into that of her odious dead brother.

'Of course I can help you, my dear,' I went over and patted her lap. 'I know a specialist in Litchfield who can do it easy as pulling a chicken's neck.'

She pulled away with a grimace on her face, and I beamed forward at her. 'But it has to be hush-hush, so does anyone know? Your parents?'

'No, of course they don't know,' she snapped, getting up and smoothing down her skirt, her nostrils screwing up as she smelt the whiff of cat about the place. 'It's not Mrs Nees, is it?'

'Not Mrs Nees?' I repeated quickly with a frown. Who'd she been talking to if she knew that name? Of course Nees is the only one round here, but I quickly had to pretend I knew someone else. 'I've never heard of Mrs Nees,' I said all innocent. 'But I'd never let you go to anyone bad, if that's what you mean. A nice lady like you. I have a much better specialist in mind, a man who used to be a doctor.'

She didn't sit back down, just looked out of the window at the banks of the pond, as if remembering something. 'Why isn't he a doctor any more?'

'You can't ask too many questions, girl. I tell it to you straight. He's done an all right job in the past. No deaths yet.' I coughed a little. 'To my knowledge.'

Her face suddenly dissolved into tears, and she ran for the door.

'Shall I ask him if he's free?' I called after her as she raced across the green, the heels of her shoes sinking into the grass as her white shawl billowed out behind her, like one of those Greek statues, like a perfect daughter.

Except I knew the devil cringing inside her dirty little womb.

I backed into my house and locked the door. I wasn't keen on getting an abortion for her anyway. No, I was interested in the much bigger prize glittering from the hand of the Brigadier. How debilitated he would be at the news of his daughter despoiled by a commoner. I would ask him for the rest of my money straightaway, and if he put up any resistance, I'd play my trump card.

I had to strike fast in case he found out from someone else first, and remembered I'd overheard Kitty at choir saying that he was in London today. You see how useful joining their ridiculous choir has been? She said he was at a supposed war meeting, more likely meeting his mistress if you ask me. I quickly worked out that he'd be on the evening train, the 9:21. So after dinner I took myself off to the station to wait.

I arrived early and stood outside the station reading the timetables, just in case I was spotted. I didn't want company for my little chat with the Brigadier. But the only person who came off the train was the Vicar back from Litchfield.

I stormed around for a few minutes and was just about to take off when I heard voices from the platform. On poking my head around the corner, I saw the Brigadier giving the guard strong words about something, the train being late, or untidy, or too jerky. He had been on the 9:21 after all.

And he was clearly not in a good mood.

I drew back outside and took a deep breath. It was almost dark, the sky a dappled dark blue with stars squinting through the gaps, and the sound of the train chuffed into the unknown. I shivered with discomfort, but the deed had to be done. I had to remember that I had the winning hand.

'Brigadier,' I called to him softly as his shadow appeared at the entrance. 'I was hoping to catch you here.'

'What? Who's there?' he asked gruffly, standing straight and looking around menacingly.

I stepped forward. 'It's your business partner.' I smiled.

He became flustered, looking around in case anyone else was witness to this. 'What are you doing here?'

'I came for a little chat,' I said. 'I thought I could give you some company on your walk home. You see, I want the rest of my money now.'

He paused momentarily. 'Don't be ridiculous, woman. You'll wait till the summer is up, if you get it at all,' he spat. 'There are rumours below stairs, so you'd better watch your step or you'll be locked up.'

Damn that Elsie. I've seen her around the village, smirking at me when she brushes past me in the shop. I knew she couldn't keep her trap shut.

'But, Brigadier, I think you should listen to me as I have some information that could send your family name plunging.'

'What do you mean?' he said, continuing his pace up the road. 'Are you trying to threaten me? Don't underestimate my temper.'

'What if it were something deeply humiliating, something ruinous?' I said softly.

He stopped. 'I know everything, you wretched woman. Now leave me alone.'

'No, you don't know everything,' I spat. 'You don't know that your eldest daughter is pregnant with Slater's child.'

I thought he was simply going to keel over in front of me. His face turned purple, and his hand went up to his heart. He staggered, then let out a long, hard bellow. 'How dare you suggest such a thing?'

'It's true,' I mumbled, edging back. I thought he was going to lunge at me. Take his anger out on me.

'It can't be true,' he yelled. 'It can't possibly be true.' And he began storming up the hill. 'We'll see about this.'

'What about my money, for keeping your dirty little secrets?' I asked, scurrying beside him to keep up.

He stopped sharply, his bony hand gripped on my upper arm, his fingers digging into my flesh. 'You stay out of this, Paltry,' he growled. 'Or you'll be a dead woman.'

The whites of his eyes glistened murderously in the moonlight. He was out of his mind with rage. I hadn't thought this through properly. He could murder me for even suggesting such a thing.

'If you breathe a word of any of your abominable lies I will have your pointless life cut short, my woman. So you'd better make yourself scarce.'

With that he shoved me back onto the road, where I fell badly on my hip, paralysing me briefly with pain. When I pushed myself up, he was gone into the blackness.

I struggled to my feet and staggered home, feeling sorry for myself. My plan had gone wrong. My tactics were flawed. I never imagined he wouldn't believe me, that he simply couldn't bear for it to be true to the extent that he would rather slaughter me.

As I sit here in my little front room, counting the half of the money, I know, dear sister, that I'll have to cut my losses and leave first light tomorrow. The Brigadier will kill me one way or another, especially with Elsie talking loose. I have sealed my doom.

I will be with you in a few days, and we will make good our plans.

Edwina

Kitty Winthrop's Diary

Thursday, 1st August, 1940

My very own war effort

More bad news today. The Nazis invaded our Channel Islands. They took the younger men away to fight and began starving everyone else. We know it's us next. Which is why I decided it was my duty to tell someone about seeing Old George and Mr Slater in the woods, and adding what I suspect about Proggett, who is certainly not just butlering. Perhaps I'll end up with a medal, the hero of the village.

At first I considered cycling to Litchfield Police Station, but it's quite a long ride, and I'm rather busy with singing practice at the moment. Then I wondered if I should ask Mrs Tilling what to do, as she's the most helpful person around here, and then the answer struck me. Mrs Tilling has an important colonel from Litchfield Park staying with her, and he quite liked my singing at the competition. Surely he would be able to give my information the proper attention it deserves.

So this evening, after dinner, I told Mama that I was to go to Prim's house for a special singing lesson, grabbed my torch, and headed down to the village in the purple and amber light of dusk. All was deadly quiet, not a stir of a bat or the usual foxes tiptoeing across to the wood – it was as if something horrid was going to happen tonight, something evil was snaking silently into our world.

I began running, and reached Ivy House short of breath, scared of invisible villains chasing me. I pulled the bell and within a minute the door opened a few inches and Mrs Tilling whisked me inside.

'Kitty, what in the world are you doing here?'

I stood in the hallway, relieved to see the familiar flowered wallpaper, the kitchen door open at the end of the passage, the smell of a casserole wafting around.

'I've come to see the Colonel,' I said boldly. 'Is he here?'

Mrs Tilling looked surprised for a moment, then shrugged. 'Come on into the sitting room,' she said. 'He's eating dinner. I'll make a pot of tea, and he can come when he's ready.'

The Colonel was enormous. I've seen him in the village and at the choir competition, but being so close to him, in Mrs Tilling's sitting room, made me inch back in fear of suffocation. He was easily the tallest man I'd ever met, heavily built, with broad shoulders and a chest as big as a bear's.

'Gosh, you're frightfully big,' I blurted before I could stop myself.

He smiled. 'Yes, I've been this way since I was a little older than you. Mrs Tilling said you needed to see me about something.'

'Yes,' I stammered. 'I'm Kitty Winthrop, from Chilbury Manor, and I think I have found a' – I glanced around and hushed my breath – 'a spy in our midst.'

He smiled briefly before quickly coughing and adopting a more serious expression, sitting down on the floral sofa and beckoning me to sit on the armchair opposite. 'Why don't you tell me all about it.'

'Well, when we were in Peasepotter Wood, Silvie – that's our evacuee – and I saw a black marketeer called Old George, and he has a bush that he uses to store all the black-market goods he has, and he was there with Mr Slater, the artist who moved into the house on Church Row next to Hattie, and I'm sure they were doing business, and then Silvie told me she keeps seeing Proggett, our butler, in Peasepotter Wood too, and I saw him once there as well, and I wonder if he's a spy or has anything to do with Mr Slater and the black market too.' I stopped and looked at my hands, clasped together on my skirt.

'Goodness,' he said slowly, coughing slightly into his big, rolled-up hand. 'You are definitely the type of open-eyed civilian we need around here!' He looked at me a moment, taking in my height and age. 'Mrs Tilling tells me you have your head screwed on properly, which means that you'll take good care of what I'm about to say, won't you?'

I nodded briskly, quite pleased that Mrs Tilling had said that I had my head screwed on, as I most definitely have.

'I want you to carry on being observant wherever you go, but not to go out of your way to find things out. You have to trust me when I say that we have a number of highly trained people keeping an eye on this, and I don't want you to put yourself in any danger. All right?'

I nodded, disappointed.

'Now, this is a very dangerous underworld we're speaking about, so I need to have your word of honour not to tell a soul about this.'

'Definitely,' I said crossly. 'I am completely trustworthy.'

'I'm certain that you are.' He smiled and his entire face lit up, making him look quite normal and even rather nice. 'You know I have a girl of your age. You must be twelve?'

'No,' I snapped. 'I'm nearly fourteen.'

'Of course you are! My daughter is twelve. She's my youngest, staying with her aunt in Oxford with her two older sisters. I think she'd keep a secret too, although she'd find it enormously hard work.' He let out a snort of a laugh, and I had to smile as he suddenly looked funny and friendly, like a big, unkempt St Bernard or a beaten-up old teddy.

'Can she come and visit some time?' I asked.

'Hopefully,' he said quietly. 'I'd like them all to come one day and see where I live, this beautiful village with the rolling hills behind us.'

'I never think of our village as being beautiful. I've lived here all my life, and it's just home to me. Do you really think it is?'

He paused, and I wondered if he'd heard me properly, but then at last he answered. 'There's a way of life here that I don't believe any war can crush, that will endure long after we're gone.' He snapped out of his thoughts and stood up. 'I'll let her know you want her to come. Her name is Alexandra,' he said, putting his giant hand forward to shake my small, slender one. 'If you come across anything else, please tell me, Kitty. And don't go to Peasepotter Wood. It's dangerous. I know you're a clever, mature sort of girl and can keep it to yourself, but especially don't let Proggett suspect that you know anything, all right?'

'Yes,' I said, pleased that finally someone was acknowledging me as mature.

Mrs Tilling came in and asked for a word with me in the kitchen. The Colonel bid me good night and asked Mrs Tilling if he might use the telephone. I wondered if he was calling HQ to tell them what I'd reported. That I was a hero after all.

Mrs Tilling began clearing up the tea things. 'Does your mother know you're here?'

'No.'

She sighed and looked round at me. 'I don't know why you came to see Colonel Mallard tonight, and I'm not asking that you tell me, but please don't mix yourself up in this war, Kitty.'

'But we're all mixed up in it, whether we like it or not.'

'Some of us are, Kitty. Some of us are.' She looked at me with a sudden sadness in her eyes, and I could see how David worries her. She gave my shoulder a squeeze with her hand. 'Now, off you go, and do please try to stay away from trouble.'

As I went into the hall, I overheard Colonel Mallard on the telephone. 'Yes, the exhaust is blown, and I need a replacement,' he was saying. 'Immediately.' All my revelations and he was busy talking about his motorcar.

Mrs Tilling opened the front door for me, and we heard the distant hum of aircraft coming from the south. I stepped out onto the path to get a better look, closely followed by Mrs Tilling, who stood behind me like a still squirrel listening for danger, Colonel Mallard silently joining us. The droning got much busier and messier, as if a lot of engines of different pitches were sputtering towards us. We watched the skyline behind the church tower, the moon suddenly appearing from behind dense cloud cover – a slim bright crescent, its silver light covering the side of the church with a heavenly gleam.

And then we saw them. The spots grew distinct, first one Nazi bomber, then two behind, a precise, forward-moving mechanical arrow of doom.

We watched in awe as they came towards us, a wave of Nazi destruction passing overhead. Had they overshot Dover? Were they heading for the Thames? The Colonel walked down to the road to better gauge their path.

The siren started blaring loudly – the first time it's gone off for a real air raid – shrill and frightening, like a ghost bellowing at us to get inside.

'Let's go to the cellar,' Mrs Tilling said briskly, ushering us back into the house. 'I think they're heading over us, but best be on the safe side, especially since we have Kitty here.'

She led the way through a slim door in the kitchen and down the narrow wooden staircase. As she switched the light on, I was relieved to see that it was decorated and cosy, not as grimy and insect-ridden as our cellar. Mrs Tilling had put a worn-out rug in front of a small old sofa and an armchair, complete with hand-embroidered cushions. A small bookshelf housed a clock, a dozen books, and a black metal box, which I hoped might be full of provisions. Rolled up to one side were some pillows and blankets, and I thought how comfortable it would be, curled up on the floor in such a snug little burrow.

The Colonel squashed himself into the armchair and asked Mrs Tilling if she had a pen and paper as he may as well catch up with his correspondence. She flustered around the bookshelf, found some, and gave them to him without a word. I wonder why she doesn't like him. He seems rather nice to me.

'Now, Kitty,' she said, 'what do we have for you?' She bent down and looked over the bookcase. '*Great Expectations*? Have you read that? Or there's Tolstoy's *Anna Karenina*, which may be a little too old for you.'

Nothing's too old for me, so I took the *Anna Karenina* from her and opened it on the first page. *All happy families are alike; each unhappy family is unhappy in its own way*. It was all too strange. Chilbury the centre of unscrupulous dealings, Proggett a dangerous spy, Venetia's Mr Slater a black marketeer. Obviously it's a good thing that the Colonel's people are on top of all this, but I confess I was slightly upset that my one and only offering to help the war effort had been trounced in a short conversation.

All happy families are alike; each unhappy family is unhappy in its own way. Our first air raid. Maybe the beginning of many, with bombs coming down on our houses, destroying everything we have. I listened hard, but the planes must have gone. And as the ticking of the clock dissolved into the background, I started feeling trapped by time itself. It was as if every moment had become both longer and shorter – more meaningful in case it's our last, yet so fleeting and pointless. And all these moments join together to build my life, like it's a patchwork quilt of different colours and shapes, good days and bad, that together make an uncomfortable, badly fitting whole.

Then the all clear sounded, a single siren call that somehow sounds comforting and friendly, even though it's the same awful air raid siren but only played once. The Colonel looked at Mrs Tilling, who stood up and brushed down her brown woollen skirt, turning to me as if he weren't even there and saying, 'Well, Kitty, I hope it's not too late for you to be running home? You can always stay in the back room if you'd like?'

'Thanks, Mrs Tilling, but Mama will worry about me.'

As she led the way back upstairs, I turned back to the large Colonel, still finishing his letter, and bid him good night.

'And good night to you,' he said lightly, looking up and smiling. 'Thank you for coming.'

I said good night to Mrs Tilling and hurried outside and up the road to the square. The moon lit the graveyard with a sinister glow, centuries of villagers buried beneath the ground, all those people rotting away until their grave-stones are the only traces left of them – the marks of their death.

I ran faster, faster, until I was halfway up our drive, the mass of Peasepotter Wood on my left, when an ear-piercing gunshot exploded from the wood. I shuddered to a halt with fear, and within a minute another frighteningly loud shot sounded. Daddy has taken me hunting a few times, but the sound was not like that. It was louder, crisper, a dead bolt through the clear night sky.

I listened for further shots, trying to calm my breath, slow my galloping heartbeat, but nothing. After a few minutes of silence, I crept farther down the lane. As I turned the bend, I sensed something ahead of me, a movement in the shadows. I froze, glaring through the traces of light to see the hunched form of Proggett making his way through the thicket in the wood.

After a few minutes of silence, I crept on, then made a dash for the house and eased the side door open. I half expected everything to be in disarray, to be different.

But it wasn't. Everything was strangely normal.

There were two fresh bread rolls under a glass dome on the table, so I pocketed them and headed for my bedroom. Mama met me on the stairs. Her eyes had that stare, like a frightened mouse unable to run. Daddy must be on the warpath again.

'Where have you been? Did you hear the sirens?' she whispered.

'I was at Mrs Tilling's house,' I said, trying to go past her.

'Did you see Venetia?' Her voice was like cracked ice.

'No, why?'

She seemed to look through me for a moment, then pulled herself together. 'I wanted to ask her something, that's all.'

'Is everything all right?'

'Yes, of course.' She smiled nervously. 'Time for bed. Good night.'

I tramped up to my room, drew my curtains, and crawled into bed. I wondered what happened to Venetia to make Mama so scared. I suppose there's always some drama or other with Venetia.

It's probably nothing.

Silvie's Diary

❦

Thursday, 1st August, 1940

Tonight the Brigadier was very angry with Venetia. He came home late and shouted at her. He said she is pregnant. That means she will have a baby. Mr Slater's baby. It is bad. The Brigadier took her into his office and shouted bad things. Then he hit her. She screamed and ran outside into the night.

'I'll kill him,' the Brigadier shouted. He went to get his gun.

I was scared. I ran out after her. But she was gone.

So I hid in my room. Then I heard Kitty coming up the stairs. And then the sound of a plane got louder and louder, low in the sky. I pulled up my blanket, scared.

Front page of the *Kent Times*,
Friday, 2nd August, 1940

Bombs Smash Chilbury

Late last night, a lone Nazi plane released three
bombs over the village. Local rescue volunteers
fought through the night to rescue the wounded
and put out fires that devastated Church Row and
other local buildings. Three people are missing,
feared dead.

Letter from Venetia Winthrop
to Angela Quail

Ivy House
Chilbury
Kent

Friday, 2nd August, 1940

Dear Angela,

I am wholly exhausted, in every possible way. No doubt you already know that Chilbury was bombed last night. I was there when it happened – watching our world explode in front of me – but let me start at the beginning.

I'd had a tremendous fight with my father – he found out that I'm pregnant and was threatening to kill Alastair. I ran out into the night, desperate to warn Alastair, desperate to tell him about the baby, our baby. Then I heard a gunshot in the woods, and then another, and thought that Daddy had found him and shot him dead. Terrified, I started sprinting down the lane to the village. I had to make sure he was all right. Whatever it took, I had to get to Alastair's house as soon as I could.

At first I tried to ignore the sound of a distant plane, but it grew louder as I reached the road to the square. It was low in the sky, a throaty roar, spluttering as it wavered in and out of the clouds. I kept on running, trying to escape this whole situation, this war, everything.

As the road opened out into the square, the plane suddenly became deafening, coming in right behind me, low, hounding me down.

I heard shouts from across the square – it must have been someone calling the Vicar to sound the siren as a moment later the slow wail swelled up, clashing with the roar of the plane that had become so thunderous that I felt my eardrums might explode.

But it was too late. It was all too late. The shadow came over me and I looked up to see a Nazi plane looming right above me, the noise overpowering, the dark grey presence making me cower with fright. It soared over me like the grim reaper and, as I glanced up to its extended black underbelly, I saw the bomb-release doors opening, and one by one the deadly load spilled into the night sky, straight towards Church Row.

I found myself racing to reach Alastair's cottage before the bombs did, desperate to warn him. The plane zoomed overhead, banking to turn back, not even waiting to witness the impending devastation.

I saw a sudden flash of bright white up ahead of me as the explosion of the first bomb ripped into the night, followed by the second, and then another as the noise of the blasts echoed into the night. Fragments of homes, furniture, people hit the air and tumbled down to earth. And the fires, soaring above the destruction: great blue-gold surges of flame gathering momentum into the smoke- and debris-filled sky.

I was knocked to the ground by the force of the explosion, and shards of glass cut my face and arms. I got up and ran to the blaze. It seemed to be centred on Alastair's cottage, although most of Church Row was wrecked, valleys of bombshell amongst surviving walls swathed with the colossal flames. Blood was dripping from one of my arms where it had been slashed, but I just ran and ran. Had there been enough time for anyone to get out before the bomb struck? Had anyone survived? Had Alastair survived? And Hattie? What about Hattie?

I screamed out, 'Alastair, Alastair!' but nothing came back. Just the immense sound of the fire, every so often an almighty explosion as the flames found something volatile.

The fire was scorching as I came closer, and I could see the outline of Alastair's cottage and Hattie's next door.

I stood for a second and watched the fire come alive, every memory and ounce of Alastair being swept up into the universe. I began crying, still shouting out his name, not bothering to cover my face, beseeching God to make Alastair walk unharmed out of the fire.

That's when I heard the cries. I stopped with horror as I listened to the high-pitched screams of a baby. Rose. Hattie's baby. I looked towards her cottage. It was more intact than Alastair's, the second storey still in place but about to collapse into the blaze.

I looked behind me. There was no one there.

'Someone, please help,' I yelled into the square, but no voice came back.

The baby screamed again. My stomach convulsed. I trod carefully over to the house and kicked the front door, which landed in an explosive heap at my feet, fires raging inside the skeletal building. I leapt back and shouted again.

'Help, please!'

There was so much smoke and dust in the air, I had to back away to get a good deep breath, and even there it was so hot and airless, almost impossible to breathe. Then I braced my arms in front of my forehead and plunged into the house. Knowing that the staircase was beside the door, I ran up and found the baby in a cot in the small bedroom, blue flames licking the far wall and a dense black smoke smothering the air. I picked her up in her blanket and darted back out the door. The heat was unbearable, and I felt the stairs melting away beneath my feet as I plummeted down, holding my breath and praying that I would get out before the whole place collapsed.

As I came to the bottom, the last stair gave way and I tumbled forward onto the floor by the door, shielding the baby from the weight of my body with my elbows, blood gushing from my arm onto the blanket and over my dress. I hauled myself up and stumbled through the doorway and over the debris, unable to see the ground in front of me because of the baby clasped to my chest. I finally came out far enough that the air was cool and clear of soot and smoke and I stopped to catch my breath, turning just in time to see the house explode into a million splinters.

Clasping hold of the baby, I watched the fire and eruptions, blood dripping from several wounds, my shoulders curved in over the tiny baby, clinging to her as if she were the last hope in the world. Suddenly, a hulk of a man came toward me, and I prepared for a new terror, but he stopped in surprise. 'Venetia!'

It was Colonel Mallard, looking incredibly anxious and intense.

'Is that a baby?' he said frantically, taking the bundle from me with great urgency, because it was at that moment that I felt the ground sway beneath me, coming up to meet my weak and bloodied body as I collapsed in a heap amongst the debris.

I must have passed out cold as I have no idea how I got to Mrs Tilling's house, or even what time it was when I finally awoke. All I knew was that I was in a strange, tiny room, on a soft, small bed. I could hardly move. My body was in colossal pain, my arm especially. I just lay there, blinking into the dark, until I made out that I was in a bed in Mrs Tilling's little back room. My arm had been thickly bandaged, and I was wearing an old white nightdress. Everything seemed incredibly blurry, and when I coughed I felt like I had a sack full of grit in my throat.

'Are you feeling all right?' Mrs Tilling asked, stroking my forehead. As I looked into her worried eyes, it all flooded back to me, and I began to cry, although not hard, as everything hurt.

'What happened to the baby?' I asked through my sobs.

'She's fine. She calmed down and now she's asleep in a drawer downstairs.'

'A drawer?'

'Yes, we don't have a crib, so Colonel Mallard emptied some clothes from a drawer in his bedroom, pulled it out, and set it on the kitchen table with a few blankets to make it soft. I dare say it's a bit old-fashioned to use a drawer,' she shrugged. 'But it's the least of Rose's problems. She has her life, which is all thanks to you.'

'And her mother? Did Hattie—'

She shook her head. 'No, she didn't make it,' she whispered, the pain catching in her throat like it was choking her. 'Prim was killed too.' A look of anger swept over her, before she quickly replaced it with her usual practicality. 'We don't know what will happen to baby Rose. She has no other close relatives. Victor has an aunt, his mother's sister, in Wiltshire, so I'll write to her.'

The news passed over me like a saturated storm cloud waiting to pour out its contents at a later time. Hattie was gone. Prim too. It was still only words.

'What about Alastair?'

She took my hand, which was also bandaged. 'We don't know what happened to him,' she said quietly. 'Was he supposed to be at home last night? Was he waiting for you?'

I looked at her, unsure what she was asking.

'He hasn't been found yet.' She went on slowly, choosing her words carefully. 'We don't know if he was in the house when it was struck. We thought maybe you'd know?'

My mind was in a muddle. Had he been there? All the other places he could have been flitted through my mind. He could have been in a meeting with spies or black marketeers, or lying in Peasepotter Wood shot dead. I remembered the tall angry man he'd met, the one with clothes too short for him, Alastair handing him the passport.

Why hadn't I thought of it before? The tall man must have been the downed Nazi pilot the Defence Volunteers have been trying to find. It explains the short clothes, why he was trying to escape the country. I couldn't

believe it. Alastair was helping an enemy soldier. How
could he do such a thing?

And how could I love a man like that?

My mind reeled with pain. Through this tangle of doubt
and fear, I still couldn't bear the thought that he might be
dead. Might he have been in his house last night? Had I
really been expecting him to be there? We'd made no
arrangement to meet. The last time we'd been together was
when I'd stormed off through the orchard yesterday
morning, without even saying goodbye.

We'd never said goodbye.

I began to cry again, softly, silently, and Mrs Tilling took
my hand between hers. It was all too much. Alastair
missing, Prim dead, Hattie – my dear friend – gone, leaving
her baby motherless. It was all too much.

Eventually I went back to sleep. Mrs Tilling must have
been sitting with me all night, as she was still there when I
awoke again in the morning, the sound of the crying baby
filling the house.

'Who's looking after the baby?' I asked. The crying made
me nervy, although I suppose that's its job, to get us
women up and moving. It stopped abruptly, as if someone
had picked Rose up.

'Colonel Mallard,' she replied. 'He seems to have quite a
knack.' She lifted her eyebrows as if surprised, although
somehow it made sense to me.

'Is she all right? All that smoke—'

'She's got a cough, but honestly, Venetia, it's a miracle
she's alive. And you too!' She looked at me crossly. 'Did you
know that the building was about to explode when you
went in to get her?'

'I didn't think.' I started getting out of bed, somehow feeling more alert, wanting to be up, finding out what happened to Alastair. 'I couldn't bear the crying and felt, well, compelled.' As I spoke, my memory flashed back to that moment. 'I was shouting for help, but no one was there, and the baby was just screaming and screaming. It was only me. I had to go.'

'I think you should stay in bed, Venetia.' She guided me back into bed, pulling the worn counterpane up around me. 'You lost a lot of blood.'

I looked at the bandage on my arm, remembering the gash. 'Is it bad?'

'I put some stitches in it,' she said in her calm way.

'And the baby? My baby?' I whispered.

'It's doing all right for now,' she said. 'But you're recovering from concussion, as well as being very battered and bruised. The baby won't stand a chance if you keep trying to get up. Shall I get your mother to come and get you?'

I looked up at her. 'But I need to find Alastair.'

She shook her head slowly. 'Venetia,' she said in a way that made me erupt into tears, knowing what was coming. She patted my shoulder, holding me down, 'If he was in that house, he wouldn't have made it.'

I heaved a few great sobs. 'What do you mean? Are you sure?'

'We don't know for sure that he was there. Does he always wait for you, Venetia?'

'Well, mostly,' I lied. Quite often he wasn't there, leaving me to wait. I would let myself in and lie back on his sofa, leafing through his poetry, or looking over my own nude

with equal measures of awe and aversion, feeling the colour
and tone of the room change as he stepped through the
door, the greys and browns transforming into golds and
bronzes. I could be late too, with difficulties getting away
from Chilbury Manor, bad weather, interfering sisters,
demanding fathers, and so forth. We were both willing to
wait, wait as long as necessary.

'Well, in that case—' She wavered, unable to finish.

After a moment's pause, I simply blurted out what had
been going through my mind. 'I think my father might have
shot him.'

She stopped mopping my head for a moment, a look of
anxiety covering her face. 'Does your father know about the
pregnancy?'

'Yes.' I looked up at her. 'Someone must have told him
last night, before he got home.'

'Could it have been Miss Paltry? Did you tell her?'

I gasped. 'She wouldn't have told him, knowing he'd kill
me?' My mouth went dry. 'Would she?'

Mrs Tilling grimaced. 'I'm not sure, my dear.' She shook
her head with wonder. 'I'm really not sure.'

She tucked me in and went to get me some hot milk to
send me to sleep again. She's worried that I'll lose the
baby, and it scares me too, more than I can say. If Alastair
is truly gone, either by the bomb or by the gunshots in the
wood, then this baby is the only part of him I have left, and
I know it sounds sentimental and ridiculous, but I miss
him as if I were dying in some way, my insides melting
into me, slowly dissolving into nothing. This baby, his
baby, is my only hope, the one bright star in a body of
hopelessness.

Oh, Angie, it's so dreadful that you're not here with me. Poor Hattie, I still can't believe that our lovely, warm, bright-eyed friend has gone. I don't know what I'll do without her. I can hear her voice in my head saying, 'Venetia, you need to learn to look after yourself.' As I listen to Rose's gurgling, I feel a closeness to her, and have decided that I owe it to Hattie, who was like an older sister to me, to be an older sister to Rose.

Do write as soon as you can.

Much love,
Venetia

Mrs Tilling's Journal

❧

Saturday, 3rd August, 1940

What a horrific couple of days. I have a truly bad feeling about this war, that we will be overtaken, lose our country, our culture, our freedom. That we will give everything, all our fight, all our hopes and dreams, our very selves. Then the Nazis will come and there will be nothing left. We will be hollow skeletons, letting them walk all over us, leaving them to run our lives, our homes, our children – if there are any left.

According to Colonel Mallard, the bomber probably over-shot Dover, got lost, and then had to drop its bombs in order to make it back over the Channel. It shouldn't have struck civilians. All that loss and it was only a horrendous mistake, an afterthought.

Venetia went home this morning and still isn't doing well. She's lost a lot of blood, and I worry that she'll lose her baby. The concussion was a bad one, and she's not herself at all. She's incredibly sad about Hattie, and is still talking about Slater as if he'll come back. No body was found in what remained of his house, and she can't seem to work out where he could be.

The square is now bereft of one side. We've been working hard – the women of the village – to clear it away, trying to make the best of the uneven pile of bricks and broken things, some of which are deeply unsettling, like Hattie's familiar dresses, Prim's broken gold ornaments. Meanwhile, a growing number of scavengers have been scouring the remains for jewellery or trinkets. Yesterday, I saw Ralph Gibbs pushing a woman aside to get to some treasure first, his eyes crazed with greed. This war has turned him into a monster.

Miss Paltry's house was also wrecked, but luckily she was pulled out of the debris with just a fractured hip. They took her to Litchfield Hospital, so perhaps when I have time to visit I'll question her about this curious baby affair.

Yesterday Mrs Quail found the remains of Prim's gramophone player and a few other items. The Vicar told us that we can give them to Prim's sisters tomorrow as they're to come for a special eulogy in the Sunday service.

We also found some of Hattie's things, including a metal biscuit tin with Hattie's letters. Everyone said I should take it with me to give to Victor's aunt when she comes to collect the baby, so I brought it home and asked the Colonel to force it open as it had been melted closed.

'Isn't that illegal?' he asked, all puffed up about doing the right thing.

'Open it,' I said. 'I will take the responsibility if you have a problem with it. And I'll find a way to open it myself if you don't oblige.'

He looked at me as if I'd gone quite mad.

'Someone has to open it eventually,' I said quietly. 'And I'm quite sure Hattie would rather it was me and not Victor's aunt, wouldn't you think so?'

He harrumphed and then set about prying it open with a

screwdriver. Once open, he handed it over to me, and I leafed through the contents.

'Don't you feel like you're rifling through someone's private life?'

'No, I feel like I have no time for questions at the moment.' I carried on for a moment and then stopped and looked up at him. 'I just want to make sure that the family loves the baby, loves the memory of Hattie. That they give her a welcome home.' I looked back down at the tin. 'We can't have them finding this love letter that's not from their nephew,' I said, taking a letter and making a pile for things I'd keep to one side. 'Or this one.'

'Yes, yes,' he said. 'I suppose you're right. How knowing of you.'

I stopped leafing through and looked up at him. 'It's only what I'd like someone else to do for me.' I thought I'd start crying, knowing Hattie like I did, knowing how she loved that baby, loved her husband. How ironic that she'd been so worried that something would happen to Victor, somewhere in the Atlantic, when it ended up being her who was killed.

'You're a brave soul,' the Colonel said gently, and he put his big hand on my upper arm and held it there for a moment, oddly comforting in the stark new light of day.

There was a photograph of Hattie and the whole group: Venetia, Henry, Angela Quail, then my David and Ralph Gibbs from the shop. They were walking down the lane towards Chilbury Manor. Someone had taken the photograph while no one was watching, Victor maybe? They'd separated off from each other: Hattie and Venetia in the foreground, smiling and linking arms; David and Ralph laughing and pushing one another, looking so young and innocent before the war came and dragged them quickly into adulthood. And then, at the back, half hidden, were Angela and Henry, holding hands. She was whispering something into his ear, her other hand touching his arm, and he was laughing. They looked like lovers. I wondered why I hadn't worked that out before. Angela was in love with Henry, but he was always infatuated with Venetia. If you look closely at the photograph, you can see that his eyes are on Venetia as she slinks ahead, while Angela's eyes are directed sideways to him. I wondered if Venetia knew. Probably not.

'What are you going to do with them?' the Colonel asked, glancing at my pile.

'I'll put them in an envelope and give them to Rose when she's old enough to understand,' I said, straightening the small pile gently, as if it was to be a precious treat for the future. 'She won't know anything about her mother, growing up with just her father. These few items will help to fill in some of the gaps.'

'You can't draw a picture of someone who's dead,' the Colonel said plainly. 'Believe me, I've tried. There's so much that is intangible about a person, all those little details, their past, those annoying little habits, the way they speak, their natural perfume. It's those things – and countless more – that gives them that fullness of life that you just can't re-create. You can use photographs, portraits, poems, scents, everything you can find to remind you of them, but to convey that essence of a mother to her children is at best sketchy.'

'Did you lose your wife? I'm so sorry—' I must have blushed furiously as I thought of the horrid ways I'd treated the poor man, when really he was widowed too. Just like me. And I'd never thought to ask him.

'Yes.' He glanced out into the garden where a breeze was catching the clematis, swaying the maturing violet blooms up and back. 'My daughters were seven, nine, and ten when Vera died. They remember her as a sick woman, demanding, queasy, often quite scary. It's a tough task persuading them that once she was a vibrant, beautiful person.' He picked up the photograph of Hattie and looked sadly down at her. 'She too had vitality and dreams, just like this poor woman.'

I was quite struck by his words. I hadn't known that he had a wife who had died, although he had mentioned his children in passing. I suddenly felt dreadfully sorry for him; after all, I knew how it felt to be all alone, bringing up the children, forging on.

'David was only eight years old when Harold died. We carried on by ourselves all right, became very close. Where are your children now?'

'They're in Oxford with their aunt, my sister, and they're older now: twelve, fourteen, and fifteen. I was thinking of renting a place down here and bringing them to live with me. I miss them, you see.' He coughed slightly to offset his bluntness. 'But now—'

'Yes, they're probably better off up there for now,' I said quietly, and I found myself struck by the fact that he had been thinking of leaving and renting a house instead of living here at Ivy House. Didn't he like it here? Why hadn't he told me? Maybe I should have made him feel more welcome.

So I made us both a fresh pot of tea, and as he sat with me at the kitchen table, I asked him all about his girls.

Kitty Winthrop's Diary

Monday, 5th August, 1940

Life without Prim

This evening we had a special choir practice, the first without Prim. I could hardly bear to walk into the cold church knowing she'll never be there again. Our choir will never be the same. Many of us won't be able to go to Prim's funeral as it's to be held in London, so the Vicar held a special Sunday service for her yesterday.

He asked me to say a few words, which was such an honour, and I decided that I would tell everyone about my time with Prim. How she was such a tremendous force in our lives. But when it came for my time to speak, I wasn't sure I could do it, trembling with nerves and sadness as I stepped up to the pulpit.

But then I remembered Prim. How she would want me to be strong.

'At my very first lesson in Prim's house, we spoke about dying. She told me how she'd nearly died of malaria. She said that she didn't mind the thought of death. That realising you're going to die actually makes life better as it's only then that you decide to live the life you really want to live, not the one everyone else wants you to live. And to thoroughly enjoy every minute.'

I paused to pull myself together. The whole village was there, and some people from Litchfield too. All waiting for me to speak. 'It's shattering that she's gone, but she wouldn't have wanted this service to be about her death, but to be a celebration of her life. She was the most vibrant person — the most energetic, the most real person — and she'll always be alive to me.'

I began to cry, and Mrs Tilling came to help me back to my seat. It's just so hard to come to terms with the fact that her immense presence is gone.

Tears were pouring from our eyes as we sang 'Come Down, O Love Divine'. Her fierce bravado will be sorely missed, and as I looked around the choir stalls, I wondered if it could have seeped into each one of our choir members. That just by being around her, we've become more fierce and brave ourselves, ready to take on the world in her place.

What happens when people die

Their souls may go to Heaven, where I might see them again when I die (although I'm unsure how they'll look by that time)

Their bodies go into the ground where they become a feast for earthworms

Their presence lives on in everyone who knew them, as if we took that responsibility when we met them, without even being asked

Their essence is refracted into the universe, where it colours the air with their hues, eventually bleeding into the sunset with the other colours, a march of the dead every evensong

The question of who will lead the Chilbury Ladies' Choir

At choir practice this evening, we had to work out what we're going to do for Hattie's funeral, which is tomorrow. Predictably, Mrs B quickly took charge in Prim's place, but her busy hornet ways seemed so brisk and artless compared to the close memories of Prim.

'After our tragic week, we're here today to rehearse for Hattie's funeral,' Mrs B began. 'As one of our leading second sopranos, we owe it to her to give it our very best.'

'It would be the very least we can do for her,' Mrs Tilling chimed in, coming forward. 'I can hardly bear for us to sing without her, but I know it is what she would have wanted. She would want us to give her the best funeral singing we've ever performed.'

There was a mumble of agreement, and then Mrs B called for silence. 'Yes, yes, everyone knows that, Mrs Tilling. Thank you for your thoughts. We'll take that into consideration.' She ushered Mrs Tilling to sit back down, but Mrs Tilling was busy looking through some sheet music at the front, and Mrs B, visibly bristling, continued. 'After much thought, I think it would be best for us to sing "Ave Maria" again for the funeral. We can try our best, with my leadership, to repeat our glorious performance in Litchfield.'

More kerfuffle. No one wanted to sing 'Ave Maria' again. Somehow it seemed wrong to simply churn out something we sang to win the competition when this certainly didn't feel in any way victorious. We looked to Mrs Tilling, who was busy looking through a pile of music scores.

'We can't sing that!' she declared, popping her head up from the music. 'It's completely wrong for this situation. No, we need something else. Something for Hattie.'

'Maybe we could try Mozart's "Lacrimosa" now that the special Memorial Service Prim was planning is ... cancelled. I know that we need to work on it, but it is meant for a funeral,' Mrs Quail called.

'No, that's not right either,' Mrs Tilling sighed. 'It's too heavy and dramatic. Hattie would have wanted something simple, like a favourite hymn.'

'Indeed, Mrs Tilling?' Mrs B snapped. 'Tell us, pray, what you have in mind.'

'Well, the Vicar left us all the old music from the church, and it's a bit dusty, but I'm sure we can find something in here.'

I went up and helped her look through. Some of the copies were very tatty, and sometimes there simply weren't enough to go around, even if we shared one copy between three or four of us. We'd never be able to get more music in time.

'What about this?' I called, holding something up. 'Handel's *Messiah*?'

'A touch too celebratory perhaps, Kitty,' Mrs Tilling said kindly, flipping on through. 'Ah, here we have it, "Amazing Grace", one of the most moving pieces of music ever written.'

Everyone murmured, and it was generally acknowledged to be an excellent choice.

'Its beautiful anthem brings the whole of life together,' Mrs Tilling said wistfully, then added decisively, 'It is just the thing.'

She handed out the sheets, and everyone began humming

the music. We went to our places and looked up ready to begin.

'Are you going to lead us, Mrs Tilling?' I asked. She was the obvious person as she can read music and has a very good voice too.

'Yes, are you going to conduct?' a voice from the altos called.

'Well,' Mrs Tilling stammered. I could see she was uncomfortable, slipping into the shoes of Prim – such a unique presence and authority – when she'd only been dead a few days.

'Go on, Mrs Tilling,' Mrs Quail called from the organ. 'You're the only one who can.'

Mrs B, who had remained at the front, moved to the centre and said, 'Now, I don't think we should force poor Mrs Tilling. After all, she only stepped forward to help us find the right piece of music, and now that has been done, she is very much needed in the altos.' She smiled benevolently at Mrs Tilling, her hand outstretched to guide her back into her place in the choir stalls.

For a moment, Mrs Tilling looked as if she was about to head back to the altos, but then something held her back, and she stood up straight and smiled at Mrs B.

'I can do it, I think,' she said. 'It won't be the same as Prim, but we all have to do our best. I'll be able to lead us in and keep us in time, and make sure the crescendos and rallentandos are done just right. I'll do it.'

'That's the spirit, Mrs Tilling,' Mrs Quail called, amongst the other voices and nods. 'You are the best we have. You'll do a fine job!'

I watched Mrs B walk back to her place, head held high to conceal her annoyance. I've never seen her vanquished like that before, especially by her usually loyal supporter, Mrs Tilling. The tables are turning.

Mrs Tilling didn't have a baton, but she raised her arms and nodded to Mrs Quail at the organ to begin. Then she looked straight at me, as if she knew that I would lead the sopranos in, and a few tears began to form as I remembered lovely Hattie, a girl who'd always been part of my world, which was slowly but surely breaking up, dissolving in a way that can never be reversed.

Venetia is the hero of Chilbury!

The village square is in chaos. The shop is closed. But worst of all, Venetia is the hero of the hour! I can't go anywhere without being bombarded with questions about Venetia. How did she save the baby? Did she get the cake Mrs Quail baked for her? Was she going to receive a medal of bravery? It's all 'Poor Venetia' and 'Well done, Venetia.'

She was lucky to be in the right place at the right time. Anyone would have done as she did. I most certainly would have had I been there. Then I would have been the hero.

But Venetia is pregnant!

Our maid Elsie told me this morning, making fresh scones to tempt me into the kitchen.

'Did you hear the latest news?' she said softly, lavishing butter onto another for me, proffering a dish of strawberry jam in my direction.

'What news?' I said through a full mouth.

'About Venetia having a baby.' She turned away so that I couldn't see her face, her apron swooshing out around her narrow frame like a ballerina. She has that tall, picturesque look that looks wonderful from a distance, only close up you get to see the sullen bitterness in her eyes. It quite ruins the effect. Today she was looking happier, however, a twinkle in her great green eyes like a sorcerer's cat on the prowl.

'I heard about her rescuing the baby,' I began. But she butted in rudely.

'No, her own baby.' She turned towards me and pushed her pointy face into mine. 'Mr Slater's baby.'

I took a step back. 'Venetia's pregnant?'

'Shh,' she quickly said. 'Don't tell anyone I told you.' She must be scared someone will say she's been gossiping, or causing trouble. She turned and dashed out of the kitchen, leaving me confounded, then dismayed.

Suddenly everything makes sense!
Why Daddy is furious with Venetia
Why Venetia is not speaking to Daddy
Why Mama is excessively concerned about Venetia's
    health
Why Venetia is extremely upset that Slater is missing
Why everyone is acting very oddly and, worst of all,
Why no one is telling me a thing about it

Yet it seems strange that Elsie should be the one to mention it. She hardly speaks to me at all – I've often wondered if she has a chip on her shoulder about being a servant. Venetia says that's why getting staff is so difficult these days. No one wants to be bossed about. Maybe Elsie was getting her own back on us, especially now that she has twice as much work since Proggett left. We hadn't seen him for a day or so, and forced open his room. It was completely cleared out. He must have left the night of the bomb. We're all baffled, except for Daddy, who's completely livid.

I decided to find Mama to ask why she hadn't told me about Venetia being pregnant, but when I found her in the nursery with whining Lawrence, I chose not to say anything. Sometimes it's best to carry on as usual so that no one suspects that I know. I've been thinking about it all day though, turning it over and over in my mind. I can't help relishing the idea that this will surely be the end of Venetia.

This will put her on a back foot for the rest of her life.

Mrs Tilling's Journal

Tuesday, 6th August, 1940

In the bleak afternoon drizzle, our small, sobbing group huddled outside the old church, chilled and nervous, for Hattie's funeral, the final switch on dear Hattie's life. The proper end that was supposed to round the whole thing off, but seemed so contrary and out of place for such a vibrant, warm-hearted character.

'It's just so hard to believe that she isn't going to come careening around the corner, her usual beaming smile across her face,' Kitty whispered with a loud sniff, and we looked over to the corner where she might appear.

'I feel that she's with us in spirit,' I replied, clutching baby Rose closer, her little face smiling on this dreadful day that would change her world forever – almost definitely for the worse.

'She doesn't know her mother's gone, does she?' Kitty murmured.

'No, and it'll be a few years till she's old enough to understand. She'll never have known Hattie, only Victor and the people who look after her.'

'Who *is* going to look after her until Victor gets back?' Kitty's eyes darted from the baby to me.

It was a good question.

Victor's aunt wrote to say they're too frail to have Rose. I hadn't realised they're in their eighties now. Sadly they couldn't even make it for the funeral. So Rose has been staying with us – the Colonel and me – at Ivy House for now. I suppose I'll have to find a home for her, a nice family to foster her.

No one's heard a thing from Victor for months, although the Colonel had his ship checked, and it seems it is doing all right somewhere in a remote part of the Atlantic. Victor probably hasn't even heard about Hattie's death; he might be still in a different reality where his wife and new daughter live happily in their small, snug home, while he is the one facing the bombs, he is the one risking his life so that they may live free. Oh, the wretched irony of it all.

Before the Vicar opened the big church doors for us to enter, he crept out to have a word with me.

'We haven't any pallbearers,' he whispered hurriedly.

I looked at him, puzzled.

'There are no men to carry the coffin,' he elucidated, coughing to cover his embarrassment. We looked around. A group of mothers and children from Hattie's school had come, but apart from old Mr Dawkins and the Brigadier, who was clearly in no mood for carrying coffins, we were all women. The world seemed to fade in front of me. Dear Hattie, who was like a daughter to me, taken from life so early, and we couldn't even give her a proper funeral.

'Sorry,' the Vicar muttered. 'Our usual bearers are at war or in the fields or making bombs. There's nothing I can do.'

'Everyone's harried these days,' I said quietly, annoyed that this wretched war is making us too busy for everything.

If something needs to be done, it's up to us women to make do.

And then it dawned on me.

'We will carry the coffin,' I announced.

A sea of faces looked up.

There was a moment of shock, when everyone seemed to look from me to the Vicar, registering the situation.

Then, after a few whispers, a few murmurs, one by one, they all began to step forward; first Kitty, then Mrs Winthrop and Venetia, Mrs Gibbs, Mrs Turner and Mrs Poultice, then Mrs B, and soon everyone had silently volunteered.

'The Chilbury Ladies' Choir will bear the weight,' Mrs B declared, taking charge in her usual manner, which for once was useful. 'We will carry Hattie, our loyal second soprano, on her final procession.'

As the Vicar led the way into the vestry, I realised I needed someone to hold baby Rose, and after looking around, I knew that I had no choice than to pass her over to the Brigadier.

'Could you hold Rose for a while, please?' I said sharply, bundling her into his arms, and he was surprised into taking the infant, looking down into the blue shawl with a frown over his face. I paused for a moment, wondering whether he registered that this beautiful girl was, if my suspicions were correct, his own child. Might he have felt a shudder of remorse?

'Lead on, Vicar,' Mrs B called, and we followed him into the vestry, where we caught our breath at the sorry sight of the coffin, a slim wooden box containing all that was left of our precious Hattie. What was once a vivacious, energetic young woman was now a pile of sad, dead remains without colour or life, set inside a still box.

'How are we to lift it?' Mrs Gibbs asked nervously.

'Everyone who feels strong can take a corner, and the rest of us will fill in around the edges,' Mrs B ordered.

The mood became sombre as we hoisted our fellow choir member up, at first a little wobbly, but then we straightened up and began to walk out into the entrance hall, waiting for Mrs Quail to begin the organ processional.

But Mrs Quail had different ideas.

At the precise moment we stepped out down the aisle, the ponderous introduction of 'Abide with Me' began to sound forthright through the old church, the simple and yet poignant tune pouring softly from the organ, urging us to sing as a united front, for Hattie, for Prim, for our small yet resilient community, for our dear, collapsing country.

> *Abide with me; fast falls the eventide;*
> *The darkness deepens; Lord with me abide.*

Thus it was that a shuddering chorus of twelve deeply saddened women, singing at first softly, then more resolutely, advanced slowly down the aisle. We sang as if our lives depended on it, as if our very freedom, our passions and bravery were being called forward to bear witness to the atrocities that were placed before us. We were united and strong, and I knew right there and then that nothing, nothing could ever break the spirit of the Chilbury Ladies' Choir.

At first, I couldn't bring myself to sing, the feeling was too immense, the extraordinary sound of our procession echoing around the empty church too tragic to eclipse the dreadful finality of death, the weight in the box making me shudder with discomfort. In front of me Kitty was struggling to hold the coffin up, her voice coming out piecemeal like fragile broken china, and behind me Venetia was inconsolable, heaving huge gulps of tears. I know that we are taught to think of death as a gentle passage of the soul from one place to the next, but the brutal bombing of a young mother seemed to contradict all of that, make it into the abominable destruction of a very real, strong spirit.

I felt Venetia's hand on my arm from behind me, and suddenly felt less isolated in my dismal reckoning of mankind, and found my voice. At first gravelly and croaky with tears, it soon gathered strength, clarity, deliberation, until I felt the sound of our combined voices encompass us like a warm halo of protection, making us aware of the precious life we all have – what it means, and however long it may last.

As we reached the last majestic notes, we stood tightly at the front, breathlessly listening to the sounds of the closing song reverberating around us.

With some effort, we gently lowered the coffin onto the low table, Mrs B hoarsely whispering, 'Gently, Mrs Gibbs. Gently!'

Then we glanced around at the looming emptiness of the space. On one side were the mothers and children from the school, and on the other was only old Mr Dawkins, the Brigadier with Rose, and now Henry, who had arrived while we were in the vestry.

Then, at the very back of the church, I noticed that the Colonel had slipped into the row on the left – my spot, the place I always like to sit. He gave me a sad, tight-lipped smile, and I nodded in the direction of the Brigadier, hoping he would get the hint and go and collect Rose from him, which he did, remaining at the front as the Chilbury Ladies' Choir went quietly into the choir stalls.

Clearly upset, the Vicar led us through the ghastly service, a series of words that seemed all too inadequate to describe the grief I felt inside, and although I tried to hold them back, thoughts of David, and what I'd do if that telegram arrived, sprang into my mind, an ominous gleam of a possible future.

I was snapped out of my miseries by the Vicar announcing, 'The Chilbury Ladies' Choir will now sing for us.'

We stood, and I took a few deep breaths before walking to the front, feeling unnerved and unable to go through with my task of leading, such a new endeavour to be making at this awful moment, at once stepping into a dead woman's shoes — and Prim's, no less, with her magical presence gone — for the sake of poor Hattie.

And then, a sudden anger shot through me: *What vicious brutes did this to them?* And a new emotion overcame me: integrity, and a feeling of pride for everything we stand for. Pride in Hattie for striving on with Victor so far away in danger at sea. Pride in Prim for having the faith to take our choir to new heights. And pride in us, the Chilbury Ladies' Choir, for carrying through with our duty: to rejoice in their lives, to be strong and resilient enough to hold off our enemies, and to make sure their deaths are not in vain.

The organ's introduction of 'Amazing Grace' filtered through the empty church, sweeping through us like a clean, crisp wind, and I took up my baton and prepared the choir to give the finest performance of our short, eventful existence. And a tragic awe overwhelmed me as the clear, crystalline voices pierced the air with all the beauty that a woman's voice can attain, a soaring white dove in the everlasting tumult of war.

When we had finished, the Vicar announced that the children of the school wanted to sing for their dear teacher. And my heart broke as I watched the children, most of them eight or nine, wondering what had happened to wonderful Mrs Lovell.

It was the most tragic scene I'd ever encountered. The children covering their faces with their small hands to avoid looking at the coffin, in shock by the raw reality of death: how it could totally destroy something so warm and alive.

At the burial, our sorry group stood silently as Hattie's coffin was lowered into the sodden ground beside her parents, before we made our way back to Ivy House for tea and sandwiches. I walked home with the Colonel, who had slipped the sleeping Rose into her pram – a black one that had been lent to me from a nurse friend in Litchfield, as Hattie's blue one had been crushed in the bombing. She'd been so proud of it. I remembered when she brought it round to show me, pleased as Punch, the first of many such memories to haunt me.

I found myself pondering about Hattie and Prim and their lives, and thinking of my own insignificant time left on this planet, and how it might be shortened by bombs or invasion, or who knows what.

Later that day, after our desolate assembly had left with tears and embraces, I found myself talking about it to the Colonel.

'That could have been my funeral,' I said quietly, sitting at the kitchen table, drawing my fingernail down a crevice in the wood. 'That bomb could have come a hundred yards in this direction and hit us.'

'Yes, but let's not think about that until it happens, eh?' the Colonel replied, and drew up a chair. It was early evening and the gloomy grey of the day was dimming into a stormy-looking night.

'But if we don't think of our death until we die, how can we decide how we want to live?' I looked at my hands, thin and wrinkled and bony, their freshness lost. 'If it had been my funeral, it would have been a sorry affair.'

'You're tired,' the Colonel said, getting up. 'Let me make you a cup of tea.' He went and filled the kettle.

'I've just been thinking about Hattie and Prim, wondering why I've spent my life working away to make other people happy. Why didn't I make my own life more fun and happy, and more purposeful?'

He sat back down. 'Now look here,' he said in a very authoritative way. 'You have a great life. You have a lovely home, brought up David—'

I broke him off to say, 'Who is at war and may not come back alive.'

'You have a son,' he went on. 'And you are an incredible help and support to everyone around you.' He put his hands on the table emphatically. 'Can't you see how much this village needs you? They'd be lost without you!'

I put my head down, feeling self-conscious, and then I suddenly got up and snatched my dishcloth brusquely. 'Enough of this self-indulgence,' I muttered. 'I need to get on with dinner. I'm afraid I'm a little behind today.'

He came up beside me, guiding me back to the table with his firm, big hands on my shoulders.

'You just sit back down,' he said gently. 'I can make dinner tonight.' And he went over to the larder and took stock of the contents. 'Excellent news! We have some eggs, and eggs are my speciality.' He took the box out and promptly started looking for a pan. 'Scrambled or boiled?' he asked, as he opened the cupboard and began banging around.

'Scrambled,' I replied, smiling. I can't remember the last time someone cooked me dinner, even if it was only eggs.

'Excellent choice, madam,' he smiled. 'My girls swear that I make the best scrambled eggs in the whole of Oxfordshire.'

Albeit a little overcooked, he made them very well indeed, singing a dreadfully out-of-tune rendering of 'It's a Long Way to Tipperary'. Of course I felt obliged to sing along, as he kept getting the words wrong and coming into the chorus too soon. It was ridiculous, us singing around the kitchen while cooking the scrambled eggs, but it cheered me up.

And so, dear diary, as I go to bed tonight, I feel that this war has become a turning point for me. I need to be more sure of myself, make the most of the time I have left.

Stand up and make myself heard.

Letter from Miss Edwina Paltry
to her sister, Clara

Litchfield Hospital
Litchfield
Kent

Tuesday, 6th August, 1940

Dear Sister,

Why has this happened to me? My house was ruddy well
bombed, and I'm stuck here in bleeding Litchfield
Hospital with no way of finding my money, which is buried
in the rubble of my house, waiting for the looters to find it
first.

You're probably wondering what happened. A sodding
great bomb did, that's what! Thursday night and there was
I all tucked up nicely in bed, when next thing I hear the air
raid going and have to hoist my exhausted body up. I was
just going for the floorboard to get the money, when blam!
Nothing, until I wake up in this dreadful place with the
biggest pain in my hip you'd ever know, and my leg in
bandages too.

'Please remain calm and quiet, Miss Paltry,' the nurse
told me in her patronising manner. 'It's only a fractured

hip. You'll be out in a few weeks. We have patients in with
far more severe wounds than you.'

What about my money? I felt like yelling.

But instead, I snivelled into my hands and started
thinking up a plan. And then it came to me. The woman in
the next bed is one of those horrible hop pickers from
Dawkins Farm, and she has a few young fellows visiting
her. Yesterday I asked her if her nephew might be able to
do me a favour, that there would be money in it for him. If
he could be trusted. The next day she got him to come to
my bed to find out what it was about.

'What d'you want me to do then, missus?' he said plainly.
I looked him over and wasn't at all sure. He was tall and
gangly, scruffy as a chimney sweep, with floppy loose hands
and a pasty, moist complexion.

'It's Tom, isn't it?' I said, trying not to crease my forehead.
Was this really the best I could do? 'Now, can I be sure you
can keep your word, Tom? As I have a great task for you, but
you have to reassure me that I can depend on you.'

'You can trust me, missus,' he replied easily, hands on
hips. Hardly the thing to fill me with confidence, but I
proceeded nonetheless.

'You see, I have an amount of money hidden in the
remains of my house. Not a large sum, you know. But, you
see, I have been saving up for my poorly sister, who is in
need of a wheelchair.'

'Maybe you'll be the one to need it now, with your leg
and all,' he said, not meaning to be impertinent. I felt like
giving up there and then.

'Maybe I will need it, and then she can use it afterwards.
But the long and short is that I am trapped here in hospital,

and my house is likely to be looted. I need you to get the money and bring it here to me. I will give you some of the money for your trouble.'

He looked at me, sucking in his lips. 'How much?'

'Ten shillings,' I said in a final way.

'Righty-ho,' he sniffed, wiping his nose with his shirt sleeve. 'Where is it then?'

I stalled, asking him to fetch some water for me. His easy attitude unsettled me. He was fine with ten shillings now, but once he saw the thick wodge he'd change his tune as quick as a jackrabbit. Would I even see the money again? His lack of haggling made me doubt him.

'Here you are, missus.' He handed me the water. Perhaps I'd got him wrong. Perhaps he was just a simple child who wanted to help.

I didn't have many options, dear sister. The money may have already gone, or been burnt to ashes. This was the only possible means I had of reclaiming it. It was my only hope.

'All right then. Listen carefully.' He bent his head closer, and I explained where the money was hidden, making sure that he understood that the bomb damage may have shifted the floor or the money to another place. He was to leave no brick unturned.

'I'll do my best,' he said with a lopsided, crooked-toothed smile, and my heart sank. What has the world come to?

And so I will keep you informed as to how it goes. He promised to return as soon as he finds it, and in the meantime I can only lie here and hope.

Edwina

Letter from Venetia Winthrop
to Angela Quail

Chilbury Manor
Chilbury
Kent

Tuesday, 6th August, 1940

Dear Angela,

You wouldn't believe what mayhem and sadness has been
going on since the bomb. I am shattered even thinking
about it and try to stay in my room resting as much as I
can, although I did make it to Hattie's funeral, which was
heartrending. I still can't quite believe she's gone. We've
been friends since we were born, together as babies, then
little girls, teenagers, and now grown women. Or rather,
now just one woman – me. It's as if a whole chunk of my
past life has been obliterated.

I'm still very weak. Mrs Tilling comes to see me every
day to tut over me as she doesn't think I'm making
enough progress. Mama has been wonderful, helping me
through with lots of soup and good food. I worry that she
has been giving me her rations, and Kitty's too, probably,
as I've had eggs every day and bacon at least three times

this week. My father is furious with Mama for being so nice to me but has stayed away, for which I can only be grateful. I think he's playing a waiting game, lurking quietly in the wings until I become well enough to deal with his wrath.

He expects me to marry someone else quickly so that I can pretend that the baby is my new husband's — by which we all mean Henry, even though no one's saying it. Sweep it under the rug once and for all. It never dawns on him that I might not want to marry anyone else. I just want Alastair back. I keep wondering if he's out there somewhere, and if he is, why he's not coming back to me. I imagine him walking through the door, putting his arms around me as if nothing happened. I know I should be loathing him right now, but I can't. I feel that I love him even more, with every ounce of strength I can muster. It's as if the bombs have made everything transparently clear: now all I want is him.

But it's been five days since the bombs, and with every day the chance that he is alive gets slimmer, as where might he be otherwise? There are three things that would account for his disappearance, none of them good. The first is that he was shot in the woods, either by my father or by a member of his underworld, and now lies dead in a ditch, and the second is that he was bombed in his house, although they tell me that no remains were found in the wreckage. The third option is that he left the village that evening, after our argument, and has not returned.

I wear his St Christopher every day, slipping the tiny sliver beneath the front of my dress so that no one can see.

It makes me think he is out there somewhere, thinking of me, whether it's here on earth or from some kind of heaven, looking down on me.

Meanwhile, Henry was back for Hattie's funeral and came to see me this afternoon. I'd seen him after the funeral, of course, where we spoke about Hattie, and I must confess it was rather nice to have him there, another one of our old childhood gang. He is so gentle these days. It's hard not to warm to him. Although he seems less keen than he was in the spring, and I wondered how much he'd been told about Alastair. Mrs B is such a belligerent gossip, although I'm sure she doesn't know the intimate details of what happened between Alastair and me. Henry's bound to disapprove of me spending time with him, but obviously he'd never show it.

Mama begged me to come downstairs to see Henry, and I leant on her arm as she brought me into the drawing room, which seemed so light and airy and formal compared to my little room. She'd opened the door to the patio, and a fresh scent of grass cuttings wafted in with a cool breeze. The sunlight reflected in the great silver mirror above the fireplace, and shimmered around the pale walls and furnishings, and I wondered how lovely it would be to live in a past era, one where people were civil and poised, one where everything made sense. One where innocent people didn't get killed by bombs, or vanish into thin air.

'Henry,' I said carefully, giving him my hand to shake and sitting on the taut grey sofa. I felt rather nervous for some reason, and had put on some lipstick and brushed my hair. He was looking excessively proper and respectable with his uniform so tidy, his handshake so measured.

'Hello, Venetia,' he said, smiling into my eyes. 'Wonderful to see you.' He glanced around the room, selected a sofa opposite me, and sat down, taking off his hat and placing it on the seat next to him. 'I heard that you're quite the hero in these parts.'

'So they say.' I laughed a little with embarrassment. 'It was rather stupid actually, running into an exploding building.'

'But it was terribly brave of you. Not everyone would have risked their own life so readily. People are saying how well you did, with your wounds and so forth.'

I flinched at the 'and so forth', wondering if for some mad reason he knew about the pregnancy. No, of course he doesn't. Not even Alastair knows about the pregnancy. I saw him register my movement and hastily pulled myself together.

'A lot of fuss, that's all,' I smiled, trying to find another topic of conversation. 'And you too. Mrs B tells us you're to get a medal.'

'Well, Mama has a lot of notions, and I'm not sure if I'll get a medal, but I have been shooting a lot of the enemy down, which is the main thing.'

'We owe so much to you pilots, fighting back against the Nazis. They would have invaded by now if you hadn't frightened them off.' I was trying to sound bold and strong, but the words came tumbling out all smattered with potholes.

I could see him taking in my attempts to be normal, as if I were less beautiful, more unkempt. As if he was thinking about how much I'd changed. And I *have* changed. But somehow I didn't want him to think that. I wanted him to think I was exactly the same.

'I'm looking a bit of a mess, I'm afraid,' I said, tossing my hair back as I would usually, putting more of a swing into my voice. 'I haven't been so well since the air raid.'

'Yes, I heard,' he said warmly. 'I hope I'm not putting you out, getting you up like this?'

'No, it's nice to see you. In any case, you'll be gone in a few days, and I wouldn't want to miss you.'

'It's funny being back, after all that's happened. The air raid, Prim and Hattie, the disappearance of that fellow, what was his name again?' He stood up and went to the mantelpiece, interested in the craftsmanship as he ran his fingers over the elaborate white edging.

'Slater,' I said quickly, trying not to put any inflection on the name. 'Mr Slater. No one knows what's happened to him.'

'I heard that you were going to his house the night of the raid.' He didn't turn around, just continued studying the mantelpiece. 'I wondered if you were having a liaison of sorts.'

'Well, I was, as a matter of fact,' I said boldly. I could hardly lie when it was now common knowledge, but I confess I really didn't care to discuss this with Henry. I didn't want him to know. It wasn't his business, and I somehow didn't think it would be useful. 'But it wasn't a big thing. Just a spot of fun.'

'Oh, I see.' He turned and looked at me, straight in the eyes. 'I wondered, that's all.' He walked towards me and sat down beside me on the sofa. A worried look had come over his face. 'Are you all right, Venetia? I mean, are you really all right? Deep down inside?'

I nearly burst out crying.

Of course I'm not all right. The man I love has gone, and I have his child growing inside me. I'm scared to death I'll lose the baby, and I try to stay in bed all day. I'm petrified of what's going to happen.

'I'm fine,' I said quietly, rearranging my skirt on my lap. 'Really, I'm fine.'

'You just look so different, not the same Venetia as you were. You seem, well' – he paused in thought – 'lost.'

I had to get up. Being so close and him being so terrifically frank with me was all too much. It would be too easy for me to cry my eyes out on his shoulder. We've known each other since we were children. He is one of my best friends, but I know that revealing everything would do me no favours. I walked over to the piano and began straightening out the music, which was all higgledy-piggledy on top.

'I lost a lot of blood, that's all. It's been rather exhausting frankly.'

'Yes,' he said, but he seemed to be dwelling on something quite different. 'What can one do?' Our eyes met, and I know he was trying to read me, trying to get inside. He must have seen me let my guard down, as he got up swiftly and took a step towards me.

'Venetia.'

I don't know if he was coming to take me in his arms or kiss me or just to be close, but I stepped back, keeping him away.

'How awful of me not to offer you tea.' I darted for the door. As I left, I registered his disappointment – or was it annoyance – at my escape, and remembered uneasily that I had been encouraging him the few times we'd last met. An awful vision of David's leaving party scorched through my head. Why had I played those ridiculous games with him?

When I returned some minutes later, he was standing by the patio door looking down over the yellowing lawn, the unpruned roses, the fountain turned off to save water. He had changed his tone completely, becoming charming and impersonal, an RAF pilot on a jaunt, keeping his buddies up to date with amusing stories. He's so terribly witty these days, getting me laughing about some prank his friend got up to asking too many girls out at the same time. I know the pilots are incredibly popular with the girls, and I imagine he has more than his fair share with his amiable bonhomie, but I somehow missed that tense moment from before, and tried in vain to recapture it, but he resolutely kept up his light and impersonal banter.

That is, until he left. I had walked him to the front door, and we stood together on the brink, the sky fading to a darker shade of its former brilliance, the sound of a barn owl piercing through the still air from the wood. He turned to me, his eyes boring into me again, his hand reaching out for mine.

'I hate to leave you like this, Venetia. Please let me help you.' He kissed my hand in an old-fashioned way, his eyes flickering up to meet mine for an intense moment, before he smiled, said goodbye, and turned down the path. I leant on the door frame and watched the back of him as he walked away into the late-afternoon haze. He looked so very manly in his uniform, all rational and not losing his head. It was hard to remember the boy he had once been, the time we had kissed by the river when we were both about fourteen. Of course it was forgotten quickly, and we never spoke about it again, but as I stood there watching him walk away, I wondered what it would be like to be Henry's wife. Perhaps not so very bad after all.

I spent the rest of the night thinking long and hard about Alastair. Where has he gone? Why did he leave me? Even though he didn't know about the baby, what about his love for me? Did I mean so little to him that he could just leave? And what if he was lost in the flames, or killed by Daddy or any number of spies or black marketeers? Or on the run from the police or the army or the intelligence service? What had I been thinking to fall in love with such a man?

And yet, when I recall the passion, the poetry—

But where has it gone, Angie? Where has *he* gone? How could he desert me when I need him most?

I began to look at it practically. If he is in hiding, or has vanished to a new safe haven, then he doesn't care for me, and I have to get on as well as I can by myself, and if he is dead, well, I need to get on too. Whichever way it is, I can't sit here in my room and wait for him to return. I have a baby growing inside me. Soon it will be too late for me to deal with this.

Tonight I took off the St Christopher and felt its lightness in my palm, and then I looked out of my open window into the night and prayed on the first star that I saw, willing him to come back with all my might.

And so, dear Angie, it is with a heavy heart that I go to bed tonight. Perhaps tomorrow will come and he will be at my door, although as every day passes that chance seems to get smaller and smaller, like a distant star gradually dying to a tiny, unfathomable glimmer of a memory.

I will write again soon,
Venetia

Mrs Tilling's Journal

❧

Thursday, 8th August, 1940

I have taken to going round to Chilbury Manor every morning to see Venetia. She is not at all well, still terrifically pale and weak from the blood loss. Anyone can see she's heartbroken. She hardly says a word without crying, and turns away most food, although Mrs Winthrop is turning the county over to get her favourite meats and fruits. I worry that she will lose the pregnancy, although I sometimes wonder whether – well, I expect we shall see how things work out.

Mrs Winthrop had a word with me as I left today, telling me that Henry had been to see Venetia. He is on leave and, with the RAF out every day fighting and fatalities growing, I can only imagine his purpose.

'Did he ask her to marry him?' I asked.

'No, but I think he may do so. Obviously he knows little about Slater, and nothing about the baby.'

'Will she accept?'

'I'm not sure.' She looked at me long and hard. 'She knows she's in a bind. She swears that Slater loves her, but where the devil is he?'

Back at home that evening, after we'd finished dinner and washed the dishes, I came to sit in the front room with the

Colonel for a cup of tea while he was reading the paper. I sat close to him, waiting for him to pause so that I could talk. In the end he smiled and looked up.

'I know you're watching me.' He laughed gently. 'What is it that you want?'

'I need to ask you a question,' I said, thinking it best to be direct as possible. 'I need to know about Mr Slater. I have a feeling that you know what happened to him.'

He glanced over the paper at me, then turned the page noisily, making a big deal about folding the pages straight. 'Now you know I can't tell you that kind of thing, Mrs Tilling,' he said calmly.

'Yes, but I really wonder if you might be able to break that, just this once, just a little. You see, there's a young woman who is completely heartbroken on his account, and she is now on the brink of accepting an engagement from another.' I paused, wondering how I could put it to best effect. 'I know you can't tell me, but if you could perhaps give me some small indication as to whether he is alive, that would be very helpful.'

'Well, I can't, I'm afraid.' He went back to studying his paper as if completely absorbed.

'Or perhaps you could simply turn the page of the newspaper if he is alive.' It was a chance. I was desperate.

He sat contemplating this for a few minutes, then turned the page of his paper.

'And is he in prison, or in some way unable to get to her?'

This time the page turned quickly, his eyes still glued to the text.

'So she shouldn't be marrying this other chap, then?'

At this he pulled the newspaper down onto his lap and looked straight at me. 'If Slater is alive, it's because he is lucky. One day he will die, or land up in some prison some-where. She stands a better chance at happiness with this other fellow, if you ask me.'

'But she's not in love with him. She's in love with Slater.'

'Well, it stands against all reason. He's not the type of fellow one should fall in love with.' He pulled up the news-paper again, giving it a hard shake to straighten the pages, then resumed his reading.

'We can't all choose who we fall in love with,' I said, rather annoyed at his insensitivity.

He pulled down the paper and looked at me for a moment, suddenly thoughtful, then replied, 'You're right.'

I poured out the tea. 'So should I tell her to wait for him?'

'That depends on how much time she has,' he said quietly, then added as an afterthought, 'And how much pain she'll go through when he puts his life at risk again and again and again, until he finally loses it.'

And that's all I could get out of him. He utterly refused to tell me anything else, even though I tried my most conniving methods. What a stubborn man!

I began pondering other ways I could find out more about Slater, and remembered Carrington, who also works in that department now. Perhaps he could find out about Slater for me. He of all people would know that I'm trustworthy.

I called his number, even though it was getting late.

'Parnham House,' pronounced the officious tones of the butler.

'I'd like to speak to Lt Carrington, please,' I said, trying to keep my voice confident and firm.

'He is not available.'

'It is a bit of an emergency,' I said quickly.

There was a pause and a small cough. 'I shall enquire. Whom shall I say is calling?'

'Mrs Margaret Tilling, from Chilbury.'

A minute later I heard the soft upper-class tones of Carrington, whispering in the echoey room. 'Hello there.' He seemed pleased to speak to me, which was a good sign. 'Hope you survived the Chilbury bombs all right?'

'I did, but a friend of mine is in a spot of trouble. It is a matter of the heart. I was wondering if you could use your connections at Litchfield Park to find out about someone?'

'I'll try,' he said quickly. 'I can't promise anything. Who is the person?'

'A Mr Alastair Slater. Could be a black marketeer, could be caught and in prison, could be dead, but almost certainly is known by your lot. I just wanted to know his story. Whether my friend should hold out for him or not.'

'Yes, quite agree. I'll be on to it straightaway,' he said cheerfully, obviously disguising the nature of our conversation. Then he paused, and I heard voices in the background. 'Look here,' he whispered. 'I'm afraid I have to leave now, but I know what you're after and I'll ask a few questions and telephone if I find anything. Cheerio.' And he was off the line.

The Colonel came downstairs and eyed me suspiciously, so I picked up my duster and gave the telephone a quick dust, beaming a cheerful little smile at him.

Kitty Winthrop's Diary

❋

Thursday, 8th August, 1940

The money

This morning, Silvie and I went to have a look at the massive pile of broken buildings in the village square. Lots of people have started digging through it, some helpfully trying to find the things of the people who lived there, but most are looters, stealing anything they can find.

Much to our surprise, we found Tom there. Hands on hips, he was standing on top of a heap of debris, dirty as a bandit.

'I'm trying to find an envelope of money,' he said in hushed tones as we climbed up beside him. 'Miss Paltry asked me to find it for her. She said she hid it under her floorboards.'

'Well, you're looking in the wrong place,' I told him sternly. 'Miss Paltry's house was next to Hattie's, over here.'

I led him to the right spot, and then we climbed around and started looking for the envelope. I was longing to find it so that I could be a hero like Venetia. And finally I did, holding it high in the air and calling over to Tom, 'Here it is!'

Of course, everyone looked around, some coming forward to see.

Ralph Gibbs was there, watching the fat envelope. 'Do you know how much money is in there?'

'Don't know,' Tom said, and much to my annoyance, he snatched it away and shoved it down the front of his shorts, of all the horrid places. 'Come on, Kitty. Let's go.'

'But I'm the new hero!'

He grabbed my hand rather roughly and dragged me away, Silvie running behind.

We sprinted down the lane and across the fields to the hop pickers' huts, dashing into Tom's and shutting the door behind us. Laughing, we opened the envelope and took out all the money.

All the money!

There was so much of it! 'Where did she get it from?'

'I don't know,' Tom whispered.

'Come on, let's have a party,' I said, getting to my feet. 'I'll go and see if the farmhands in the barn have some biscuits or milk.'

'I'll come too,' Tom said. 'Look after the money, Silvie.'

Off we ran, Tom beating me by a fraction, although I hadn't been racing at all. But the place was deserted, and after a spot of searching we quickly realised there wasn't anything to be had.

I was just checking one last corner, when Tom decided to grab me around the waist, pulling me to him, and planting a rather soggy kiss right on my lips.

'Stop, stop!' I yelled, thrusting him away. 'Don't you know I'm engaged to be married?'

'No, are you?' He laughed in a disbelieving way, wiping his mouth.

Silvie was suddenly there, innocently enquiring, 'What are you doing?'

'Nothing, Silvie.' I took her arm and walked to the door. 'We couldn't find any biscuits, so we'll have to go without, won't we, Tom?'

He came up beside us and took my other arm, grinning in an annoying way, and we strode back to the huts.

When we got back, Tom's door was hanging open, squeaking as it swung to and fro.

'Silvie, did you bring the envelope?' Tom said.

She shook her head, unable to speak.

We ran inside to check for the money, but I think we already knew.

It was gone.

There was no sign of anyone, but we looked at each other, knowing who must have followed us. Silvie and I went sulkily back home, leaving Tom to work out what he was going to say to Miss Paltry.

'Well, at least it wasn't our money,' I said as we rounded the wood.

'Why didn't you kiss Tom?' Silvie asked. 'He's nice.'

I stopped dead in my tracks. 'I am engaged to Henry, Silvie. I can't go around kissing hop picker boys, can I?'

How could she possibly think otherwise?

Letter from Venetia Winthrop to Angela Quail

Chilbury Manor
Chilbury
Kent

Thursday, 8th August, 1940

Dear Angela,

A dull feeling of dread lurched in the pit of my stomach when I woke up this morning, as if I knew how the day would evolve, what events would take place, what decisions would be made.

The doorbell rang at ten, and I wasn't surprised when Mama knocked on my door to tell me that Henry had come again. I knew straightaway that I wanted everything to be different from yesterday. I didn't want his sympathy or his comments on me looking, how did he put it, 'lost'. So I put on my yellow sundress to make me look more cheerful and brushed my hair until it shone golden. I wanted him to treat me the same as he'd always done, as if nothing had changed. As if everything were exactly the same as it had been six months ago, and I was the undisputed empress of the village.

I looked at myself in the mirror and put on my old red lipstick, feeling encouraged by the transformation. Isn't it extraordinary how one can look like an empress yet feel like a frail shadow?

He was sitting on the same sofa as the other day, immaculate in his uniform. I tried to make an entrance, like I would have done before all of this, swinging my yellow skirt so that it cascaded around the door frame, raising my hand alluringly up to my hair, jeering loudly, 'Oh, Henry. I see you simply couldn't stay away.'

But it all felt a little flat and overrehearsed.

He stood up and stiffened, although still smiling in a polite way. Henry is always polite – I can't work out whether it's adorable or tedious. I stopped swishing my skirts and struggled to work out what my approach should be. I was self-conscious, wanting him to adore me as he always has done, yet not really wanting him to. I'm sorry if this doesn't make sense, Angie. I confess it doesn't make a lot of sense to me either. I really don't know what to think any more.

'How are you today?' he asked, coming and taking my arm and leading me over to a chair, as if I were an invalid.

'I'm fine, Henry,' I muttered, lifting his hand away and standing beside the sofa. 'Look, let's please not talk about me today. I'd much rather hear about you and your plane and how many dogfights you've won.' I looked up at him beseechingly, and he gazed at me for a moment, and then he smiled gently, tilting his head slightly to one side.

Then he lowered himself down on one knee.

I froze. I'm not exactly sure what I had been expecting from this meeting, and I knew that Daddy felt certain that

Henry would come running if only I said the word, but I didn't feel so sure any more. I didn't feel so sure about anything. Why would I be suddenly interested in his marriage proposal had not something happened that had made me more eager, more in need of it? Why did he suddenly think he stood a chance?

Was he walking the tightrope between being the best of friends, helping in a bad time, offering support and love, or being a man who sees an opportunity, a weakness, and seizes the moment?

'Venetia, my darling,' he said, taking my hands in his, pressing them lightly, with the merest suggestion of urgency. 'Please let me take you away from this, and encompass you with all the love and happiness that I have in my heart.' He smiled in such a wonderful warm way, his eyes caressing mine with hope and happiness. My eyes began to water, and a tear spilled out and down my cheek. *If only I could love this man*, I thought. If only I'd never met Alastair, never known what real love was. But then I wouldn't be in the state I was in now. I'd be the old Venetia, and there's no damn way I'd be settling for Henry Brampton-Boyd.

'Will you do me the honour, Venetia, of accepting my hand in marriage?' he asked in a half whisper, taking my hands to his lips. 'I have a wonderful life to offer you, with the heavenly Brampton Hall, a very comfortable living, and, not least I hope, my very dear and enduring love for you.'

A series of pictures flickered through my mind in quick succession: a heavily pregnant shadow being hidden away in her parents' house and then swept into a nasty nunnery, her beloved baby snatched from her grasping arms, never to be seen again. I couldn't bear the thought of giving up my baby. I knew that this was my alternative. I was being given a way out, a brutal compromise between two sacrifices, and I knew how I had to act.

'Yes,' I uttered, hearing my words as if spoken by another, more practical Venetia, a Venetia who wanted an easy life, with wealth and status and legitimate children, living in the grand Brampton Hall in the style to which she had grown accustomed. A Venetia who always looked at her eldest child with regret and guilt sliding uncomfortably together in a swell of discontentment.

Could this Venetia be me?

I took my hands away and sat down, using all my force to stop myself from crying, steadily putting a smile on my face, keeping my chin up, facing the music. And I realised that this is what it's like to be an adult, learning to pick from a lot of bad choices and do the best you can with that dreadful compromise. Learning to smile, to put your best foot forward, when the world around you seems to have collapsed in its entirety, become a place of isolation, a sepia photograph of its former illusion.

I stiffened as he sat down on the sofa beside me. Shifting over a fraction, I rearranged my yellow skirt, scared of what was coming next.

I saw his face come towards mine and worked hard to prevent myself from shrinking away. He gently placed his lips on mine and – although the world didn't stop turning – it was not unpleasant. He has vastly improved his kissing since the orchard experience, which had been rather wet and gagging. It was a gentle kiss, no pressure, no passion, nothing like the kisses I shared with Alastair, which were torrid, fervent episodes. It couldn't have been more different.

'My love,' he said, and it sounded so odd coming from his lips. 'This is the happiest day of my life.' He smiled and looked sincerely overjoyed. I managed to smile, trying to mirror his joy in my face and my bearing. It was extremely awkward.

'We will need to set the date soon,' he whispered, leaning into my ear, kissing my neck, my throat. 'I don't know how long I can bear the wait.'

'No, let's not wait too long.' I agreed with frail enthusiasm, wondering how long I could hide the pregnancy. 'The sooner the better.'

'So, we're agreed!' he exclaimed, slapping his hands on his knees with pleasure. 'I will tell my Group Captain as soon as I return to base. They should be able to give me a few days off later in the month.' He took my hand and brought it to his lips, kissing first the back of my hand and then turning it over, opening up my fingers, and kissing inside.

The room was closing in on me, clammy and stifling, and I felt like leaping up, throwing open the veranda doors, and letting myself run, run, down the lawn, escaping down into the valley like a wild horse, and on, on, forever. And I knew that it would always be that way. I would spend the rest of my life running.

'Let's tell Mama,' I cried, snatching my hand back and heading for the door. 'I can't wait to see her face.'

I strode out into the hall, and he followed me as I went up the grand staircase, clutching the sweeping banister with every step, desperate for some kind of reprieve.

We found Mama in the nursery with Silvie, helping her mend a doll's dress, carefully showing her how to backstitch to make it stronger, the way she had with Kitty and me when we were girls. So very long ago.

'Mama,' I called, breathless from the door. 'We are to be married.'

She got up, a look of panic quickly turning into a smile as Henry came in beside me. 'Oh! That's good!' she said, rushing to open a window and letting in a fresh breeze. She took a great breath of air, then turned and came over to give Henry a kiss on the cheek. 'I'm so very pleased.' She looked me straight in the eyes, only seven or eight inches from mine, and her mouth said, 'I'm sure you'll be the talk of the village', but her eyes looked as if they were about to be crushed by a ton of black, heavy coal. I know she's never been happy with Daddy, was forced to marry him for the sake of her family. The weight of all those years was packed into that look. She wanted me to do the right thing, but she couldn't help but think of herself, the loveless, persecuted life she'd led.

She looked back round to Silvie, her new protégée, and then she said to Henry, 'You must go straight away and tell your mother. She'll be furious if she finds out she wasn't the first to know! Venetia, you must stay here and discuss plans.'

'You're right, she'll be livid. You know how she is!' he chortled in his good-humoured way, and I found myself already disliking him. 'So, my darling.' He took my hand again. 'I'll bid you goodbye and come again this afternoon. Maybe we can go for a long walk together and make some plans, the wedding, the honeymoon.' His eyes sparkled, darting uncontrollably over my body.

He disappeared out with alacrity, and we stood in silence listening to his footsteps down the marble stairs, echoing through the hallway, and then the massive dull clunk of the front door being slammed. Then silence.

I crumpled. Mama helped me to the nursing chair, and Silvie was sent out to get some tea.

'I had to do it, Mama,' I whimpered. 'You know I did.'

She didn't say anything, just a long, quiet 'Shhhhhh', as if she had learnt that the troubles of the world could be absorbed and deafened out by slow, steady wishfulness, and I suddenly understood that she'd been silencing out the noise for the past twenty years.

Silvie returned with some tea, and we sipped quietly, talking about how things were going to be. Weddings happen with great pace these days, which one must see as a blessing under the circumstances, although we exchanged withering looks at the prospect that it might even be as soon as next week.

'Of course, you may wish to, well, consummate the marriage before the event, so to speak,' Mama said in a bit of a hurry, rather embarrassed. I must have looked at her as if she'd lost her mind, as she quickly added, 'So that he doesn't doubt the parentage of the baby.' She smiled at Silvie, who was looking especially alert, and I couldn't believe that either of them was keeping up the ridiculous charade that Silvie doesn't know exactly what's going on, and how it had come about.

After a while I dragged myself out of the comfort of the nursery and headed down to my room, where you find me now. My mind is going round in circles: Why am I here, what was I thinking, why is this the best choice, surely there are alternatives, and where is he? Where is Alastair? Doesn't he hear my pain expanding exponentially through the universe, covering multitudes of galaxies with a never-ending scream?

Where *is* he?

I sat at my dressing table and took out the pendant, wishing on it that he would arrive, like a knight in shining armour, and whisk me away. Or that I would wake up and find it was all a horrid dream, happening to a different Venetia, on a different planet, somewhere high, high above us in the brutal, dispassionate universe.

I will write soon.

Much love,
Venetia

Letter from Miss Edwina Paltry
to her sister, Clara

Litchfield Hospital
Litchfield
Kent

Thursday, 8th August, 1940

Dear Clara,

What a day! First of all, the stupid boy came in to tell me
he lost my money. I cannot believe I entrusted my fortune
to such an incompetent idiot. He found it, took it to his hut,
and then someone ruddy well stole it. He thinks it was
Ralph Gibbs, so I'll be having words with him when I'm
out of this place.

Next, there I was, lying in the lumpy hospital bed, when
in jaunts the Tilling woman, her beady eyes on me as she
strode down the ward, a bright and shiny new look of
determination about her. She was all fitted and buttoned up
in a navy-blue coat I'd never seen on her before – a far cry
from the baggy old grey thing she usually wears – and
carrying a brown leather handbag that looked like it could
give someone a nasty bruise if she took a good swing
at them.

'Enjoying your break?' she chirped in her singsong way, putting on a forced, unfriendly smile, the one you might see on a magistrate's face just before he finds you guilty. 'Nice to put your feet up, isn't it?' She patted my leg, and I winced at the thought of how much pain she could inflict should the mood take her. I thanked the Lord that she was such a wimp, although I have to say that she's not the downtrodden widow any longer. This war has given her a real boost. You can tell by the way she holds herself, more upright now, none of the slouching shoulders and moping face. Where once she was always running little steps to keep up, now there's a purpose to her stride, like she's more worthy than the rest of us, doing more, giving up more for this war, for our community. And we'd better show a little respect.

'Ah, Mrs Tilling, what a lovely surprise!' I pulled out my syrupy smile. 'How good of you to visit poor little me, wrecked up in hospital. I was just thinking that you were the only person decent and kind enough to come.'

'Well,' she sighed. 'I actually came to ask you a few questions about the day the two babies were born.'

I kept a calm smile glued on my face, but I never dreamt she'd jump to the chase like that. 'I'll be glad to help you there. Quite a day it was!' I took a sip of water from the glass beside my bed for sustenance.

She pulled up a chair, sitting her narrow behind on the edge.

'I've been thinking,' she began in an ominously lowered voice, 'how strange it was that both babies appear to have had the same breathing problem that required resuscitation, at your house, no less.'

'Yes, it was a very trying day, but one has to do one's best. You see, these things are a lot more common than you think. It was fortunate I had the correct apparatus. It's incredible how ten years of experience can mean the difference between life and' — a pause, creasing up my eyes for effect — 'death.'

'How very fortunate that you were there,' she said, raising a skinny eyebrow. 'Although perhaps if you hadn't been, the babies would have stayed with their rightful mothers.'

All I could think was, *We're done for!*

But then a nauseating little smile touched her lips, and I could see that she thought she'd won, and of all the things I am, Clara, I am not a loser, so I pulled myself together and did a spot of clever thinking. For her to just come out and say it means she thinks she can scare me into an admission, and she ain't getting no admission out of me, no matter how close to the truth she gets.

'What can you mean?' I smiled.

'Only that having both the babies in your house at the same time would have made it possible for you to have swapped them. You could have given the boy baby to Mrs Winthrop, and the girl to Hattie.'

'What a preposterous suggestion,' I sputtered, feeling my voice cracking a little. I decided to try to laugh it off, make her sound like the crazy one. 'How could you dream up such a monstrous idea, Mrs Tilling? Have you lost your mind?' I shook my head in a disgusted way.

'I didn't dream it up, Miss Paltry.' She looked directly into my eyes, her voice calm and collected, a judge revealing the final sentence. 'The facts led me to believe it to be true.'

I took a deep breath, searching for some facts of my own. Then I remembered. 'Both of the mothers already knew the sex of their babies before I took them away. They'd been delighted. I'd been so pleased. Why would I have needed to do such a terrible thing?'

'Neither of the women actually saw her child close up before you whisked it away, Miss Paltry.' Her voice was mellowing, like an overripe plum, lowering in tone, gaining confidence. 'Both told me that the only reason they knew the sex of their baby was because you had announced it.'

'Oh now, don't be putting ideas together from different stories. I know you're just upset because you weren't there, but it can't be helped.'

She leant forward and her eyes bored into me, and that's when she came out with the one thing I would never have imagined she knew. 'You made a deal with the Brigadier, didn't you?'

I was scared. If she knew the Brigadier was involved, and let him know that she knew, then I'd be dead meat. 'What are you talking about?'

'I know you met him the night of the bomb, and I have a good idea of the information you were attempting to sell.'

I gazed up at her with shock. How could she have known that? There'd been no one around. I swear on it. Just me and the Brigadier, alone. 'We just happened to cross paths. Had a chat about the trains. The delays are appalling—'

'Wasn't it a little late for you to be catching a train?'

Something inside me snapped. What right had this stupid woman to walk in here and pester me with accusations? In any case, my nicey-nicey approach wasn't getting me anywhere. I was just a sitting duck for her. I needed to get her out of here.

'I can catch a train whenever I like, Mrs Tilling.' I glowered, my voice rising. I sat up more straight, adjusting my leg on the bed. 'How dare you come in here and start accusing me of these ridiculous crimes. How dare you, of all people a nurse! You should know to let a convalescing person stay quiet and calm.'

She sat poised, watching my gathering annoyance, a serene calm on her face.

'It was the moment I saw Venetia with baby Rose in her arms that I knew,' she said, showing off how clever she'd been to work it all out, just like bleeding Miss Marple. 'The baby looked so very much like her. Venetia could have been her mother.' She looked at me, an eyebrow tentatively raised. 'Or her sister.'

God damn that baby, and that wretched girl. If she weren't so beautiful no one would have noticed a thing. I felt trapped, like a weasel in a poke hole.

With a sudden burst of ingenuity, I knew exactly how I could smash her little intimidation to smithereens. I reached for the glass jug next to my bed and shouted as loud as I could, 'Nurse! Nurse!' And with a tiny laugh, I let the jug slip from my fingers, sending it tumbling to the cold, tiled floor.

A colossal crash broke the silence as a thousand splinters of glass soared into the air before cascading down, silvering the floor, the beds, the furniture with a delicate crust of icy glitter.

It would take hours to clean.

The nurses came rushing over, dashing here and there with brooms and mops, moving Mrs Tilling out of the way, taking the chair, changing my blankets, reassuring me that everything was going to be all right.

I tried to look dishevelled and innocent, nodding to the nurses apologetically. When I peeked over to Mrs Tilling, she was standing away from the bed, hands clasping her bag, fury on her frowning face. She remained smouldering from afar, until a nurse went and had a word with her, fetched her navy coat, and led her to the door. Her long face turned to me as she was marched off, annoyance in her eyes and perhaps a ghost of the Mrs Tilling of old, being pushed and shoved around again. Only this time she wasn't happy about it. She wanted her own way now. I felt a chill over the back of my neck as the door swung shut behind her.

But what will she do next? My first thought, of course, was that she could try to blackmail me, extract some kind of reward for her silence. Thing is, it's not the Tilling woman's style. She has enough money for her practical little lifestyle. She would be more likely to do something for morality or decency, or some equally nauseating reason. She has a sickening desire to be an upstanding member of the community, and this little victory could perch her on a new throne.

Of course there is a chance she could do us all an almighty big favour and let the whole thing go. Why should she bother taking it further, after all? She has no proof. Her precious Hattie is now dead. Mrs Winthrop is overjoyed with her boy. Swapping the babies back is not in anyone's interest. It would just break up their little community and cause more trouble than it's worth. Everyone would hate her. She's not such a fool that she doesn't know that.

Which brings me to my final, most alarming outcome. She might go and blab to the Brigadier, tell him I betrayed him, use it to get power in this little place.

And the Brigadier will come in here and break my bleeding neck, as he promised to do if anyone found out. Lord, I feel like a trapped fox with the hounds circling.

I made sure they moved my bed next to the nurse to be on the safe side, and just as I was settling in, who should walk in but Elsie. All fancy in a green floral dress and looking pretty as a young swan, until she opened her gob.

'I heard it off Kitty that a lad was looking for your money.' She leaned close. 'And I know some of that is rightfully mine.'

'Don't threaten me, my girl,' I said. 'In any case, I ain't got no money. It's gone. It was found and then stolen. If you want money, you need to look elsewhere.'

She tidied her hair, preening. 'I've got that in mind too,' she said. 'Got a plan to get a rich husband. Need a little pocket money, see? Make myself look the lady.'

I gave a snort of a laugh. 'You'll have to do better than look good if you want to get a nob.'

'I'll show you,' she sniffed. 'But I need cash, and I know things about you that'll make you cough up.'

I was getting cross. 'Elsie, I haven't got any money to give you.'

'Well, where's the money gone then?'

'Tom thinks it was Ralph Gibbs, if you want to let him know I want it back.' I was angry now. 'It's my money and he ruddy well knows it.'

A thoughtful look came over her beautiful complexion, her lips twisted. 'Well, best be off then,' she said, a resolution clearly made, probably to go and snatch it off him herself. And with that she pranced out, a confident smirk on her wide mouth like she'd swallowed a toad.

I rolled my head back on the pillow and groaned. That's all I needed. Another person in search of my money as well as the Tilling woman and the Brigadier after me.

You'd better burn this letter, Clara, and the rest, in case the old you-know-who gets wind of it. You never know which walls have ears these days.

Edwina

Kitty Winthrop's Diary

Thursday, 8th August, 1940

What not to do

I heard about Venetia and Henry. Silvie told me, running up to the stables to find me.

'There's news,' she called as she saw me in the stable yard saddling up Amadeus, who started shuffling away nervously.

'What news?'

'Venetia is going to marry Henry,' she panted, coming up next to me, an intense expression on her face. 'She said yes!'

'What?'

'Henry asked Venetia to marry him, and she said yes,' she repeated, her face creased with worry.

'She can't,' I said matter-of-factly. 'She's pregnant with Slater's baby.'

'I know. That's why she's marrying him.'

'That's not fair!' I said, struggling with the enormity of it all. 'Poor Henry! Won't he find out? Won't it all have to be called off?'

'I don't know,' she answered, coming up beside me.

'But why would he ask her to marry him when he's engaged to marry me?'

'Maybe he forgot,' she said softly. 'He likes Venetia a lot, Kitty. He always wants to talk to her.'

I turned and screamed at her, 'You don't know what you're talking about.'

She ran, faster than I've ever seen her go, and I was left stroking Amadeus, convincing myself she was mistaken, that this was just some ludicrous joke.

'Come on, Amadeus,' I whispered into his neck. 'Let's go for a ride.'

Once I had climbed onto his back and sat above my surroundings, looking over the green-and-gold patchwork of countryside, I felt more at ease to consider the possibility of Silvie's news.

Reasons why Venetia can't marry Henry
She's in love with Mr Slater
She's pregnant with Mr Slater's baby
Henry's supposed to marry me

It simply wasn't the way things were meant to be. When I look into the future, I always see Henry and me, living at the Hall with four children, three cats, and a big dog called Mozart. I don't see Venetia there. She wouldn't suit living in Brampton Hall, I don't think she aims to have quite so many children, and she doesn't even like dogs, or Mozart.

It just wouldn't work.

I trotted Amadeus down the path and broke him into a racing gallop over the pasture. I wasn't really thinking about which way I was going, but it didn't surprise me when I found myself in front of Brampton Hall, the sprawling redbrick, Gothic-style mansion gleaming in the brilliant sunlight. It was built a few generations ago by the original Brampton trader who got rich in India. Now they're a grand local family, with Mrs B determined to make them even grander.

It was Henry himself who came to the door when I rang, looking rather flustered, and I remembered that all their servants had left.

'Henry.' I beamed.

'Kitty? Nice to see you.'

'I thought you might like to go for a walk?'

He glanced back into the house. 'All right. Let me just tell Mama.'

He left the door open and strode off.

I returned to Amadeus. 'You see, he's not engaged to Venetia. Silvie was wrong.'

He reappeared, and off we went, walking up the path to the lane, while he hastily buttoned his collar and smoothed his hair. I was on foot, running slightly to keep up with his long strides, Amadeus trotting beside me. We quickly reached the lane, with steep grassy banks up each side, and the sky blue and cloudless over us.

'I'm afraid I can't walk for long today, Kitty,' he started. 'You see, I have some wonderful news.'

'Oh, about the war?' I asked, feeling the earth beneath me uncertain, like a tremoring earthquake waiting to rupture open the ground.

'No.' He looked at me with a grin. 'I suppose I need not keep it from you, of all people. Venetia has made me the happiest man in the world by agreeing to marry me.'

I stopped, rooted to the spot, terrified. 'It's true,' I uttered, the sunshine piercing a blinding light into my eyes. 'It's true.'

'Yes.' He stopped and turned to me. 'Did you already hear about it? I say, are you all right, Kitty?'

I looked up at him. 'But we were supposed to be married, Henry,' I cried out. 'You said we would be married once I was old enough. You said so.' Tears had begun forming fat, pointless fingers of water that rushed down my cheeks.

Henry looked horrified. 'But, Kitty,' he said quietly. 'I never said that. When? Where?'

'By the river on the picnic to Box Hill. You said if I helped you find Venetia you'd marry me.'

'Did I really? What a dreadful thing to say. I'm so sorry, Kitty. It must have been a misunderstanding, or a joke, or, well, something.' He spread out his hands, and a short, embarrassed laugh escaped him. 'But now you'll be my sister, and I'll be your brother, and that'll be even better than being married, won't it?'

'No, it won't,' I shouted. 'I don't want you to be my stupid brother, even if you do end up marrying my sister, which I doubt very much.'

'What do you mean?'

'She's pregnant with Slater's baby,' I yelled into his face, spit flying out of my mouth with every word. He took a step back, his face empty, looking at me.

'Now, Kitty, you shouldn't joke about things like that.'

'Just go and ask her. She's in love with him. She wants his child. But he's disappeared. So she has to take you instead.'

His shoulders fell forward, and his eyes grew hollow, and like a mirror of horror, I saw my utter distress pass from me to him, coursing out of me like a thick jet of yellow and black and surging into his body with a flood of rage and despair.

He sat back on the grassy bank, his knees up before him, and his head in his hands, murmuring something to himself. I stood and watched him for a while, my hero deflating before my eyes, and I began to sense the enormity of what I had just done.

'Go away, Kitty,' he said, quietly, calmly, not looking up at me.

'Henry, I'm sorry, I—'

'I'll say thank you for telling me, and now leave.' He raised his head, his eyes suddenly angry and wild.

'But, Henry—'

'Stay away from me,' he snarled under his breath, getting up and standing above me. 'If I told you what I'd like to do with you right now, you'd wish you'd never met me. Now go. Leave.' He was shouting, threatening. I could never imagine he could be like this, his beautiful blue eyes turning black like a fury of snakes.

I grabbed hold of Amadeus's reins and ran, sobs heaving uncontrollably from my mouth, feeling like the end of the world had truly come.

Once I was back in the dark, shadowy stable, I laid an old horse blanket on the floor in the corner and curled up on it as tight as a shell. I stayed there sobbing, Amadeus nudging me with his soft nose in sympathy.

Why had I done this? Why had he done this?

A few hours later, I heard the sound of a small voice behind me. It was Silvie peering into the shadows.

'What do you want?' I demanded.

'I have sandwiches,' she said in her quiet voice.

'Put them on the bench outside.'

'Everyone is looking for you,' she said.

I didn't say anything, just let the words flow in and be absorbed. Of course Daddy will be furious. He wanted Venetia to marry Henry. It had all fit into place. Venetia staying in bed. Daddy trying to talk to her. Mama trying to negotiate. Venetia changing her mind about Henry and agreeing to marry him. Mama weeping late into the night. And next? Daddy will surely kill me, if Venetia doesn't get to me first.

'Thank you for the sandwiches,' I said quietly to Silvie, remembering she was now my only ally. She backed away into the dusk, unsure whether I was a wise choice of friend.

It was night before I went back to the house, cold and hungry, shivering with fear. The pantry door was left unlocked for me, and someone had left a roll in the bread bin. I scooped it up and crept up the back stairs into my bedroom, which is where you find me now, dear diary. The house is in silence. I had anticipated the family waiting for me, everyone shouting, everyone crying. But this, this stillness, is somehow more disturbing.

I think that tonight, when it's past midnight and everyone is asleep, I shall pack a few things together, and vanish.

Letter from Venetia Winthrop
to Angela Quail

Chilbury Manor
Chilbury
Kent

Thursday, 8th August, 1940

Dear Angela,

I write again, this time to tell you that the engagement is dramatically off. I can only thank God for a narrow escape – how was I to know that Henry Brampton-Boyd could be such a monster? I feel numb and exhausted, and the whole business has given me a fever. I am to stay in bed, which I confess I am more than happy to do.

It was with mixed feelings that I heard his arrival early afternoon. He hadn't been due to come back until late afternoon – Mama had insisted that I needed to rest, and I was looking forward to a chance to recover from the whole ordeal. But abruptly, at around one, I heard the bell pull hard, and then again, and the sound of raised voices rang through the hallway, my name being called, shouted.

I knew that something had happened. I knew he must have found out. I took a deep breath, smoothed down my

yellow dress and padded out onto the landing overlooking
the hall, where I could see him looking up at me, red-faced
and furious, his fists clenched, his fair hair dishevelled, his
uniform open at the neck, skewed and fraught.

'Venetia,' he yelled. I've never known Henry to be angry,
but not in a thousand years would I have imagined him as
ferocious, as crazed, as he was then. He's always been so
gentle, so dignified. It was like seeing a Labrador
transformed into a wolf.

I walked down the great staircase slowly, holding my
breath, praying for this encounter to be over quickly.

'I need to have a word with you, my girl,' he said under
his breath, grabbing my arm and dragging me into the
drawing room, where he closed the door so that Mama,
who had been hovering in the alcove, couldn't follow.
As it happened, it made no difference, as she could hear
every word out in the hallway. I never knew he could
raise his voice to such a level. The whole house vibrated
with his bellowing, the crystal chandeliers thrumming in
his wake.

'Now tell me,' he demanded, shoving me down on the
sofa, standing over me raging. 'Are you pregnant?'

I nodded slowly. To be honest, Angie, I was so done in by
the entire drama that I simply couldn't find the energy to
fight back. I was petrified of him, in a way I would never
have thought possible, and frankly overwhelmed with relief
that he was going to break it off. That I would be free,
whatever burdens I knew this would entail. I knew then, at
that moment, that I was strong enough to get through this,
with or without my family's support.

'Yes, Henry,' I said louder. 'I am.'

'What?' he roared, his whole face red and contorted with rage. 'You were going to marry me knowing that you had another man's child inside you?'

'I'm sorry, Henry. It was a mistake. I can see that now.'

'Did you really feel you could get away with this?' He stood over me, looking down threateningly.

'I don't know,' I said plainly, looking at my hands. 'I thought it would be for the best, but now I see I was wrong.'

'We could have been married! We could have gone for years without me ever knowing! I wonder when exactly someone might have informed me, had not Kitty told me this morning?'

'It was Kitty,' I said quietly. Of course it was Kitty. She's in love with him. She was using the only card she had left. Yet I couldn't help feeling rather pleased she did it. Proud of her almost, in an odd kind of way. Although this was probably due to my immense relief that *someone* told him and put an end to this dreadful charade. I can't believe I'd let myself think it was the best thing to do.

'Is that all you have to say? "Oh, it was Kitty!" As if you don't care at all?'

'I'm glad you know,' I said stiffly.

'Are you feeling some sense of remorse?' he said sarcastically. He sat beside me and leaned over, his face right in front of mine, threatening and vengeful. 'Did you discover that deep down you may even have a conscience?'

'I suppose I do,' I said uneasily. 'I felt that the whole thing was wrong.'

'Oh.' He stood up with a start. 'The lady realises that getting married while pregnant with another's child is

"wrong". Well, well, Venetia.' He laughed sarcastically.
'Now I think of it, that was half of your attraction: your
lack of conscience. Your complete, unremitting self-
absorption. I wonder now how I never saw through it
before. You're nothing but an empty shell, Venetia. A
beautiful girl without a soul.' He strode over to the veranda
doors, looked out over the fading wisteria and broken
cobbles, then added quietly, almost to himself, 'I'm glad I
finally see you as you really are.'

There was a gap, a silence, where I should have said
something, defended myself, apologised, soothed him. But I
didn't. Alastair had shown me that I was a flesh-and-blood
human, more than the façade Henry thought he knew.
Everything he said was irrelevant. He didn't know me now,
perhaps had never known me. I was only angry with myself
for agreeing to marry him in the first place, silently
wishing this entire ordeal were over. I was aching all over,
my head was throbbing, and I felt the chill of an invisible
wind whisking through the room behind my neck, under
my hair.

'But, Venetia!' He turned, his voice different, now
pleading, a sorrowful yearning. 'Why did you do this to
me? You know how much I love you. We've known each
other all our lives. Why did you do it?'

Waves of nausea began rippling over me. 'I thought it
might be all right, Henry. I never meant to hurt you. I
thought I was doing you a favour, marrying you – I know
you've always wanted that. I know it wasn't perfect, but I
thought I'd get over the past, begin again. I'd get pregnant
quickly, and no one would know the baby wasn't yours.
Lots of people do it.'

'But we aren't "lots of people",' he roared, storming towards me. 'I am an individual, Venetia. Sometimes I wonder if you've ever realised that.' He sat down on the sofa next to me. 'Look at me, Venetia. Take a good, long look at me.' His voice was firm, abrupt, and he looked straight into my eyes as I raised them to his. He looked different from every other time I'd seen him; open, alive, as if bringing everything he had left to this moment.

'Yes, I know,' I murmured. As his eyes met mine, they altered, relaxing, narrowing, his rage replaced by hunger.

'Venetia, I want you so badly. I almost wanted to ignore the baby and continue with the wedding. I tried to push it to the back of my mind, but I could never live with that. I hate Kitty for telling me. If she hadn't come and ruined it all, it would have been perfect. I would have been the happiest man on earth. You would have been mine.' His eyes swept down over my body, and his hand moved to my waist. 'You would have been mine,' he repeated, his hands moving fast, running up and down my side, his thick, clumsy fingers grappling over my thighs. I was calling for him to stop, trying to get his hands off me, but he carried on, yelling, 'Is this the kind of girl you are, Venetia? Is this what you like?'

I realised that I needed to get out, so I used all my force to push him away, standing up to flee from the room. Only he regained balance fast and strode after me, his hand slapping my face so hard that I fell to the floor with an almighty bang.

Then Mama was there, standing over me, screaming, 'What's going on? What on earth are you doing?'

He promptly stopped and began to smooth down his hair.

'I think you should leave now, Henry,' Mama said briskly, feeling my forehead and helping me up.

He pursed his lips in annoyance. 'Yes, I've had enough of her now,' he said with meaning, and strode out of the room haughtily.

Mama's sad eyes caught mine as we listened for the second time that day to his footsteps hard across the marble hall, the voice of the maid showing him out. The great thud as the front door slammed, sending a shower of tiny dust particles slowly rippling through the air like a vanished apparition being laid to rest.

I began to cry; the pain in my body was immense and my head was pounding. Mama helped me upstairs and I collapsed on the bed.

I slept for a while, and then I heard Daddy shouting downstairs. Mama, who was sitting beside my bed, quietly got up and turned the key in the door. I knew she was scared for me, far more scared than I was. He can come for all I care. I know that I can cope with his temper; I know I can cope with anything. I am completely numb.

And that's where you find me now, Angie, sitting in bed, trying to make head or tail of this whole miserable mess. Mama says I have a fever, and I confess I feel incredibly tired, so I must leave you here and get some rest.

Venetia

Mrs Tilling's Journal

Friday, 9 August, 1940

What a sad night this has been.

It was past midnight when Kitty scratched on the front door. The Colonel answered and came up to get me, and I opened my bedroom door in Harold's old brown dressing gown and pattered down to find out what was afoot.

'Something's very wrong with Venetia, and I think you need to go to the Manor,' she said quietly, adding, with a vague tremor, 'And may I stay here for a while, please?'

I told Kitty she could have the small room and hurried back into my bedroom to throw on some clothes and grab my nurse's bag before darting out into the night. I ran all the way to the lane, stumbling over twice as my thin torch roved over the uneven path ahead of me. At the Manor, I let myself in the side door and headed up the back stairs, stopping to catch my breath for a few moments before knocking.

My main dread – that Venetia was having a miscarriage – was confirmed as I entered the room. It was a tragic scene. In the dim mauve light of her bedside lamp, I saw Venetia sprawled in pain, weeping that she'd never forgive herself. There was a lot of blood and a strong smell of plasma. Mrs Winthrop was dashing around with towels and cloths.

I sat next to Venetia on the bed and spoke quietly to her, gauging what she was going through, what needed to be done, whether we should take her to the hospital. It was early in her pregnancy, so at least she wasn't going through labour, and slowly, throughout the early hours of morning, the entirety of her pregnancy was gradually ejected from her frail body.

'Is she going to be all right?' Mrs Winthrop asked.

'Yes,' I said, although inside I couldn't be certain. She was underweight, exhausted, and traumatised. She was running a fever and had lost a lot of blood.

'There was a scene with Henry,' she went on. 'He found out about the pregnancy and hit her. She fell hard on the floor.'

I put my arm around her as we sat down beside the bed. Henry's explosion must have been the last straw, after the blood loss, the weakness, the heartache. We watched her in silence, and I was relieved when the situation began to stabilise around dawn, and she fell into a light sleep.

'Go to bed now and get a few hours' sleep, as I'll have to leave at eight,' I whispered to Mrs Winthrop.

'I'm far too awake to sleep,' she said. 'But I'll make us some tea.'

I stayed, quietly monitoring Venetia's fever while Mrs Winthrop crept in and out, bringing tea and a vase of purple hydrangeas from the garden. She opened the curtains a few inches as the sun rose over the wheat-clad hills, allowing a pastel amber stream to flicker into the room.

It was all over, and Venetia was alive.

When she woke, she lay despondently on her bed for a long while, her large eyes wide open, fixed on the ceiling, or closed shut, tears billowing out.

'What have I done?' she would whisper from time to time. 'What was I thinking? I could never have married Henry. What have I done?'

Mrs Winthrop and I glanced at each other. It was as if the culmination of the whole situation had finally broken her inside.

The Brigadier was throwing a tremendous racket downstairs, as if it were yet another battlefield, the sound of crockery breaking and doors slamming in utter contrast to our quiet little corner of grief.

After eight, I trod sadly back to the village to get some rest before morning surgery, feeling light-headed from the lack of sleep. I reached Ivy House just in time to see the Colonel leave for Litchfield.

'Is she all right?' he asked, although I hadn't mentioned it to him, and I have no idea how he knew where I had been.

'Yes,' I replied. 'She'll be fine.'

'And you?' He stopped right in front of me, his bulky mass hovering over me.

'I'm—' I began, about to say as usual that I'm all right. But it wasn't true. 'I'm tired. It's all been rather traumatic, to be frank.' I looked at him and gave him a frail smile.

'Why don't you go and lie down for a while.' He leant his head down slightly. 'I'm sure the surgery can do without you this morning.'

I could have cried on his large, friendly shoulder, but I just stood there, trying to be practical, holding in my tears. 'But what about all the people waiting for me?'

He stood looking at me for a moment, and then he put both arms out, perhaps to put them around me, but then stopped himself midair, deciding instead to plant his hands firmly on my arms. 'You need to rest for a while, otherwise you won't be able to help anyone.'

'I'll try,' I said, then pulled away, embarrassed by our closeness. 'But where's Kitty? I need to make her breakfast.'

'Kitty has already made me breakfast and, if you ask very nicely' — he smiled, raising an eyebrow — 'I'm sure she'll rustle up some for you too.'

Kitty Winthrop's Diary

Friday, 9th August, 1940

The sharp light of day

When I opened my eyes this morning, I found myself blinking at Mrs Tilling's small back room, and spent a few abysmal moments piecing together the gruesome events of the last day, my fast and furious demise into a pit so deep I'll never be able to struggle out.

> My future
> Daddy's unleashed fury – I'll have to leave home in disgrace
> Venetia's anger, and her unremitting torment
> My utter and complete disgrace that will follow me like a shadow of death
> My broken heart dissolving my insides into molten lava
> My shattered dreams – the end of everything I've ever known and wanted

I wandered downstairs and into the kitchen to find some breakfast.

'Is Mrs Tilling up yet?' I asked the Colonel.

'She's still at the Manor,' he said, starting to poke through the cupboards for something to eat. 'She's been there all night.'

'Oh dear,' I muttered as I reached for the oats. 'It must be Venetia. I hope she's all right.'

As I made tea and porridge for the Colonel, I couldn't stop thinking about Venetia, and how it was all my fault she had the dreadful row with Henry. He must have been furious with her. I shouldn't have told him. I really can't think how bad people can live with themselves and their guilt. I felt it lurking in me, like a poisonous slime slushing around my body, making everything I do or say come out all yellowy-brown and stinking of sick.

The Colonel sat down at the table, reading yesterday's paper and giving me a running commentary.

'Well, it's officially called the Battle of Britain now. The Nazis are bombing all our airfields and factories.'

'Really,' I said, not listening.

He glanced up at me as I slowly stirred the porridge. 'Let's see if they have something more cheery.' There's always a couple of those humorous or nice-ending stories to lift spirits, and he read one out to me about an air raid warden who was patrolling the village of Upper Leigh when he felt a gun in his back and thought the Nazis had invaded. He put his hands up quickly, and as he gradually turned around, he realised he was being held up by a huge heron – he had backed into the bird's beak thanks to the blackout.

I smiled, but my spirits remained unlifted, and he gave me a heavy pat on the shoulder before leaving for Litchfield Park. I'm sure he wouldn't be so nice to me if he'd heard the full story.

I went back to tidying the kitchen, and heard Mrs Tilling come in. They spoke quietly as they passed in the hallway, and then I heard the front door close as he left.

'Hello,' Mrs Tilling announced as she breezed into the kitchen. 'The Colonel tells me you made him breakfast, which I must say was immensely good of you. Now put the kettle on and let's have a little chat.'

'Is she all right?' I said hastily, busying myself with filling up the kettle.

'I think she'll be fine,' she said, to my immense relief. 'But she lost the baby.'

I know what that means. And I know that my telling Henry was the last thing she needed. She's been so weak since the bombing. This must have tipped her over the edge. I plonked myself down on a chair, laid my arms on the table, and sank my head into them. 'It's all my fault.'

'It's not your fault, Kitty,' she said, putting her arm around my shoulders. 'Henry should take responsibility for his own actions, although it probably wasn't helpful of you to tell him. The scene was monstrous. It was too much for her in the end.'

I began crying, trying not to, of course. Poor Mrs Tilling has so much to deal with at the moment, and I'm sure she doesn't need some infuriating tattletale girl crying on her shoulder, but each time I stopped, there was another wave behind it, waiting to surge to the front and break apart, as if my entire life had been a series of horrors waiting to be released.

Mrs Tilling stroked my back. 'We all need to remember that you're young, with so much to learn in life. Henry should never have led you to think he might marry you, but there's a lot more to it than that. Your mama should have talked to you about Venetia's pregnancy, rather than pretending that nothing was happening. Venetia should never have deceived him into proposing. Your father should not have put so much pressure on Venetia to accept Henry. Henry should not have hit her. Slater should not have disappeared, leaving Venetia so heartbroken. It's all a mess. You shouldn't bear the whole of it on your own shoulders.'

'But why does Henry love her when he could love me? I'm the one who wants to marry him. Why can't people love other people who love them back? Why is everyone in love with the wrong person?'

'Kitty, look at me,' she said, and I raised my bleary face from my arms. 'Being a grown-up is a tough thing. We can't choose who we fall in love with, or who falls in love with us. Whatever happens in your life, Kitty, you need to remember that you can't change the way someone feels about you. Love is a terribly odd emotion, and can have very little to do with common sense. Sometimes it's a cosy, comfortable feeling, like tucking yourself up in a lovely warm blanket, but other times it just washes over you completely, and you simply can't help yourself.' She paused for a moment, dwelling on something, and then snapped out of it. 'I'm sure that Henry loves you like a sister, but he feels a very different kind of love towards Venetia.'

'But I know what it feels like to be in love,' I wailed. 'Don't tell me that what I feel isn't real!'

'It is real, Kitty.' She put her arm around my shoulders. 'It's very real.'

I cried and cried, because I had ruined everything, because Venetia would hate me, and because Henry would never love me now. He was out of my life forever.

'You'll find someone new,' Mrs Tilling said.

'No.' I shook my head. 'I'll never find anyone else. Not like Henry. No one else is as handsome and funny, and looks at me in the way he does. When he's here it's like the sun comes out and everything bad in me, everything bad in the village, the country, the world, is not evil after all. Then it's perfect and wonderful and heavenly.' I opened my mouth for air before howling into my hands. 'And it's not going to be heavenly any more. He's gone, and everything bad is always there and will never be taken away.'

Long after Mrs Tilling went to the surgery, I remained sat at the table. But by the middle of the afternoon I decided I needed to get out, and so I set out in no particular direction. As I was walking, I found myself going home. I had a nagging need to speak to Venetia. The closer I got the more adamant I became that this was what I had to do. I needed to apologise to her.

But would she ever forgive me?

As I opened the side door, I realised that I'd been forgetting my main opponent. My father. He'd kill me if he saw me. All the pent-up rage he had for his darling Venetia would be taken out on me. After all, I'm the youngest girl, the least able to stand up to him, the one he habitually takes it out on. Why break the pattern of a lifetime? That hurricane of violent retribution would pound me until there was nothing left but the oozing silence of a crushed soul.

I shuddered with fear as I crept over to the back stairs. The house was still, the hallway echoing with the mismatched tocks of the grandfather clock. I slid soundlessly up the back stairs and knocked cautiously on Venetia's door. It was opened by Mrs Tilling, who had gone straight over after morning surgery.

'Kitty,' she whispered. 'What are you doing here?'

'I have to talk to Venetia.'

'But what if your father sees you?' she said anxiously, pulling me inside the dark room.

'I have to see Venetia.' I looked around me. The curtains were drawn tight, and only a small bedside lamp – Venetia's purple one – shed a bruised light around the room. The place was cleared of the usual debris, the discarded clothes, the spilt perfume bottles, the books and the jewellery boxes. Even the dressing table was orderly, sterilised for a new tomorrow.

Venetia stirred in the bed. Mrs Tilling went to her side and explained that I was there, and she would make some tea for us.

'Please let her wake slowly,' she said to me. 'And remember what's happened, Kitty. You are not foremost in her mind at the moment, so don't get upset if she's angry with you.'

I stood where I was for a few minutes after Mrs Tilling had left.

'Come and sit down, Kitty,' a weak voice mumbled from the bed.

I went and sat down.

'Venetia, I'm very sorry. I can't tell you how bad I feel about it. I know how wrong it was of me. I know now, you don't need to tell me. I know that Henry was in love with you, and I understand that you meant the best for everyone. I know it all now, but I didn't yesterday. I'm so sorry.'

She lay still, and I wondered if she was well enough for this conversation. Her dazed eyes locked into mine, glassed over with thought or confusion or delirium. I couldn't make out what she was thinking.

'I despised you at first for telling Henry, do you know that?' she said in a croaky voice. 'But I came round to thinking it wasn't so very bad. I know you didn't intend it that way. In any case, now we know that Henry's a vile person, a cruel, unkind man, despite how handsome he looks on the outside. You deserve better, Kitty.'

I didn't say anything. I was just looking at her. Her face was emaciated. Her hair clung to her head and clumped around her shoulders. Even though someone had sprayed some lavender water around, it didn't cover the smell of something bad, blood maybe. The bed was moist with tears and sweat. I had never seen her like this.

I began to cry.

The door opened, and Mrs Tilling hurried in. 'You need to get out, Kitty. Your father's home, and he knows you're here. He saw you walking up the drive as he pulled in.' She picked up my arm and yanked me up. 'Go, leave now. He's threatening to thrash you.'

She pushed me out of the room, and I ran as quietly as I could for the back stairs. My heart was pounding, and I was feeling incredibly flustered, all fingers and thumbs, as I went to grab the banister. As soon as I reached the bottom, I clung to the side to make sure the coast was clear. The most hazardous part of my journey lay before me – the dash across the back of the hall to the kitchen, passing the door to Daddy's study.

I heard a movement in the study as the door stood ajar. I couldn't see all the way into the room, but he was most definitely in there, looking through papers by the sound of the rustling. I decided that speed was of the essence, and counted silently one, two, three, and darted out across the bare marble floor. In my haste my foot slid off to the side, sending me crashing to the floor. I scrambled to get up and run forward but found myself barred by a violent and volatile man – my father.

At the sight of me, he lunged down, his maroon face in a crazed snarl. His hands grasped towards my throat as if to strangle me outright. I backed away terrified, scrambling to my feet.

'Ah, it's the little traitor, is it?' he bellowed. 'I want a word with you.' He grabbed me by the arm and hauled me into his study, where he dropped me on the floor in front of his desk. 'I want to know precisely why you want to ruin our family's name.' He strode around to the other side of the desk, picking up his horsewhip and coming back to where I was cowering, whooshing it rhythmically onto his boot, where it cracked with every step he took. Whoosh, crack. Whoosh, crack. Whoosh, crack.

'Please, no,' I muttered, terrified. Once Daddy had whipped a horse to near death – it had to be put down as a result – and frankly I didn't reckon my chances. 'Please, let me talk. Let me explain. Stop!'

But he had already started. In no particular place, and with no particular finesse, he lashed me as furiously as he could. I hunched forward so that my shoulders and back took the brunt, and I could feel the back of my dress being slashed and the sharp wince of pain when he broke through the fabric, then broke through the skin, the wet trickle of blood coursing down my back, mingling with the sweat and tears that I couldn't hold back. I was sobbing, yelling, moaning, not knowing what to do. Every time I tried to rise, his foot would come out and boot me back down. I was completely at his mercy, and I tried to crawl towards his shoe and grip his ankle, pressing him to stop, but he shook me off, further enraged. 'You worthless' – whip – 'disloyal' – whip – 'fickle' – whip – 'miserable' – whip – 'wretch.'

Then I heard another voice.

'Brigadier, what are you doing? Put that whip down at once.' At first I could hardly recognise who it was, so different was it from her usual soft enunciation. Today it rang out loud, strong, calm. A woman with power.

It was Mrs Tilling. She was standing at the open door, her demeanour upright and poised, like a disgusted school head-mistress stumbling on the pranks of a naughty boy.

'Get out, you nosy little woman,' he raged. 'This has nothing to do with you.'

'I think it does,' she said crisply.

There was a pause. Daddy turned around, as did I, and saw Mrs Tilling, the gentlest and meekest of women, carefully closing the door and taking an authoritative step forward.

'What are you talking about, woman?' Daddy bellowed, making a move towards her, the whip thwacking menacingly on his leg.

'Don't mess with me, Brigadier,' she said sharply. 'You wouldn't want to make an enemy of someone who knows so much about you and your immoral little deal.' Her voice clipped sharply like an efficient sewing machine drilling up an old hem.

Daddy stopped in his tracks, fury over his scowling countenance.

Astonished does not convey how I felt. Never in all my life have I ever known Mrs Tilling to stand up to anyone, let alone Daddy. Now, in my hour of need, she had found the strength – the oomph! – to walk in here and save my life. I wanted to run and throw myself into her arms with love and gratitude, and warn her that we should get ourselves out as quickly as we could!

'Don't threaten me, Mrs Tilling,' he spat. 'You don't know anything.' His eyes narrowed threateningly.

'I'm not afraid of you, Brigadier.' Mrs Tilling stood resolutely where she was, upright and composed, as if she had gained a new position of strength and righteousness. 'I know enough to have a full investigation set into motion. If that's what you want?' She said every word carefully. 'All it takes is one small telephone call.'

'Give the game up, Mrs Tilling,' Daddy ordered. 'You don't know what you're playing with. How irresponsible it would be for you to mess around with this. Put our little community in jeopardy, crush us in this awful war.'

Daddy can be extremely frightening when he's in this kind of temper, and I was worried for a moment that Mrs Tilling would back down, ease herself out of the room, and the thrashing would be resumed without delay.

But she stood firm. I could even see a flicker of a smile on her lips, a small, quiet kind of smile, the type you might see at a chess tournament when someone knows they've won a long time before anyone else realises.

'Don't get all patronising, Brigadier.' She took two steps towards him, so that she was only about a foot away. 'I have nothing to fear from you.' She lightly swept a little dust from his shoulder. It was a damning gesture, dismissive. 'Quite the contrary, I assure you.'

Daddy was visibly perturbed. He took a step back and looked across the room as if for inspiration, some kind of solid ground. His brow was fraught and his eyes darkened, and his thin lips drew down at the corners, a schoolboy thwarted.

I cowered further into the corner. That Mrs Tilling could stand up to Daddy was one thing, but that she held something over him was quite another. I was unsure how he would react. He doesn't like women at the best of times, merely tolerates Mama and us girls. What was it that she knew that could force him to back down? I've never known Daddy to concede defeat. Not once amongst his many, varied combats. Even Mrs B treads carefully around him, and we all know how relentless she can be.

Mrs Tilling looked over to me, beckoning me to get up.

I got unsteadily to my feet, looked around at the small dark drips of blood on the parquet floor, and tried to straighten my shredded dress and tidy my hair.

'Now say you're sorry,' she calmly said to him.

'Say you're sorry, Kitty,' he bellowed at me.

'Not her,' she shouted – yes, Mrs Tilling shouting! '*You* say you're sorry to her. She's thirteen years old, and you're battering her with a horse's whip. You should be ashamed of yourself.'

'Now, Mrs Tilling, I don't know why—'

'Apologise.' There was a look in her eye I had never seen before, like Justice weighing the balance and finding him wanting.

'I'm sorry, Kitty, Mrs Tilling appears to have gone quite mad,' Daddy said, a little embarrassed.

'No, don't apologise for my actions. Lord knows I am capable of doing so myself should it become necessary. Apologise for whipping her, of course.'

'Sorry, Kitty.' He struggled, his hands scrunched in tightly knuckled balls, furious and not looking at either of us. 'Now, I think you can go, Kitty, and I think you've done enough too, Mrs Tilling,' he said sharply.

'No.' Mrs Tilling came over and put her arm around me, guiding me to the door. 'I think your family has had enough of your tyranny. They've put up with your cruelty for years, and I don't see why they should put up with it for a minute longer.' She stopped in her tracks and turned towards him, pointing a finger to the window. 'There's a war going on out there. A real war. People are being killed defending our precious country, and all you can do is beat your own children into submission. Well, it's not going to happen any more. Do you understand?'

She turned to me. 'You can go and clean yourself up now, Kitty. He won't be threatening you again, and if he does you're to tell me straightaway.' She looked at him as she said this, making sure he understood. I nodded and scurried out quickly. Holding my breath, I leapt up the stairs two at a time and nipped quickly into Venetia's room, quietly closing the door behind me.

'Kitty, I heard the screams, what happened?' she whispered.

I showed her my back.

'Oh no! Not again!' She sighed, motioning me to bring a flannel from the dressing table.

I brought it over, with a cup of water to make it moist, and sat on the bed next to her so that she could prop herself up in bed and clean up my wounds. It was pitiable – one victim helping another. But it felt normal somehow, as if we were each other's natural allies.

I told her about the standoff.

'Who'd have thought Mrs Tilling would have it in her?' Venetia exclaimed, confusion over her face. 'I wonder what she knows.'

'Perhaps he's having an affair?' I said. 'Although I can't imagine he'd be so worried about keeping it quiet – he has such little regard for Mama. Or maybe it could be his buying black-market gas from the man in Chartham, although I'm sure his status and army connections could override any manner of criminal offences. He tells me everyone does it anyway. No, it has to be something else. Something much, much worse.'

'Yes, it has to be something else.' She paused, still dabbing my wounds, making me wince with every touch. 'Mrs Tilling has been so different lately. It's as if she's discovered there's more inside her.'

'It's the war,' I replied. 'It puts everyone on a different footing, doesn't it?'

'Yes,' Venetia said quickly, with a small laugh. 'It's us women in charge now,' she said in more of her old cavalier style. 'The Chilbury Ladies' Choir will rule the world.'

Through all the pain as she cleaned my wounds, I found myself grinning, and through all the background noise and darkness surrounding us, I had a strange feeling that everything was going to be all right.

Letter from Elsie Cocker
to Flt Lt Henry Brampton-Boyd

Chilbury Manor
Chilbury
Kent

Saturday, 10th August, 1940

Dear Henry,

I could dance for joy as you have made me the happiest girl
in all of England, comfy and warm in the knowledge that I
am now your girl. When I remember this afternoon, after
you left the Manor and I walked you home and got you out
of that horrid temper in the little outhouse in the wood, I
can't imagine such happiness could truly be mine. And no
matter what happens, I'll know that you're there thinking
of me, waiting to be with me again once this silly war
comes to an end.

So I've handed in my notice at Chilbury Manor, just
as you said I was to do. I thought they'd ask what I meant
to do next, but they didn't seem bothered, which was
just as well as I didn't know how they'd react when I
told them that you and I were to be married. The
Brigadier is so old-fashioned that he'd have a heart attack at

the maid marrying one of the nobs. Now that would be a sight!

I'm a bit unsure where I'll go for now. I have only to stay my notice period, and then I'll have to move. I have a good mind to ask your mother if I can come and live with her, as we are now together. I know she won't like the idea of you marrying me, but she'll have to get used to it. I thought maybe you could write her a letter, telling her about us and asking if I can stay.

That's all for now, my love. I think of you all the time and our beautiful afternoon together. Please write soon.

All my love,
Elsie

Letter from Miss Edwina Paltry to her sister, Clara

Litchfield Hospital
Litchfield
Kent

Saturday, 10th August, 1940

Dear Clara,

I am lucky to be alive! Although I fear this may not be the case for much longer. I am terrified, Clara. Terrified, and unable to think what to do.

In walked the Brigadier at morning visiting time, frothing at the mouth like a poisonous toad. Dressed in his usual army uniform, his medals and paraphernalia showing the world who's boss, his shoulders forward ready for a fight, he looked around the beds of worried women until he spotted me, even though I was half hiding beneath the blankets. Striding over to my bed, he stood towering over me seething with fury, his face reddish purple and the veins in his throat and temples blue and throbbing like sinewy snakes.

'What have you told Mrs Tilling?' he roared at me.
'I might have known you'd mess it all up, land us in

trouble with your shoddy stupidity. I should never have trusted a woman.' He bent forward and leant his fists on the bed, his face hovering just above mine, his breath like spoiled meat or some other animal flesh in a state of unrelenting decay.

'I didn't tell her a thing, you stupid man,' I whispered loudly to him, spitting the words out with pent-up anger. 'She ruddy well guessed.'

'How could she have guessed?' he shouted, standing back up and putting his hands on his hips, looking like a brutish dictator. 'How could she have guessed unless you didn't do the job properly?'

I offered him a meaningful look at the nurse, who was sitting at her desk taking a keen interest in our exchange.

'Hello, there.' I smiled at her cheerily, a small wave.

His voice lowered to a brutish whisper. 'How could Mrs Tilling have guessed if it weren't for you leaving clues everywhere?'

'The girl baby is the spitting image of Venetia,' I said matter-of-factly. 'The other baby looks like Hattie. The rest of the pieces just fell into place. A lucky guess.'

'She knows too much for it to be a guess.'

'She has no proof of anything, and there is no conceivable way she can get any unless one of us tells her.'

There was a pause, and he looked at his hands, pink and wiry, like some form of dried-out seafood, a shellfish crawled loose from its shell and left to crust over. Then he turned and sat on the bed with a defeated thump.

'She's threatening me,' he said quietly.

'Bribery?' I asked softly.

'Nothing as base as that. Trust your rotten mind to leap to such conclusions!' he muttered angrily. 'Exposure.' He looked out of the window, at the hefty clouds collecting as if there might be rain later. 'Prison.'

'Well, we'll just have to make sure we deny everything and admit nothing,' I said sharply. 'No one has any proof. They'd have to get an admission from one of us. We have to stick together.' And, with this as my final conclusion, I turned to the nurse. 'My companion is leaving now, and I need some help with my leg,' I said evenly, and she came round to see what I wanted in a most obedient manner.

He shot me a look of disgust, getting up briskly. 'I can't think of anything worse than being stuck with the likes of you. Just you wait until you're out of here, Miss Paltry.' Then he added, all menacing, 'There'll be a proper discussion about this waiting for you.' With which he turned on his heel, gave first me and then the nurse a vile growl, and strode purposefully towards the door.

I let my heavy body fall back into the pillow, like a body launching off a great cliff and hurtling down towards a rocky sea.

My only plan is to disappear the moment my hip is mended and they let me out of hospital. I'll have to go to Chilbury first and try to get my money back from Ralph Gibbs. I know it won't be easy, but I have my ways, Clara, and I'm desperate enough to bargain for half the way things stand. Then I can make my way to Birnham Wood and meet you there. It doesn't fill my heart with joy, but all I'm asking is simply to stay alive. Lord, I'm livid that I got into this mess. I wish I'd had nothing to do with it.

Pray for me, Clara, that I might come out of this in one blooming piece.

Edwina

Letter from Flt Lt Henry Brampton-Boyd to Elsie Cocker

Monday, 12th August, 1940

My dear girl,

How terribly surprised I was to receive your letter, both for its actuality and, more strikingly, for its content. Please allow me to unburden you of any misapprehension you may have about my feelings towards you and the nature of our relationship.

Firstly, the 'beautiful afternoon together' of which you speak is merely that, one beautiful afternoon. There was no intention on my part for it to lead to more beautiful afternoons. In fact, that was quite its beauty: that it was a single escape from the bounds of reality. Any references I might have made to your change of occupation were concerned with the growing need for women to join the war effort. Would it not be more correct for you to train as a nurse or join the forces instead of wasting your energies as a civilian parlour maid?

Secondly, it will consequently not be necessary to contact my mother, and I must tell you that should you choose to ignore my warning, her wrath will be overbearing, and your livelihood in the area will be at stake.

I wish you well in your new career.

Yours, &c.
Flt Lt Brampton-Boyd

Letter from Venetia Winthrop
to Angela Quail

Chilbury Manor
Chilbury
Kent

Monday, 12th August, 1940

Dear Angela,

Isn't it strange that momentous things happen –
catastrophe, sickness, death – and then a week or two later it
seems that everything has gone back to normal. I went back
to work today, catching the 7:40 bus to Litchfield and
walking past the telephone box on the corner, the same
faces, the same clouds settling above us. I headed for our old
office. Elizabeth was there making tea and gave me the
chipped cup as usual. I sat down at my desk and went
through the new papers. I've only been away for a few weeks,
yet it feels like eternity. No, actually it feels like I'm just a
whole different person. The old Venetia left and now a new
person has come who looks like Venetia, and remembers
how to do Venetia's job, but she isn't the same person at all.

No one knows what happened, except for Colonel
Mallard, who came and asked how I was doing in rather a

lovely way. They know about me saving the baby, as that was in the papers. But they don't know about me losing a different baby. I shudder every time a new person comes in to congratulate me. 'Well done about the baby!' they say, or 'You must want one of your own now!' I know they mean to be good-humoured, but I have become quite annoyed at having to rush to the ladies' every few minutes to check my mascara.

After work, Colonel Mallard gave me a lift to Chilbury, and I popped in to say hello to Mrs Tilling and baby Rose. She's such a cuddly baby, all plump and giggly. I sometimes get to feed her too.

'I want to help look after her – it's what I owe to Hattie,' I said, as I rocked her on my lap.

'Yes, I can understand that,' Mrs Tilling said, smiling, and I found myself blushing at the selfish, snippy person I used to be – especially to Hattie.

'Perhaps I could have been a nicer friend to Hattie, but at least now I can help her child.'

'Well, you'll have more of a chance, as your mama has agreed to take her until Victor returns. So she'll be living with you at Chilbury Manor.'

I beamed with joy, and held her especially tight. But then I remembered. 'What about Daddy?'

'It's all right, Venetia. You have nothing to worry about from him any more.'

I remembered what Kitty said about Mrs Tilling knowing something. How incredibly useful!

Overjoyed, I hugged Rose tightly. She is to come with her belongings on Friday, and I'll be able to feed her every night.

Chilbury Manor remains terribly quiet for now. Kitty has been excruciatingly apologetic and really quite sweet. Daddy has been exceptionally absent and has thrown himself wholeheartedly into defending Chilbury from the Nazis. He has the Chilbury Defence Volunteers meet every other day to exert his authority. We're incredibly relieved he's found another focus for his energies.

Mama ordered me to rest as soon as I got home from work, realising at last that she can leave baby Lawrence with Nanny and he'll be just fine. After dinner, Kitty and Silvie decided to bring the gramophone into my bedroom to cheer us all up. We listened to the records Prim lent to Kitty before the bomb. She tried to give them back to Prim's sisters when they came to collect her belongings – what was left of them. But they insisted that we keep them and enjoy them as much as we could in honour of Prim.

It was a cosy little evening, the four of us sitting around the player flipping through the records – there must be over forty of them, many of them from America. Mama brought up some tea and I had some biscuits from work, so we had a small party.

'This one is my favourite.' Kitty took a record out of its cover. 'Prim told me it was one of her favourites too, so I hope she's looking down on us now, listening to her music.'

'What is it?' Mama asked.

'You'll have to wait and see,' she chimed, putting it on and lifting the needle.

The notes began, after a little crackling. It was a band playing a fast little American number, quite amusing. Kitty and Silvie have clearly been listening to it as they knew all the words.

'Keep young and beautiful,' they sang, strutting around the room. Kitty scooped up a small towel, pretending it was a feather boa.

It was highly entertaining, and we fell about laughing. Then I found 'Blue Moon', so we put that on. It was sung by some sisters from America. We joined in, with Kitty singing a harmony, such a magical song.

Mama chose an older one called 'Putting on the Ritz'.

'It reminds me of when Daddy and I went to dances. Sometimes people would do the Charleston. I always wanted to have a go,' she said shyly.

Kitty and Silvie got up and did a few dance steps, back and forth, pulling Mama up to join in. Silvie was rather good, but Kitty was so pathetic that I felt obliged to get up and show them how to do it properly. Mama, for once, didn't tell me to get back into bed.

'Let's do this next.' Kitty put on an English favourite that we all knew called 'Kiss Me Goodnight, Sergeant Major'. We sang along, sitting in a line on the bed, linking arms and swaying from side to side, until Kitty swayed too far and fell off, collapsing with laughter on the floor.

'We should put on a show!' Kitty said, her little face lighting up. 'We should learn all the words and put on a show!'

'Why don't you write the words out, and maybe we can try and sing along another time,' I said, hoping Mama wouldn't be a bore and say it was too much for me.

But she said, 'What a lovely idea. Perhaps we'll ask some of the ladies from the choir to come along too.'

'Hurrah!' Kitty cheered, and Silvie clapped her hands, jumping in her seat.

'It could be our new resurrection,' I said. 'The Chilbury Ladies' Choir becomes a singing show!'

I'll keep you informed about our show, and if it ever comes into fruition. I'm sure with Kitty at the helm it'll be difficult to put her off.

Much love,
Venetia

Mrs Tilling's Journal

❦

Tuesday, 13th August, 1940

Hitler has clearly resolved to make a decisive air attack on England, as there's been a frenzy of fighter formations hurtling across our skies the past few days. The Nazis have been targeting military places, and we're petrified they may hit Litchfield Park or Parnham Airfield.

When I arrived home this afternoon, Carrington was there waiting for me, his slim form perched neatly on the whitewashed bench on the front veranda appreciating the orangey glow of the late afternoon. He was wearing army uniform, but had taken off his hat, holding it in his hand and enjoying the warmth on his face, closing his eyes against the golden sun.

He got up when he saw me, and hurried over to give me a hand with my bicycle.

'How lovely to see you, Carrington,' I said, cheered to see his warm smile. 'Is your leg doing any better?'

'Yes, it's all right. They say I'll never be able to run properly again, but these days I feel lucky to still be alive.'

'Come and have a cup of tea,' I said leading him inside. 'How is work at Litchfield Park?'

He followed me in, and we went and sat in the front room. 'They've put me in intelligence, which is fascinating stuff. I'm hoping they might move me to London.'

I made some tea and brought it in, sitting down opposite him and waiting to hear if he had any news for me.

'I found out a few things,' he said after I poured the tea. 'It took a little prying, but at last I found a lead, someone who knows how these chaps operate, and bingo! We have a few answers.' He looked jolly pleased with himself. 'But, Mrs Tilling, I must ask you to promise never to repeat what I am about to tell you to anyone. It really is top, top secret, and we will all be in trouble if anyone finds out this knowledge has been shared.'

'Of course,' I said quickly, knowing he should trust me after the dealings with Berkeley's ring.

'Slater is a spy. One of the best we have. He came down to break a strong Nazi intelligence ring that was focused on Litchfield Park. He found one of the sources – someone's butler, I believe – and escaped with him and another one to London, where he uncovered a complete network of Nazi spies. Bit of a hero, really.' He picked up his tea and sat back in the armchair while I absorbed this information.

So I'd been wrong about Slater all along. But at least I had been right about one thing: there most certainly was a lot more to him than meets the eye! All the things that the Colonel said to me last month came flooding back, about how much pain Venetia will go through when he puts his life at risk again and again, until he finally loses it. Of course, everything makes sense now.

'Did he leave the night of the bomb?'

'Yes, but it wasn't to do with the bomb. It was because that was the night he abruptly left for London. They had reason to believe someone suspected them, a girl.'

That would be Kitty, I thought, remembering that night, her conversation with Colonel Mallard, his telephone call afterwards, then the planes, the sirens, the bombs.

'Once in London they were put in touch with a senior organiser, and Slater nailed the whole ring. Some of them have been "turned double", so they're back on the street but working for us.'

My head was spinning with questions. 'If he was undercover, am I right in thinking he wouldn't have been able to tell the woman in question anything about himself or what he did?'

'That's right.'

'Which is why she was always so confused about it.'

'Indeed. Apparently he was involved with the black market to bolster his position. In effect, he was an intelligence agent pretending to be a Nazi spy, who was pretending to be a black marketeer, who was pretending to be an artist. Clever chap.'

'Why did he have to be a black marketeer?'

'He needed to get illegal papers for them so that he could provide food and ration books. He needed to give them a service, to prove he was one of them.'

'So what's he going to do after he's finished with this? Will he be able to tell her about it all?'

'They're sending him away next. He won't be allowed to tell her the details, but I'm sure he can explain a certain amount.'

The sound of the front door opening and voices came from the hall, so we quickly stopped talking, which was lucky as within a moment Venetia herself stepped into the front room, followed by the Colonel. She was looking a picture of beauty in a dress with lavender flowers. Her eyes still have that haunted look, and she's altogether too slim, but strangely more striking now than she ever was before, when she was 'empress'. She came in and perched on the arm of the sofa.

'Colonel Mallard gave me a lift in his motorcar, and I thought I'd drop in to say hello,' she said, smiling beautifully.

'This is Lieutenant Carrington. Perhaps you two know each other from Litchfield Park?'

Carrington, who had stood to attention when the Colonel came in, was looking at her, captivated. He was staring rather at her face, and then from head to toe. I thought it rather odd that he of all people might be in awe of her, but then I saw the look on his face. It was more one of complete and utter astonishment than admiration.

She stayed and chatted for a while, telling us about how they contrive to get some work done squashed into the long underground shelters.

'Everyone is washing themselves far more than usual as we're in such close proximity and it's easy to notice if someone hasn't bathed.' She laughed and Carrington joined in politely, although I don't think he was actually listening to a word she was saying.

After she left, I had to find out why he looked at her like that.

'Do you already know Venetia?' I asked.

He blushed and looked at his hands. 'Did I stare rather? I'm so terribly sorry.' He smiled. 'You see, my father recently procured a new painting for his office, and—' He hesitated over his words. 'And it happens to be a woman who looks exactly like Venetia.'

'How marvellous,' I said. 'I hope it does her justice.'

'Well, yes,' he said, covering a laugh. 'You see, it's a nude.'

I tried to stop myself laughing, but couldn't help it, and when the Colonel came down the stairs, he found the two of us, by the door, whooping with laughter.

'Slater must have painted her. How very funny. Where on earth did he get it?' I giggled, leading him out to the front path.

Carrington laughed. 'He bought it from a rather thuggish-looking dealer called Gibbs.'

'Oh! I wonder how Ralph Gibbs got hold of it. I can't imagine Slater gave it to him.'

'I very much doubt it. Although I must say I'm rather impressed with his artistic skills, for a spy that is.'

We were still laughing as we walked down to the road. He had left his bicycle leaning against the wall, beside my creeping roses.

'Thank you for coming,' I said, 'and for the information, although Heaven knows what I'm to do with it. I suppose I'll just keep it to myself and see if he shows up.'

'Yes,' Carrington said, climbing onto his bicycle. 'Better to be circumspect.' He gave me the loveliest of smiles and a 'Cheerio', and was off down the road to Litchfield.

I wandered back into the house trying to absorb this news. Should I tell Venetia about Slater? I decided to leave it for the moment. She seems to be improving, and I wouldn't want to build up her hopes again.

The Colonel gave me a knowing look as I walked into the sitting room.

'I didn't know you were friends with young Carrington.'

'Yes,' I said, shooting him a sidelong glance. 'It's good to have friends in the right places.'

Kitty Winthrop's Diary

Thursday, 15th August, 1940

This hideous war!

It all started early this afternoon when Silvie and I arrived back from riding, Silvie galloping headlong across the fields as if her life depended on it. Having let ourselves in the side door, we wandered through the kitchen to the hall, hoping to catch Mama having tea with maybe a few sandwiches to spare. The sound of her meandering voice, then Venetia's languid tones, echoed crisply through the galleried marble hall, and Silvie and I exchanged small smiles. We were in luck.

How wrong could I have been! As we approached the door, I felt Silvie's cold little hand touch my arm, holding me back. I looked back to her quizzically, but she put her finger to her lips. 'Shh.'

'I know,' Mama was saying. 'I honestly don't know how to break it to her. Let me read you what he says.' She coughed slightly, then came the sound of paper unfolding – a letter. '"We are sorry to say that Silvie's parents have been found. For the last few months they were hidden in a neighbour's barn, the Dornaks'."'

I looked at Silvie, and she nodded, whispering, 'They're our friends. I played with their daughter.'

"'But they were found, the Dornaks taken out and shot dead as punishment.'"

Silvie's eyes dropped from mine to the floor, her face as white as a sheet. With all this information flying at us through the open door, I decided to make our presence known and took her arm forward. But she held me back angrily, giving me such a hard look that I didn't dare.

"'Her parents were taken to a work camp for Jewish people in northern Czechoslovakia. There is no mention of her brother.'"

For a haze of a moment, Silvie's face looked translucent, as if she was a pale ghost of a child here from antiquity, and then – quick as a wisp – she turned and fled. Out through the hall, through the kitchen and side door, and out into the wide open space of nature, the emerald and amber of late summer enveloping her, a tiny figure under the vast blue sky. In a few strides she was gone, into the thicket, into the wood, like a small creature under perpetual attack.

We spent the rest of the afternoon looking for her.

The first places I looked for Silvie
She wasn't in the stables, cuddling up with Amadeus
All the horses were still there, so she hadn't galloped
    off somewhere
She wasn't at the dam in the stream, or by the beehives
She wasn't at Old George's bush in Peasepotter Wood

Mama and Venetia had hurried into the village to get help, and by the time I returned home, exhausted and worried, a group of ladies were being debriefed by Mrs B on the front lawn.

'Today we have a vital mission,' she began, marching up and down in front of them. 'Our task is to find this defence-less young girl, who has been placed in our care, before the day is out. We need to show her that although she has lost one family, she can depend on us, her new community, to look after her, to protect her from those Nazi brutes.' At which point she threw a menacing look towards the coast. 'And to show her that there are still some places where good, decent people welcome her into the fold.'

A round of 'Hear, hear' followed, as Mrs B began shouting orders, as if advancing into battle. 'I'll cover Peasepotter Wood with you, you, and you' – she pointed at various women who stepped forward – 'and the rest of you comb the fields. Mrs Quail, you take a group towards Dawkins Farm, and Mrs Gibbs, you take a group over to the west side of the village. We'll reconvene here at half past four for tea.'

With that, everyone disbanded, and I was left standing, hands on hips and still out of breath, with Venetia looking at me with a puzzled expression.

'There's got to be a way to work out where she's gone,' she said quietly, almost as if she was talking to herself. 'Let's think this through, Kitty. Where would you go if you were her?'

'The stables. But I already checked there.'

'Let's put ourselves in her shoes.' She took a step closer. 'You've just found out that your parents are still alive and in a camp. You're at once overwhelmed that what you've been dreading – that they're dead – hasn't happened, and yet more afraid than ever that it might be coming next. Your baby brother is gone. The cornerstones of your world are on the verge of collapse, and this would be such a massive catastrophe that you're unsure if you'll survive.'

'I'd want to run away and find Mama,' I said. 'It would be unbearable to stay, sit still, simply waiting for more bad news.'

'Exactly,' Venetia said. 'I'd want to go to her too.'

I began to cry. It was just too much. Poor Silvie, the ridiculous horror of the choices she has to make. She must be thinking she can either stay here and possibly never see her family again, or risk her life making it back across Europe to be with them. What a decision to make!

'She'd have gone to the train station,' I muttered between sobs. 'Although I'm not sure she'd know where to go, or what to do, or where to get money for the fare. She'd have to go through London, of course.' My forehead creased in thought, the nuance of a clue coming to me. 'Tom!' I exclaimed. 'He comes from London. She would go to him for help.'

Without another word, I turned and set off, darting straight past the wood, skirting around the edge of the orchard, and down the hill, spreading my arms open wide to balance myself, like a swallow swooping down into the valley.

As it was a Thursday afternoon and everyone would have been busy in the fields, the hop pickers' huts were deserted, the usual bric-a-brac of prams and firewood lying dormant in the central scrub, a game of cans kicked to the side. A wind blew through. It was like a ghost town. How strange that within a few hours forty or fifty people would be back, chattering and singing, ready for the evening.

I wondered if I'd been wrong. Maybe she wouldn't have come here. Looking around, I wasn't sure I'd want to hang around. And what if Tom couldn't help her get to London? He was only a child himself, after all.

Feeling like an intruder, I walked cautiously down the central scrub, remembering that Old George had been living there, fearful that he was still lurking around, ready to jump out at me with a knife in his hand. A sudden bang made me jump, but it was a door swinging shut in the wind, loose on its hinges. I walked over and closed it properly, just to be on the safe side.

That's when I saw her.

Her eyes were the first thing I noticed, huge and black like a petrified mouse. Crouching at the end of the row, huddled between that and the next one, she sank lower and shifted back into the shadows, and I heard a whisk of movement before I realised that she'd escaped me, scooting off behind the huts and away into the cornfield behind. I raced after her, finding a new speed that I never knew I had, my legs shooting forward with newfound strength. Behind the huts, I found myself looking down a long avenue of grass, spying the blue skirt and a back leg vanishing behind another hut back to the central scrub.

I sprinted down and around, just in time to spot her flying across to the huts on the other side and swiftly opening a door and leaping inside, pulling it closed behind her.

I had her trapped.

Out of breath, I walked to the hut where she was hiding, then tried the door. It was locked.

'Silvie,' I said. 'Open the door.'

There was no answer.

'Silvie,' I said more softly. 'I want to help you.'

Still no answer.

'Silvie, please come out. I can help you get back home. I promise.'

There came a shuffle of movement, and then the metallic click of a bolt sliding over, and the door slowly creaked open, a musty smell of dirty clothes emanating from the dark interior. She sat crouched on the floor, her eyes big and red and unbearably sad.

Why should such a small girl have to go through so much grief?

I climbed into the doorway next to her and put my arm around her, and she cried great heaves of tears as she turned her face into my shoulder and wept. I looked out over the shabby scruff of land. What a miserable world to be born into.

'I need to get back to them,' she sobbed. 'I must go.'

'I don't know the best way,' I said, unsure if I should be aiding her escape, but feeling trapped as I'd promised her I would. I couldn't imagine trying to get to Czechoslovakia. It seemed so distant and dangerous. Then it struck me, my only hope of getting her to stay would be to convince her of how hazardous the whole escapade would be. So I sat down in the doorway and pulled her down beside me. 'I suppose our best bet is to go to Dover and see if we can get a boat to take us over to France.'

Her little body gave a shudder. 'Aren't the Nazis in France?'

'Yes,' I said slowly. 'It might be hard to find someone to take us – I'm not sure many boats are heading that way – but I'm sure we have spies and such going over there, stowing away in a boat or pretending to be smugglers.'

'What is a smuggler?'

'Nasty criminals who steal things from other countries.' I paused, wondering if I was taking this too far. 'We would stay hidden all the way, as they'd probably kill us if they found us.'

'How do we get from France to Czechoslovakia?' she whispered.

'Once we're in France we'd have to hide away, probably in bushes and forests, because if we're found we'd be taken to some kind of work camp—'

'Then I'll be with my mother?'

'No, they would take us to a different one.'

'But once they knew who I was, wouldn't they put me with my parents?'

'No, they like to keep everyone separated. So we'd have to stay hidden, which means we might end up being very hungry, as we wouldn't be able to buy food. Now, do you speak French?'

'No,' she murmured despondently, and I could tell it was beginning to work.

'I suppose we could take some food with us, although I'm not sure it would last more than a month.'

'A month? Would it take that long to get there?'

'We couldn't take trains or buses. We'd have to walk.'

She put her head back into my shoulder and began to cry again. 'We will never make it! We will both die. We'll starve or the Nazis will kill us.'

I held her to me as she wept with the futility of it all. 'Silvie, I'm so sorry about your family.'

She snivelled a little longer, and then drew a finger to her lips and let out a quiet, shaking 'Shhh'. Her eyes were boring into me with fear. 'I know what has happened to my brother.'

Her voice was tense and choked with tears, and she looked around trembling that someone should hear.

'What?' I whispered.

'My mama gave him away.' She put her face in her hands and began to cry, her narrow shoulders hunched and shuddering under the turmoil. 'She gave him to her friend who is not Jewish.'

I held her closer as tears began coming from my own eyes. So that was her secret.

'It was terrible, she loved him – us – so much. He was too young to get the train with me. She knew it was his only chance. The day she came home without him, she pretended it was fine. But it was not fine. She cried all night. It was the end of her world.' Her voice trailed out to a frail whimper, and all I could think was how desperate these people were that they had to give away their children to save them.

I pulled back and looked at her. 'You'll always know that your mother loves you and your brother. You'll always remember that. And just think, when this dreadful war is over, we can go back to your mother's friend and find him. Do you know where she lives?'

Silvie nodded.

'Let's do that, then. This war can't go on forever. We can't let it take everything away from us.'

She nestled into me, and we sat like that, huddled together, looking out, as the clouds began to form above us, darkening the world like a grim shadow, and slowly, quietly, the gentle pitter-patter of raindrops began to sound around and above us.

A kestrel circled and swooped around in the rain, his wings like a great spread of hands, black and dishevelled against the dark sky. And then, without any warning, he was gone.

Softly, Silvie began to chant, slowly in a whisper at first, but then more rhythmically, more lulling, her throat catching with tears as she repeated the Kaddish, as if mourning her own loss. I joined in with her where I could remember the words, and our voices echoed strangely around the deserted huts as if we might have been living today or a thousand years before, feeling the same horror of uncertainty.

It might have been twenty minutes later, maybe an hour, when the shouts and whistles of the hop pickers came from the hill. Soon a few boys raced in front of us down the scrub of land, Tom in the lead, slamming up to the last hut with a deft halt. He threw his hands in the air to declare victory, which was somewhat ridiculous as the other boys were at least a year or two younger. It was almost cheating.

'What are you two doing here?' He trotted over to us.

'We were out for a walk and took cover when it started to rain. Hope you don't mind.'

'No, course not,' he said, looking at Silvie's red eyes, my arm around her shoulder. He perched down beside her, putting his big, thin hand on her arm. 'You all right, girl?'

'They took her parents to a camp,' I said, unsure if I should be telling Tom, but as Silvie lifted her gaze to him, her lips pursed together with unhappiness, I remembered how much she liked him. How much we both liked him.

'We need to get home,' I said, starting to get up.

'I'll come with you,' Tom said, his lanky body dancing around us like a skinny clown. 'Try and cheer you both up a bit.'

Without a word, Silvie slipped her slim, white hand into his, and let him help her up. Then, taking my hand too, Tom led us back to the Manor.

True to his word, he entertained us with his news from the day, which amounted to someone finding a half-decomposed dead rabbit (which we heard about in gruesome detail), a boy who ate an apple that was full of maggots, and one of the families having to leave early because the mum's having a baby.

We had cheered up somewhat by the time we got past the orchard, and as we rounded the side of Peasepotter Wood and onto the drive, we saw the crowd of women in front of us, back on the lawn, sitting on benches and drinking tea. Mrs B was striding around taking notes on her clipboard, until she spotted us coming towards them, announced something, and then they leapt up and began to clap and cheer.

'You found her!' Mrs Quail shouted.

'Well done!' one of the Sewing Ladies chimed in, and someone even promised some sweets.

'Good to have you back, Silvie!' Venetia came over, relieved and smiling.

They heartily slapped our backs, and then Mama put her arms around Silvie, who promptly burst into tears again.

'You have to promise to stay with us,' Mama told her, crouching down to her level. 'And never, ever run away again.'

Silvie nodded and buried her face in Mama's neck.

'What about Daddy?' I whispered to Mrs Tilling, who had come over to stand next to me. 'He'll never let Silvie stay.'

'Oh, don't worry about him, Kitty.' She smiled, as smug as a cat with her paw on a mouse. 'He won't be a problem any more.'

I turned to quiz her, but she was gone, off to herald the return of Silvie, and I was left wondering what's at the bottom of it all.

Tom bounded over, interrupting my thoughts. 'You're quite the hero after all.' He stood beside me, almost touching.

'Of course I am!' I huffed. But then I remembered about my recent mishaps with Venetia and Henry. 'Do you really think so?'

He laughed and slapped me on the back, sending me lurching forward a few paces. 'You're the best, Kitty. The fair damsel who saves the day!' Then he took my hand and gave it a rough squeeze.

Front page of the *Kent Times*,
Sunday, 18th August, 1940

Air Raid on Litchfield

Last night at around nine o'clock, twelve enemy
aircraft came over Kent and released
approximately 60 bombs over the town of Litchfield,
most of them devastating Litchfield Park. Fires
raged throughout the night, and it is feared that
over a hundred are dead, with many more
homeless.

Mrs Tilling's Journal

❦

Sunday, 18th August, 1940

As soon as the all clear sounded, I was on my bicycle and heading through the darkness to Litchfield. I had to be there for the medical team, to help the wounded, but I was mostly worried about the people I knew. Venetia had started work again, and of course there was the Colonel. Might he have been careless enough not to go to the bomb shelter? He mentioned to me only last night how he was fed up with leaving his desk when he was busy, how he'd taken to staying put during the raids.

I cycled fast the whole way, praying he didn't do so tonight: if there was one time he went to the shelter, please God, let it be this time.

As I came over the hill, I saw the blazes over Litchfield Park. You couldn't miss them. Surging gusts of flame soared high into the sky, covering most of the main building, with more fires over what had been the outbuildings. I wondered how many people were trapped in the blaze, and I knew right then that, before I went on duty, I needed to see if I could find the Colonel.

I rode in through the gates and asked a man in uniform watching the blaze.

'What happened to everyone? Did they all get out?'

'Not really,' he said in a daze. 'One of the shelters gave way, and a lot of people are still missing.' He looked around at me, dismay in his eyes. 'They say some people didn't use the shelters.'

'Where are all the people who work here? How can I find out if my friend is all right?'

'They told them to go home, or to one of the rest centres if their homes have been bombed. Obviously a lot of them have stayed to help though. Who are you looking for?'

'Colonel Mallard,' I said. 'He's billeted at my house. But he wasn't there when I left.'

'I can't say I've seen him since the bombs hit. Can't remember seeing him in the shelter neither.' He pondered for a moment, and I wanted to shake him ruthlessly. *Think, man. Think!*

But all he did was shake his head.

'Thank you,' I said quickly, hopping back on my bicycle. If the Colonel had made it, he'd have stayed to help the wounded. But where? Litchfield isn't a big place, but with hundreds of bombed homes to evacuate, who knew where he might be?

I resolved to cycle on to the hospital and look out for him on the way. As I cycled through the miserable pandemonium, I could hardly bear to see the number of injured and homeless shuffling around the streets. It was a horrendous scene, people weeping beside buildings, perhaps knowing who had been crushed beneath, women stopping me for help, and me having to tell them that I was a medic and had to get to the surgery as fast as I could. I couldn't help catching sight of every man to see if he wasn't a little too tall, a little too clumsy.

Litchfield Hospital was already packed. I found the supervisor, and she set me up at a canteen table at the front, where I was supposed to assess patients' needs and send them on to a specific doctor or treat them myself if I could. I was immediately bombarded with a long line of wounded, some of them with deep gashes oozing quantities of blood, others with larger limb injuries. There was a man with concussion, a baby with breathing problems, a severed hand that I tried to sew back on and we'll just have to wait and see how it takes. There were a lot of cases of really bad burns, one all over a poor woman's leg. She said it was trapped under a fallen beam in her house, and she had to wait for the rescue team to lift the beam, even though it was on fire.

The noise and panic amongst the crowds were immense, and the smell of soot and burning flesh horrific. I tried to listen for the familiar tones of the Colonel, and glanced around me when I had the chance to see if he was one of those being carried in on a stretcher. The space was busy and I could only see narrow slots between moving bodies, and once or twice had to leave my table to double-check when I had been sure I'd caught a glimpse of him. But he was nowhere. My stomach was churning like a hot whirlpool.

Where was he?

At last, around midnight, they gave me a short break, and I raced outside and found my bicycle. I didn't know where to go, I just knew that if he was alive, he would still be out there, helping people. I cycled from street to street, looking at every bomb site, trying to see him through the darkness. I saw people running to and from buildings, gathering possessions, moving furniture, looting.

After ten minutes of frenetic cycling, I knew I had to get back, so I began tracing my way through the maze of destruction back to the hospital.

And then I saw him.

I had to look twice. His large silhouette stood before a rampant fire, a collapsed school building, a fire truck attempting to subdue the flames. I flew off my bicycle, leaving it to crash to the ground, and ran towards him, calling, 'Colonel Mallard, Colonel Mallard.'

He turned, first his head, and then his body, seeing it was me, taking great strides forward, opening his arms to meet me, calling my name. 'Mrs Tilling!'

I plunged down onto the forecourt, faster, faster, and then, quickly, frantically, pulled myself to a stop just short of him, a foot or so away, suddenly shy, afraid.

Was he about to embrace me?

'I thought you were dead,' I said, panting and quite unable to handle the whole situation.

'I thought you might have,' he said, folding his arms around in front of him, as if that was what he'd intended to do all along. 'I asked Venetia to go and see you when she got home, but of course you were here, weren't you?'

'Yes,' I said, letting out an embarrassed little laugh and looking at my feet. 'Of course you're all right.'

He unfolded his arms and stepped towards me, and as I looked up at his large chin, he took me in his arms and held me there for a space of time that felt like a thousand years and a single millisecond simultaneously. I couldn't think, although several dozen questions were colliding inside me, none of which seemed to have answers. But life is not always about questions and answers. It's about things and feelings, like the sensation of someone's arms around you, on a chilly night, beside a monstrous burning building. These things are real. Yet now I can't quite put my fingertips on it. It has gone, subsumed into the past, gone with the moment.

I drew apart before he did; I knew that he would take it better than I would. He looked down at me and smiled, taking one of my hands in his.

'It's nice to know that someone cares enough to miss me,' he smiled.

'I'm glad you think that racing around like a demented rescue dog marks me out as caring,' I laughed back. 'In any case, who knows what kind of person I'd get billeted with next time.'

'When did you get here?'

'Around quarter past nine. Litchfield Park was a ball of flames. I heard that one of the shelters had given way.'

'Yes, horrendous. We lost half our aerial defence team, truly wonderful people. An absolute tragedy.'

'But you weren't in it?'

'No, I was one of the lucky ones. I was in a different shelter on the other side of the compound.' He looked at me with remarkable sadness. 'It's just a case of luck, isn't it?'

'Sometimes,' I answered, and then more slowly, 'Sometimes.'

A thunderous explosion went off in the burning school, an unexploded bomb perhaps or something volatile that had just caught light, a bottle of paraffin or paint or something. I saw men running out, some with new flames on their clothes, and we ran forward to help them.

It was a long night, arduous and distressing. I had to head back to the hospital and my line of injured. A different atmosphere had taken over the place, a quiet resignation, with the grunts and groans of those in pain combined with the odd snores of those who fitfully slept. The lights had been dimmed to get everyone to calm down and go to sleep. Lines of people and children on blankets of all textures and wear paved the floor, the white bandages of limbs and heads standing out in the darkness.

'How utterly dismal,' I said to a fellow nurse.

'At least they're not in the morgue on the other side of town,' she replied. 'They haven't enough room inside so they've lined them up on the pavement outside. The munitions factory said they can put them in their warehouse, but no one's keen. It's better than being left on the pavement, but I'm not sure I'd want to be surrounded by bullets after an awful death.'

I cycled home slowly at dawn, leaving the hospital in a state of relative calm. When I got back, I had a wash and went to bed. The Colonel wasn't home, and I wondered if he'd found a place to sleep for a while. He would have to be at work today, after all, taking charge of the pile of rubble that used to be Litchfield Park.

Letter from Miss Edwina Paltry
to her sister, Clara

The Vicarage
Chilbury
Kent

Monday, 19th August, 1940

Dear Clara,

Today they kicked me out of hospital as they need the beds
for the new lot of wounded. Trembling I was when they
brought in some clothes for me to wear. Strange to think I
have nothing except the slightly singed nightie I came in
and these wretched old slippers. The secondhand skirt and
blouse they brought were all right, but the shoes were too
tight, rubbing my bunion something rotten. I didn't
complain though. Too petrified of what was out there.

I had the whole day planned out in my head. First, I
needed to get that money back from Ralph Gibbs. Without
it I have nothing, no way of running away from Mrs
Tilling, who threatened to hand me in to the police, or the
Brigadier, who promised to kill me.

But I had to get the money before Mrs Tilling or the
Brigadier saw me. I had to be quick, quiet, resolute.

Of course I wasn't expecting Ralph Gibbs to just hand over the money. I'd decided I would threaten him with telling the police about his black-market business and the ration book stamping being quietly forgotten for under-the-counter favours.

I also had the scissors. I stole them off the nurse's desk when she wasn't looking, a big clunky pair as heavy as a hammer. Although they weren't as threatening as a knife or a dagger, I knew how to wield them to best effect.
I wasn't thinking of killing him or anything, just brandishing them around to let him know I meant business. I'd asked for my old nightie, ration book, and gas mask to be put in a paper bag for me to carry, and I slipped the scissors in between, a comforting security in their solid weight.

As I stepped out into the warm August morning, I took a deep breath and set forth, getting on the bus for Chilbury (they'd given me the fare at the hospital – my last pennies in the world), and chivvying myself on as we circled the fields before pulling up on the square. I limped off the bus and set my sights on the shop. Pushing open the door, setting the bell jangling loudly, I watched the solid form of Ralph Gibbs appearing at the counter, appraising me with malice.

He looked different. I remember him as always being a slight, small kind of lad, tagging along behind the big kids, playing silly tricks and making a fool of himself. Well, that had changed all right, there was no fool here. He looked bigger, bulkier, more muscular and rugged. A long uneven scar raged red down his face beneath a growth of tawny stubble. His eyes were marbled and ringed with the deep maroon of blood, a theme that was repeated in the little scrapes and cuts on his face and hands.

It hadn't crossed my mind how the army might have changed him, how fighting on the front line can make a young man dangerous. I recalled someone saying that he'd been damaged in the brain, that Mrs Gibbs was having trouble with him. I'd thought that meant he was a bit down.

But now I could see precisely what kind of trouble they'd meant.

'What are you doing back around here?' he growled.

I stood firm, clenching my paper bag.

'I want my money,' I said with more determination than I felt.

'And what money would that be?' he said gruffly. Mrs Gibbs slipped in behind him, remaining half hidden by the till as Ralph stalked lazily around the counter into the main shop in front of me.

'You know exactly what money I'm talking about,' I spat, my hand itching to get out the scissors. 'The money you stole from the hop picker boy. It's my money, Ralph Gibbs. You have to give it back to me.' I was shouting at him, shouting and crying, spelling each word out as if it was the end of the world. 'I've lost my house, I've lost everything. I need my money.'

He stood watching me for a moment, half bored, half amused. Then he said, 'Or what?'

'What do you mean?' I cried.

'What, exactly, do you plan to do?' His tone was flippant, jokey. 'If I can't – or don't – give it back?'

'I'll tell the police about your dealings with the black market.' I planted a firm look on my face, as if that would be that. 'What with that, and your very casual use of rationing in the shop, you'll be behind bars in no time.'

'Oh really, Miss Paltry?' He seemed undaunted, leaning his hand on the counter, glancing around the shelves. 'I don't think they'll do any such thing without proof.'

'I'm sure they'll find it soon enough,' I sputtered, feeling the situation rushing out of my hands.

'Is that the best you can do, Miss Paltry?' He smirked, a pitying look on his face. 'Is that really the best you can do?'

That did it. I rummaged into my paper bag as fast as I could and closed my fingers around the scissors. 'I'm going to make you,' I said with relish as I brought them out, swooshing them in the air in front of his face.

He laughed, yes, laughed, and took a step back away from me. 'You don't want to do that, Miss Paltry,' he said lightly.

'I want my money,' I screamed, making a sweeping plunge towards his shoulder.

'Oh no you don't,' he said sharply, and, quick as a flash, he grabbed the end of the scissors with one hand and my arm with the other, and within the space of a few seconds he had my arm twisted around my back, the scissors dropping to the floor with a smattering metallic clatter. I felt something sharp, pointed, jabbing under my chin, the wincing pain of blood seeping out. It appeared that he had a knife of his own. I uttered a squeal, terrified that he would kill me, slit my throat like a pig's. I squirmed to get out of his grip, but it only threw my neck further into his blade.

'I warned you, Paltry,' he growled into my ear all sinister. 'When I get angry I lose control of what I'm doing.'

A tiny clang of a bell at the door made him lurch around, spinning me around in front of him.

Who do you think it was? None other than Mrs Tilling, who was clearly listening in, trying not to let the bells sound as she eased the door open.

For a split second we all froze – Ralph uncertain whether to let me go, Mrs Tilling sizing up the scene, Mrs Gibbs still peeking out from behind the till, and me unable to move for the ruddy blade beneath my chin.

'What's going on here?' Mrs Tilling demanded in a razor-sharp voice, striding forward to Ralph, who had decided to relax his grip, calmly slipping the knife into his pocket.

'Nothing,' he said, rubbing his hands against each other to blend the spots of blood. 'Just teaching Miss Paltry here one or two lessons I learnt in the army.' He cocked his tongue into the side of his mouth flippantly.

'You appear to have gone too far,' she said crossly, coming over and looking at my cut. 'Do you realise that you've drawn blood?'

'Have I?' he said, feigning surprise. 'I might have got a little carried away.' He folded his arms in a rebellious manner, half of him the man who went to war, half still the schoolboy afraid of his friend's mum.

'Well, that's quite enough.' She looked him over in a disapproving way. 'I'll be back later to deal with you. I'm sure that Constable Richards would be interested to hear about this.'

Ralph slouched into his heels. Was she going to turn him in? I half hoped she would, as it would serve him right, but that would also mean that the origin of my money would no doubt become known, and I would end up in jail with him. I let out a long breath.

Mrs Tilling turned to me, and I cringed back into the shadows. 'Why don't you come home with me, Miss Paltry?' Her tone was lighter, gentler, filling me with a searing trepidation of the horrors awaiting me. 'I'll help clean that nasty cut.' With that she picked up the scissors and put them in the brown bag, took a firm grasp of my elbow, and marched me out of the door.

We'd turned the corner out of the square and were heading down the road towards her house before I could shake her off.

I stopped dead, dug my heels in. 'Mrs Tilling, let me go!' I snarled. 'You can't make me go with you.'

'No, of course I can't, but under the circumstances I imagine you might realise that it's the preferable choice.' She didn't say she was going to call the coppers, but I knew she could. The little charade she just witnessed was evidence enough to get me put away for something, if not everything.

I stood away from her, grimly realising that my only hope of escape was to hobble frantically down to the train station, and with my hip the way it is she could easily stop me. I was well and truly cornered.

'Oh, all right,' I said, plodding alongside her like a disgruntled five-year-old.

At least she was taking me into her house, away from the road where I might be seen by the Brigadier. I let her take my elbow again as I stumbled over the stone path to her front door. She opened it wide and walked me into her sunny front room, where I slumped down on the nearest sofa, desperate to ease the pain in my hip.

Mrs Tilling disappeared for a minute, arriving back with tea and sandwiches, further alerting my suspicions about her motives. 'Why did you bring me here, Mrs Tilling?' I blurted out.

She didn't look dismayed, just sat neatly on the edge of an armchair and began to pour the tea. 'It was a good thing I came into the shop and rescued you when I did,' she said, completely ignoring my question. 'Ralph Gibbs is a brute these days.'

'Yes,' I muttered. 'I suppose it was lucky you came when you did.'

'Fortune had nothing to do with it,' she proclaimed, looking up from the teacups. 'I saw you on the bus and guessed where you were headed.'

I sat up, alarmed. 'Ralph Gibbs?' I uttered. How the devil did she know that Ralph bleeding Gibbs had my money?

As if reading my thoughts, she said, 'Kitty told me.' It was as simple as that. She had the whole bleeding village informing on me. 'Don't worry,' she added, picking up her little teacup. 'I'm not going to hand you in.'

'If you mean you're going to stop accusing me of some kind of baby swap, then I can only say it's about time,' I snapped.

She made a long, audible sigh. 'It's all right, Miss Paltry. I know you did it. I've just decided not to do anything about it. Now do you want me to help you or not?'

We sat in silence for a minute or two. I was busy trying to work out how she could help me, and whether she was bluffing about not handing me in. She, meanwhile, was eating a cucumber sandwich in the most irritatingly calm way. I felt like punching her delicately chewing mouth.

'It's not that it's right, what you did,' she added, after swallowing her dainty mouthful. 'But it was done, and exposing it would end in far more harm than good, especially for the poor babies. I dislike the dishonesty that this entails, the deceit that your little scheme has led me to, but I can't see any other way. I must put the stability of the community above my own integrity.'

I stopped myself from raising my eyes to Heaven, but, Lordy! Her moralising makes me want to give her a hearty slap.

'I do wonder sometimes if you ever felt any remorse about the action though?' she asked, her eyes creased up in thought. 'Do you think it's wrong to put the babies with the wrong parents?'

I looked at her blankly. One baby is much the same as the next, as far as I'm concerned. But I did feel rotten that it had all come to nothing. And I was certainly wrong for having touched it in the first place. So I put on a nice smile and said, 'Of course it's wrong. Says so in the Bible, doesn't it?'

She looked oddly puzzled, then continued, 'Well, the babies are both doing well at the Winthrops', and that's the main thing. Venetia is taking her godmother duties to heart and helping to look after Rose until Victor returns, and I must say the whole situation of her being surrounded by her real family makes me more comfortable.'

'Well, I'm very glad for them, and pleased you're drawing your accusations to an end,' I said brusquely. 'Not that anything happened, mind.'

'Come, come, Miss Paltry. All three of us know that you did it – you and I' – she paused, narrowing her eyes – 'and the Brigadier. He told me about your corrupt little scheme. I know everything – the meeting, the money, the swap, the bomb, and your clumsy efforts to retrieve and then lose the money.' She gave her little Miss Marple smile. 'You have nothing left to hide, you know.'

I have to admit that at this point the fight had gone out of me. It was as much as I could do to keep breathing, a fear gripping me like a snake tightening round my throat.

'Calm down, Miss Paltry.' She came and sat next to me, put her hand on my arm. 'I'm here to help you.'

I drew a deep breath, wondering what was coming next. 'What kind of help?'

'Well, for a start, I've found you somewhere to live. I'm the Billeting Officer, so it's my job.' She smiled, and I got the oddest feeling that this boring WVS stalwart was actually trying to help me. She got out some forms. 'This is the billet information. You're staying with the Vicar and Mrs Quail for now. I've got some things for you too, clothes and household things. They're secondhand, but they'll be fine for the time being.'

I sat sullenly looking into my cup, unable to grapple with the situation. What was going on? Why wasn't she turning me in?

'Look, Miss Paltry, perhaps we could go about this a little differently.'

'What do you mean?'

'What if you told me all about it.' She paused, looking at me curiously. 'On the basis that I promise not to expose you?'

'Why do you want to know if you're not going to hand me in?' I asked shiftily.

'I want to know how it happened, to understand it all. I want to know the truth.' There was a tense pressure of her hand over mine. 'And in return, I can make sure the Brigadier stays away from you.'

Now that made me sit up. How could this squirrel of a woman get one over on a man like that? I must have had the question on my face, because she smiled and said, 'Don't worry about the details, Miss Paltry. Just know that he won't be bothering you any more.'

Then it all fell into place. She was threatening him with exposure, which was why he was threatening me, and that's when it dawned on me that the more Mrs Tilling knew what happened, the more she could ensure that he never laid a finger on me.

And I know you'll think me wrong, Clara, but I told her. I told her everything. Once I began my story, about the Brigadier pulling me into his office after the funeral, it all came tumbling out so fast I could hardly stop it. But then I went on, I told her more. How it wasn't my fault, it was having to steal for food and shelter when I ran away from Uncle Cyril and found myself in King's Cross. Thank God the Great War came along and I got that job in Bart's Hospital, where they let me train as a nurse. But I was always broke, always running, taking chances when they came, however low and grimy. And as it all tumbled out, I realised that I had become a specialist in exactly that. Low and grimy had taken over my world.

Low and grimy was me.

She didn't say anything, just nodded and occasionally creased her forehead, offering me sympathy of all things. When I'd come to an end, she calmly patted my hand and told me they were expecting me at the Vicarage.

And you'd be surprised at me, Clara, as for once I was

relieved. I needed to rest my hip, and Mrs Quail is a down-to-earth sort. And a good cook.

'I thought it would be a good match for you,' she said, tidying my things into a bag. 'At least until you find a place of your own.'

'And they don't know about—' The truth seemed so open now, so loose and uncontained and out of my control.

She laughed, not a big laugh, but a laugh all the same. 'No, no one else has ever suspected a thing.'

I let out a nervy kind of laugh too, from pure relief, and that by some incredible stroke of luck I was still alive and free, that I had a roof over my head, a job.

I looked Mrs Tilling square in the face and said, 'Thank you.'

She must have known I meant it, as she put her warm thin hand on mine and squeezed it.

'Why are you being so helpful, Mrs Tilling?' I asked, wondering what's in it for her.

'We have to stand together and look after each other, Miss Paltry, or we'll never have any chance against the Nazis.'

Funny, I'd completely forgotten about the war.

Leaving her looking on from her front door, I made my way up to the Vicarage. But as I limped up into the square, there was one thing I hadn't been expecting. The sight of my old house, now a pile of rubble settling amongst the other piles of rubble that were once the houses on Church Row, lay strewn before me. My life had been in that place for years, and although I was never especially happy there, those were still my years.

A shiver of horror ran over me as I found myself drawn to the carnage. All that was left of my house was a mush of bricks and debris, pieces of wall still with my blue-striped wallpaper and those hideous green tiles from the kitchen. A fire had carried half the contents of my house to oblivion, and the ransackers took the rest.

There were still a few children out, nosing through the wreckage and showing off if they found anything. One of them held up a piece of a photograph, still clinging to part of a frame.

'Give me that,' I yelled, grabbing it from the little thief. 'That's mine. Now, get out of here.' I swatted them away, flailing around and giving them each a clip round the head. 'All of you, get off my house.'

I have to confess that when they'd gone I slumped down and cried. Everything that I owned was in that house, now destroyed or burnt or nicked.

I looked at the broken picture in my hand. It's the one I have of you and me with Mum, less than a year before she died. You were about sixteen, and I was twelve, happy and innocent to this wretched world we live in. We were in the garden at Birnham Wood, I could see the house in the corner, the gables where the wisteria grew. Mum loved that wisteria. I wondered what had brought me so far away from that moment. How could I still be the same woman as the girl in the photograph? What has become of me?

After an hour or so of picking through my things, finding a fork and a spoon, some hairclips, a broken ornament, that dancing-couple statuette I always loved, I heard a voice behind me on the footpath.

'Miss Paltry, are you all right?'

It was the Vicar, come to take me home with him, and I realised that it had begun to rain without me noticing, fat drops of water splattering on and around us, getting harder as we made our way across the square to the Vicarage.

He showed me to the comfortable room they'd prepared, 'Especially for our midwife guest.' After I settled in, we had a fish supper, and then I sat listening to the wireless with news of the war, of the Battle of Britain, Nazi planes dropping bombs over the southeast, and I was suddenly struck by how precious it all is, how much we have to protect.

So here I am, in the most unlikely of places, writing this sat up in my soft, warm bed, as the rain falls outside my window. I feel like I need to write it all out tonight so that I can start afresh tomorrow, move on to a new day, a new beginning.

I know that you will be cross with me, Clara, and I know you're planning to come and give me a piece of your mind. But please stay away. My hip is sore, and I need to rest for a time, and then I need to earn a little money from a few births, find a small place of my own somewhere.

And then I will turn my attention to Ralph Gibbs. Make no mistake, Clara, I will get my money come hell or high water.

Until then,
Edwina

Notice pinned to the Chilbury village hall noticeboard,
Monday, 19th August, 1940

Anyone who wants to join the Chilbury Ladies'
Choir for a singing concert to cheer up the
homeless people of Litchfield next Saturday, please
come to the practice tonight in the Village Hall,
7 o'clock prompt.

Mrs Tilling and Kitty Winthrop

Letter from Venetia Winthrop
to Angela Quail

Chilbury Manor
Chilbury
Kent

Monday, 19th August, 1940

Dear Angela,

Since my office at Litchfield Park was obliterated by the bombs, they're moving me up to London. The bombing was horrific, a lot of people's homes destroyed, and a lot of those beautiful Tudor buildings. I feel terribly guilty for being excited to leave, but I need to be away to take my mind off everything that's happened.

I do still pine for Alastair, but I can't get over him leaving me like he did. The more I think about it, I feel that he was two different men, the one who was a villain and a spy, and the other Alastair – the one I knew – who was gentle and clever and decent. I wonder if he's somewhere out there, thinking of me.

In the meantime, Kitty has got us involved in a singing concert for the people who were bombed in Litchfield. At first it was just us singing along to some gramophone

records at home, but then Mama suggested that we make it
for the Chilbury Ladies' Choir. I could make a joke about
the Litchfield people needing cheering up, not burst
eardrums, but I won't as I'm sure they'll love it. There
aren't a lot of good things you can give people these days,
now that everything's rationed or not allowed, but at least
we can still sing. It's amazing how much better it can make
you feel. Prim always used to tell us it's because of all the
blood flowing through our bodies, the extra air in our
lungs, making us feel alive. Poor Prim! It'll be sad to have
the concert without her here. She would have loved it.

Mrs Tilling arranged for us to use a church hall in
Litchfield this coming Saturday, and Kitty made some
colourful posters to put up around the town. They think
that over seventy people might come, and we're beginning
to feel quite nervous.

There was a practice this evening in the village hall, and
we arrived wondering how it would all work out. Halls are
nothing like churches, and the music we were singing was
certainly not 'Ave Maria'. But we're terribly excited. What
better way to cheer us up after cleaning up first Chilbury
and then the rather larger job at Litchfield.

'Hello, everyone,' Mrs Tilling said jovially. 'Let's start by
getting into place then, shall we? Everyone up on stage.'
She whisked her hands up to hurry us along, and then
began to position us. 'Sopranos on the right, altos on the
left,' she called, and then began pulling the shorter people
forward and pushing the larger ones – including a much
befuddled Mrs B – to the back. Then she dashed back off
the stage to admire her handiwork, coming back a few
times to make small adjustments.

'Perfect!' she finally announced, and handed out a few pages to each person. These were Kitty and Silvie's masterpieces. They had managed to fit the words of all twenty songs onto two sheets of paper, and then copied them out lots of times.

We began by singing along to the gramophone records, as we had back at Chilbury Manor, and there was a lot of stumbling over words.

'Not to worry if you haven't got the words in time to the music yet,' Mrs Tilling said. 'Just muddle through for now. Remember that you can practise on your own at home, and we'll have a full rehearsal on Wednesday.'

Kitty is singing a wonderful solo, 'Somewhere over the Rainbow'. She sang it perfectly at practice, which is hardly surprising since we haven't heard anything else in the house since Sunday.

Then Mrs Tilling stepped forward and said, 'I'd also like to ask Venetia to sing a solo. Would you do that for us?'

I was bewildered. 'Well, I'll give it a try,' I said uncertainly.

She gave me the music for a song we sang at home last week, 'Blue Moon'. My fingers began to shake as I looked over the words. It's about a girl, like me, who is now alone, like me, and waiting for someone new. This last part is not like me, and my eyes began to water. I don't want someone new, I want Alastair back. I know he's a scoundrel, and that I should never want to see his face again, but I can't get over him. I don't want to get over him.

'You don't have to sing it if you don't want to, Venetia,' Mrs Tilling said softly, putting her hand out to take the page away from me again.

'No,' I said, standing straight. 'I can do it.'

And so I did. Mrs Quail started the introduction, and I sang, clear and low, my voice filling the hall. Everyone clapped and cheered at the end, so I must have done a reasonable job. I have been practising at home, and think it'll work fine on Saturday.

After that, I shall be London-bound, and we shall have fun like the good old days, and hopefully I'll begin to forget about Alastair. Would it be all right if I stay with you until I find a place of my own?

Much love,
Venetia

Letter from Colonel Mallard to his sister, Mrs Maud Green, in Oxford

Ivy House
Litchfield Road
Chilbury
Kent

Tuesday, 20th August, 1940

Dear Maud,

It appears that my department is to be moved to London since a bomb neatly destroyed our entire office. My desk is woodchip, and I can hardly bear to imagine the state of me had I been sitting at it. They aim to start moving us up as soon as they can find accommodation. I have been told that we've been prioritised, so it may be as early as next week.

I have yet to tell my landlady, Mrs Tilling. I'm sure she'll be upset to have to find a new person for her room, although with Litchfield Park bombed and Kent on the front line, she may find herself spared the effort. I know she'll miss having the company though, and I rather worry about how I'm going to break it to her. We've become quite good friends, what with our makeshift dinners in the kitchen and our air raids together in the cellar. I must confess I'll miss our little chats.

Nevertheless, the war carries on, and we must step to. I'll write again once I have a new address for you. Send my love to the girls.

Much love,
Anthony

Mrs Tilling's Journal

❦

Wednesday, 21st August, 1940

The Chilbury Ladies' Choir will perform again! We are to sing in a concert in Litchfield this coming Saturday. A lot of the ladies were very upset that the choir competition was cancelled, and now we have our very own stage. What a marvellous idea it was of Kitty's.

The rehearsal went quite well, although I am hoping that certain members put in some extra practice. Our plan is to begin at seven. We will perform for an hour by ourselves and then do songs that everyone knows and can sing along to, like 'My Old Man Said Follow the Van', and 'Roll Out the Barrel', and 'We're Going to Hang Out the Washing on the Siegfried Line'. The church said they may be able to find some tea for afterwards, but I'm not counting on it. Following that, well, back home, and back to reality.

The Colonel has to move to London, probably next week or the week after. He told me over dinner last night, at the kitchen table. All we had was oxtail soup and some bread and butter, but it didn't seem to matter.

'I'd really rather stay here, you know,' he said, looking rather crestfallen. 'I've grown to like it, and all that.'

'Yes, I suppose I've grown used to you being here too.'

'Have you?'

'Yes.'

'Will you miss me, then?'

'Of course I will.' I carried on eating my soup, even though he'd put down his spoon.

'Will you write to me?' he asked carefully.

'Of course,' I replied. 'I love writing letters. I do hope you'll reply, tell me how things are in London, whether we're going to win the war, that kind of thing.'

'No, I mean it,' he said more quietly, seriously.

'So do I.'

We watched each other for a few moments, the spoon midway to my mouth, and I suddenly felt like we were in some sort of battlefield. It was clear that he liked me and I liked him. We had grown to fit around one another, fill the gaps of space between us. The comfort and support, the lively conversation and banter, the fleeting feeling of passion, love even. I knew he felt it too. It had woven its way around the pair of us together, in unison, each move of the one bringing the other closer, and vice versa.

He brought out a gift for me, 'a thank-you-for-having-me-stay gift', he called it. I took off the newspaper wrapping and beheld a new dressing gown, soft and blue.

'Thank you,' I said, embarrassed, thinking of my battered brown one, wondering how he'd come across such a lovely item in the thick of war.

'Oh, it's nothing. I just noticed that your old one was, well, old,' he murmured, also embarrassed.

After dinner we sat in the front room and listened to the news on the wireless, and then I put on a few gramophone records Kitty lent me from Prim's collection. The first one was called 'Cheek to Cheek', that lovely dance number sung by Fred Astaire. Much to my surprise, within the first few bars, the Colonel was on his feet and asking me to stand up with him, right there in the front room.

At first I laughed. 'Don't be ridiculous.'

'Why not? When do we ever get to dance these days? In any case, goodness knows when we'll get the chance again.'

I thought of him living in London, the chance that something might happen to him too. His near hit in Litchfield had given me a bit of a jolt. I began thinking that one by one all the people I've ever cared for will be taken away from me. He must have seen my face, as he said: 'Now stop thinking miserable thoughts and enjoy the moment.'

He hauled me up out of my seat and pulled me towards him, and began to gallantly waltz me around the small space. I laughed nervously. He was a surprisingly good dancer for such a large, cumbersome man, light on his feet and competently leading me around and around, one hand firm on my waist, the other clasping my slender hand. I'm medium height, or thereabouts, so my eyes were level with his chest. We must have looked quite comedic, spinning around the dim little room in our own world.

When it finished, we were left standing in the centre of the room; the deep red glow of the curtains and rug was warm, close. He pulled away from me and looked down, bent his head a little to one side, and I knew he was about to kiss me.

I panicked, pulled back, started flustering. It's not as if I'd never thought about him in this way. Or that I'd never dreamt about kissing him. I just didn't ever see it actually happening. Now I panicked even more. Perhaps he mistook my panicking for not wanting to kiss him. What would happen if he never wanted to kiss me again?

So I stopped panicking, stepped up to him, reached my hands behind his neck, and pulled him down to kiss me. It was all a little clumsy, but we got there in the end, and it was well worth it. An incredible sense of bliss and fortitude drenched my body. I'd never thought that kissing was so divine. I suppose I must have forgotten, parcelled it up in a storage box in my brain with a large label: *Do not open.* Now it's open. Well and truly exploded.

We continued kissing for quite a while. I think he must have been enjoying it as well, as he had a dreamy look in his eyes. It was a late night, with very little time spent studying the music for the concert.

What a strange turn of events. Perhaps he felt that since he was going, he needed to take stock of the situation. Perhaps he wanted to secure my affections. Possibly his near death in the Litchfield bombing made him realise something too. Maybe he's just never had the nerve to do it, and now, since he'll be gone next week, it made it so much easier for him. All I know is I'm glad he did do it. Whatever happens in the future, last night will always be ours, an isolated piece of Heaven in this chaotic world.

Kitty Winthrop's Diary

Saturday, 24th August, 1940

The Litchfield singing concert

We hadn't had enough rehearsals, at least two sopranos had come down with a nasty cough, and then when we arrived the hall was as dirty and dingy as a deserted mansion.

Our hearts fell.

'Well, it's a good thing we got here early,' Mrs Tilling said, looking in cupboards for some brooms. 'And did anyone remember to bring decorations?'

Mrs B had brought along the coloured bunting from Henry's leaving party, and began handing it out and ordering people around. 'We'd better hurry if we're to make this place fit for a concert at seven o'clock.'

We scurried around, and I have to confess that by a quarter to seven the place looked a lot better. The red, white, and blue streamers really cheered the place up, and we made some newspaper chains to bulk it out. We set up the chairs for the audience, then went and took our places at the side of the stage, and waited, whispering last-minute tips for nerves.

But the place remained deserted.

'How many of those posters did you put up, Kitty?' Mrs B boomed over to me from the altos, as if it were entirely my fault that no one had turned up yet.

'A lot more than you did!' Mrs Tilling snapped back at her. We all giggled. Fancy Mrs Tilling getting the better of Mrs B!

But the clock ticked on, and still no one was coming in. Our lines of chairs looked sadly out of place, with only the church porter bumbling around with a hammer doing some odd jobs. It was now five to seven. I couldn't believe no one wanted to come to hear us. I'd plastered the city's lampposts with my posters.

'I'll just have a word with the porter,' Mrs Tilling said. 'Perhaps the church cancelled it and forgot to tell us.' She trotted down the steps at the side of the stage, down the aisle, and disappeared into the entrance hall.

'One would hope they would have the decency to let us know!' Mrs B said, sniffing slightly, as if the whole thing were very much beneath her.

All of a sudden from the entrance there came a frenzied commotion as a torrent of people surged through and into the hall, some racing to get a seat near the front. The porter must have forgotten to open the door. There was a caco-phony of chattering, people calling to one another once they had reached some seats, or on recognising a neighbour. There were a lot of people in military uniform, but predominantly it was women, as we've got used to these days. I couldn't believe they were so excited. They'd all come just to hear us sing! I could feel butterflies exploding all over my stomach. Why had I agreed to do a solo? Was I really cut out for a life on the stage?

At last the hall was bursting at the seams, and the porter closed the door and indicated to Mrs Tilling that it was time to begin. She got up and walked purposefully to the centre of the stage, raising her arms to indicate that we were to stand up and take our places. After a little confusion and Mrs Gibbs standing on Mrs B's foot, we found our spots. Mrs Tilling looked serenely around the massive hall, waiting for everyone to be silent. The voices lowered amongst some shushing, and then disappeared completely, especially as I could see Mrs Tilling's eyes focusing on one or two perpetrators to give them a what-for look.

Then she returned to us, raised her baton, and gently ushered Mrs Quail to begin the introduction of our first song. It was a lovely lazy jazz song called 'Summertime', and we all began swaying a little as we sang, as it just seemed so dreamy. We were so enjoying singing that I think we almost forgot about the audience out there, hundreds of faces listening, some swaying, some tapping a foot, some forgetting for a moment about the bombs and the blood and the bodies.

At the end there was an eruption of applause, and even a few whistles. We beamed with delight and then saw that Mrs Tilling indicated that it was Venetia's turn to sing 'Blue Moon'. Venetia had wanted me to go first, but Mrs Tilling insisted. 'You have such a marvellous stage presence, Venetia,' she said. 'I want you near the beginning.'

'Good luck,' I whispered as I went to stand at the side of the stage with the rest of the choir. 'You can do it, Venetia.'

And then it was just Venetia, alone at the front of the stage. She looked nervous, in her beautiful way, her great blue eyes staring out into the crowd, her yellow dress trembling slightly, and her golden, curled hair rustling on her shoulders. Her carefully painted mouth was open slightly in fear, her chest flittering up and down with fast breaths. The introduction began, and she spread her fingers out down by her side and sang out the first notes, 'Blue Moon', at first quiet and nervous, but then growing in strength with the first few lines. She was doing it. She was singing in front of all these people.

I looked around the faces, smiling, enjoying it, and I felt her becoming more comfortable, letting her voice ring out to fill the great hall. Before I knew it, she was in the second verse, her hips swaying slightly as she sang, smiling at the audience.

Then I saw someone vaguely familiar.

He was standing at the back, slightly to the right. I couldn't work out if it was really him at first. He looked different. His hair was shorter, his clothes less formal. Was he an apparition?

He smiled and winked at her, slow and measured, and I knew that it truly was him. That he was alive. Come to find her.

She stopped singing. Her words just petered out as she gazed over at him. I saw his mouth move, saying something silently through the air. *I love you*. And *I love you too*, she mouthed back to him over the crowds.

Mrs Quail had carried on playing, even though Venetia had stopped singing, and I quickly found my feet and darted across the stage to her, carrying on from where she left off. She turned and looked at me, trepidation in her eyes, and headed to the steps off the stage. I carried on singing as she made her way through the crowds, people parting to let her through, making a path for her, until she reached Mr Slater.

There they stood, a few feet apart, looking at each other, until someone nudged her forward, and they fell into each other's arms, kissing like people do in the movies. It was the most romantic moment I've ever seen. Everyone around them cheered, and soon the whole hall was alight with a roar of celebration. In this bleak world, there is at least one thing that we have left. Love.

He took her hand and led her through the crowds to the door, and they disappeared into the night together.

I carried on singing, thinking of being alone, the end of my future with Henry. How ridiculous it all seems now, that I was so smitten that I'd do something so stupid and childish.

But then I thought of all the wonderful people that I have in my life: Mama had suddenly become more herself, Venetia had become a friend, Silvie was part of our family for now, and Rose too, and even Tom, in his small, adoring way, could be considered a new friend. And the choir, almost like a family of friends and neighbours all standing by each other. You see, I'm not alone any more. None of us are.

The crowd roared with pleasure as the song came to a close. It took a minute for me to realise that they were clapping for me – I had quite forgotten my butterflies.

'Let's go straight into your solo, Kitty,' Mrs Tilling said, turning to Mrs Quail for the introduction, and before I knew it I was smiling around the crowd waiting for the moment to come in. It was that wonderful, soaring song, 'Somewhere over the Rainbow'.

After the sweeping low-high of the first notes, the audience cheered their approval, and I couldn't help beaming a smile through the entire song, the words spilling seamlessly out of my mouth and filling the hall with a glowing, radiant hope.

At the end, the applause burst forth like thunder, with people calling and whistling. I felt my eyes fill with tears. My singing had been a success!

Soon I was surrounded by the rest of the choir, congratulating me and getting their music ready for the rest of the show. Mrs Tilling took her baton and led us into the next tune, another jazz number, and we found ourselves swinging our hips to the rhythm, the crowds joining in. It was so much fun. Following that, we had the sing-along, finishing off with a very hearty version of 'There'll Always Be an England'.

'You were right, Kitty,' Mrs Tilling said, as the applause continued and we took bow after bow. 'There's nothing like a good song to cheer us all up.'

'Thanks to you, Mrs Tilling, for taking over the choir.'

The calls for 'More' and 'Encore' continued, and Mrs B bustled forward and nudged Mrs Tilling. 'Shall we give them another one?'

Mrs Tilling looked around at our eager eyes. 'I don't see why not,' she said, and raised her baton one final time. 'Let's sing "The World Will Sing Again".'

We'd only rehearsed it a few times, but it was one of the most tearful songs, thinking of the bereaved and filling them with some kind of hope. Mrs Tilling waited for the hall to be completely hushed before holding up her baton and leading us in. We sang it plainly, letting the words speak for themselves, their intertwining mixture of despair and hope, of smashed dreams and brave smiles, of the blackest night quietly overcome with the new light of daybreak. It was a magic moment – you could have heard a pin drop, the audience was so quiet. Respectful, I'd say, of everyone there who'd lost someone, or with loved ones away, in danger.

When we finished, there was a long moment of silence, a prayer perhaps, before a slow applause began, rippling around the crowded room like a growing tide. There were no cheers, no whistles, just the dense resonance of hundreds of people sounding their support to those who'd lost someone, to those who didn't know how to carry on.

After it had died down, we went to see if there were any refreshments (which there weren't) and meet people. All of Chilbury had turned up, including Henry (who Venetia and I have renamed Horrible Henry), who was talking animatedly to a uniformed woman who looked like an especially brutish bulldog.

'That's Lady Constance Worthing, Lady Worthing's daughter,' Mrs Tilling whispered, a little laugh trembling her voice. 'I am surprised Henry's succumbed to Mrs B's wishes.'

'Is he courting her?' I was amazed. She didn't look like his type at all. I couldn't even be jealous!

'Their union would make their families very formidable indeed. The Brampton money and the Worthing title.' She smirked, and I could see she thought the whole thing ludicrous. 'But look over there!'

I followed her gaze to see Ralph Gibbs with none other than our former maid Elsie. 'Are they courting?' I asked again.

'It looks like it,' she replied. We watched as he leant in and whispered something in her ear, and they both laughed. She took his arm, leading him back to the door. Whoever would have thought such a pretty girl would want to be with such an ugly thug.

People came forward to congratulate us, everyone saying how marvellous it had been, and how grateful they were. One woman told me about her ruined house. She and four children have been squashed into a neighbour's house ever since. Quite a few people are still living in various halls, sleeping on floors. Blankets have become scarcer than pork chops. They're becoming tradable commodities, like shillings or silver. I've decided to make a collection around Chilbury, and Mrs Quail said she'd help.

Tom was there, his hair combed for once, and looking rather handsome. 'You were incredible, Kitty. For organising everything, and for singing so beautifully.'

'Do you really think so?'

'All the people here think so,' he said, and everyone around us began cheering. It was a little embarrassing.

'I was right, wasn't I?' Tom went on.

'What about?' I asked, wondering what was coming.

'You have become the big hero after all!'

I leant forward and gave him a peck on the cheek.

Then Daddy appeared out of nowhere. 'What's all this about?' he grumped. 'Kitty, it's time to leave. Come on. We haven't got all day. What happened to Venetia and that blasted chap? I'll have a few words with both of them when I find them. Should have shot him while I had the chance.'

'I didn't know you'd come to hear us sing,' I said, wishing he hadn't.

'I had to come to see how much of a mess you'd make of it,' he bellowed, then gave a snort of a laugh. 'But you weren't actually that bad.' He glanced around, eyeing the surroundings, possibly for Mama or Mrs Tilling. 'Although I do hope that your ambitions stop at local charity shows, young lady.

It really wouldn't do to have a Winthrop on the stage, you know.'

I smiled at him like the Cheshire Cat. 'Don't worry, Daddy. I'm still your little poppet,' I said, and skipped off into the crowd.

It seems Venetia has taught me a thing or two after all.

Letter from Venetia Winthrop
to Angela Quail

Chilbury Manor
Chilbury
Kent

Wednesday, 28th August, 1940

Dear Angela,

I simply can't believe it! Alastair came back, he is alive! I am beside myself with incredulity, and keep having to shake myself to make sure it's not a dream.

It all happened the evening of our concert. Can you believe, I was standing alone in the centre of the stage singing 'Blue Moon'? And everyone was enjoying it! The crowd was swaying along to the music, smiling, and I was beginning to get used to being up there, singing louder, when my eyes flickered over to a man standing at the back. At first I thought I'd dreamt it, and then I thought it must be someone who looked like him, but the more my eyes darted to his, the more I knew for sure.

It was Alastair.

He was watching evenly, a vague smile on his lips, like he always had, and I felt something inside me buckle up and snap. I stopped singing, stopped breathing, as if I'd seen a mirage. Mercifully, Kitty came up beside me and took over the singing, and I found myself walking across the stage, down the steps, and through the throng, as if the rest of the people in the room had vanished. It was just him and me, walking towards each other, our eyes connecting, and then him taking me in his very real arms.

We missed the rest of the show, as we disappeared outside to take a walk together. The evening was warm and balmy, the smell of burnt-out buildings still settling in the air, an almost-full moon hanging mindfully in the purple hue above the horizon.

'Good choice of song,' Alastair said, taking my hand. I felt that extraordinary sensation of happiness flooding through me. I know I should have been cautious, but I simply couldn't help myself. I had been deprived of something so crucial to life, and someone had just given it to me, reminding me of how it is to be happy.

'"Blue Moon",' I said, looking at the moon, a small smile escaping. 'And now you're here. Finding me alone. On a stage, of all places.'

'You were terrific,' he said, steering me into a small park, a pond with some benches, swans in pairs, curving their necks into their plumage ready for sleep. We sat down, holding hands, like an old couple on holiday.

'Alastair,' I said quietly, looking at his hand holding mine in my lap. 'Where have you been?'

'I had a job to do, unfortunately,' he whispered, as he turned his head to nuzzle into my hair. 'I didn't want to go, nor did I realise that I was going to have to leave so quickly.'

'It was to do with the Nazi in the wood, wasn't it?' I asked. 'Were you worried you'd be caught?'

'No, Venetia.' He smiled and kissed my hand. Then he told me all about it, but swore me to secrecy, so I really mustn't tell you, my dear! Suffice it to say, he is not the villain I thought him. Rather he is one of the good guys.

When he finished, I ran my fingertips over the collar of his coat, which was a little scruffier than the suits I was used to him wearing. 'But why did you leave me?'

'I had to go. I had to follow Proggett. He led me to the others. I had to make sure I had them all.'

'And the shots in the wood that night—' I began.

'Yes, that was an altercation between Old George and Proggett. I saw it all as I was following Proggett.' Then he added with a smile, 'Both are disastrous shots though. Never stood a chance of harming each other. And after that they both fled.' He paused, looking down at my hand. 'I never got to say goodbye, but I always meant to come back as soon as I could. Believe me, Venetia, I wouldn't have left for anything less.'

'You're a pretty good liar though, pretending to be an artist. Was that part of your prep for the job? Like seducing local beauties?'

'Now, Venetia. It was you who seduced me, remember? I was trying to maintain a professional distance.' He gave me a knowing smile.

I suddenly felt that I didn't know this man at all. Well, rather I know him in one sense, but not the details about him, and little by little he began telling me. He comes from Somerset and was sent to a boarding school and then went up to Cambridge, where he studied philosophy of all things.

It was there that he was approached to 'work for the country', as he puts it.

'I moved to London, and have a flat in Bloomsbury for in between missions. It's got much more intense since the war. We've had a feeling it was going to get rather messy for years before the war actually started, tracking the buildup of German military and espionage. Frankly the war seemed almost inevitable from about 1936. The Government never listened to us, of course,' he laughed. 'But they're listening now.'

I took this in with vague confusion, especially when he began to elaborate on the simplest details of his life: his parents being old and strict, his love for fishing, his twin brother dying in infancy, him never feeling quite right afterwards, 'as if there's always someone missing'.

'That's how I felt about you,' I said, feeling estranged from this new man. 'I don't feel that I know who you are any more. I mean, who is my Alastair Slater anyway, the man I loved?'

'I'm still here, Venetia,' he said, taking me in his arms. 'I'm still the man who loves you, the real Venetia. I'm still the man who loves cooking candlelit dinners for you, and loves art and poetry and painting your portrait. I'm still the man who wants to love and cherish you from this day forward.' He paused, pulling back and looking at me. 'But there is one thing you need to know.'

I pulled back again. 'What now?'

'My name isn't actually Alastair Slater. That was made up for me for the mission.'

'So what is your real name, then? Mr Nobody?'

'No, it's John—'

'John MacIntyre,' we both said together, then laughed.

'The same as your grandfather,' I said, and took out the battered pendant, on a necklace under my dress. 'I've been thinking about him, you know.' Then I began to tell him about all that happened since he's been away, and he was horrified and utterly guilt-ridden.

'I wish I'd known, then you wouldn't have had to go through it all. I am so incredibly sorry I wasn't here, and that you were forced to go to that scoundrel.' The light from the moon reflected in his eyes. 'Will you ever be able to forgive me?' Then he scooped up my hand, turned it over, and kissed my palm. 'Venetia, my darling, will you do me the honour of marrying me?' he asked, a seriousness in his eyes taking me back to that moment when we were hiding behind the tree, his fingers interweaving mine, his eyes so sad, so intense.

My heart broke, as I slowly shook my head. 'There's a war on, and we've both got lives to live. In any case, I need time to get to know you better, Mr MacIntyre.' With that, I stood up from the bench and offered him my hand, and we continued our moonlight walk together, careful not to disturb the swans.

We've spent all our days together since. He's on leave to be briefed for his next job – he's not allowed to say where he's going, but it's abroad, and he promises it's not dangerous, although I can't imagine it isn't. Well, where isn't dangerous these days? He's been staying in a barracks in Litchfield and spends a lot of time here at Chilbury Manor – Mama said it's all right as it's good for my health.

We'll both be leaving next week, him for his secret destination and me for London. I can't wait to be there with

you, Angie, and be free to live my own life. I dread the
thought of Alastair – I mean John, of course – leaving, so
we'll just have to keep incredibly busy, shan't we? That's all
for now, my dear Angie. Until you see me next week.

Much love,
Venetia

Silvie's Diary

❈

Wednesday, 28th August, 1940

There was a singing show and everyone joined in. There were silly songs, like 'Run Rabbit Run' and 'Knees Up Mother Brown'. For that we have to do a dance. Mrs Tilling was bad, but Mrs B was very good. We laughed as it was so funny.

The Brigadier said I could stay, so I am part of the family. I call Mrs Winthrop Auntie Lavinia, and Venetia and Kitty are my new sisters for now. Everyone is very kind to me, especially the choir ladies. Mrs Poultice always gives me an apple and a special smile.

I think about my parents a lot. I want to go to them. I want to see them, hug them. It is hard. I dream about them and wake up crying. Kitty comes in with her map book and we plan our trip after the war.

I hope it ends soon.

Mrs Tilling's Journal

❧

Wednesday, 28th August, 1940

What a few days we've had! Last Saturday was the Chilbury Ladies' Choir's first ever singing concert, and it was a massive success. Venetia's Mr Slater arrived back and they had an extraordinary reunion at the concert, which quite added to the spectacle of the whole event. They've been virtually inseparable since, although she is going to London next week and he is to go abroad.

Carrington was at the concert too, and is also being sent to London. He was incredibly happy about it, whispering to me, 'It'll be marvellous to get away from the old man', which made me laugh.

Another amusing occurrence at the concert was that Lady Worthing was there with her appalling daughter, Lady Constance, who is so terribly bossy she quite competes with Mrs B, who has her in mind for a daughter-in-law, just because she's titled, of course. It's hilarious to think of Henry with her though. I had a chance to have a short chat with her after the concert.

'I've always had a notion that marriage is not unlike getting a new hound,' she said to me, loudly and in an instructional way. 'It takes a lot of whipping them into shape before you can get them to do what they're told.' She slapped her thigh with enthusiasm, and I had to purse my lips to stop myself hooting with laughter.

I couldn't wait to tell the Colonel about it when I got home, but he wasn't there. I assumed he had to work late, but felt the chill of loneliness in the house without him, and my little story quite lost its charm. I decided to give the kitchen a good tidy-up, rather than plodding despondently to bed, and soon found myself sitting at the kitchen table, wondering how much I was going to miss him. By the time he walked through the door at one, I was quite miserable and pathetic.

'What's all this, then?' he said as he came in. He bent down and gave me a kiss on the cheek. 'Have you had bad news?' he said, anxious that I'd received a telegram about David, and I began a new set of tears.

'If I did get a telegram about David, who would be here once you leave?' I sobbed. 'It's just me in this old house now, alone with my thoughts. They'll kill me, you know. They'll gang up on my brain and take over, thinking all the worst things and never getting anything done.'

'You'll be fine,' he said, dragging a chair over and sitting down so that he could put his arm around me. 'You're a strong woman, Mrs Tilling.'

'But I don't want to always be the strong one. Who can, in these dreadful times? I'm sick and tired of holding it all in, putting on a brave face, living an inner misery behind a frail smile. It's simply not going to work any more.'

We sat in silence for a minute or two, him rubbing my shoulder, and me looking into nowhere, enjoying a last feeling of warmth and comfort from him before he leaves.

'Why don't you come with me, then?' he said in a perfectly matter-of-fact way, as if he were suggesting a picnic or a day at the beach.

'Don't be ridiculous,' I muttered.

'I don't see why not. I mean, they've found me a nice flat in London, and there'll be plenty of room. There's a need for nurses everywhere at the moment, so you'll find a job up there. It'll be like a new start. An adventure. We'll have to get married, of course, but that'll be easy.'

'Don't be ridiculous.'

'Look at me, Margaret.' He'd never used my name before, and it made me feel strange, like he was talking to the real me, the one inside, not the one who rushes around cheering people up and making things better. 'I mean it. I'd love it if you'd marry me. We've been living together these past months blissfully, so why leave it there? I love you.'

I was suddenly finding it hard to breathe, so I decided it was about time to tidy out the cupboard under the sink. Making a loud scraping sound as I pushed back the chair, I strode to the sink, got down on my hands and knees, and started to drag everything out.

'Don't you love me too?' he demanded, crouching down beside me and helping me take out a rather grubby old metal bucket with several holes.

'Of course I do,' I replied, carefully bringing out an old pot with candles poking out the top. 'But we can't just get married. What about David? He'll come home and find I've gone.'

'He's a man now, although he'll always be your boy. He can always come and stay. You can't just sit here waiting for him to come home.'

'And what about your girls?'

'They'll adore you. Everyone does.'

I got up to find an old cloth to wipe the shelves inside the cupboard, then knelt back down, proceeding to give it a severely hearty scrubbing down.

'And what about me? My independence? My home, my village? Ivy House?'

'We can come home after the war, if you want.' He took my hands in his, prising out the old scrubbing cloth and throwing it on the floor. 'I don't want to take over your life. I just want to be part of it. Living together, just like we have been. Two people together, happy.' He took a deep breath, his fingers lacing between mine. 'There's a war on, and everything seems to be getting a lot worse out there. You never know what's going to happen to any of us. We need to grab any happiness we can while there's still time.'

I sat gazing at him for a long moment.

'I need time to think it over. I'm not one of those people who can jump into something new straightaway.' I leaned into him, tucking my hand behind his neck and bringing him close. 'And yet,' I began, pausing for a moment with the truth of it. 'I'm not sure I can just let you leave.'

We sat there for some while, on the kitchen floor, holding hands and kissing, talking about it all – the war, David, his girls – until the sirens went off at around two, and we headed downstairs to the cellar.

Kitty Winthrop's Diary

Friday, 6th September, 1940

An unexpected wedding

What an extraordinary week this has been! With astounding decisiveness, Mrs Tilling married the Colonel yesterday in our little church before they vanished off to London. I know whirlwind weddings are the thing at the moment, since we don't know if we'll all be here from one week to the next, but I was impressed with Mrs Tilling making such a forthright move. She stepped forward to conduct the Chilbury Ladies' Choir one final time during the ceremony, choosing 'All Creatures of Our God and King', a magnificent smile across her face as we sang the words:

> *Thou burning sun with golden beam,*
> *Thou silver moon with softer gleam.*

Mama threw a party of sorts for them afterwards, a few cucumber sandwiches and cardboard cake, as usual. Yet there was a joviality about the place, as if our choir felt somehow responsible for giving Mrs Tilling a new lease on life.

'It's what we have to do these days, Kitty,' she said as she kissed me goodbye. 'You need to find where you fit in this world, where you are happiest, where you can make a difference. And don't be afraid of change.'

'But you can make a difference here in Chilbury,' I told her. 'You don't need to go to London.'

'I've done what I can here, and now it's time to go and help out elsewhere.' She smiled in a way I don't think I'd ever seen – not like her usual caring smile, or her polite smile, but a whole deeper level of smile, as if radiating a force of sunlight breaking through a stormy sky.

'We'll miss you – you will write to me, won't you?'

'I will. And you keep the choir going. I know you will though, but somehow it seems a lot to be asking a thirteen-year-old.'

'I'm almost fourteen,' I snapped. 'And I'm planning on taking the choir to bigger and better things. Just you wait.'

The Chilbury ladies' choir

With Mrs Tilling leaving, the choir voted for me to take over concert planning, which is an extraordinary honour. To her utter relief, Mrs B was finally voted to take over the conducting, so she and I have become quite a team, visiting bombed towns to offer our services. Can you believe that the Mayor of Dover has asked us to perform there? They've had more than their fair share of bombs and hundreds of people are now homeless. Mrs Quail and I have started collecting blankets for them.

I'm sure there'll be other places in need of our blankets and singing concerts soon, as there seems to be a never-ending stream of Nazi planes flying over to bomb us, our Spitfires fighting fiercely back. They're saying that the more we shoot them down, the less likely they are to invade, so we're putting our all into it.

Our new additions

Now that we have two babies in Chilbury Manor, Mama and Nanny Godwin are busy all the time. Mama is overjoyed, of course. They're like twins as they were born on the same day, except they couldn't be more different – Rose all cheerful and angelic and Lawrence small and perplexing. Silvie has been helping to look after them, saying it reminds her of looking after her baby brother. She still has that wistful look but has been talking more, and has attached herself to Mama quite fiercely. Silvie and I have been busy planning our expedition across Europe after the war to find her parents and her brother. She said she'll show me around her old house and neighbourhood, and has begun to tell me more about her life. How lovely it was before this horrid war began.

News from the shop

The village shop was bustling again with news this morning. Ralph Gibbs has bought the old mansion across the square, Tudor Grange. It must have cost a lot, and no one knows where he got the money, as surely the black market isn't doing all that well. Quite the village lord he is now, with Mrs Gibbs saying she's to sell the shop. Elsie is glued to him, the attraction now more obvious. I can't help wondering if it has something to do with the money that we found with Tom.

Tom's departure

Sadly, Tom is returning to London as his school is starting up again (as is ours in Litchfield). He promised to write to me, and if he doesn't I'll be incredibly cross as Silvie and I have both become quite fond of him. He says he'll miss us too, and he'll be back next year, if not before for a visit.

The newcomer

We have another newcomer to our village, and quite a character she is too, with her shoulder-length wavy hair brushed back like she's spent too long on a very windy cliff or has undergone a tremendous shock. She's older than Venetia, maybe even thirty, and taller too, wearing a tweed skirt and striding around looking at everything with determined interest like an unruly horse.

'I'm a journalist,' she told us in a nasal upper-class voice. 'Endeavouring to root out the real stories behind the war. The stories of us women, left alone in these little places to fend for ourselves and deal with the devastation. How we all pull together to help the war effort.'

Obviously I introduced myself to her promptly. 'Let me be the one to show you around,' I announced, taking her arm and marching her off to see the remains of Church Row. 'You see, we've had quite a summer with it all!'

'Is that where the bombs hit?' she asked, putting on her black-rimmed glasses and taking a notebook out of a large leather handbag.

'Yes, two women were killed, and one badly injured. One of the dead was the magnificent new choir mistress, the other our wonderful school teacher. Luckily her baby was rescued.'

Her face snapped around to me. 'How fascinating!' She glanced around and pulled me to the little wooden bench by the duck pond, the September sun sending a glowing golden hue over the gently yellowing leaves.

'Tell me about it. What time did it happen?' she asked.

'About half past eleven.'

'And a clear night?'

'A crescent moon, I think.'

She sat transfixed for a moment, murmuring to herself. 'Clear black skies with a shimmering moon, the stars flickering like a thousand innocent bystanders.'

'That sounds beautiful,' I sighed. 'It must be marvellous to write like that.'

'I can teach you if you have time,' she said, and I found myself transfixed as she rose from her seat and began pacing around the pond twiddling her pen. 'But first I want you to tell me all about how the women are coping with war.'

'Well, I don't think we were doing very well at all, until one spring day the new choir mistress arrived and got us singing again. She resurrected the choir, making it a women's-only choir – the Chilbury Ladies' Choir. It seemed such an unthinkable idea at first, but then we won a competition and realised how much better we were, and how we could transform ourselves into a charity singing show, or anything we liked. Well, after that we all began looking around and realising we could do a lot of things better by ourselves, or with the help of each other, and together we became stronger, better. A force to be reckoned with.'

The woman watched me, and then gazed over at the crumbling church.

'The Chilbury Ladies' Choir. It has a ring about it.'

'Yes,' I nodded, smiling. 'The most inspiring group of women you'll ever meet.'

Acknowledgements

My jovial grandmother, Mrs Eileen Beckley, always regaled
me with hilarious stories from the war, most of them funny
or racy, some of them touching on the horrific and sad reali-
ties. But through it all, her tales showed how the women
came together, working hard and keeping cheerful, to form
the solid Home Front that played such a crucial role in the
war. My warmest gratitude goes to her and the women who
fought on through the bombs and the heartache. This book
is dedicated to you.

At the beginning of the war, an organisation known as
Mass Observation began, encouraging ordinary individuals
to keep diaries and journals and send them into the head-
quarters, where some would be published in a newsletter.
These diaries filled in many gaps in my understanding of the
war years, notably one by Nella Last, and my thanks goes to
her and her fellow writers for allowing us to look not only
into their lives, but also into their minds and hearts. Letters,
biographies and memoirs have also provided details of the
era, and my thanks go to their authors, as well as to those
who spoke to me personally about the war. A wealth of books
about women in the war have provided background, as well
as books and articles written during the era. *Henrietta's War*,
by Joyce Dennys, includes wonderfully witty stories written

by a journalist of the era, and was invaluable for gauging the voice and spirit of the time.

After this book became a work-in-progress, a multitude of people helped to see it through. Wholehearted gratitude goes to my beloved critique group, Barb Boehm, Emmy Nicklin and Julia Rocchi, for providing excellent critiques and plenty of wine and warmth to help the process along. Thanks go to my teachers at Johns Hopkins, especially to Mark Farrington, whose intuition for plot, character, and narrative is legendary, and also to David Everett, Ed Perlman and Michelle Brafman. Other people who added information, personal stories, or helped along the way, include: Irene Mussett, Jerry Cooper, David Beckley, Chris Beckley, Louise and Charlie Hamilton Stubber, Tomas Ryan, Cheryl Harnden, Colin Berry, Breda Corrish, Annie Cobbe, Elaine Cobbe, Lorraine Quigley, Seth Weir, Douglas Rogers and Grace Cutler.

From the very first time I spoke to my phenomenal editor at Crown, Hilary Rubin Teeman, I was taken aback by her intuitive understanding of the book. Her vision and exceptional editorial skills have made Chilbury into the book it is today: thank you so much for all your work and expertise. My thanks go to the publisher, Molly Stern, and all at Crown, including Annsley Rosner, Rachel Meier, Maya Mavjee, David Drake, Kevin Callahan, Rachel Rokicki, Dyana Messina, Amy J. Schneider, Patricia Shaw, Heather Williamson, Sally Franklin, Anna Thompson, and a special mention to Rose Fox for all your help. Thanks also to Mark Wiggins for the stunning cover illustration.

Cassie Browne, my outstanding editor at Borough Press, has blown me away with her ability to bring the book to its true potential: thank you for your invaluable perception and insight. Big thanks also go to Kate Elton and Suzie Dooré, and the wonderfully welcoming and enthusiastic team at HarperCollins: Ann Bissell, Sarah Benton, Katie Moss, and the excellent Charlotte Cray. And for the ingenious cover, my gratitude goes to renowned illustrator, Neil Gower.

My magnificent agent, Alexandra Machinist at ICM, combines editorial wisdom, publishing instinct, and immense charm in a truly spell-binding way. Thank you for your razor-sharp guidance and expertise. Thanks also to the invaluable Hillary Jacobson.

Special gratitude goes to Karolina Sutton, my brilliant and distinguished agent at Curtis Brown in London: thank you for your tremendous skill and support. Huge thanks also go to Sophie Baker, my dynamic translation rights agent at Curtis Brown in London, and to my publishers around the world, including Martin Breitfeld at Kiepenheur & Witsch in Germany and Anne Michel at Albin Michel in France.

Finally, to my sister, Alison Mussett, thank you for your invaluable ideas and first-class editing. Hearing your reassuring voice at the end of the phone has made this book as much yours as mine. Thank you more than I can say. My warmest gratitude also goes to my mother, Joan Cooper, for her ongoing support and keen reading eye. And lastly, massive thanks go to my family, Lily and Arabella and my wonderful husband Pat, without whom this book would never have been written.

Interview with Jennifer Ryan

Charlotte Cray, editor at The Borough Press,
interviews Jennifer Ryan about her inspiration for
The Chilbury Ladies' Choir.

Charlotte Cray: This book came from a very special place, with pretty big inspiration behind it, and a pair of fantastic grandmothers. Tell me about Shakespeare, and Party Granny, and their involvement in Chilbury.

Jennifer Ryan: When I was growing up I had two grandmothers. One was Shakespeare Granny, who was very into her literature, and every time we went to see her we had to study a new tragedy and dissect it, and the awful question would come, which was: what is it *really* about? So we would always lean back and say: oh it's about – life is a big show, isn't it? Because that's what quite lot of them are about! So a lot of it was stabbing in the dark, really.

But our other granny we called Party Granny because she just loved parties. She adored getting everything ready, putting on the high-heeled shoes – she was quite a plump lady as well, so she used to totter around – put on a nice frock, get her hair done, and put on the lippy. She would cook huge amounts of food, and drink lots of Pink Gin, and tell hilarious stories. A lot of her stories were about the Second World War. Her and her beautiful friend Lettie – Lettie is the inspiration for one of the characters in the book – would get up to no end of mischief. They actually belonged to a choir during the Second World War, but their choir was not so good, and Party Granny used to tell us hysterical stories about how bad they were. They lost a carol competition because they all had very bad colds and instead of singing *Ding Dong Merrily on High*, they sang *Dig Dog Merrily on High*. Once they went to the hospital to cheer one of their members up, and the nurses thought that they were so bad that they paraded them around every single ward to cheer everyone else up. My grandmother said with great pride: 'Of course, we hammed it up hugely!'

CC: You're a non-fiction editor, so fictionalising source material must have felt quite natural to you. It's as if [the book is] an archive. It is made up of documents. So, you wanted to go back to source material but fictionalise it. Why? Because it allowed you to get into those voices? Was it only going to be in that way, in that form, or can you imagine having done this with a traditional authorial voice?

JR: It never really crossed my mind to do that actually. I read a lot of books in first person written during the war, letters, diaries, and memoirs, and that was an extensive part of my research. So it came second nature to me to present the material in that way. During the war there was something called the Mass Observation, where a couple of sociologists decided that it would be interesting to ask the public to document their day-to-day lives throughout the war. So they put out a message to the British public: Anyone who wants to write a diary and send it in, please do so, and we'll archive it for you, and we'll publish parts in a newsletter. And surprisingly, 700 people signed up straight away. Some of them would write every day and some of them once a week and some of them once a month, so it was all very sporadic. But actually that grew throughout the war, and by the end of the war there were a few thousand people who would submit Mass Observation diaries. It's fascinating to read the everyday lives of these people. Of course the result was that it was used for propaganda, just to see how well the propaganda was working, but also the rationing – they used it to gauge how people were dealing with the shortages and hardships of war. It gave the government a direct insight into people's lives and how they were being affected.

CC: Do you think British people would have been able to express themselves so freely had it not been anonymous? Would anyone have signed up?

JR: In a lot of ways I think people were using the diaries as a form of catharsis and also a kind of method of complaints. They would say, well, this is how things are with me and it's not all great!

CC: Can we talk about Kitty and Miss Prim, and her sweeping black cloak and her halo of frizzy glorious grey hair? Their relationship really took me back to those absolutely essential teacher-student relationships that can make a person: when someone sees you for who you are, and wants to build you up. I found that very profound, and I wanted to ask, did that stem from any relationship in your life?

JR: I did actually have a music teacher and Prim is *very* loosely based on her. She had that sense of magic about her, as if anything bad happening in my life wouldn't matter now that I have walked into her room and we have music. She taught me a lot about how you can put aside the bad things in the world and just let music carry you away.

CC: If there's any message from this book, it's certainly that. And every time any one of your characters walks into the rehearsal room or into a competition, I feel them shucking their lives and their war experience and being enveloped in this safe world of music, and a *glorious* world of music as well. So, do you think music can heal us?

JR: I do. When they come into the choir it's a safe place that they can express their emotions. When they sing for their grieving members, there is a colossal sense of community and them all coming together.

CC: Talk to me about how you unpeeled the gender normative role and why you wanted to explore female empowerment in Chilbury.

JR: The choir is a metaphor for the women finding their voice. Mrs Tilling, a middle-aged widow who is the nurse of the village, is almost the backbone of the book. One of the first things she says is that she has been told as a girl not to say very much, and certainly not to say what she feels, or thinks, or to complain about anything. Then as the book goes along and she's given more power within her life and within the community, she starts to challenge what's going on around her, and she finds her voice, and starts standing up to some of the authority figures. The whole book is a metaphor for that. It's how women during that time frame really did start questioning the authority and finding their voice, saying what they believed.

CC: And was that part of the storytelling that came from Party Granny?

JR: Not only Party Granny – I actually interviewed quite a few old ladies about their experiences during the war, and I was amazed by the number of people who said that it was the best time of their lives, the Second World War. Through all the bombs and the nastiness and the blitz and everything – all the tragedy – there was such a sense of community in freedom; freedom of expression; sexual freedom as well. They were allowed to express themselves. They were allowed to take their own abilities further.

CC: In the book, Kitty can intuit people's colour — do you know what colour Kitty would say you were?

JR: Well, I would like to think that I'm a pale but bright sunshine yellow. A kind of early morning sunshine yellow.

CC: Like first light.

JR: Yes, that's what I would like to be.